Night Pilgrims

NIGHT PILGRIMS

A Novel of the Count Saint-Germain

Chelsea Quinn Yarbro

TOR®

A TOM DOHERTY ASSOCIATES BOOK
NEW YORK

NIGHT PILGRIMS

Copyright © 2013 by Chelsea Quinn Yarbro

A Tor Book
Published by Tom Doherty Associates, LLC
175 Fifth Avenue
New York, NY 10010

www.tor-forge.com

Tor® is a registered trademark of Tom Doherty Associates, LLC.

Library of Congress Cataloging-in-Publication Data

Yarbro, Chelsea Quinn, 1942–
    Night pilgrims : A Saint-Germain novel / Chelsea Quinn Yarbro.—First edition.
        p. cm.
    "A Tom Doherty Associates book."
    ISBN 978-0-7653-3400-8 (hardcover)
    ISBN 978-1-4668-0771-6 (e-book)
    1. Saint-Germain, comte de, -1784—Fiction.   2. Vampires—Fiction.
3. Egypt—Fiction.   I. Title.
PS3575.A7N54 2013
813'.54—dc23

                                                                    2013006327

Tor books may be purchased for educational, business, or promotional use.
For information on bulk purchases, please contact Macmillan Corporate
and Premium Sales Department at 1-800-221-7945 extension 5442
or write specialmarkets@macmillan.com.

First Edition: July 2013

Printed in the United States of America

0   9   8   7   6   5   4   3   2   1

This book is for

Deena *and* **Jon,**

the best landpersons one could wish for.

Author's Note

Northeastern Africa is one of the most tectonically active places on the planet. Three tectonic plates meet there, and are in the process of pulling a slice off the east side of the continent, beginning where the Red Sea meets the Indian Ocean, splitting Ethiopia and Kenya in two at the Great Rift Valley, continuing on through a series of mountain-backed lakes to the Zambezi River, where it enters the Indian Ocean. This long valley is the place which a very long time ago was home to the earliest humans, and a much longer time from now will be a sea. At the northeastern base of the Ethiopian Highlands on the north-east end of the rift, in a place now called the Danakil Depression, a cluster of volcanos punctuates the landscape, a stark, low-lying desert. To the west-southwest, the ancient crags of the Ethiopian Highlands rise up between the Great Rift Valley and the Nubian Desert in what is now Sudan. Even today the volcanos are remote, part of a blistering landscape that is almost as empty now as it was eight hundred years ago. The amount of travel across the Nubian Desert has increased in the intervening centuries; there are roads and oases throughout this territory in the disputed region between Ethiopia and Eritrea; there are scientific and commercial projects going on at this time that did not exist in the thirteenth century, but even in the distant past, the trade routes from oasis to oasis carried a great deal of traffic in spite of the harsh conditions of the region.

It is in and around the north side of the Great Rift Valley and through the plateaux of the Ethiopian Highlands that a large number of underground Coptic churches are located: underground in this case is a literal description, for they are carved out of living rock below ground level, and are unique in Christian architecture. Many have the means to serve as cisterns and sluices as well as churches, suggesting that they were not only intended as places of worship, but of refuge. Built—or, more accurately, carved or excavated—about the same time that Europe was building major Gothic cathedrals—in the twelfth century and the first half of the thirteenth—these African churches were unknown to western Europeans until the Fifth Crusade, which was fought against Islam in Egypt, when occasional meetings with African Copts informed the Europeans of these remarkable structures, along with reports of most unusual peoples and animals rarely, if ever, seen in Europe at that time, among them two species of what the Crusaders called dog-monkeys and we call baboons, Ethiopian wolves, and African wild cats.

In the thirteenth century, most Europeans had few opportunities to travel. Peasants and serfs were bound to the lands they farmed; artisans and builders rarely went far beyond their native towns and villages; even apothecaries and notaries and similar city-dwellers were rarely encouraged to wander. A few of the non-clergy scholars often traveled significant distances between the small group of recently founded universities, or to centers of learning in the Middle East and Egypt. Soldiers had the option of Crusading: the Crusades were military ventures promulgated by the Church with the supposed purpose of saving the Holy Land from the rising tide of Islam, but certainly were as much an exercise in rapine and pillage as they were in defending Christendom. As an adjunct to the Crusades, a small number of European Christians headed toward the Middle East in the wake of the armies; over the length of the Crusades, the number of pilgrims increased from a trickle to a steady stream. With the Crusades there also came an increase in trade and a fashion for silks and other fine fabrics among the European upper class, encouraging travel among merchants, and expanding pilgrimages to the limits of African Christianity.

During the early Crusades—notably the First and Third— Jerusalem was the usual goal of pilgrims, with Bethlehem coming in a close second, and a great many other Christian holy sites in the Middle East saw a considerable increase in foreign Christian visitors, for although travel was dangerous, expensive, and time-consuming, when done for reasons of faith, it was acceptable to undertake far-away journeys. After the Fifth Crusade (1218–1222), the possibilities of more extensive pilgrimages lured many European Christians to Egypt, for the thrill of tourism and for spiritual exercises; the pilgrims expanded their travels into the partially Christian lands to the south of Egypt. Many of the Coptic religious buildings became destinations for penitents as well, in particular, the Chapel of the Holy Grail in Ethiopia—it is still there, by the way, and now, as then, only the senior priest of the chapel is allowed to enter the chapel and see the Grail. During the hectic pilgrimage years of the thirteenth century, the realization that pilgrims would not be allowed to enter the chapel led to unpleasant confrontations between priests and pilgrims, but that did not stem the tide of Europeans, as more holy sites were found that were rather more hospitable to European Christians than the Holy Land was, which in turn brought an increase in their presence. For the first time since the Roman Empire fell, parties of Europeans became relatively commonplace in northeastern Africa for a period of nearly twenty years, giving trade a boost and creating a small but profitable industry that we would today call tourism.

The Fifth Crusade, conducted primarily in Egypt, had a second military presence to compete for the military attention of the Ayyubid (Sons of Job) Sultanate: Jenghiz Khan and his Mongols were moving into Islamic territory from the east, and headed toward eastern Europe through the Crimea, causing much unrest in the loosely federated Emirates and Sultanates throughout the Middle East, and causing many eastern European rulers to keep a good portion of their armies at home rather than lending them to the Church for the Crusade; there was a marked effort to kick the Crusaders out of Islamic territory so that the forces of Islam could turn their attention to the impending threat of the Mongols. Crusaders no longer served as pilgrims' escorts. The Knights of Saint John Hospitallers, whose mandate was the protection of pilgrims, were dragooned into fighting the Islamic forces, leaving the pilgrims to find their own guides and guards. While the Knights of the Rose in this novel are fictitious, there were a number of military monkish Orders that operated clandestinely in Islamic territory, most of them as spies and assassins.

The Poor Knights of the Temple of Jerusalem, otherwise called the Templars, always battle-ready, were often placed at the lead of Crusading armies, where they could do the most damage if they got near enough to the Islamic cavalry to engage it. Templar knights constituted roughly 10 percent of the membership of their Order, which included foot-soldiers and engineers as well as financial officers, since the Templars handled monies for all manner of travelers. After the Fifth Crusade, guide and guard duties no longer applied for the Templars any more than they did for other European combat troops; the Hospitallers continued guarding some but not all pilgrims.

And guides and guards were needed: not only were the pilgrims crossing deserts to reach the Ethiopian Copts, they were prey to robbers, slavers, and kidnapers, subject to being killed, sold, or held for ransom. One of the reasons for the extreme vulnerability of the pilgrims was that they were not allowed to carry weapons of war or defense, only hunting weapons—simple spears, bows and arrows, slings, hatchets, and small knives or daggers; no swords, crossbows, maces, lances, pikes, halberds, caltrops, morningstars, battle-hammers, battle-axes, mauls, armor (human and horse), or shields were allowed. As a result, most pilgrims traveled in groups, or joined other groups, undertaking the dangerous journey across the Nubian Desert. Many trading-merchants—meaning those going overland from market to market rather than those using the sea for a highway, as did Venice, and Genoa in the Mediterranean, and the Hanseatic League in the Baltic and North Seas—took advantage of foreign travelers, offering to allow the pilgrims to travel in their company, and then refusing to release them without receiving a significant bribe. Travel itself, when the pilgrims left the Nile, was done on camels, horses, and asses. For desert crossings, asses, usually ridden unsaddled and unbridled, were given pack-saddles for cargo; riders used a blanket to keep the sand from rubbing their clothes to bits against the asses' backs, and the asses were provided reined halters, not unlike modern hackamores (bitless bridles) for the journeys, which were linked together. Standard bridles were used with horses, which were usually Arabs and Barbs, not the heavier European breeds, for since the pilgrims were not permitted to have armor, the smaller, lighter desert breeds could carry the pilgrims more easily through the sands, were lighter keepers (they ate less than European war horses), and were bred to accommodate the heat more readily than their European cousins.

Not all of the scattered villages along the ill-defined pilgrims' route were willing to receive Christians, being populated by followers of Islam, for although Ethiopia was mostly Christian, Islam was making steady inroads from what is now Sudan into the territory that was the last Coptic Christian stronghold of the largely collapsed Empire of Axum. There were even a few settlements of Jews who were reluctant to receive Christian pilgrims due to their excess of zeal; pilgrims had been known to kill Jews in a demonstration of the depth of their faith. In addition, the weather was never mild; heat and sand made travel slow as well as enervating, and although most pilgrims followed the Nile a good portion of the way and therefore had water to drink, finding enough to eat while traveling was difficult; in the eyes of the Christian Churches of the time, this added to the spiritual value of the exercise; danger, rationed food and water, and general suffering were commendable risks for pilgrims to endure. Occasionally pilgrims enlarged the difficulties of their pilgrimages when recounting them, resulting in accounts of low reliability, but exciting adventure. Although some of the villages along the Nile retained their names from the days of the Pharaohs, by the time of this story, a few of these villages had both Arabic as well as older, Egypto-Coptic ones; sometimes the old names remained but the villages were relocated, as in the case of Syene Philae, originally two separate towns, at the First Cataract, or Dofunj, which was a trading village that had once been an important trade center. Its exact location is unknown, so I situated it at a place convenient to the story but within the stretch of the Nile where accounts of the period place it.

There were less dangerous but equally important problems to such travel: for one, the need to carry a fair amount of money, most food for humans, all food for animals, all shelter, sufficient clothing for conditions which ranged from heat that rivaled Death Valley and cold that was numbing, and such medicines as were available at the time. Pilgrims took oaths to maintain their virtue while traveling on pilgrimage; the punishments for failure to do this were quite severe: adultery was punished by stoning the woman and, occasionally, castrating the man. Sodomy, which at the time was numbered among the Seven Deadly Sins, earned abandonment, which was tantamount to a death sentence. Pope Honorius III, who promulgated the Fifth Crusade, was particularly strict about upholding pilgrims' oaths, and insisted that special clergy accompany all pilgrims in order to report upon them at a later time.

Then there was the problem of languages: most of Lower Egypt—the part in the north—spoke Arabic and some Greek—Upper Egypt—the part in the south—spoke some Arabic and some Coptic, a tongue descended from the languages of ancient Egypt. It was not too difficult to find a translator who knew these languages and Church Latin, but once the pilgrims passed the Second Cataract, the picture changed: the Nubians had a language of their own, as well as their own version of Coptic, and many secondary groups within Nubia had regional languages, most without a written version of the language. Arabic was spoken, at least secondarily, by the steadily enlarging Islamic population, but once the Christian communities were reached, languages and dialects became a much greater jumble, even among those religious communities. The Coptic language could be found among a large number of those communities, but often as a secondary language, as Church Latin was in many parts of Europe, or English is in much of the world today. The demands on translators often exceeded their capabilities, and so chains of translators became necessary as the European pilgrims entered the Ethiopian Highlands.

European languages were also more chaotic then than now; spelling had not been regularized since the Roman Empire gave way to Gothic invaders, and all writing was phonetic, which often meant considerable variations in vocabulary from region to region, with extensive variances not only in dialects, but in spellings and pronunciation of place and personal names. Even Church Latin was more irregular than Imperial Latin had been, and subject to regional idiosyncrasies; in many parts of Europe, written language combined elements of Church Latin with local dialects, which complicated communications among Crusaders and pilgrims alike. In terms of pronunciation, the phonetic approach is closer to the conventions of the time than following modern rules: basically, if the letter is present, pronounce it. Due to the strong central control of Constantinople, Byzantine Greek was somewhat more cohesive, but equally subject to regional variations, and to influences of the Orthodox Church.

Although some Orthodox Christians undertook pilgrimages into Africa at this time, by far the largest group of pilgrims were Europeans, constituting more than two-thirds of the non-Africans venturing into the farthest extent of Christianity in that continent. It is likely that the reason for this can be directly linked to the Crusades, and their promulgation by the Roman Popes with the participation of European military forces. Seafaring states, such as the Republics of Venice and Genoa, used the Crusades not to stop the spread of Islam, but to expand their regions of trade and to broaden their markets throughout the Mediterranean; the increased popularity of luxury fabrics from India and the Middle East in Europe was directly connected to the markets opened up as an offshoot of the Crusades. Venice in particular, and Genoa to a lesser degree, increased their fortunes by carrying Crusaders and pilgrims as well as cargo on their galleys; the Venetians accommodated the Crusaders to the extent that they created a special ship for the transportation of horses, since armed knights were too heavy for the small, quick Middle Eastern horses, and the Crusaders had to bring their larger, heavier mounts with them, and all the tack and bard (horse armor) required in battle.

In the thirteenth century, Christians as well as Moslems kept slaves, and the slave trade was a highly successful enterprise throughout most of Europe, Africa, and Asia. It was understood that slaves were necessary to maintain not only social order but to provide for the time-consuming-but-boring-yet-essential domestic routines that most of us today assign to appliances. In traveling, slaves did the preparation and clean-up for everything from meals to campsites to procuring food, drink, and other supplies as well as looking after the welfare of their owners. Among Europeans, servants, or paid staff, were usually the supervisors of slaves; in the economic structure of Islamic culture at that time, which had a larger use of slaves at all levels, servants as such were comparatively rare, that function belonging to a socially higher order of slaves, ones who often owned slaves themselves, something not often seen in the Christian West, but occasionally encountered among pagan Europeans.

About titles: the title Sidi is Middle Eastern, and means, roughly, lord or master. The Moorish invaders of Spain gave the title to the warlord Ruy Diaz de Bivar, conqueror of Valencia, and we know him by that title to this day—El Cid. The title Sieur is French and Anglo-French, and given to knights; it was not associated with specific fiefs or grants of land, which had other titles for minor landholders, although a knight, a Sieur, could also have titles to fiefs and estates. The title Vidame is French and is the equivalent of Baron, but was bestowed by the Church on those men of noble birth who managed Church estates for a cut of the wealth generated by those estates; the title and position could pass through several generations, but would never convey title to the land—the Vidamie—to the Vidame.

Coptic Christianity at that time, while distinct from other forms of Christianity, had more in common with the Greek Orthodox Church and the Gnostics than it did with Roman Catholicism— though all these Churches have changed their liturgy and rituals through time: upper-class Catholics no longer ride their horses into cathedrals and churches for Mass, Greek Orthodox penitents do not crawl on hands and knees from church to church to gain absolution for usury, and Copts no longer chant the *Gospel of Thomas* and dance to it on major holy days as some communities of monks did in the thirteenth century. Reconstructing these by-gone religious exercises has not been easy, and I freely admit that there are many sources that contradict one another in regard to the particulars in various communities. Where there is uncertainty or differing ceremonies, I have chosen the rites that best suit the purposes of this book and followed their descriptions when presenting some of the rites of the Copts at that time.

The Ayyubid Sultan, Malik-al-Kamil, a Sunni in charge of a largely Shia army, and the nephew of the great Salah-al-Din (called

Saladin by Europeans), ruling Egypt at the time, was tolerant of most pilgrims, but unwilling to provide any special protection for them; his policy was that Christian pilgrims should look to other Christians for housing and supplies. He apparently lost some of his cordiality with the European presence in his country, twice ordering all non-pilgrims and non-merchants to leave, dictates that were sporadically enforced and that led to an upsurge in conversions to Islam among the Europeans wishing to remain in Egypt. Islam granted access to Christian holy sites to pilgrims since Christians and followers of Islam were "people of the Book," meaning that they both traced their religious origins to Abraham and Judaism. This genial policy was often more observed in the breach than in practice, but that did not mean that open hostility was a common response to pilgrims; there was a lot to be gained through acceptance of pilgrims in the country, including an influx of money as well as access to information about conditions in Europe: in the fifty years before the time of this book, money was slowly replacing service and barter as the rate of exchange, a development much favored by mercantile states active in international trade, a shift that made the expansion of pilgrimages more readily accessible for many with an urge to travel. Money as much as the European Crusaders made the Crusades a viable venture, and the expanding wealth from mining in central Europe fueled them both militarily and commercially, for the Crusades were a vastly profitable enterprise, and when the pilgrimage craze caught on at the end of the Third Crusade, the floodgates opened. The pilgrims came in droves, in spite of cultural, linguistic, and religious differences; the chance to see the new and wonderful overcame almost all difficulties.

Languages and customs were not the only confusing factors impacting travel: calendars were not coordinated, and although the Middle East lacked the one hundred or so calendars being used in China at this time, there was also no regulatory body to adjust and correct calendars as there was in China, where distributing an erroneous calendar was a capital offense. The Orthodox Christian calendar did not align with the Roman Catholic one, and neither meshed well with the Islamic lunar calendar. Parts of Egypt kept to the old

calendar left over from Pharaonic times, observing three seasons
(Planting, in the autumn and winter, Harvest, from early to late
spring, and Inundation, the annual Nile flood through the summer)
and dating an event by the number of years of the reign of the present ruler. Working out when a thing was to be done, or when a specific occasion had taken place, often required careful calculation,
and even then, accuracy was not guaranteed. Almost all Christian
rulers at the time maintained an astrologer or two, as much to sort
out dates as to decide what stellar influence was impacting the rulers' lives. Many Christian countries did not begin the new year on
January 1st: Russian Christians' New Year was September 1st, several
of the Italian city-states began the year on the Vernal Equinox,
March 20th or 21st , depending on the calendar being used, or on the
Feast of the Virgin Mary, then celebrated on the 24th or 25th of
March. The Coptic Church kept to its links to Pharaonic Egypt,
starting the year on August 29th or 30th, and identifying three seasons, although during the height of the Crusades, the Copts also applied the Gregorian Calendar in documents involving Roman and
Orthodox Christians, and I have followed their excellent example.
Rome followed the old Imperial Roman calendar—as we do today,
with a few post-Gregorian adjustments—so dates could easily become confused. For the sake of clarity rather than historical accuracy,
this book keeps to the modern Western calendar in most instances.

These events took place during the Medieval Warm Period,
which allowed agricultural expansion in Europe, thanks to the slight
rise in world temperatures, but in hotter climates, the impact was
less beneficial: the Sahara and other deserts expanded and many
oases dried up as streams went underground, and the savannah mar-
gins to the fertile regions along the Nile narrowed to strips or dried
up and blew away as sand encroached on scrub-grazing land, creating new areas of depopulated villages as well as driving more of the
population to the river for their livelihoods as fishermen, watermen,
boatmen, and bird-hunters. Fortunately, the Nile still provided the
annual Inundation and brought a new load of topsoil to the narrowing band of the arable land which was developed with intensified
farming techniques. This led to an increase of irrigation in the fer-

tile swaths along the Nile, and made stored granaries and similar caches the target of military seizures, Islamic and Christian alike, as armies sought out food for their men and animals, as did bands of robbers and unlucky farmers whose lands had been claimed by the desert. The Crusaders were supposed to provide or buy their supplies, not steal them; the Popes who called for the Crusades made that plain, but no one actually expected the Crusaders to live up to this high moral stance, and they were as eager to pilfer and raid as the most experienced bandit. Food was seized whenever possible, and the Crusaders themselves had established squads within their companies whose sole job was procuring food for humans and animals, and were recognized for their skills in pilferage. Another aspect of the Medieval Warm Period that imposed on Crusaders came from the obduracy of the Crusaders themselves: they brought European-style warfare to the Middle East and Egypt, meaning they fought in iron and steel chain-mail—though by the Fifth Crusade, solid iron or steel breastplates were becoming the upper-body protection of choice—worn over thick padding, with metal helms and coifs to protect their heads, and went into battle so armed in 115-degree or higher heat, where they succumbed to heatstroke and dysentery in significant numbers, conditions that often proved fatal, since the monks who served as nurses had no practical means of treating either malady beyond administering salted fish and prayers.

During the later Crusading years, England still owned a large slice of western France, and the English King, starting with Richard I "Lionheart," encouraged English knights and lesser nobility to accept fiefs and estates in the English lands of France to keep the territory English. These Anglo-French titled men and promoted soldiers were largely centered in the Aquitaine, and were heavily tied into French politics as well as English, which occasionally led to disputes between the French and English that erupted into brush-fire battles. To ensure the Pope's support for maintaining the English presence in France, the English Kings usually encouraged the nobility and knights to participate in or financially support the Crusades. Even in the interbellum years when no Crusade was actively going on, the English and Anglo-English presence in the Holy Land and Egypt continued, through trade and pilgrimages, and various kinds of chicanery.

All through the Crusades there was a thriving black-market business in holy relics, and with the increase in pilgrims, the relic business exploded throughout the Middle East, into Egypt, and, for a century, south into Nubia and Ethiopia, where the remoteness of the source added to the value of the relics obtained. One especially sought-after relic was the hand of the Apostle Philip: several mummified hands were accepted as the real thing, including one that had come from a baboon. Not only did pilgrims seek all manner of relics out for themselves, but for the pilgrim bringing back an important relic from the Holy Land or from any sacred Christian site to donate to the Church, prestige and indulgences—religious documents exonerating and forgiving the holder from sins committed or forthcoming sins—would be the rewards. One of the most popular relics that pilgrims bought was pieces of the True Cross; whole forests must have been used to supply the demand for that relic, for thousands of wooden bits were sold to Crusaders and pilgrims throughout the Crusading decades, all purporting to be genuine. Vials of the Virgin's milk were also much sought after. Very important relics were so valued by the Roman Church that often agents were dispatched to steal them from other churches, a risky act, since most Medieval Christians would kill to protect their relics. The Orthodox Church was not as focused on relics as the Roman Church was: the Orthodox churches valued icons with much the same fervor as Roman churches regarded relics; icons deemed to be especially powerful were also targets of theft; many households had a private iconostasis, or screen for icons, which was constantly guarded by a slave. In Orthodox churches, novices guarded the icons, and the penalty for failure to stop a robbery was immurement—being walled up alive in the monastery's foundation.

In 1228, a Sixth Crusade was undertaken, led by the excommunicated Holy Roman Emperor, Frederick II, who dealt with the contending successors to the Sultanate of Egypt more through diplomacy than force of arms, and with greater success than he brought to his attempts to reconcile with the Pope; Frederick II spoke fluent

Arabic and lived in a Middle Eastern manner. He culminated his successes in the Middle East by crowning himself King of Jerusalem in the Church of the Holy Sepulcher on March 18, 1229, which title he claimed through his 1225 marriage to Iolande, daughter of King Jehan, Count of Brienne, who had claim to that kingdom; Frederick's wife did not live to see him crowned, and Frederick returned to Italy three months later to continue his disputes with Pope Gregory IX, a conflict which ended in July of 1230 with the Treaty of San Germanno—no relation.

There are a number of people who provided information and insight to the preparation for this book, and I am taking this opportunity to thank them: to David Blaize for information on the logistics of the Crusades; to Amelia Crowley for information on the Medieval Coptic Church, in particular its ties to ancient Egyptian rites; to E. J. Eduard for explaining the pilgrims' routes from Egypt to Ethiopia, and where the riskiest places were on those routes, and who believes that the Europeans of the period called those who lived in the highlands Ethiopians and those who lived in the lowlands Abyssinians; to J. G. Jeffers for information on various boats, barges, and other water-craft used on the Nile in this period; to Leslie Kim for information on the environmental shifts during the Medieval Warm Period, particularly its impact on northeastern Africa; to Walter Mendip for statistics on the demographics of European pilgrims; to Maria Obdach for information on languages and language proliferation in Ethiopia, Somalia, and Sudan in the thirteenth century; to Shawnia Visson for steering me toward two useful Web sites on Coptic and Ethiopian sacred texts, and then answering my questions about changes in the liturgy and rites over the centuries; and to Ingmar Wellerhavn, for explaining Medieval pronunciation of and spelling variations in regional personal names. I'm grateful to all of you for your time and expertise; any errors I have made are mine, and should not reflect badly on these good people's knowledge and generosity.

On the publishing side, my thanks to the incomparable Wiley

Saichek, who does so much to publicize these Saint-Germain books online; to my agent, Howard Morhaim, for handling the business end, and for negotiating the e-publishing contract for the electronic reprints of much of the Saint-Germain backlist and the Olivia books; to Robin Dubner, attorney-at-law, who protects Saint-Germain; to Elinor Wainwright, for helping me chase down spare copies of the books in this series; to Paula Guran, the diligent webmastrix (webmistress sounds so black-leather-and-riding-crops) for my Web site, www.ChelseaQuinnYarbro.net; to the Yahoo chat group; to my recreational readers Angelica S. Johnson, William Penbury, and Glen Yao; to good pals and Ph.D.'s all, Sharon Russell, Stephanie Moss, and Elizabeth Miller and her Canadian chapter of the Transylvanian Society of Dracula; to DragonCon; to the Horror Writers Association for listing *Hotel Transylvania* among the six novels nominated as Vampire Novel of the [Twentieth] Century; to Lindig Harris for her continuing support of this series; to the Albuquerque crowd, Libba and Spencer in particular, with a second thanks to Libba for proofreading my pages; to Peggy, Charlie, Steve, Marc, Jim, Patrick, Mary-Rose, Megan, Shawn, Christine, Cheryl, Robert, Alice, Maureen, David, Bill, Suzon, Marsha, and Gaye, as well as Peter, Ingrid, and Eggert; to the Costco Angel; to Libba and Spencer again, and to Beth, Glenn, Rini and Barrett, Angelique, and Christine; to Tom Doherty and Tor; my editor, Melissa Singer; and to the readers and booksellers who have supported the series for more than three decades, and counting.

CHELSEA QUINN YARBRO
Richmond, California
15 March 2012

PART I

RAKOCZY, SIDI SANDJER'MIN

Text of a letter from Sieur Horembaud du Langnor at Alexandria to Rakoczy, Sidi Sandjer'min, written in Latin, and carried up-river to the Monastery Church of the Visitation; delivered twenty-three days after it was written.

To the renowned European teacher known here as Rakoczy, Sidi Sandjer'min, greetings from Sieur Horembaud du Langnor, once Crusader, now penitent, bound for the churches and shrines in the far south, on the Feast of the Circumcision, in the Year of Grace, 1225.

I am told by several well-informed Christians here in Alexandria that you are the man I must address in this predicament. I am seeking a translator and guide to assist in my pilgrimage to the south, into the mountains beyond the ancient Empire of Axum, which will set out from your monastery within a month of my arrival in that place. You, I am informed, know well the ways of the Nile and have many languages at your command, which will be most useful: I am intending to find a number of like-minded Christians to accompany me and my servants on my journey to the Christians of the Horn. As few Europeans are willing to guide us, lacking sufficient knowledge to undertake this pilgrimage, I believe it is God's intention that you will accept the commission, for it is said you understand the risks of journeying beyond the limits of Egypt; you are vastly traveled, or so I have heard, and that would mean that you are especially well-prepared to supervise our journey. Also, you know the customs of the Christians of the region, and will be able to assist us in showing proper regard for their ceremonies, and to be able to lead us to the holiest shrines and churches.

I would expect that we will be gone on this pilgrimage for a year or so. Those who have made the journey themselves have told me that it will take that long to travel into the mountains beyond the desert, to visit the holy sites, make proper obeisance at each of them, and to return; I have heard that after we leave the Nile to cross overland, we must travel at night, due to the fierceness of the sun in the day, which I trust will not lessen your ability to guide us, until we reach the mountains, where, I have been told, at the height of summer, rains begin, and until autumn, the rainfall continues, and slows travel in those distant places. All those going must be prepared for hardships, but such devotion is pleasing in God's sight, or so the priests have said.

It is important to me to do this, for unless I perform this penance, I may not lead my troops again, by order of the Bishop of Acre. This was due to an error from local guides who assured me that there were Islamites in the town we had reached, and said they were preparing to poison the wells. As soldiers loyal to the Church and Christ, we went in and killed the people, and only then discovered that the people of the town were Christians of the Eastern Rite, and that we bore their deaths on our souls. I am eager to rejoin my troops so that we may stem the tide of Islamites that plagues the Holy Land, as any true Christian in this place would be, and therefore I have decided to address a European to guide me and my pilgrims, so that we should not be tempted to sin again, and who could offer testimony that the terms of my penance have been fulfilled. All those who have been on Crusade know to their costs how easily one can transgress. To that end, I am hoping to secure relics for Saunt-Adrien-le-Berger in the Aquitaine, where my fief is located; relics will surely help me in being restored to command of my troops and bring distinction to my family. I long for battle in the cause of Our Lord, Who made me to be a warrior in His Name. To wear armor again, to wield my sword in the name of the Savior: what Christian knight can ask for more?

Not that pilgrims can go armed into those lands beyond Egypt, for that has been forbidden since the First Crusade, when only unarmed Christians were allowed to enter Jerusalem, which stricture is still in force there. Hunting weapons are allowed, but the weapons of war and the armor that goes with them are not, and failure to comply with this order of disarmament brings a most unpleasant death. Enforcement of these restrictions is severe, by all reports. We will need to find men to accompany us who are skilled hunters, not Europeans, which would make us more vulnerable to attack and capture, but from Egypt and Christian. I am not minded to trust any Islamic hunter in our numbers, for they will put their faith ahead of ours. Since you are already among Christians, the search should not be a difficult one. I will leave such things up to you. God has pointed the way to you, and I will bow to His Will, as will you, for the sake of our faith—if you are the man I have heard you are: you are the man I seek; if you will pray, you will learn what God has revealed to me, and you will place yourself in my service, for it is the service of God.

In recognition of your station, I authorize you to bring with you up to six men, and will bear the cost for their travels; food, water, and shelter will be their concern, and yours, to the limits of my purse. When I and my pilgrims arrive where you are, you will advise us on what we need for our journey and where to obtain it; I have two servants with me, one of whom is a fine judge of camels and should be able to find worthy beasts for us once we need them. This is an endeavor worthy of any Christian, and one that many saints have undertaken. It is unfortunate that we must travel in summer, and therefore at night, as I have stated, but God has willed it so, and we must take His Gifts as He offers them. Be ready to receive us and we will welcome you to our numbers as a guide and translator, although we must ask that you do not associate in too familiar a fashion with the pilgrims, for that might distract them from their holy purpose, to the successful conclusion of which we now must turn our prayers and our purpose.

Sieur Horembaud du Langnor

by the hand of Frater Anteus, Ambrosian

1

Set back from the Nile on the east side of the river by more than half a league, the Monastery of the Visitation stood at the edge of the desolation of the desert. Not unlike the village between the monastery and the river, it was a collection of stark, mud-brick buildings surrounded by a thick stone wall that enclosed simple herb-gardens, a stand of trees, a mill, a chapel, a church, a scriptorium, a dormitory, and a well. Two small barns, a small stable, three pens, and a paddock were attached to the outside of the wall. The place smelled of dust and dung and the restless, relentless sands that poured over the ridge behind the monastery, slowly and inexorably besieging it, promising with every wind that it eventually would press on to the village and its fields, covering the monastery and its grounds as it moved.

In the far corner of the enclosure, nearest the encroaching dunes, in the thickest of three spinneys of broad-leaved sycamore trees, there was a two-room house where the foreigner and his foreign servant had lived since their arrival, away from the monks and the pilgrims, though the leader of the monastery made it a habit to visit Rakoczy, Sidi Sandjer'min, once a day before sunset. This evening the monks would dance and chant to celebrate the coming of the Twelve Magi, and that would mean Sandjer'min would have to remain inside, for only Copts could witness the ritual.

A hint of a breeze was coming off the Nile and making its languid way around the monastery when Aba'yam came to the remote house late in the afternoon of Epiphany, a little earlier than usual; he was walking slowly, favoring his right foot. He was a square-built man of forty-four, with a formidable beard going white, an aquiline nose that made his eyes seem deeper than they were, and two deep lines running from his thick eyebrows toward his receding hairline; his ears were large and stuck out from his head like the handles on a pot. He was dressed in a simple hooded habit of dark-brown wool with only his pectoral crucifix to show his position of leadership. He blessed himself before he crossed the threshold, and found Ruthier, Sandjer'min's manservant, at his tall work-table, an array of herbs on drying mats spread out across it. "God give you a good evening, foreigner," he said in the language of his people.

"And you," Ruthier answered, turning around to face his visitor; his Coptic was a bit stilted; he had not learned the language until he had been with Sandjer'min for five centuries, and had not ever become easy with it. He wiped his hands on one of a stack of cotton cloths at the edge of the table. "Have the Thessalonians gone?" He set another raised, woven mat on the table and began to sort out a knot of feathery leaves. Behind him on the wall hung many bunches of herbs already dried and wrapped in twine.

"They will stay in the village tonight and take a boat down-river in the morning," said Aba'yam. "I came to thank the Sidi for translating their words for us. He was most helpful to us, and to them."

"He was pleased to do it," Ruthier answered, a bit surprised that Aba'yam would want to talk with him. "They went a long way to the south, those Greeks."

"As many pilgrims are doing since the Egyptian Crusade ended," said Aba'yam. "We're likely to see more returning pilgrims between now and the Mass of Resurrection; then their numbers will diminish through the heat of summer and increase again as the nights grow long."

"Hardly unusual: the summers turn this land into an oven," said Ruthier.

"We see fewer Orthodox Christians on pilgrimages than Roman ones; I suppose it's because the Crusaders are Roman Christians for the most part." He glanced around the room. "The Sidi is out?" He was used to seeing Ruthier in the house, making preparations for his evening meal, or sorting herbs as he was doing now, but to have Sidi Sandjer'min away was disconcerting.

"Yes. He'll be back shortly," said Ruthier. "I'll be pleased to send him to you when he returns, or you may wait here until he comes, whichever suits your purpose." He did not add that Sandjer'min had gone down to the river, for that might lead to questions that would trouble Aba'yam.

"No matter. I was only surprised not to see him." Aba'yam folded his hand atop his crucifix. "I was hoping to get more of that unguent for my foot; the wound is slow to heal, and it keeps me from dancing with the monks. The Sidi has eased its discomfort before, and I trust he will do so again." He pressed his lips together. "Furthermore, there is the matter of the Sultan's messengers."

"The men who came this morning?" Ruthier continued to create order with his collection of drying mats and their contents.

"Yes." He paused, uncertain if he should go on. When he could not make up his mind, he said, "But, also, I've come to ask that neither he nor you leave this house during our celebration of Epiphany." He had given the same warning at every outdoor celebration in the eighteen months the two foreigners had lived there. "You are not Copts, and though you show us great respect, it is not fitting that you should be with us for our rites. You cannot dance with us, and we do not want observers here while we celebrate."

"I understand; the Sidi and I have observed your Rule before and will now," said Ruthier. "You may be at rest. My master has not gone far; if for some reason he is delayed, he will remain outside the walls until you have finished your celebration of Epiphany, and treat your foot then."

"I am most thankful," said Aba'yam. "What have you there on your table?"

"Herbs for medicaments," said Ruthier, moving so that Aba'yam could see them.

"To treat what ailments?" Aba'yam inquired with interest.

"This"—he held up a thick-leaved dark-green mass of leaves— "will diminish fever and help clear the skin when made into a paste. And this"—he pointed to a handful of bulbous pods laid out on another raised mat—"will ease pain and help reduce panting for those with gasping sickness. It is not to be given to pregnant women."

"Poppy syrup. He has given the monastery a good supply." He

pulled the larger of the two chairs in the room a bit nearer to the work-table and sat down.

"This is used for cough and wet lungs. This is for problems with the eyes. This is for women with severe monthly bleeding. This helps burns to heal. This relieves itching. This restores the eyes when they are tired. This clears the bowels. This reduces inflamation of the joints. This will settle the digestion. This and this in equal portion stops sores on the skin. This will relieve sore muscles. This is for teething infants. This eases sleep. This treats insect bites. This with this mixed together draws putresences." He pointed to a jar. "There's moldy bread in there, from which my master makes his sovereign remedy, which he keeps secure in his medicaments chest."

"But nothing for the bite of a mad dog, or for a cobra's venom," said Aba'yam, sighing. "If we had such medicaments, we could save so many from a suffering death. It is always hard to see such suffering before death."

"If I had such medicaments, you would have them as well," said Sidi Sandjer'min, coming through the door bearing a pair of jars filled with water from the Nile hanging from a wooden pole on his shoulder. His black linen short-sleeved cotehardie was damp around its calf-length hem; his heavy-soled Persian boots were wet, and there was a smear of mud on the back of his left hand. Unlike the monks', his dark hair was cut short, and his attractive face was clean-shaven. "When I first started to learn to heal, I had a woman come to me who had been bitten by a mad dog. Nothing I tried could help her, and nothing I have used since can stop the madness the bite brings, or the death." That had been more than twenty-seven centuries ago, but the experience could still bring a sense of failure to him.

This revelation troubled Aba'yam, so rather than pursue so discouraging a matter, he offered a standard greeting. "God give you a good evening, Sidi," he said, rising and blessing the Sidi.

"And to you," said Sandjer'min, inclining his head and showing his palms as he had learned to do in the Temple of Imhotep, more than twenty-seven centuries ago; this ancient courtesy amused Aba'yam.

"Some day you must tell me where you learned that form of greeting," said Aba'yam, shaking his head.

"I learned it here, in Egypt," said Sandjer'min, setting down the wooden pole and bending to retrieve the jars. He did not add that the time he was remembering was more than a thousand years ago.

Aba'yam laughed. "If you insist," he said, glancing toward the open window. "Our rite will last through sunset and into night so long as the wind doesn't rise." He coughed diplomatically. "I was hoping you might have a salve for my foot, before the ceremony begins. I prefer to dance than limp."

"I do." He turned to Ruthier. "In my red-lacquer chest, the chalcedony jar with the dragon on the lid, and three lengths of linen."

"At once," said Ruthier, and went into the second room.

"During your rite, Ruthier and I will remain here," Sandjer'min agreed; he wiped his hands on a damp linen towel that hung at the end of the work-table. "We will not leave this house until your chanting is over."

Aba'yam cleared his throat and spat. "The Sultan is worried about the warriors from the East, for it is said no army can stand against them. Great kingdoms fall to their horsemen every year, and they are coming westward," he went on apologetically. "The Sultan is ordering the young men in the village to join his troops to defend this land from the might of—the name escapes me."

"Jenghiz Khan," said Sandjer'min; images of T'en Chih-Yu filled his mind, and her appalling death at Mongol hands, a little more than a decade ago.

"That is the name," Aba'yam said, relieved that the foreigner knew.

Ruthier returned with the jar and two rolls of linen and handed them to Sandjer'min. "Do you need anything else? The rest of the cloth is in the clothes-chest."

"Not just at present," said Sandjer'min. He took a clean length of cotton and knelt before Aba'yam. "If you will raise your habit so I can see your foot?"

"You will find it a little puffy," Aba'yam warned.

"Um," Sandjer'min said, lifting both feet to make a comparison. "Have you been soaking it as I have recommended?"

"Not as often as would be wise, but as often as I can spare an hour to do it," Aba'yam said. "At this time of year, the holy feasts demand my presence; there are so many observances, celebrations, and rites . . ."

Sandjer'min removed the sandal on the swollen foot, wiped it with the cotton cloth, and examined it closely; the small, open puncture on his heel was dark-red around the edges, and some bits of skin were sloughing off. The top of the foot felt spongy, like dough, yielding easily to touch, and marked deeply with the impressions of his sandal-lacings. "You need to soak this more often, using water from the well, not the river, and with the tincture I gave you added to the water." He wiped the foot again, more thoroughly. "It has heat in the flesh and there is an odor of skin putrescence."

"How long will it take to heal?" Aba'yam did his best to sound unconcerned about the answer.

"It's difficult to say; you are on your feet much of the day, and that slows your recovery; if you could lie abed for half the day, the wound would be likely to close," Sandjer'min answered, opening the chalcedony jar and scooping out a little of the honey-colored contents; it smelled a bit like camphor and a bit like mustard, and it slipped down Sandjer'min's fingers to his palm. As he smoothed the unguent over Aba'yam's heel, he said, "Tonight, after your final prayers, I would like you to soak your foot for as long as you can bear it in heated water with double the usual amount of tincture."

"That may be difficult; our Rule requires that we go to sleep immediately after final prayers."

"Surely God won't mind if you take time to treat the wound on your foot," Sandjer'min said. "And you are Aba'yam. You can allow yourself to do this."

"That would be lax in me, so I cannot do it, for I must set the example for all the monks here," said Aba'yam. "I am Aba'yam, and the monks are sworn to me. For as long as I am Aba'yam, I am as much their servant as their leader. To set such a poor example—no. I could not." There was no pride in this statement: Aba'yam was the name all the monks promoted to the position of Superior took upon their election to the post, and it became both their title and their identity within the monastery; it brought with it both authority and responsibilities. This Aba'yam was the ninth to hold that name and title.

"I understand that," said Sandjer'min, "but I have my duty to perform as well as you: if you continue to walk on this heel without soaking it, you risk getting a severe putrescence that could eventually require the removal of your foot."

"Flesh is weak," said Aba'yam, watching Sandjer'min wrap his foot. "I will try to do as you recommend," he said in another, more resigned, tone.

"Very good," said Sandjer'min, knotting the end of the second strip of linen to the first and going on with bandaging Aba'yam's heel.

While Sandjer'min worked, Aba'yam said, "The Sultan's men said they will return after the Inundation to gather more young men for Malik-al-Kamil's army unless the Mongols stop their advancement, which would mean moving troops from their present locations in order to fortify the eastern frontiers. He is also concerned about foreigners in Egypt, his messengers told me. Now that the most recent Crusade is over, he is anxious to restore his sovereignty from the Second Cataract to Alexandria, and to spread Islam everywhere."

Ruthier looked up from his drying plants. "You say the Sultan is worried about foreigners: does that include European foreigners? Do Europeans trouble him?"

"Yes. His messengers told me he believes that Europeans still in this land, unless they are religious, are spies and criminals, or men willing to be suborned by the agents of the Mongols, who must surely be in Egypt by now. The Sultan has declared that he cannot allow Egypt to be drawn into another Crusade at a time when other foes are moving against us." Aba'yam made a gesture to show that he did not share the Sultan's belief. "With the Mongols approaching, he may decide that all foreigners must leave, and on short notice."

"Is that the current rumor?" Sandjer'min asked, feeling suddenly very tired; he had seen the same response to the Mongol invaders in China a dozen years before, and finally had traveled into the Land of

Snows in search of safety. He finished the bandage and tied it off. "There. You may put on your sandal now."

"It is what the Sultan's men told us," said Aba'yam as he picked up his sandal and set it in place along his sole, then took up the laces and secured them while he went on, "I have no desire for you to leave; between your knowledge of medicaments and your facility with languages, I would be pleased to have you here for as long as you wish to remain, but that may not always be my decision to make. For the most part the Sultan has left us alone, as he has left the Jews alone, but if there should be another Crusade, or the Mongols get nearer, then—" He shrugged. "It is in the hands of God."

A rattle of the shutters revealed the shift in the wind; it had swung around and now came off the desert, bringing a steady trickle of sand with it.

Sandjer'min nodded his understanding. "So it hinges on Jenghiz Khan: again." He wondered where he would have to go this time.

Aba'yam got to his feet and turned his hands toward Heaven. "It hinges on God's Will," he corrected his foreign guests. "May you receive the gifts of Epiphany," he said, blessing Sandjer'min and then Ruthier. After a formal gesture of farewell, he left the little house, going out into the deepening sunset to join his monks in their celebration.

"How bad is his foot?" Ruthier asked in Imperial Latin.

"Bad enough. If he had the Bending Sickness, it would be worse, but not by much. However he got that puncture, it isn't mending properly. There may be something lodged in it which ought to be removed," Sandjer'min answered in the same tongue.

"Would Aba'yam allow that?"

"I don't know. He would have to be in more pain than he is now, but he would heal in time, and the pain would fade. If he stays as he is, the pain will persist." He took the cotton cloth he had used to wipe Aba'yam's foot. "This will need to be washed in boiling water with astringent herbs." He had learned that from the Romans when Nero was Caesar and had found that it did help to contain the spread of putrescences.

"I will do it in the morning, when the dancing is over. Do you want me to draw water from the well or the river?" Ruthier asked.

"The well. At this time of year, the river teams with animacules. Once the Inundation comes, the animacules will disperse, but for now, they are increasing. That's why I brought those jars here, so I may test the water to learn which of the animacules are present. I can treat the well-water to keep it clear, but not the Nile."

Outside the first droning chants accompanied the lighting of torches around the front of the monastery's chapel, where the monks would dance to exhaustion. The ragged flames leaped and fluttered at every gust of wind.

Ruthier almost smiled. "How many leagues do you suppose they walk in that dance-circle?"

"By the end of the rite? Perhaps three or a bit more." Sandjer'min thought back to the many processions he had witnessed in his centuries at the Temple of Imhotep, and saw echoes of those in the stately dance of these monks: right foot forward, left foot up behind, a slow turn to the right on the ball of the right foot, when the rotation was complete, left foot forward, right foot up behind, a slow turn to the left on the ball of the left foot, always moving in a large circle, the sequence repeated for hours, accompanied by the chanting of gospels and psalms.

"Most of the new-gathered herbs are sorted, and ready for hanging," Ruthier said when Sandjer'min remained silent. "I have a plucked chicken, and I'm about to eat. Is there anything you need me to do first?"

"No," said Sandjer'min, reaching for the tall stool in the corner and pulling it to the work-table. "For now I'm going to spend a little time making up medicaments."

"Do you need anything for that?" Ruthier inquired.

"No; I have wool-fat to use in ointments, palm oil for infusions, olive oil for lotions, honey for unguents, and will gather eggs for poultices, as I need them." He gave a half-smile, his dark eyes somber. "Enjoy your meal."

Ruthier took flint-and-steel and lit the rush-lamp that hung over the work-table. "There. The monks expect you to need light for your tasks." He knew Sandjer'min well enough not to question the reason for his sudden reticence; the prospect of having to travel again during the year ahead was making him fretful.

"It may be a long night," Sandjer'min said. "Last year they chanted and danced until well past midnight."

"They danced until dawn before the Paschal Mass," said Ruthier. "Only half the night for the Feast of the Martyrdom of the Baptist."

"And for the Annunciation," said Sandjer'min, looking toward the door with mild curiosity. "I don't think they will go on so long tonight."

"Why?" asked Ruthier.

"There is a wind coming up, from the east, and that will blow sand into the monastery grounds. That cannot be a good surface for dancing. As the monks grow tired, they may slip and fall." He set the second latch on the shutters, and the rattling stopped.

Ruthier considered this. "I don't know. Monks aren't the same as holy-day worshipers; if it serves their faith, they will undertake all manner of demanding acts. A little sand in the courtyard would not be enough to stop them." He ducked his head. "I will be finished with the chicken in a little while. If you have need of me then—"

"Yes, I know; I will call you; but I doubt that I will. Go along and enjoy your meal, and afterward, rest if you like." He nodded in the direction of the second room.

Ruthier put his right hand to the center of his chest, then turned away.

Over the next hour the wind rose, going from a whispered tapping to a persistent drubbing; Sandjer'min sat at his work-table grinding dried herbs and mixing them with various oils and honeys, distantly aware of the monks chanting from the *Gospel of Thomas,* "I am the dancer and the dance. I am the singer and the song. I am the way and the wayfarer. I am the lamp and the flame," and other verses from the millennium-old text. By midnight the wind was promising a sandstorm, and the monks were chanting less steadily in the irregular torchlight; Sandjer'min watched through the small gap in the largest shutters—luckily facing away from the wind—as the monks slowly circled in front of their chapel, their steps unsteady, their voices more harsh than when they began. He could see that the wind was taking a toll on them, and wished he could recommend they cease their rite for now, but knew his intrusion would not be tolerated. "There'll be sprained ankles tomorrow," he said to the room. "And dust-coughs." With a fatalistic sigh, he went and set out the medicaments he would need to treat the monks in the morning.

But the morning brought higher winds and more drifting sands; the monks kept to the chapel until mid-day, when they huddled into a group to scuttle to the refectory, where a meal of lentil soup and simple bread awaited them.

"The nights are growing shorter," Ruthier observed as he swept the sandy floor with a broom of stiff reeds.

"And will do so for the next six months, less ten days," said Sandjer'min, pausing in his on-going work of labeling his medicaments.

"True enough," said Ruthier. "It will be easier to travel in the dark of the year."

"I'll send word down-river to Kerem-al-Gamil to see how trading is going now that the Crusaders are gone. He should be able to give us some useful information." There was a grim note in his voice; Ruthier knew why.

"Do you mean to travel by water?" Ruthier asked, his usually impassive face revealing his shock; Sandjer'min rarely boarded boats, for crossing running or tidal water was an ordeal for him that left him almost immobilized if he endured it for more than a day.

"If necessary." Sandjer'min extended his hand to a knot of dried reeds, removing them from their hook. "I'd prefer to hire a messenger."

"There are roads to Alexandria," Ruthier reminded him.

"There are," he agreed, putting the reeds on a chopping board. "But getting away from Egypt may require speed, and that means the Nile." He took up a knife, but paused to add, "Fortunately we do not have to decide now. Though it would probably be sensible to leave at the end of the summer, when the heat isn't so extreme."

"The nights are longer, as well," said Ruthier, and swept himself and the sand out the door into the shade of the sycamores.

"They are," Sandjer'min agreed; he finished writing on the jars he had filled the night before, then went to an iron-bound chest in the corner, opened it, and removed a sheet of vellum, a vial of ink, and a broad-tipped Persian stylus with which to write.

"Kerem or Olivia?" Ruthier asked as he came back inside.

"Kerem," said Sandjer'min, setting his supplies on the corner of the work-table. "I'll write to Olivia when I have decided where we are to go, and when. I have no desire to cause her anxiety."

Ruthier gave a rare chuckle. "She'll chastise you for making her worry."

"That she will," Sandjer'min conceded with a faint smile. "And no doubt I'll deserve it."

Ruthier nodded, then said, "There is a great deal of sand inside the walls. I'd like to spend the afternoon shoveling as much as I can out of the monastery's grounds."

"You don't need my permission to do that," Sandjer'min said, amusement in his tone.

"Possibly not, but the monks will want to know," Ruthier responded as he went to get his shovel from the tall cabinet near the table.

As soon as Ruthier was out the door, Sandjer'min opened the vial of ink and set it at an angle in a wooden stand made for it. He was cleaning the broad point of the stylus when he heard someone calling, "Sidi! Sidi! Come at once!" He got off his stool and went to open the door, shading his eyes with his hand against the sunlight.

A young monk was standing there, his face worn from the previous night's celebration. "It's Aba'yam," he said without any greeting. "His foot is swelling, it stinks, and his face is red."

Sandjer'min nodded. "I will bring my medicaments. Where is he?"

"In the chapel. He stayed there to pray when the rest of us went to eat. He said he wasn't hungry."

"That's unfortunate," said Sandjer'min, stepping back inside the house; in the second room he opened his red-lacquer chest, where he took down three jars and two rolls of bandages. Then he took a vial of opalescent liquid from a drawer set under the shelves, and put all these things in a small leather case. He closed and latched the chest, then went back to the monk. "You are . . ."

"Dinat."

"If you will come with me?" Sandjer'min saw the young monk wince.

"I should." He swallowed. "I will."

Sandjer'min stepped outside and pulled his door closed; the weight of the sun struck him with the force of a blow, and he was once again grateful that Ruthier had taken care to replace his native earth in the soles of his Persian boots just two days ago. "The chapel, you say? Not the Church?"

"Yes." Dinat started off down the gentle incline; every step kicked up sand, and he had to steady himself twice to keep from falling.

"Tell me," Sandjer'min asked as he kept up with Dinat, "when did this begin for Aba'yam?"

"He was limping at Mass this morning," Dinat told him. "He had trouble dancing toward the end of the rite."

"I don't suppose he soaked his foot afterward, or do you know?"

"I am not aware of it." They had passed the refectory and were almost at the chapel. "I had to feed the goats this morning; he might have done it then."

"It doesn't seem likely," Sandjer'min said.

Dinat shook his head, and hurried ahead to open the chapel door for Sandjer'min, his eyes flicking nervously. "Near the altar, out of the light," he said, standing aside to permit Sandjer'min to pass.

The interior of the chapel was dark but for a pool of light beneath the square dome atop it; heavy, greenish glass let in sunlight through this oculus, but lent it an underwater quality. The altar itself was shadowed but for the lamp that hung over it, providing faint illumination to the Coptic crucifix at its center.

Aba'yam was lying in a heap at the base of the altar, his knees drawn up to his chest, his arms encircling his knees. He was reciting prayers rapidly; his eyes were squinched shut, and his face was plum-colored. As Sandjer'min approached him, he let out a little cry and sketched a blessing in his direction. "God is merciful," he said as Sandjer'min knelt beside him. "Praise Him for His mercy."

"From what Dinat told me, this is more a worldly problem, or a fleshly one." He helped Aba'yam to unfold himself, saying over his shoulder to Dinat, "Go and get a bucket of water from the well and have the cooks boil it, then bring it to me while it is hot. Do you understand?"

"I will do it," Dinat said, and left the chapel with alacrity.

"My foot has swollen," Aba'yam said.

"So I gather," said Sandjer'min as he pulled back the hem of Aba'yam's habit, revealing the unbandaged foot, distorted now by massive swelling in the arch, heel, and ankle. "Why did you unwrap it?"

"It hurt," said Aba'yam, regarding Sandjer'min with fretful eyes.

"And no doubt it is more painful now," said Sandjer'min, bending over him and inspecting the inflamed injury. "When did this begin?"

"Mid-way through our dancing." He stifled a cry as Sandjer'min gently touched the puffiest part of his foot; a drool of yellow pus seeped out of the puncture in his heel.

"You would have done better to leave the wrappings in place," said Sandjer'min, bracing him so he could sit up.

"I realize that," Aba'yam said. "I am very hot."

"You have a fever. I will give you something for it in a moment, and then I will deal with your foot." When he had wiped away the pus from the wound, he opened his case and pulled out the vial of pale liquid. "I want you to drink this. I'll bring you more later on today." He broke the wax seal and removed the stopper, then handed it to Aba'yam. "Drink all of it. It is the sovereign remedy." As he handed the vial to Aba'yam, he felt the heat in his palms. "I've been told that it doesn't taste very good."

"So many medicaments don't," said Aba'yam, and drank, pursing his lips against the remedy's sourness.

"As soon as Dinat brings the hot water, you will soak your foot; I'll add salts to the water to help draw out the putrescence. Then I'll dress the wound with linen that is spread with willow, hyssop, and pansy, to lessen the pain and promote healing. Tomorrow I will give you syrup of poppies, and then I'll search the injury to discover if there is anything remaining in the wound that is causing this putrescence. If there is, I will remove it, and close the wound with silken threads." He had brought a good supply with him on his return from India, but he was careful not to squander it; with Jenghiz Khan marauding along the Silk Road, Sandjer'min did not know when he would be able to get more of such quality.

"That will mean I won't be able to walk for some time," Aba'yam said, his frown deepening.

"No, not for many weeks, and you will have to soak it daily until the swelling is gone and the wound is healed, but if we are diligent, you will keep your foot," Sandjer'min told him levelly.

"There is no other way?" Aba'yam sighed as Sandjer'min shook his head. "If you must, you must."

Sandjer'min moved a bit so that Aba'yam could lean on him, and took more containers out of his case, trying to decide how best to proceed; it would take time for Aba'yam to recover, and that could keep the Sidi at the monastery well into summer to tend Aba'yam through it. If the wound continued unhealed, and the monks blamed Sandjer'min for it, he and Ruthier would have to be gone sooner, traveling in the long days of oppressive heat. "I must," he said.

Text of a letter from Wilem van Groet, farrier with French forces remaining in Egypt after the Fifth Crusade ended, to Emmerico Cammaro, Captain of the Venetian ship *Diadem,* both at Alexandria, written in Church Latin on papyrus and delivered the day after it was dictated to Frater Giordano.

To the great Captain Emmerico Cammaro, of the trading ship Diadem, *the greetings of Wilem van Groet, farrier, presently residing in Alexandria, on this, the third day of February in the 1225th Year of Grace,*

Most esteemed Captain Cammaro,

I am hoping you will read this and give me the honor of your attention: as you know, Malik-al-Kamil, the Sultan of Egypt, has asked all foreigner residents of Alexandria, with the sole exceptions of merchants living in the walled quarter and religious pilgrims, to leave this country by the Vernal Equinox, or face imprisonment until the threats to the country have gone.

I am among those who will have to depart by then, being neither merchant nor pilgrim. Since I came here as a volunteer with the French knights, they are not obliged to aid me in returning home, and they have said that they can do nothing to assist me, which would mean I will have to find a band of pilgrims returning to Europe by ship, or try to travel overland through the summer; unless you are willing to allow me to go aboard your ship as far as the Serenissima Reppublica, the great port of Venezia, I will starve or be taken captive when I try to return through the regions held by Islamites.

As a farrier, I am a capable metal-worker and would be pleased to bring my forge and put it to your use on the seas. I have many years of experience to offer you in regard to smithing. I can repair all manner of metal objects, from cooking stoves to runners for block-and-tackle, to batons for hold-covers. I am capable of doing other work as well, no matter how humble. I have very little money, but my back is strong, and I would be at your service for the whole of the voyage. The reason I am appealing to you is that I have heard that your company, the Eclipse Trading Company, has accepted such arrangements in the past; I hope you will do so now.

It is seven years since I have seen my home and my family. You are one of the few Captains who have extended themselves to men in my position in the past. You are scheduled to depart in three days. If you consent to take me aboard, send me word by the messenger who carries this, and I will present myself to you before sundown with my possessions, such as they are, and my pledge of honest labor. I ask you to consider my request with the concern that all Christians should have for one another.

With my most sincere prayers for your travels and the hope that I will travel with you,

Wilem van Groet
farrier

by the hand of Frater Giordano, Trinitarian

2

Sandjer'min studied the letter that a monk called Yaboth had brought to him in the scriptorium behind the chapel. "Sieur Horembaud du Langnor, in the Aquitaine," he mused as he read the message a third time. "He certainly knows what he wants."

"Is it important?" Yaboth asked, hesitating a bit as he spoke while he peered at the letter he could not read. He was middle-aged, about thirty-five, with a long, tangled beard and fingers gnarled from his years of copying.

"It may be," said Sandjer'min. He set his stylus aside and looked down at the page of formulae for medicaments, part of a book of remedies he was preparing for the monastery. "But that depends on Malik-al-Kamil more than on Sieur Horembaud."

Yaboth looked askance. "What does the Sultan of Egypt have to do with a Christian knight?"

"Directly, I would think very little, but if the Sultan has decided to banish most Europeans from Egypt, then it may have everything to do with him, and me."

"There has been no word of such a ban yet, Sidi," Yaboth said, not looking directly at Sandjer'min.

"But if it comes, then I must consider Sieur Horembaud's request seriously." He gazed out through the unshuttered window into the warm afternoon. "I shall be sorry to have to leave here."

"Do you want to send this Sieur Horembaud an answer?"

"It seems unnecessary. He is planning to stop here on his way south in any case." Getting off the writing stool, he began to refold the letter, sliding it into the sleeve of his cotehardie when he had done, then closed his dish of ink and covered his ink-cake, a mixture of powdered charcoal, rat-skin glue, and ground marsh-berries. "It's time I go to Aba'yam."

"He is improving, isn't he?" asked Yaboth, more doubt in his voice than he liked.

"Yes, he is improving, but he still needs to become better: why do you ask?" Sandjer'min regarded Yaboth with a penetrating gaze. "Is Tsura'gar persisting in seeking to replace him as Aba'yam?"

"He says not, but who knows the hearts of men but God," Yaboth said unhappily. "He has said that the continuing pain in Aba'yam's foot is a sign that he is no longer fit to lead the monastery and that we should elect a successor."

"An unfortunate situation," said Sandjer'min.

Yaboth scowled. "Has he said anything to you—Aba'yam, not Tsura'gar? Do you know what he is planning to do?"

"What would he say to me? I am a foreigner not of your faith. It would not be advisable for him to speak to me about the monastery or the monks. For the most part, we discuss his progress and the treatment I provide." This was not entirely true, but he did not want to break Aba'yam's confidence. He gestured his farewell for the day and left the scriptorium, walking around the front of the chapel, past the refectory to the dormitory, where he knocked to summon the monk who supervised the building. "I am here to—"

"I know what you are here for, Sidi," said Tsura'gar, his head slightly lowered, not in humility, but like a bull preparing to charge. He was the biggest man in the monastery, almost a hand taller than Sandjer'min, bigger framed than most of the Copts, with dark-brown hair hanging in disordered curls to his shoulders, and honey-colored eyes. "Aba'yam is waiting for you in the wash-room."

"Very good," said Sandjer'min.

"Shall I escort you?" His stare challenged Sandjer'min to refuse.

"As you like. I do know the way," said Sandjer'min with no indiction of annoyance. "But do as you think best."

"Then it is best that I show you," said Tsura'gar. He set out to trudge along the narrow corridor and up the half-flight of stairs at the end of it.

"Did Aba'yam soak his foot this morning?" Sandjer'min asked as they went up the steep steps.

"He did, and prayed while he did it." There was an edge of defiance in his answer, as if he regarded Sandjer'min's medicaments as a kind of rival to God's capacity to work miraculous cures.

"Very good," Sandjer'min said, refusing to be drawn into an unnecessary dispute.

Near the top tread, Tsura'gar stopped and rounded on Sandjer'min, on the step below; taking full advantage in the difference in height this gave him, he loomed over the foreign Sidi. "You will not suborn him with your strange wizard's tricks. He will not forfeit his soul to be spared suffering of the body."

"I have no wish to do other than return him to good health," Sandjer'min said calmly, his enigmatic gaze meeting Tsura'gar's stare.

"That is God's work."

Sandjer'min studied Tsura'gar's face, wondering to whom the monk had been talking, that he so reviled the Sidi's determination to help Aba'yam; whoever it was, his influence must be growing stronger for him to condemn Sandjer'min's efforts so rigorously. "Which is why God gives us medicinal plants and treatments, that His Will may be done. It would be irreligious not to use what He has given for our good." He saw Tsura'gar's frown deepen to a glower. "Why do you doubt this? You, a man of faith."

"Because you are not a Christian!" Tsura'gar burst out, his face thunderous. "You have not been baptized! You have not Confessed!"

Sandjer'min favored Tsura'gar with a sardonic smile. "At least I am no hypocrite. You monks have known that I am not of your faith since I came here, and raised no cry against me, until now," Sandjer'min reminded him with unflustered calm. "None of you protested my being here before the Sultan's messengers arrived."

"Because Aba'yam welcomed you, and Venerable Minseh made no objection."

"What do you hold against me, then, if Aba'yam and your Venerable have accepted me?"

"Because I know the Devil sent you." There was absolute certainty in Tsura'gar's deep-set eyes. "You are his servant."

"If I were, what good would it do for me to treat monks and your fellow-Christians for injuries and illnesses. How would that serve the Devil?" He waited to hear Tsura'gar's answer.

"You seek to turn us away from God," Tsura'gar insisted. "To mistrust His Mercy."

"How could treating the sick do that?"

"There are things in your medicaments that will cause us to turn away from faith. You are a corrupter of holy men, with your foreign ways and your—" Tsura'gar folded his arms so he could more completely block the last two steps to Sandjer'min. "You have come here to lead us to tergiversation."

"By treating your ills?" Sandjer'min persisted.

Tsura'gar had no answer for this, and barreled on, "You have insinuated yourself into Aba'yam's good graces and you are using that to destroy him. You think I haven't been watching you, but I have, and I see what you are doing."

"I am treating Aba'yam for a deep putrescence in his heel which—"

"You *put* it there, with your potions and ointments and soaking! You are slowly poisoning him." He raised his fists, trembling with the effort to keep from using them.

"Aba'yam had the end of a thorn sunk deep in his heel; sand worked itself further into the wound and irritated the tip of the thorn. That is what caused the putrescence and made it impossible for the wound to close. Now it is almost—"

"There was a thorn, probably poisoned, because you—" He stopped abruptly as Sandjer'min came up next to him, took him by the shoulder and held him against the wall without apparent effort.

"Listen to me, Tsura'gar: I have done all that I know to do to return health and strength to Aba'yam, as I have done for other monks, and those of the faithful who have come here for succor. I do it out of my obligation to you for giving me a safe haven here. No one has complained of either my work or my reasons for doing it, not even those among you who are suspicious of me, or not until now." He spoke softly, almost gently, but with such purpose that Tsura'gar goggled at him and squirmed in his relentless grip. "I have no reason to do any of you harm." He took a half-step back—all the narrow stair would accommodate—and released Tsura'gar. "But rest assured, I will shortly be gone from here. You haven't long to wait."

"How long?" Tsura'gar asked, the question itself an accusation of lying.

"A month at most." As he said it, Sandjer'min knew he was committed to leaving. "I have been asked to join a group of pilgrims going south."

Tsura'gar showed his teeth in what was not quite a smile. "I will inform Venerable Minseh of this. He will be much relieved," he said nastily.

"I would have thought it was Aba'yam's responsibility to do that," said Sandjer'min with maddening calm. "If you will excuse me, I have to attend to Aba'yam now. If you feel you must, you may lambaste me again when I am finished." Without waiting for any response, he climbed the last step and entered the wash-room, to find Aba'yam waiting for him, his foot plunged into a large bucket of steaming water; the room smelled of salts and wet hemp. Next to it Sandjer'min's medicament case was sitting, its straps unbuckled.

"I heard you talking with Tsura'gar," Aba'yam said, keeping his voice low. "He will have to do penance for his accusations."

Sandjer'min pulled up a low stool and sat down next to the bucket. "If you would help me, say nothing to him: he is looking for reasons to think ill of me, and such penance would give him another injury to increase his rancor. Any attempt to hold him to account will strengthen those who oppose you." He lifted Aba'yam's foot from the hot water, examining it carefully, testing the skin around the ruddy new scar on his heel. "Are you having much pain from walking?"

"A little, but as you told me would happen, it is decreasing. I walked twice as far yesterday as I had been able to the week before. In a month, I hope to be fully restored. In the meantime, I will continue to wrap my foot before I don my sandals when I must walk across sand—even a little sand. I think you were right in fearing that sand in the wound was making it worse." He flexed his foot. "You see? Now that the swelling has gone down, I can move much more easily."

"Good, but not quite as supple as it could be," Sandjer'min told him.

"How long do you think it will be before it is fully strong again?" Aba'yam asked this without any show of worry, though his eyes were a bit too bright.

"A year, perhaps a bit more," Sandjer'min said. "The putrescence has been deep, so it will require time to leave your body completely."

"A year? So long," Aba'yam marveled unhappily.

"Such obdurate putrescence can take longer than that to heal. If it had spread, you would have lost your foot and perhaps your life."

"So you warned me," Aba'yam said, letting his foot sink into the bucket again. "But a year seems a long time for a man of my age; I have fewer years ahead than behind me."

"I suppose it must," said Sandjer'min distantly, trying to recall how it had seemed to him before his unsuccessful execution, when he was thirty-three breathing years old, thirty-three centuries ago.

"It may not appear to be so long a time to you. You are a grown man but not sunken in years, as I am," said Aba'yam.

Sandjer'min smiled faintly. "I am older than you may believe."

Aba'yam shook his head. "I will accept your conviction, but I can't imagine you are much more than thirty-eight or -nine."

Not wanting to continue on such potentially dangerous observations, Sandjer'min asked, "How long have you been soaking your foot?"

"Not as long as you would prefer, I suspect." He lifted the foot. "The skin isn't shriveled yet."

"True enough. Keep it in the water a little longer." He unbuckled the strap that held his case closed. "Have you been eating lemons with your mid-day meal?"

"Not every day, but most of them." Aba'yam yawned, then blessed himself so that his soul would not escape his body. "I could have more if you require it, though I don't like the taste."

"If you dislike the taste, then don't eat more than you're doing already."

Aba'yam shook his head a second time. "Thank you. My mouth puckers at the thought of lemons. Why do you want me to eat them?"

"They bring the sun into your body," he said, giving the explanation he had heard in Persia when he and Ruthier had traveled into China almost two decades ago.

"Haven't we sun enough in Egypt?" Aba'yam joked feebly.

"Not for the inside of your body," Sandjer'min said seriously. "I hope you will continue with the lemons, for your sake."

"Very well," said Aba'yam.

"If your teeth start to hurt, you may stop for a while, say for a week at most," Sandjer'min told Aba'yam, then gave his attention to laying out his medicaments. When he was satisfied with his work, he asked, "How much longer will you be able to continue not leading the monks in the rites of your monastery?"

"Before Tsura'gar confronts me for Aba'yam?" he asked. "The Procession of the Annunciation to Holy Marya is in a few weeks; I will have to participate fully. As you may be aware, the monastery takes its name from what followed that holy occasion, and therefore I must lead or become Bulo'the again, and go into one of the old desert caves to fast and pray for salvation from my failure."

Knowing it was useless to argue about this, Sandjer'min said to him, "If not leading a procession is your greatest trespass, you may count yourself a most fortunate man."

"All sins, even the smallest, are abhorrent in God's eyes," Aba'yam said sternly, looking directly into Sandjer'min's dark eyes. "Repentance is needed, or salvation is meaningless."

"Surely God understands the nature of your errors and assesses them with that in mind," said Sandjer'min, remembering how different the teachings of the earliest Christians had been from those that now predominated the liturgy and the tenets.

"God's sacrifice of His Son demands our repentance," Aba'yam insisted.

Sandjer'min wondered what Aba'yam had done that made him believe years of isolation and penance was required of him; he kept the question to himself, and instead broached the matter that had claimed his attention for most of the day. "I have received a letter from a Christian knight who is escorting a group of pilgrims into the lands to the south. He has . . . asked that I go with his company, and I am inclined to acquiesce; he wants someone who can speak to the peoples of the south."

"Do you know those tongues?" Aba'yam asked, startled.

"No," Sandjer'min admitted. "But one of your monks must, and may be willing to go with us. I should know the languages of the pilgrims." He took a deep breath and continued, "It is time my manservant and I were gone from here; it would be poor repayment for your hospitality to bring the Sultan's men down upon this place because of my presence." It was true as far as it went, but there were other factors that had become pressing—there were few women in the village that he could visit in dreams and none whom he could as knowing lovers—and spurred him to decide on leaving. With Tsura'gar and his faction against himself and Aba'yam, the protection the monastery afforded the three of them—for surely Ruthier was equally at risk as Sandjer'min and Aba'yam—would not last long.

"Is there any way I might dissuade you?" Aba'yam asked, the vertical lines between his brows deepening.

"I doubt it; it wouldn't be wise of you," he said. "Let me treat and bandage your foot, Aba'yam, and then I will arrange with Ruthier to make ready for our departure, so that when the knight arrives with his pilgrims there need be no delay."

Aba'yam's sigh was a complicated one: resigned, exasperated, regretful, fatalistic, and slightly bored with the process of treating his foot. "For now, I will say nothing, in case you should change your mind," he said as Sandjer'min anointed his foot.

"I do not think that will happen," said Sandjer'min.

"Then I will pray for you," said his patient.

It was two days later when Zekri, a monk from up-river near the Second Cataract, whom Sandjer'min knew from his work in the scriptorium, came to Sandjer'min's little house and asked if he could have a word with him.

"If you'll step in out of the sun," Ruthier said, "I will ask him if he's—"

Sandjer'min appeared in the doorway to the second room. "It's all right, Ruthier. I'll talk to the monk."

Ruthier nodded. "My master." His glance in the monk's direction told him the young man needed to speak privately with Sandjer'min, and so he turned to him and asked, "Would you object to my leaving you alone while I go fetch a rabbit? I shouldn't be gone long. I'll be back as soon as possible."

"By all means, fetch the rabbit." He indicated the door; Ruthier left promptly. "Now, Zekri, why are you here?" he asked, taking his place on the tall stool at the work-table.

"I was hoping you might need a guide for your travels to the south," he said with unusual directness; he blushed and stammered, "I have h-heard that you're g-going up-stream. I-I know t-the way. It's not-t easy to f-follow the Nile. I c-could help. My v-village is south of h-here. I've b-been beyond the F-fifth Cataract with my f-father, and I know s-some of the t-tongues along t-the way. I know some f-few words of Umo and Barwa." He tugged at the sleeve of his habit, his black eyes moving uneasily; he was lean and angular, a young man still showing the awkwardness of youth. "I c-can vouch for wat-termen along the river."

"Indeed," said Sandjer'min, his face and eyes revealing nothing of the flare of curiosity that had ignited within him. "And how do you know about this? About my coming journey?" He knew Aba'yam had said nothing about his plans, which meant they had been overheard when he was treating Aba'yam's foot.

"Monks t-talk," said Zekri.

"So they do," said Sandjer'min, and motioned him to continue.

"Yes," said Zekri, continuing with more confidence. "I have been that far t-twice, to the Fifth Cataract. My f-father had been across the Nubian Desert into the mountains four times; he would have g-gone a fifth time, but he took ill and d-died before he could leave again."

"It is true that it would be useful to have a guide. I have been to the Third Cataract, but it was some time ago." It had been more than a millennium since he had made that journey; he kept that to himself.

"The river changes over time. My knowledge is no more than five years old, and should be adequate to the pilgrims you will guide.

It is pilgrims, isn't it?" He looked at Sandjer'min directly, and then his eyes flicked away. "I know men in the stops along the river, which I doubt you do."

"You would be correct," said Sandjer'min. He waited, curious to see how long Zekri could go without speaking.

After a short silence, Zekri said, "I have other knowledge, some from my own travels, some from my father's accounts. For my own, I know what animals dwell along the Nile, and in the Nile, and I have been taught how to deal with the dangerous ones. I have been told of the dog-faced monkeys and the wolves in the mountains." He saw Sandjer'min's dark eyes widen. "Oh, yes, there are wolves. They are high up, and they hunt in packs. There is more I've learned that can help you: I know what to look for to be safe from c-crocodiles and hippopotami, and where snakes go to nest. I have heard of all the animals in the mountains and the d-deserts, but have not seen them all."

"I know some of these things, as well. I have seen dog-faced monkeys, but not, I admit, the wolves you speak of. I know jackals and snakes and many kinds of birds." He considered the monk carefully, aware that a second pair of well-informed eyes could be useful as they traveled; he shrugged. "Still, if Aba'yam and Sieur Horembaud are amenable, you may come with me as one of the men I am allowed to bring."

Zekri smiled uncertainly. "Shall you tell Aba'yam that?"

"If you like," said Sandjer'min. "I will see him again tomorrow and will bring this up to him. I'll let you know what he decides."

Zekri ducked his head. "Thank you, Sidi."

"May I ask why you want to go with us?" The question was little more than an impulsive afterthought, but he saw alarm in Zekri's face. "Is there some trouble?"

"No; I seek to avoid trouble, Sidi," the young monk answered, flushed deeply, and went silent.

Sandjer'min wondered what the trouble might be, but decided not to ask; if Zekri wanted to tell him, he would wait for him to speak. "Very well. But I will give you two days to change your mind, if you should decide to stay."

"I won't," said Zekri with such force that Sandjer'min realized that the monk was not simply asking to journey up-river with him, but was seeking to escape something or someone within the monastery itself.

"Nonetheless," Sandjer'min said calmly, "I would be easier in my mind if you gave yourself a little time to consider what you're undertaking."

"If you insist, I'll p-pray, but I won't change my mind; if I do not go with you, I will still leave this place," said Zekri, his hands clenching, punctuating his determination. He studied the few remaining dried herbs on the hooks behind the work-table. "You will bring your medicaments, won't you?"

"I will," he said.

"G-good." Zekri stood awkwardly, trying to summon up something more to say, then muttered a few disjointed words of thanks before he turned abruptly and left.

A bit later in the afternoon, Ruthier returned, a skinned rabbit hanging from a cord around his wrist. He stepped through the door, pausing as he crossed the threshold. "What did Zekri want?" He spoke in Imperial Latin.

"He wants to join the pilgrimage," said Sandjer'min in the same language, pausing in his loading a wooden chest with his clothes.

Ruthier cocked his head. "Interesting. Did he say why?"

"He knows the river for a considerable distance to the south, and thinks he can be useful," Sandjer'min said with supreme neutrality.

"Then there is more than that," said Ruthier, taking the cord from around his wrist and slipping it over a peg, the rabbit hanging against the wall.

"It would seem so," said Sandjer'min, then changed the subject. "How are things in the village?"

Ruthier knew Sandjer'min would not discuss Zekri again for a while, so he said, "There's much concern about the Sultan's messengers. The villagers are afraid they'll lose all their young men to the Sultan's army. A few are planning to enter this monastery to keep from having to serve the Sultan." He hesitated. "Would you want to take any of them with us? It would remove them from the Sultan's grasp without having them resort to entering the religious life."

"To go south with the pilgrims? That would be for Sieur Horembaud to decide, not I." Sandjer'min was aware that Ruthier's dismay came from something more than the plight of the local villagers, but said nothing.

"What if you were to recommend a few of them? They're Christians, and there would be merit in helping them, would there not?"

Sandjer'min shook his head. "No, not as things stand. It could cause problems for the villagers and the monastery if we did."

"What do you think it would lead to?" Ruthier asked, not as convinced as Sandjer'min was that there could be trouble. "The village is small. The Copts are important to the village, but not much beyond its limits. Sese'metkra would seem hardly worth the effort to conscript its young men. At most there would be twenty young men who could be taken for soldiers, leaving the village without the means to plant and harvest as they have done."

"I agree. This is the sort of place where an example can be made, where opposition can be cut short with little effort on the Sultan's part," Sandjer'min said. "There aren't enough villagers to stand against the Sultan's men, so it is comply or be crushed, which would serve as a warning to other Coptic villages to do as the Sultan commands. It would also mean that many of the people would be pressured to convert, so they would be allowed to keep one son at home."

Ruthier took a deep breath. "And that would imperil the monastery and the village, having such conversions."

"Very likely," said Sandjer'min.

"To lose children or to lose one's faith," Ruthier mused. "Not an easy choice for these people."

Sandjer'min nodded. "And our presence makes it more complicated, for if the town turns away from the monastery, we will have to leave quickly."

"I agree. But do you think that would spare the young men of the village?"

"I don't know, but I would guess not." The world-weary tone of Sandjer'min's answer reminded Ruthier of their days on Cyprus and in Spain.

"You're probably right." Ruthier took a short while to think. "I was thinking of my children, my master. Had this happened in Gades when I was still alive, I would have wanted the chance to keep them out of the hands of those who fought against us, and that wouldn't be possible if I joined with those enemies." It had been almost twelve centuries since Ruthier had been restored to life by Sandjer'min, and longer since he had been separated from his family, but the poignance of the loss had never left him.

"You understand the impasse here," Sandjer'min said.

"And I sympathize with every villager family with boys between fifteen and twenty."

Sandjer'min nodded slowly. "I have no doubt of that, old friend."

"Why would the Sultan not spare a few of the—"

"—villagers' sons? It would be a false delivery, I fear." Sandjer'min stared thoughtfully into the middle distance. "Who would decide which boys were to be exempt and which were to be taken? There would be dissension and the village would face reprisals if there were any kind of refusal."

"Arbitrary selection of young men would not gain the villagers' approval," said Ruthier.

"I don't believe Malik-al-Kamil is worried about the approval of a few Copts," said Sandjer'min. "He needs to strengthen his army."

"A pity he won't spare a few Copts from the war," said Ruthier, more sharply than was his habit.

"But where would it stop? He would end up having to excuse all Copts from his conscription, and that would compromise his forces. I am not defending him," he added, seeing Ruthier's glower. "I am only describing the Sultan's predicament. If he does not take all the young men he can, he will lose before the first battle occurs. That does not mean that I am in favor of what he believes he must do, but my opinion means little here."

"Then you think Jenghiz Khan will get this far?" Ruthier asked.

"No, but I didn't think he'd get so far into China, or the west," said Sandjer'min.

Ruthier took a long moment to think this over. "You're right: it is time we were gone," he said at last, and went to take his dinner into the second room.

❄   ❄   ❄

Text of a letter from Paulos Aristadese, Superior at the Orthodox Christian Church of the Holy Redeemer in Tyre, to Eukratos Kirieki at the Orthodox Church of the Eucharist in Alexandria, written in Greek on vellum and delivered by two monks nine days after it was written.

> *To my most dear brother in Christ, the blessings and greet-ings of Paulos Aristadese, Superior of the Church of the Holy Redeemer in Tyre, on this, the Feast of Saint Porphyry of Gaza,*
>
>> *Most reverend Eukratos Kirieki,*
>
> *I can make no promise about the amount of protec-tion we can provide the European Christians who are now required to depart Egypt, for the ban upon their presence is expected to be extended beyond Egypt itself and into other lands where the might of Islam holds sway, Tyre being one of the places where such bans are consid-ered a possibility. I have asked the priests and monks serving here to vote on what we should do, but have not yet achieved a full counting of the ballots cast. I have not been able to determine which way the votes will go, for the monks and priests here are reluctant to discuss their posi-tions in this matter.*
>
> *As we approach the Paschal Season, we do so with more trepidation than we should, but as things stand, it is unlikely that we will be able to protect our Christian com-munity here, let alone add more to those to whom we already minister, for much longer; the followers of Islam grow ever more determined to assert their strength in our affairs, and God has not seen fit to instill tolerance in their hearts. We have had to inform other churches that our re-sources are at their limit, and God has also not seen fit to extend His Mercy to us. I have recommended to many priests and monks in your situation that you apply to Venezian*

merchant ships for space on their decks for those Europeans required to leave; it is difficult travel on the open decks of a galley, but it will serve as a means of getting away from Egypt without the dangers of attempting to reach Constantinople along the trade roads. If enough of our faith arrive in Constantinople, an appeal may be made to the Patriarchs and Metropolitans there on behalf of those unable to leave in the allotted time, and in turn, it is possible that some action may be taken to assist your flock, but Roberth de Courtenay rarely sets foot out of Constantinople except to ask the Roman Pope and the Christian rulers of Europe to come to his aid, and therefore he may be ill-disposed to your cause.

We are finding our circumstances straitened: in the last few weeks we have seen a number of pilgrims returning from the distant south, and they, too, are seeking the means to get home; many are tired from their travels, and a few of them are ill. A small number of them have fared well: one pilgrim had procured a jar of ochre-colored dust which he claimed was Our Lord's blood spilled by the spear in His side. He has pledged to carry it to Saint-Peter's Basilica in Roma to demonstrate his faith and to prove that his pilgrimage has earned him the absolution of his sins. He is adamant about his need to reach that city as quickly as possible, and we have put his name about to many of the European traders who might carry him to Neapolis or Ostia. Most of the Venezian traders avoid those ports, so it will have to be the Genovese who carry them. You may find some among them who will take pilgrims back to France, for those bound to that kingdom. There are some English among the pilgrims who may have to return to their island in stages; in that case, either Venezian or Genovese ships should be able to get them on their way.

I pray for the delivery of all Christians; for those called to martyrdom, I extol them and abjure them to hold fast to their faith that they may wear crowns in Paradise.

In the name of God the Father, Christ the Son, and the Holy Spirit, Amen

Paulos Aristadese
Superior
The Orthodox Church of the Holy Redeemer

3

Five sailing boats and three rowed barges swung in at the landing at the village below the Monastery of the Visitation as the residents came out of their houses and fields to see what and who had come to such an insignificant place as this. Half a dozen men ran onto the dock, shouting instructions to the boats while gesticulating where they might tie up. Most of the passengers had donned hoods against the sun, and could not easily be seen, though their blue garments marked them as foreigners on pilgrimage, as did the palm-fronds many of them held. Along with the waterman manning the steering oar, a European man with a short, ruddy beard, dressed in a pilgrim's blue linen surcote blazoned with his family's device—vert, a stag couchant proper, crowned or—with a Crusader's cross sewn on the short sleeve, stood in the rear of the open boat, next to the man handling the oar. Six other foreigners were in the lead boat, with others in the remaining five boats, all in all about twenty pilgrims; the barges held all manner of chests and cases as well as a dozen white asses and five horses. It was not quite mid-day and the Nile shone as if it was made of shards of constantly shifting polished glass.

Zekri was the first to make it to Sandjer'min's little house with the news of the arrivals. "There are foreigners of every kind! There has never been such a day here!" he exclaimed with more excitement than truth. "Five boats and three barges, with asses and horses as well as many chests. Nothing like this has happened in many years. Boats that bring pilgrims go to Edfu or Elephantine, not Sese'metkra.

The whole village is going to meet them." His eyes were excited, and he moved as if all of him itched.

Dreading the brilliance of the sun overhead, Sandjer'min tightened the lacings on his sandals and stepped out into the blazing day. "Quite a company," he said, shading his eyes.

"Such a number of them," Zekri said, doing his best to count them all against the shine of the Nile.

"Pilgrims do well to travel in large groups," said Sandjer'min. "As do merchants."

"And armies," Zekri interjected.

"Yes, and robbers, for that matter."

"And I shall be one of the pilgrims," Zekri declared, a look of happy disbelief making him look younger than his years.

"I trust you have your garments packed; from what Sieur Horembaud told me in his letter, I believe he will want to set out in a day or two," said Sandjer'min, feeling a hint of dismay at the thought of going so far over running water; the prospect troubled him now as it had for the last four days. "I will see to your other needs as Sieur Horembaud orders me, but clothing and footwear are your responsibility." He watched the trapizoidal latine sails snap in the freshening wind, and wondered how long he would have to travel over water this time; the very thought filled him with vertigo so that he had to take a moment to steady himself. "I had better go down to the landing and speak with Sieur Horembaud before he brings all his companions and their belongings into the town."

"He'll have slaves to tend to that," said Zekri, not quite tagging after Sandjer'min as he started down the hill.

"He will watch them in any case," said Sandjer'min, lengthening his stride and moving through the crowd of monks making for the entry-gate of the monastery.

"No doubt you are right," said Zekri, a bit out of breath. "I have a pair each of Roman peri and sandals, another habit and a pluvial for when we reach the mountains. I have a bed-roll for sleeping, and a canvass sail, for when the winds blow hard."

"Very wise," said Sandjer'min, pressing forward and slipping through the bottleneck of the gate with no sign of difficulty; moving relieved some of the discomfort of the running water as well as the inexorable sun. He went down the sandy street, passing the first stacks of newly mown wheat piled on the threshing floor behind the civic house of the village, where the council met and supervised the rules of market-day, took care of official transactions, received foreigners and the messengers sent from the Sultan, and held official feasts and celebrations. At the marketplace, he took the track to the river, catching up with two of the village's three leaders; he took care not to get ahead of them.

"Pilgrims," said the older of the two leaders to Sandjer'min. "You said they would be coming."

"Bound to the south," Sandjer'min agreed, making a gesture of respect toward the man.

"And you are going with them—Tsura'gar has told me." There was a critical edge to this remark, and a sharp glance in Sandjer'min's direction.

"That is the plan," Sandjer'min said with unruffled calm.

"Just as well," the leader said. "Though it will be a pity to lose your skills with your medicaments. My oldest boy would not be standing straight without you."

For an instant, Sandjer'min felt a sharp pang of loneliness that slid through him like a knife; he concealed this with an equivocal chuckle. "Those of us in exile have to be willing to go about the world. This is neither the first nor the last time that I shall have to seek out a new place where I can live in peace, and my manservant will not be suspected of nefarious doings."

The leader had the sensitivity to make a gesture of regret. "If the Sultan were not pressing us, perhaps it might have gone otherwise, but your very presence provides him an excuse to—"

"I am aware of it, and I am sorry it has come to this," said Sandjer'min, sorry to appear rude. "The first of the pilgrims is coming ashore."

The leader went forward along the broad stone landing, calling out greetings slowly and loudly in his Coptic tongue. "You are welcome here, in the name of the Christ and our God."

Sieur Horembaud answered in the dialect of the Aquitaine region of France where the English ruled. He, too, spoke loudly but not as slowly. "My pilgrims and I seek a place for a night or two, with pasturage for our stock. We will thank God for what you provide."

The two men went quiet, staring at one another. Then the village leader began again, this time in clumsy Arabic; his efforts were met with much the same perplexity and frustration as Coptic had. "I know little of Islam's language," the leader said in his limited Arabic.

Sieur Horembaud frowned, and motioned to the rest of the pilgrims to stay where they were. "I must speak to this man," he announced in Anglo-French. "Tell him that," he added to Sandjer'min.

"Leader," said Sandjer'min politely in Coptic, "if you will permit me to speak for you, I think this misunderstanding may be remedied." Before the leader could answer, Sandjer'min moved a bit closer to the two men, and said in unpolished but very acceptable Aquitanian English, "You are Sieur Horembaud, I gather, and these are your pilgrim companions. I am Rakoczy, Sidi Sandjer'min. This is Aste'on, one of the village leaders here in Sese'metkra. He is in charge of greeting newcomers. You may address him for your wants." He returned to Coptic. "Aste'on, this is a French knight called Sieur Horembaud du Langnor, who is to lead the expedition." He looked directly at Sieur Horembaud. "This man, Aste'on, will see you and your comrades are made welcome. If you will hold up your hands, palms outward, and bow slightly . . . ?"

"To such a man as he?" Sieur Horembaud challenged.

"Since he is the one who will decide if you or your animals will eat tonight, yes, it is as well that you show him courtesy." He showed him how the thing was to be done.

"Oh, very well," said Sieur Horembaud, and copied Sandjer'min's bow with neither grace nor much attention. "Tell him I and my companions thank him for receiving us." There was no hint of gratitude in his manner.

Sandjer'min turned to Aste'on. "He asks you to forgive him, but he is weary with travel, as are all those in his company. He thanks you for receiving him and the rest of the pilgrims."

"Long hours on the river can be tiring," said Aste'on, losing some of the forbidding scowl that had been gathering like storm-clouds on his face.

"He will appreciate your understanding." Sandjer'min once again spoke to Sieur Horembaud in his own tongue. "You will have to allow the village to honor you with a feast, but if you want to bring your people and their animals and things ashore, you should be assigned places to sleep."

Sieur Horembaud scrutinized Sandjer'min for a long moment, then nodded. "I'll take your word for it. What do I call you?"

"Sandjer'min will do, or Rakoczy, whichever you prefer."

"Not much to choose between them," Sieur Horembaud grumbled. "Still, Rakoczy sounds more civilized than Sandjer'min. Could it be similar to some of the names of the knights from the east of Europe."

"My native earth is presently Hungarian." Sandjer'min gave him a half-bow, and stepped aside, saying to Aste'on, "He and his company are eager for rest, but they seek the honor of joining you and the people of your village, in dining together."

Aste'on smiled for the first time. "For our fellow-Christians, it will be our honor," he said, then raised his voice. "All of you, our visitors seek the chance to share our evening meal. Let all of you hasten to prepare what will please our guests. For the Glory of God and the honor of Sese'metkra."

A general shout went up from the villagers; some of the pilgrims on the boats exchanged uneasy glances until Sandjer'min raised his voice and called out in Church Latin, "The villagers of Sese'metkra and the monks of the Monastery of the Visitation bid you welcome. They rejoice that you have come to them during your holy journey."

Sieur Horembaud studied the foreigner's face. "I hope that is what he said, Rakoczy. I would not want you to play me false."

The villagers pressed onto the landing to help the five boats tie up while the slaves from the barges clambered onto the landing to secure their crafts.

"What would that benefit me, Sieur Horembaud?" Sandjer'min asked without rancor. "I may express what you, or the leader, wishes me to convey in terms neither would use as such, not knowing the language and customs of the other, but the intent of your words must always be at the heart of what I say." It was a little too accommodating, Sandjer'min thought as he reviewed what he had said, but he decided Sieur Horembaud would prefer that to anything he assumed smacked of disrespect.

Behind them, two of the boats were helping their passengers to disembark: two men, one fairly young, the other older, with the du Langnor arms on their surcoats, were the first on the landing; immediately after them came a nun and a young man; behind them, a woman in half-mourning; last, a servant, about twenty-five, with massive shoulders. As soon as they were all off the boat, the oarsman steered it away from the landing to give more room to the other boats.

"See you stay within my meaning, Rakoczy. I have no wish to be held accountable for your misrepresentations." He swung back toward the boats. "Follow the villagers," he said loudly. "The slaves will handle the animals."

"How many slaves do you have with you?" Sandjer'min asked.

"Eleven; they're on the barges with the animals. I own two of them. They can sleep in the stalls, the lot of them. Tell Aste'on, would you?" Sieur Horembaud reached out to take hold of Sandjer'min's arm. "And tell me if you think we should post guards around our cases and our stock?"

"If you fear that you might be robbed, then ask Aba'yam if you can keep those things inside the monastery. The monks are sworn to keep everything within their walls protected. There are a few paddocks behind the rear wall, and that should be a safe place if you believe the villagers would take them." He kept all emotion from his voice.

"We're pilgrims. Better the monastery for our property, but the village for beds," said Sieur Horembaud, releasing Sandjer'min's arm. "Arrange it. Don't promise them too much—they should be honored to receive us as guests."

Sandjer'min nodded. "I'll speak to Aste'on now, and then go to the monastery to make arrangements for you."

"Very good," said Sieur Horembaud, then, as Sandjer'min moved away from him toward the village, Sieur Horembaud signaled to one of his company; a surprisingly handsome young friar came up to him. "Well?"

"I don't know the local language, but his Arabic is very good," said the friar in Greek. "He has a manner about him. You can tell he was born to better than sanctuary in a monastery, especially one like that." He pointed to the open gates.

"There must be a story behind his choice," said Sieur Horembaud, rubbing the stubble of his beard. "You're right, he does have a manner."

Frater Anteus followed Sandjer'min with his eyes. "You won't be able to bend him to your will so easily."

"So long as he obeys me, why should I care how submissively he does it?" Sieur Horembaud looked about him. "What would bring that man to a place like this, do you think? Is he on the run, or something worse?"

The second boat was nudged up to the landing, and a third on the other side of the stone pier. Both were unloading their passengers, who went along toward the village; all of them looked tired, and one seemed to be suffering from the sun. One of the pilgrims was wearing a loose linen tunic over laced leggings, a modified version of what most of the Egyptians wore; he appeared more comfortable than the others.

"He hasn't the look of a fugitive," said the friar. "Jiochim Menines said he had heard that the Sidi is in exile."

"But why? And from where?" Sieur Horembaud asked the hot, sandy air. "I'm damned if I'll call any man Sidi."

"If he is an exile, we should be able to find out the reason, in time," the friar declared. "Do you want me to befriend him?"

"If you aren't obvious about it," Sieur Horembaud said, then walked more swiftly as the slaves began to lead the asses and horses off the barges. "I must deal with the village leader, that Aste'on, and I suppose, the Superior at the monastery."

"Keep Rakoczy with you when you do. He appears to be trusted."

Sieur Horembaud gave him a hasty wink. "Ah, Frater Anteus, if your father had had any sense about him, he would not have abandoned you to the monks when he left for Normandy. Bastard or not, you do him proud."

Frater Anteus managed to conceal the flare of temper he felt, and ducked his head. "A great compliment, Sieur."

Oblivious to the sneer in the friar's voice, Sieur Horembaud returned the slight bow and strode on, following Sandjer'min, who was some distance ahead; he paid no heed to the sandy-haired, middle-aged man who came up from the river, a brace of ducks hanging limply from leather thongs; he knew a slave or a servant when he saw one.

Ruthier watched the Anglo-French knight increase his speed from a saunter to a brisk walk. He had heard enough of Sieur Horembaud's exchange with Frater Anteus to be concerned. He would have to inform Sandjer'min of Sieur Horembaud's opinions and intentions, and Frater Anteus' knowledge of Arabic and Greek, and possibly other tongues as well. He waited while more of the pilgrims disembarked and the boats moved up-river to the pier where they could tie up for the night; this would provide room for the slaves to lead the horses and asses up into the village where they could be turned out in paddocks. When the animals with the servants and slaves assigned to them were on the shore, Ruthier went up the hill, past the chapel, to the little house in the stand of sycamores.

Sandjer'min returned a short while later, saying as he came through the door, "I need my case of medicaments. One of the pilgrims—some kind of disgraced Crusader—is suffering from too much sun. His skin is fair and now it is badly burned and fevered." He went into the second room and came out with his case.

"Yes. I saw him. He looks like a half-cooked roast." Ruthier interrupted his plucking of the ducks and turned toward him. "You understand his problem."

"Far too well," said Sandjer'min, recalling his ordeal on the road to Baghdad, and the months it took his skin to recover. He was almost out the door when Ruthier stopped him.

"Sieur Horembaud doesn't trust you."

"Nor I him," said Sandjer'min. "But what makes you say that?"

"I have just heard him talking to that friar, that Frater Anteus?

Sieur Horembaud has assigned him to befriend you so that he may report on you to the knight."

"That's odd. Sieur Horembaud made it clear in his letter that he didn't want me fraternizing with his company."

"Then this may be some kind of test. By the way, Frater Anteus speaks Arabic." He said all this quietly, but with genuine concern.

"I thought he might," said Sandjer'min. "A friar—is he a friar or a monk?—from Alexandria would find it helpful. He probably knows Greek and a few other languages—and Church Latin, of course."

Ruthier nodded. "Be careful with him, my master."

"I will, old friend, and with Sieur Horembaud." He shook his head slowly.

"Is there anything I can do for you while you treat this burned pilgrim?" Ruthier asked as Sandjer'min started toward the door.

"Only if you can conjure up some ice. Otherwise, I must use the medicaments I have, and hope to bring his fever down." He opened the door. "The wind's picking up."

"I'll make sure all the shutters are closed. It will be dark soon." Ruthier waited while he listened to one of the asses being led to the small stable beyond the rear wall bray loudly. "Will you remain for the welcoming feast, or do you plan to leave early?" There was an anxious note in his question.

"I'll remain only if I must. I will have to discuss a few things with Sieur Horembaud, but they will wait for morning. I think Sieur Horembaud is more tired than he supposes he is." He stepped out into the stinging wind, wiping the fine film of sand off his face as he closed the door. Making his way down the hill, avoiding the animals being led up it, Sandjer'min went to the scriptorium, hoping to find Yaboth, but he and most of the monks were gone.

"They're in the village, with the pilgrims," one of the monastery's slaves informed him.

"I will look for them there," said Sandjer'min. He left by the side-door of the scriptorium and went on down the hill.

The doors of the civic house were wide open despite the wind, and the building was filled with pilgrims, monks, and villagers, most of them talking at once. Sandjer'min threaded his way through them to where Aste'on sat with the other two leaders; he made the gesture of respect as he came up to them, and raised his voice to be heard. "I have come, as you asked. What is it you want me to do?"

"Oh. You're here," said Aste'on, motioning to Sandjer'min to come closer. "The poor man is in the counting-room, on the bench there."

"I'll go tend him, and will tell you what his condition is when I am done." He went toward the cluster of small rooms at the back of the main hall; he saw the counting-room door was open, and he made for it.

"Rakoczy!"

Sandjer'min stopped at the sound of Sieur Horembaud's voice. "Bon Sieur," he said, trying not to seem impatient.

"They told me you can fix Torquil, that you can restore him to health," he said as he approached, effectively blocking Sandjer'min from going on.

"I hope I can. It depends on how badly burned he is."

"It's bad. I've seen men in his condition before. I had Florien give him some salted fish in gruel—that's what the Crusaders use for such burns—but I don't think Torquil ate it, or if he did, that it didn't do much for him. Florien's still with him. Send him out to me if you don't need him for your treatment." He paused. "You may speak with Torquil, and the rest of my company, as your duty requires of you, but I must insist that you indulge in no idle chatter; we are on a holy mission, and we must not have our thoughts turned from our goal. Be sure you bear that in mind in our travels as well as now."

"I will send Florien out, then, unless you want him to observe my treatment," said Sandjer'min; he had the disquieting sense that Sieur Horembaud had been waiting for him. "If you will permit?"

"Permit?" With the appearance of mild surprise, Sieur Horembaud stepped aside. "I hadn't noticed that I was blocking your way."

As Sandjer'min went on to the counting-room, he began to think that Sieur Horembaud could be just as arbitrary in his demands as Tsura'gar was in his, and as difficult to accommodate.

✿ ✿ ✿

Text of a letter from Aba'yam to Venerable Minseh at Edfu, written on papyrus and carried by Dinat, delivered four days after it was written.

> *To the Venerable Minseh, from Aba'yam of the Monastery of the Visitation, the most reverential and covert greetings, on this, the sixteenth day before the Vernal Equinox:*
>
> > *Venerable Minseh,*
> >
> > *This is to inform you that yesterday a company of pilgrims arrived at Sese'metkra, seeking a place to rest and to receive treatment for one of their number who had been badly burned by the sun. Aste'on arranged for places for them to sleep, gave them permission to eat in the civic house, and generally made them welcome. I have told them that they might come to our chapel for Mass, though they are not Copts, but I doubt any of them will. Because their burned companion will need a few days to be able to travel again, the company will remain here for another three days, and when they leave, Sidi Sandjer'min and his man will go with them. This is not a sudden decision, for the Sidi and I have discussed this possibility for some time, as he was asked to join the pilgrims some weeks ago. Much as I dislike losing his skills, I agree with him that it is appropriate that he depart, for his continued presence may cause us problems if he is still here when the Sultan's messengers return. I have given permission for Zekri, one of the younger monks, and Olu'we, a tertiary from the village, to go with the pilgrims, with the understanding that they will provide us regular reports, which they will entrust to pilgrims bound downriver to deliver to you at Edfu. Both have pledged to honor my instruction, and for that reason, I believe we will all benefit from their traveling with the pilgrims.*
> >
> > *My foot is much improved, but it will be some time yet before the healing is complete, with God's Will to bring about a full recovery. I pray daily for His Mercy. For those among the monks here who doubt I will be able to resume my duties, I know their fears are groundless, and that in*

good time they will see that they have no cause to worry. It troubles me that their doubts should so work upon their Brothers that discontent is disrupting the harmony of the monastery, and I pray that you will not be swayed by the rumors that have become rife in regard to my capacity to fulfill my office here. Venerable Minseh, you have no reason to question my abilities, or to consider putting another in my place. In God's good time, I will mend, and do all that is required of me with a whole body and a thankful heart.

May God's Grace be upon you,
in this life and in the life hereafter,
Aba'yam
The Monastery of the Visitation

4

"What do you want to do with the sword?" Ruthier asked Sandjer'min as he set the metal buckles on their clothes chest over the tongues, then pressed down the cap that would keep the buckles from opening. As they usually did when they were together alone, they spoke Imperial Latin. "Pilgrims can't have swords." Outside the sun had barely begun to rise, its golden rim sliding above the line of hills to the east; cocks were crowing, goats and sheep in the monastery pens and the village below bleated for food, and activity had increased at the water's edge in preparation for loading the barges and boats to resume the voyage up-river. The wind was steady, coming up from the north, promising good travel for the day.

"I'm not going to carry it in plain sight, but I won't leave it behind." Sandjer'min almost smiled. "I have wrapped it and its scabbard in leather and put it in the back of my medicaments chest, under the metal belt that keeps it closed. I've designed it to look like the leather padding on the inside of the belt. I've installed a pair of leather staples to keep it in place."

"What if anyone should discover it?" Ruthier pursued.

"I don't know. I suppose I will have to think of some explanation for it being there. For now, I will trust that it won't be discovered. But I will not leave so valuable a sword here in the care of monks, who would not know what to do with it, or how to take care of it." The sword had come into his possession as the result of single-combat in the mountains of western China a decade ago; Saito Masashige, the foreign warrior he had bested, had presented Sandjer'min with it in recognition of his victory.

"They'd probably use it to kill chickens," said Ruthier.

"Or cut the limbs off of the trees," said Sandjer'min with genuine sadness.

Ruthier was able to shudder at the thought. "You must bring it with you."

"And hope for the best." Sandjer'min nodded. "Have we everything else ready?"

"The tent is in a heavy cotton casing, your medicaments chest is ready, our other chests and cases are set outside on the sledge. All I have to do is finish loading them on and tying them down. Your mattress is rolled and tied on your chest of native earth."

"Very good," Sandjer'min approved. "Then we need not linger."

Ruthier hesitated before he asked his next question. "Did you visit the widow at the edge of the village last night?"

"I did. She had a wonderful dream," he said, a hint of sadness in his answer.

"But you would prefer a knowing partner," Ruthier said for him.

"Yes; but such a woman isn't to be found here, and if there were, it wouldn't be safe for either of us to be intimate." He waited for the next question; when none came, he said, "Still, I will miss her."

"There are women among the pilgrims," Ruthier pointed out.

Sandjer'min shook his head. "In such a group, I would be a fool even to visit one of them while she slept; there is too much familiarity among them for my actions to go unnoticed, and among pilgrims, my true nature would be seen as diabolical. No, for now, I must content myself with taking a little from the asses and horses. There may be places along the way where I can find sleeping women."

"Where might that be?" Ruthier asked.

"I will know when—or if—we find such a place," said Sandjer'min at his most distant. After a short silence he added, "The monks and the villagers have remembered we are foreigners and are relieved to have us gone, as useful as we have been to them."

Ruthier nodded and changed the subject. "What of Zekri and Olu'we? Will they want to put their cases on the sledge with ours?"

"They're probably going to be assigned to help the slaves bring the horses and mules down the hill; they should have their cases at the landing already if that's the case. You and I can handle the sledge ourselves. We won't have to ask for any additional help." Sandjer'min was strong enough to carry all their luggage himself, at least at night, and by day he would have been able to bear most of it, but that would draw attention he did not want, and so he put the last case on the sledge, and signaled to Ruthier to leave the little house and the shelter of the sycamores, and begin yet another journey.

"Are you ready?" asked Ruthier as he shoved the door all the way open.

The sky was brightening to a purplish red; Ruthier closed the door behind Sandjer'min and said, "Windy today."

"The signs are for it; it should help speed us up-river," said Sandjer'min, going to the front of the sledge and taking the broad loop of hempen rope in his hands, giving it an experimental tug. "I'll need you to hang on to the rear once we start down the hill. I don't want this running away from me, or knocking me off my feet."

"Do we wait for the animals to be led down?" Ruthier gathered up a length of rope, wrapping it from hand to elbow, then stowing it under the ropes holding their belongings on the sledge.

"Yes. They should be on their way shortly; the slaves went up to get them a little while ago." He heard one of the horses whinny, and added, "They're on the move."

Ruthier glanced toward the stout gate that led to the barn, the stable, the pens, and paddocks behind the monastery wall. "I have been told that Sieur Horembaud bargained for more food last night."

"He has got more of it for the animals than the pilgrims. He said keeping the stock fed will be more important than keeping the pilgrims fed, that fasting will benefit them if it comes to that." Sandjer'min watched as the four horses were the first through the gate, frisking on their lead-lines, tails flagged over their rumps.

"Do you know which boat we will ride in?"

"I believe he intends to separate us while we are moving; I have told him that you and I will usually dine apart from the rest—that it is the custom among those of my blood, and among yours, and he has agreed to allow us to do so, though I'm not sure how he sees that happening," said Sandjer'min, watching the horses come to order and mince down the hill, the nine asses coming along behind them, stolid and dependable. All of them were dusty and a few showed bare patches of skin where the sand had worn the hair away.

"Why?" Ruthier inquired. "Does he suspect us of nefarious dealings?"

"If he does not, Frater Anteus does," said Sandjer'min. "We should let Sieur Horembaud tell us where he would like us to settle for the voyage to Edfu; he will be more comfortable that way, making assignments and directing the travel," he went on, more to himself than to Ruthier, then added, "I have asked him to permit me to attend Torquil in the shelter that has been rigged for him on one of the barges; that will ensure that Torquil is given treatment for his burns, and it will keep me out of the sun. If I can keep the chest of my native earth, I shouldn't be too exhausted."

"You mean he consented to letting you travel with Torquil to care for him?" Ruthier was somewhat surprised to hear this, for he had thought that it was unlikely that the knight would be willing to see Sandjer'min so coddled when others were not.

"Consent is too strong a word; he has been willing to consider it, and told me last night that he thought it would be best for Torquil that I attend him. And since he intends that you and I should travel in separate vessels, he has assigned the nun—Sorer Imogen, the Englishwoman?—to assist me with Torquil," said Sandjer'min, recalling his discussion with Sieur Horembaud from the previous evening; his expression darkened. "Once we start across the desert, we will travel at night, so that should be no difficulty. But while we are on the river, sun and running water will enervate me by the time we stop for the night."

"You convinced him to use the old trade route, then?"

The last of the asses clattered by, their tails already flicking at flies; the slaves leading them kept them to a brisk walk, holding the leads to the simple halters with care, for the asses were still unused to them, and inclined to fret and resist if tugged suddenly. They progressed down the hill and out the heavily planked gates, then along the main road through the Sese'metkra to the landing.

"I showed him the maps of the river, including that loop to the southwest, and how we could take several days off our travels if we went on the Gold Road." He gave an ironic smile. "I think *gold* caught his attention."

"Then we will have to buy or engage camels. Horses and asses alone cannot make that journey," said Ruthier. "This company of pilgrims will need camels to get across that part of the Nubian Desert."

"That they will." Sandjer'min sighed. "Camels. Perhaps I can persuade Sieur Horembaud to let me ride one of the asses."

A glint of amusement lit Ruthier's faded-blue eyes. "If he refuses, you'll have to ride a camel."

"If only there were Bactrian camels here, not Dromedaries," said Sandjer'min, and tugged the sledge into motion. "I'd better arrange for a horse."

"It's the wrong desert for Bactrians," said Ruthier, and took hold of the main rope, preparing to keep the sledge to the pace Sandjer'min set.

"Sadly, it is," said Sandjer'min, making sure his efforts to lug the sledge appeared genuine, for he could see Tsura'gar standing a short distance above the chapel, watching him. Sandjer'min ducked his head respectfully.

Ruthier saw him, as well, and fell silent until they were past him. "It is unfortunate that Aba'yam did not come to offer you his blessing."

"I asked him not to," said Sandjer'min.

"You did?" Ruthier was so surprised that he almost stopped moving.

"Tsura'gar has been urging the monks to support him to be Aba'yam, and to compel the present Aba'yam to retire to a cave to pray. If Aba'yam were to offer any kind of farewell short of a curse, Tsura'gar would use it to discredit Aba'yam, and that would be poor thanks for the haven this place has been." He could see Tsura'gar raise his arms in prayer, and briefly wondered what the monk was praying for.

"Are you certain that that would happen?"

"Not absolutely, but certain enough, and that would be poor compensation for Aba'yam's kindness to us; he has trouble enough without our adding to it," said Sandjer'min, reducing the speed of his walking as he felt the weight of the sledge shift with the steepening of the slope. "Hold on, old friend."

Ruthier tightened his grip on the rope. "Do you need more help?"

"Not yet, but don't let go of your rope," was Sandjer'min's reply. He lifted the front end of the sledge a bit, not only to get it over the uneven ground more easily, but to keep the sledge moving more slowly than it was straining to go.

As they passed the chapel, Zekri and Olu'we came out, both with the Cross marked on their foreheads in oil, and each with two large cases slung over their shoulders. They fell in beside Ruthier. "We were told to go to the boats with you," said Zekri.

"Good morning, Brothers," said Sandjer'min in their own tongue. "A good day for traveling, wouldn't you agree?"

The monks muttered a response, showing how much they were trying to contain their excitement; Zekri pressed his lips tightly to-gether to keep from smiling.

A moment later, Olu'we said, "I'm going to tell them to keep the gate open for us," and all but ran down the hill.

"He's been worried that we will not be allowed to leave, after all, and now that the animals are through the gate, he fears the slaves will close us in," Zekri explained quietly.

Sandjer'min gave a single laugh. "Many of the monks want us gone, as well you know. They're more inclined to drive us out with whips than keep us in."

Leaving the monastery behind, they went on through the town, passing the civic house and the market-square, heading toward the landing where the barges were drawn up to take the animals aboard. Rowers stood near their various barges, most of them eating dates and flatbread, paying little attention to the loading going on, or the people who were gathering at the foot of the landing. On the nearest barge, a simple tent of dark wool had been set up, with a pallet lying under it; Sandjer'min realized this was where he was bound, and where Torquil would be laid. A number of trunks had already been lashed to the deck of that barge, and three large nets filled with fodder for the asses were tied atop them.

Sieur Horembaud, who had been shouting to the men at the end of the landing, now came toward the four new arrivals. "In good time. The watermen tell me that we should make swift progress today, with the wind so brisk."

"It is brisk," Sandjer'min agreed, dragging the sledge onto the landing. "There are two chests and my mattress I would like to take aboard the barge with me, and my chest of medicaments. The rest can go where it suits you."

For a long moment, Sieur Horembaud looked as if he would like to refuse, but then he shrugged. "You're the one who will have to treat Torquil; you know what you need to do it. If you require those things, I'll take it you know your business: you may have them." He rounded on Ruthier and the two monks. "You will go with the English widow— well, not really a widow, but as good as one—Margrethe of Rutland, in the third boat; she has her husband's half-brother with her—he's young enough to be impatient with everything. Her sister-in-law, Sorer Imogen, will ride with the Sidi, to aid him." He glared at the river. "As we concurred last night."

"Yes," said Sandjer'min, letting go of the pull-rope and working to untie the chests and cases from the sledge.

"The slaves will load your goods for you; leave the chests and cases and the rest of it to them. Your manservant may go along to the end of the landing." He nodded to Zekri and Olu'we. "You monks go with him; with Ruthier." Sieur Horembaud shaded his eyes and looked toward the rising sun. "We go to Edfu with good signs."

"How long will it take? We've been riding these waters for a long time, and still have far to go, haven't we?" asked one of the pilgrims;

he was a man of moderate height and fulsome manner; his accent was that of central France, and his clothes marked him as a man of modest fortune. "To get to that place?"

"The watermen say two, perhaps three days. We'll sail through the night tonight, and that should bring us to Edfu in two or perhaps three days." Sieur Horembaud pursed his lips, as if trusting that repetition would indicate he was deep in thought. "It will be hard on the horses, but it can't be helped. Even horses as light-bodied as these don't like standing for hours on end."

"A pity you couldn't bring a destrier or two," said the Frenchman.

"The heat would make them useless, and they'd eat double what these horses will. And they wallow in sand." Sieur Horembaud laughed contemptuously. "What do you know of destriers?"

"I know enough to see that these horses are little more than ponies," the other man protested.

"Ponies would be able to endure the rigors more than a destrier could"—he thought back to the hardy ponies of the Jou'an-Jou'an in the Year of the Yellow Snow, and wished he could summon a few up now—"and since we're not allowed to have armor, there is no reason to bring heavier mounts than these are," said Sieur Horembaud, and held up his hand to silence the Frenchman before he could advance another argument. "All you advocates think about is winning your points; you have no mind for practicalities—not even you, Noreberht, though you may think otherwise." Sieur Horembaud's smile was more a show of teeth than an expression of good will.

Noreberht chuckled ill-naturedly. "You will not let me forget why I am a pilgrim, will you?"

Sieur Horembaud turned away from him. "You know which boat is yours. Get aboard the second boat. And take that fussy Italian slave of yours with you."

Noreberht signaled to the young man who served him. "Come, Baccomeo; the Sieur wants to be gone."

Another of the French contingent came up to Noreberht. "Sieur Horembaud wants me with you."

"Why? Because we are French?" Noreberht asked at his most ungenial. "He could claim as much himself."

"It is what he told me to do." The man had a brand on his forehead, identifying him as a violent felon; at forty-one, he was regarded as the oldest of the pilgrims. He wore a penitent's dull-blue habit, and his graying hair was cut close to his head so that he looked to have a narrow halo of silvery bristles. Almost every one of the pilgrims was afraid of Micheu de Saunte-Foi, which pleased him more than he liked to admit.

The riverman who was serving as their guide, a middle-aged Coptic Egyptian returning home to Edfu, came up to Sieur Horembaud. "How much longer? We want to be underway as soon as possible," he said in poor Greek, the only language he and Sieur Horembaud had between them.

"As soon as everyone and everything is loaded. Talk to that man—Rakoczy. He knows more tongues than I do."

Sandjer'min had already got aboard the barge and was directing the slaves in placing his chest filled with his native earth next to the pallet, the rolled mattress tucked in next to it. As the riverman came up to him, he looked around. "Yes? What do you want?" he asked in Arabic, and then in Coptic.

The man answered in Coptic, bowing slightly, "Sieur Horembaud said I should speak with you. I am Iri'ty—"

"A name of excellent omen," said Sandjer'min. "What are we to speak about?"

Iri'ty answered with formality. "Matters that he and I cannot; you have both our tongues, and you will explicate what he cannot. He says we are to leave when everything and everyone is loaded."

"No doubt," said Sandjer'min.

Iri'ty shook his head. "He wants me to talk to you rather than to him. And after our voyage from Alexandria, I would rather speak to you, Sidi." He smacked his hands together to show his frustration with the Aquitanian knight. "Well, at least I know there is someone here who understands my speech. That's something to be thankful for."

"How have you managed so far?" Sandjer'min inquired, wondering what it was that Sieur Horembaud was up to now. "By the sound of it, coming up the river with him was not easy."

"Sieur Horembaud is not an easy man. Frater Anteus did his best to provide translations, but neither of us was satisfied, nor was Sieur Horembaud," said Iri'ty, his demeanor showing that this had been a trial for them both. "You do speak Coptic fairly well, and that will make the last part of the trip easier. I wish I could ride aboard this barge, not in the first boat."

"There are two monks with my manservant. They can speak to you as well as I, if not better." Sandjer'min gave Iri'ty an understanding look. "Do not be vexed by Sieur Horembaud: he has been deprived of the means of making war, and that makes him peevish." He shifted his stance, already feeling the debilitating drag of the water.

Before Iri'ty could agree, a nun came up to the barge and said in Church Latin, "I am Sorer Imogen. I have been told I must assist you in caring for Torquil des Lichiens."

"That is what Sieur Horembaud has told me, as well," said Sandjer'min, exchanging short bows with Iri'ty before the riverman returned to the boat that would lead the way south. "You are most welcome, Sorer."

Two slaves approached the barge with the shelter, carrying between them a man lying on a plank and covered by a linen sheet, with a broad strip of linen across his eyes; one hand had slipped from beneath the sheet, showing ravaged skin marked, like his face, with weeping blisters. They stood, unspeaking, until Sorer Imogen stepped aside, and then they carried the plank onto the barge and moved to the shelter, where they lifted the covered man and set him onto the pallet, stood the plank on end against the stack of chests and cases at the rear of the shelter, and left the barge. The man on the pallet sighed.

"I believe our charge has arrived," said Sandjer'min to Sorer Imogen, wanting to discover what degree of care she was prepared to give, and in what manner.

"Gratia Dei," she exclaimed, and carefully stepped aboard. "Tell me what I am to do."

"Have you done any nursing of burned men or women?"

"No; I have prayed. We Annunciationists pray and weave."

Sandjer'min showed no sign of the disappointment he felt, saying to Sorer Imogen, "Then for now, we should take turns watching him, for we will be underway shortly. I will attend to him until it approaches mid-day, during which time, I urge you to rest," said Sandjer'min, struggling a bit with Church Latin.

"I will pray," she announced.

"Not aloud; we must give Torquil every opportunity to sleep." He said it kindly, but saw her stiffen. "There is room on the barge for you to find a place to pray without—"

"The oarsmen will hear," she said.

"Then they may be uplifted by your piety," said Sandjer'min, doing his best to keep the asperity from his tone.

Her face softened. "How true," she said as she came up to the boarding-plank. "For even a seed dropped on a stone may yet take root."

Sandjer'min took a moment to collect his thoughts, and wondered what he would have to do to achieve Sorer Imogen's approval; he had seen women like her in many places and in many times: ones who placed their commitment to an idea above all else, including good sense, and felt vindicated for doing it. He had a brief recollection of Tamasrajasi, of Csimenae, and of Rhea, which he thrust aside. "Perhaps you should have a look at our patient?" he suggested, offering his hand to help her onto the barge.

"It will be fitting that you pray with me," she told him, ignoring his hand. "God will guide us if we pray."

"If you like," he said at his most conciliating, "but I pray to other gods than yours." He went into the shadow of the simple tent, and looked down at the man lying on the pallet there, only his face showing, and looking like spit-roasted pork. "Most of the skin on his arms are burned, and his legs to the knees."

Sorer Imogen crossed herself, her face paling to the color of her gorget and wimple. "Saints and Martyrs," she whispered, staring, appalled at what she saw. "I was told he was . . . But I did not think he . . ."

"Not all the blisters have broken yet, and when they do, they must be medicated promptly or it is possible that he will develop putrescences, and those could endanger his life." Sandjer'min spoke levelly and with a great deal of attention on the nun, hoping to see her understanding. "He must be given water regularly; in this heat, he will have—"

"I will pray, and be sure that the water is blessed to his use," she told him, and went to kneel at his side, unaware of Sandjer'min's brief frown. "Poor young man," she whispered before she crossed herself again, pressed her hands together, lifted her rosary from her belt, and began to recite her beads.

On the third boat, Ruthier helped Margrethe of Rutland onto a low bench, then held out his hand to the young man who accompanied her. "There's room enough for both of you on the bench," he said in careful Anglo-French, hoping she would understand him, and moving to occupy the bench opposite them; Zekri and Olu'we took their seats on the bench at the rear, flanking the steering oar.

The young man regarded Ruthier with the arrogance of one born to privilege, but also revealing astonishment that this foreigner's servant could understand his language. "We will do as Sieur Horembaud tells us."

"As will we all," said Margrethe quietly. "Sit down, Heneri. The manservant is right." She pulled her veil around her face, the fine, gray linen dulling her pale-blue eyes.

"A fine day for our travels," said the next arrival at the boat: unlike the rest of the pilgrims, he wore the same garments that the Egyptians did, a loose djellaba of pilgrims' blue cotton, belted in leather; instead of boots, he wore sandals. His close-trimmed beard was brassy, and his hair was carrot-red. He looked directly at Ruthier. "I am Nicholas Howe. Frater Giulianus, who travels with me, will join us directly. You're with the foreign physicians, aren't you?"

"Ruthier," he said, ducking his head politely. "I am Sandjer'min's servant."

"The physician they brought along for Torquil des Lichiens." Howe sat down.

"Yes." Ruthier inclined his head.

"Why does Sieur Horembaud bother? Clearly Torquil cannot

live, so why prolong his suffering?" Howe directed his stare at the river. "I hope you have something interesting to tell us," he went on, his Anglo-French more strongly English than French. "We've almost worn out what we have to relate to one another."

"I will do what I can," said Ruthier, moving a bit farther down the bench to provide room for Howe and his comrade, Frater Guilianus.

Three boatmen came aboard, and immediately behind them, Frater Giulianus scrambled aboard, the wide sleeves of his habit exposing his hirsute arms. He was about to look for a seat when Sieur Horembaud came up to them. "Howe, you and Frater Giulianus, get into the second boat. You'll be overloaded otherwise."

Howe scowled briefly, then rose. "Of course, Sieur Horembaud. It wouldn't do to sink, would it? Come on, Frater."

Frater Giulianus coughed once. "Certainly."

The two climbed out of the boat; Ruthier noticed that Margrethe gave a little sigh of relief. "Now we will have a little peace," she murmured.

"Are you troubled by him?" Ruthier asked, revealing only a faint interest, although he was most curious.

"He is inclined to speak at length about his many adventures, most of which are difficult to believe. And he has a rough way about many things." She put her hand to her lips. "I should not speak so of him; he is on a pilgrimage for his faith."

"As are you all," said Ruthier, hoping to learn more.

She looked at him, her eyes growing wide. "And you are not? For a man living at a monastery, how can you say—"

Ruthier shrugged. "My master has decided to travel, and it is my duty to go with him. We have gone many places during the time I have been in his service." It was a simple explanation, and had the advantage of truth, but the reality was vastly more complicated, something he kept to himself. He studied her briefly. "If you would be willing to tell me, why are you on this pilgrimage? A well-born Englishwoman like you I would expect to go to the cathedrals of Europe if you wished to see holy places."

"She's doing it for her husband," said Heneri, in a tone that did not encourage discussion. "The Bishop said she had to."

"Heneri," Margrethe chided him gently. "As one of our company, he has every right to know."

"He's a servant. All he needs to know is his master's wants; he said as much just now." The young man pointed to the shelter on the barge. "Why aren't you with him?"

"It is Sieur Horembaud's wish that we travel in separate vessels for now." Ruthier retreated behind his habitual reserve.

"And he has ordered my sister—my half-sister," he corrected himself, "to assist your master, so that she may discover more about him. I heard Sieur Horembaud tell her to do this," Heneri declared.

Ruthier refused to be lured into a squabble. "As well he might. We have a great distance to go, and it is to Sieur Horembaud's advantage to know as much about his companions as he can learn." Then, indulging himself in a moment of retaliation, he added, "It is what my master would do in his place."

There was a silence among the pilgrims in boat three, and then Heneri folded his arms and said, "I don't think you should talk to one so far beneath you, Bondame Margrethe."

"We are all one in the eyes of God, and while we are on this journey, we will be humble," she said.

"Your husband would not like it," said Heneri.

"If my husband could like or dislike anything, I would not be here," she responded more sharply.

"Don't!" Heneri snapped, rounding on Margrethe.

Ruthier was about to move from his place on the bench to the opposite one Howe and Frater Giulianus had vacated when Sieur Horembaud came to the edge of the landing. "Heneri! Mind how you speak to this man. Bondame Margrethe is right. You will be entering the Templars when you return home, boy, and you will need to be more reconciling in your behavior when you do." He pointed to Ruthier. "Stay where you are. The other bench is for Viviano Loredan and his servant."

"He's moving us around a lot," said Heneri quietly.

"He is our leader," Margrethe reminded him. "If my husband's sister is with this man's master, other adjustments should be expected." She smiled as she turned to Ruthier. "Forgive my husband's half-brother, good man."

"My name is Ruthier," he said.

"You are French?" She sounded surprised.

"I was born in Spain," he said, "but I left it long ago," when Nero was Caesar, he added to himself.

"And your master? Is he also from Spain?" Margrethe asked, striving to smooth over the discord.

"No; he is from lands ruled by Hungary," said Ruthier, and volunteered nothing more.

A man of twenty-seven came aboard, his blue surcote with the Lion of San Marco on his sleeve identifying him as a Venezian, as did his accent even in Anglo-French. He made a casual greeting to all on board and sat down on the bench that faced Ruthier. "My man will be along shortly. He is procuring some jars of wine."

"Excellent," said Heneri, his sullenness fading. "Something to make the river less boring."

"You'll give me two coppers for every cup you drink," the Venezian said genially.

"Why should I?" Heneri challenged.

"Because it's my wine," said the Venezian. He glanced at Ruthier. "You're one of the new ones, aren't you? I'll ask the same of you as I do of the lad."

Ruthier took a little time to collect his thoughts. "That's most kind."

A flurry of activity on the landing served to warn all the travelers that the rowers on the barges were getting ready to cast off; Sieur Horembaud shouted, "All slaves and rowers, make ready to leave!" while he climbed aboard the first boat.

A wiry man in a pilgrim's habit rushed aboard the third boat, wine jars in both hands. "I've got five of them, Signor' Loredan," he said, panting, as he plopped down on the bench beside the Venezian.

The oarsman came on board behind him, and two boatmen

followed him, each taking his place with the ease of habit, paying little attention to their passengers. On the landing slaves were unfastening the lines that held the boats in place. Sails were raised quickly, and the wind shouldered into the sails; the oarsman took hold of his broad steering oar and set out for the center of the Nile, the third boat to move away from Sese'metkra. The last two boats set their sails and moved up the river, with the rowers on the barges coming after, their oars moving at a steady, regular beat under the ruddy sun.

Text of a letter from Atta Olivia Clemens at Lecco on Lago Como, written in Imperial Latin on linen, delivered by the Eclipse Trading ship *Fair Winds* to Kerem-al-Gamil, factor of the Alexandrian office of Eclipse Trading Company, who sent it up-river to Sese'metkra and the Monastery of the Visitation; delivered there on March 19th, 1225, where Tsura'gar burned it.

> *To my most dear long-time and much-absent friend, the greeting of Olivia on this, the fourth day of the Christian year 1225.*
>
> *My esteemed Sanct' Germain,*
>
> *Before I do anything else, I want to apologize for some of the things I said to you when last we met. It was inexcusable of me to be so ungracious and uncaring. My only excuse is my on-going concern for you; every time you visit me, I feel your compassion and I know how much you have endured because of it, including what you went through because of me and the accusations my wretch of a husband made against you, all those centuries ago. I hope you will not hold my deplorable tongue against me; I give you my Word as one of your blood that I will do my utmost not to take you to task next time we meet, although I cannot promise that I will not let you know why I am worried for your safety.*
>
> *I am still at Lecco, in your wonderful villa, and it is*

ferociously cold this winter, unlike many of those before this year. Perhaps it is as you have told me, and the weather is constantly changing. Whatever the case, the snows are deep in the passes, and often our water-troughs have ice on them in the morning. The peasants working the land have all complained that many of the trees in the orchards and grapevines on the south slope are damaged and will need severe pruning before the end of winter if they are to bear fruit for the year. The livestock are being confined to barns and stables and pens and styes. But I must tell you that the house is sound, and your Roman bath has been repaired. I will send you a report on any problems brought about by the winter before the summer arrives, and I will hope to hear from you before then if you have any instructions you wish to pass on to me.

After what you went through in your travels in the East, I cannot entirely fault you for wanting to go to ground as you have done at that remote monastery, but I must tell you that I am looking forward to the day you return to Italy, or France, or even your native earth. I cannot help but worry while you are in such a distant place, and one where there has been so much unrest. You've assured me more than once that with so many Europeans in Egypt and other points of the Holy Land, few of the native people take notice of them except to sell them food, water, clothing, and such other items as these travelers will require. I know from my days in Tyre and my long journey back to Roma that while you are generally correct, it is still possible to be singled out as a foreigner and because of that, made a target for unfriendly actions. I myself know of Crusaders kidnaped and held for ransom, or worse, and servants, slaves, and campfollowers who, to preserve their own skins, betrayed their soldiers to the regional warlords, or went over to Islam and remained in the Holy Land when the Crusaders left. You have said this will not happen as long as you are within the monastery, but if that is true, you might as well be in prison as a monastery. Come back to Europe, Sanct' Germain, and be as safe as the world will let such creatures as you and I be. Be persuaded by me for my sake if not your own.

Niklos Aulirios has come upon a breeder of horses some six leagues from here and has recommended that we bring a number of mares to be bred to his stallions. He has told me that these horses have great stamina, are light keepers, and have steadiness of temper, though they will not do for war-horses, because they are not big enough; most of the studs stand at little more than fifteen hands. Most of them are black or very, very dark bay. I am minded to see what kind of get they will produce in our strongest Spanish mares. The foals should grow up to be more active than those English palfreys that everyone praises, and for travel over distances, they will quickly show their worth.

I have taken many of your books and secured them in your strong-room under lock and key; the Church is having one of its spasms, banning and destroying books that are not in accord with the present teaching; much of your collection would be regarded as heretical, and so it seemed prudent to remove them from view. Niklos assisted me, and we moved the books late at night so that none of the servants at the villa can reveal where the books are, other than they are no longer in your library. If any of the Bishop's men should come searching, you may be confident that they will find nothing objectionable on your shelves.

There has been fever among the peasants, one that brings a cough and putrid lungs to many, and in such a winter as we are having, what can one expect? I have authorized any ailing to rest at home until health returns, for as you have taught me, sending the ill to labor among the well is a sure way to spread sickness throughout the region and to increase its virulence. The priest at Santo-Andrea-in-Bosco has objected, saying that this will encourage sloth, but I will remain firm in my commitment to keeping the illness contained as much as I am able.

*When summer comes, I may return to Roma, not only
to revisit my native earth, but to make sure there have been
no more encroachments on my title to Sanza Pari. I miss
my breathing days, when I could own my land and estates
without question or condition, and although I have that
very useful Papal deed, I still find it necessary from time to
time to make sure its conditions are being met. What folly
to believe that women are incapable of maintaining their
own property! But I will not indulge in a harangue. You
know my sentiments, and I know you agree with my stance.
And before I give way to another such outburst, I will send
you my heartfelt hope that you will come to bear me company, wherever I am.*

Your most devoted and loving,
Olivia

5

As they approached Edfu in the deepening shadows of evening, they
passed a huge wall of carvings, showing a procession of figures with
human bodies and the heads of birds and animals, all facing southward. The massive structure was cracked and weathered, revealing
its age by the damage the elements had done over time as much as by
the enigmatic figures carved on it in low relief. Nearly all the pilgrims stared at the wall, and began to speculate among themselves
what the animal heads might mean.

Jiochim Menines, riding in the lead boat with Sieur Horembaud,
dug his thumbs into his belt and prepared to expound; the stocky
Spanish pilgrim had lived in Egypt longer than any of the other Europeans and so was credited with knowing the most about the place
of all of them. "Many of the people of Egypt say these are the gods of
those who built the pyramids, and that walls like this show the stories of their acts, and their powers over men. It is tempting to think

that this is true. But with such heads, what can they be but demons and the monsters from the time before the Flood? A Greek priest I knew in Alexandria told me that he believed that these figures depict the sons of men who had turned away from God and were not saved. I found his explanation most convincing. These are the ones washed away when Noah saved the creatures of the world."

"They're big enough to be gods, or archangels," said Sieur Horembaud, "or Emperors of Egypt." He studied the strange beings, shading his eyes to make out their shapes, for the wall was largely in shadow. "That one in the front? the one with the long head and the breasts? Is that male or female, or can you tell?"

"I think it is probably a eunuch," said Menines. "The people in this part of the world have a liking for eunuchs and see no shame in the state."

Sieur Horembaud nodded. "So we were told when we came here. Strange. I would guess that they have not been taught to see castration as an insult. I have been told that some of the Sultan's military officers are eunuchs." He looked away from the wall as the boat moved beyond it. "Perhaps I should ask Sandjer'min about them. He seems to know a great deal about these things."

Stung, Menines shook his head. "I wouldn't put too much faith in what he tells you: a foreigner like that isn't beyond inventing tales to mislead us, relying on our ignorance to lend him false credibility."

"I'll bear that in mind." Sieur Horembaud looked ahead toward the landing at Edfu; it was larger and more substantial than the one at Sese'metkra, having three stone piers running a short distance out into the river, and better facilities for tying up. A net of heavy cord stretched from the end of the most up-stream of the four piers to a place some three-dozen paces south on the bank, where it was secured to a stout pillar of local stone. Torches lit the piers, and a number of slaves stood ready to help the boats and barges to places among the other vessels already secured to the landing.

"A fine evening," Iri'ty called out to the gang of slaves waiting for them with ropes and boarding-planks. "Where are we to go?"

The leader of the slaves—distinguished by his copper pectoral—came to the end of the second pier and pointed to the upstream side and called out in Arabic, "The boats here. The barges on the other side. We have boards for disembarking. Let us bring them to you."

Iri'ty smiled, and answered in Coptic, "We will." He turned to Sieur Horembaud and relayed this very basic information. "I will leave you once I am ashore. My wives and children will be eager to have me home, and I don't want to keep them waiting; they have been waiting for my return since the end of the last Inundation," he said in hesitant Arabic, and waited while Frater Anteus translated for Sieur Horembaud, then Iri'ty added, "I want the last of my money now, Sieur."

"I'll give it to you tomorrow," Sieur Horembaud said through Frater Anteus.

"Now,"' Iri'ty insisted. "My family is depending on it."

Sieur Horembaud steadied himself as the boat turned into the quiet water between the piers. "My strong-case is on the second barge. I won't be able to get your money until that barge is unloaded."

Iri'ty glowered at this information, and said to Frater Anteus, "Tell the Sieur that I will wait. Or I will come to the travelers' quarter later tonight. I will be paid."

"You'll have to pay him before you retire," Frater Anteus told Sieur Horembaud in Greek. "He won't be willing to wait until tomorrow. Let me tell him you will expect him when you have finished your evening meal."

"I was afraid he might make such a demand," said Sieur Horembaud in an undervoice. "We don't know what the good people of Edfu will charge us for the use of their landing, or our lodging and food. And we still have to buy camels when we cross the desert. Still, you're right. I gave him my Word, and I must pay him."

The prow of the boat nudged into the pier as the large latine sails were furled, the lines creaking as they ran through their block-and-tackles. The activity on the landing intensified as each vessel pushed toward the stanchions to which they were directed. Boarding-planks were set in place, and the pilgrims began to leave the boats, most of them moving stiffly from their long hours of inactivity, and were pointed in the direction of Edfu, a bit more than a hundred paces away. From what they could see from the landing-piers, in the town itself, many of the buildings glittered with light, and the travelers' quarter had a galleried market-square that still sizzled with activity. A slave was dispatched to lead them into the town.

The barge on which Sandjer'min rode was the first of the three allowed to tie up, and as soon as it did, Sieur Horembaud jumped aboard, saying without greeting, "I need you to talk to the landing-master. We have to arrange for our animals and goods as well as a safe place for Torquil—how is he doing, by the way?—and the nun."

Sandjer'min stretched, easing the ache in his muscles that running water brought him. "Torquil is not doing as well as I hoped. It has proven more difficult than I anticipated to keep him watered, and he suffers because of it; his skin that should be healing is cracking instead. His unburned skin is loose and dry. Where his blisters have burst, the skin weeps, and I have much to do to keep him from thrashing about and tearing those ruptures. He needs to sleep in a cool and sheltered room, and given water through the night. I have added a little syrup of poppies to what water he will drink so that he can rest without dreadful pain." He came to the edge of the barge as the boarding-plank was set in place; he did not look down into the water, for he knew it would make him more light-headed than he already was. "The nun is at her prayers. She wants to see her sister-in-law and her half-brother as soon as possible."

"I can understand that," said Sieur Horembaud and raised his voice. "Sorer Imogen, if you will come with me, I'll take you to Bondame Margrethe and Heneri." Then he addressed Sandjer'min again. "Go and speak to the landing-master. I'll join you there directly."

"I'll fetch my case of medicaments first, if you don't mind," he said, turning back before Sieur Horembaud could give him permission.

"The slaves will bring it," Sieur Horembaud shouted, annoyed.

"They do not know how to handle this case, and I haven't the facilities to make more of these medicaments if any of these should be spilled or broken," Sandjer'min said with unflustered calm as he slung the case's broad leather strap over his shoulder and went back to the boarding-plank, where Sorer Imogen now stood, ready to go ashore.

Sieur Horembaud's glance flickered in Sandjer'min's direction. "The landing-master is at the end of this pier. He's a Copt; you can tell by the crucifix he wears. I'll send Frater Anteus to join you, and I'll be along when I have attended to Sorer Imogen."

Recognizing this rebuke for what it was, Sandjer'min only said, "I look forward to it." He waited until Sieur Horembaud and Sorer Imogen were on the landing before he left the barge; he signaled to the leader of the slaves, and speaking in the Coptic dialect of Upper Egypt, he said to the man when he came up to him, "There is a man lying in the tent." He pointed to it. "The man is badly burned and not fully conscious. You must bear him into the town, without adding to his injuries in any way. He needs to be in a protected location, and you will need four men to carry him on a pallet if he is not to be in danger of further hurts."

The slave-leader nodded, and answered, "It shall be as you say, Sidi."

Sandjer'min blinked at the slave-leader, surprised to hear that title used; to cover his confusion. "When he is bestowed safely, find me and tell me how he is faring. If he should bleed from any of his wounds, fetch me at once."

"Yes, Sidi." The slave almost smiled. "We, too, have heard of the foreign Sidi at the Monastery of the Visitation, and we know you have saved many lives. We are honored to have you here. We will do as you request, Sidi."

"Thank you," Sandjer'min said simply, reminding himself that these slaves expected no commoda, as Roman ones had done throughout the Empire, because these slaves, unlike the Roman ones, were not entitled to purchase their own freedom or the freedom of their families.

The slave called to three of his fellows as Sandjer'min moved away to seek out the landing-master. As he stepped off the stone pier onto dry land, the first easing of his muscles gave him an instant of weakness that made his legs wobble.

"Stand still a moment, my master," said Ruthier in Imperial Latin, appearing at his side. "Let me take your case until you are accustomed to earth under your feet again."

Sandjer'min handed his case to Ruthier. "I am most grateful."

"I thought you might find your first few steps on solid ground a bit tiring; you're overcompensating in balancing your steps," Ruthier went on, recalling the number of times he had seen Sandjer'min struggling to keep his footing after a prolonged journey by water. He moved a bit ahead of the Sidi, working to find a place among the pilgrims bound for the town.

"Sieur Horembaud instructed me to find the landing-master," Sandjer'min said suddenly. "He desires information from the landing-master, and seems convinced that I must gain it for him, because of my grasp of the language."

"The landing-master is over there," Ruthier said, pointing to a tall, gangly, middle-aged man with an aquiline nose and a receding chin, seated at a table three or four paces off the road into Edfu. "Frater Anteus described him to me as we were disembarking."

"Let me speak to him. I don't want to find myself in Sieur Horembaud's bad graces." There was a sardonic glint in his dark eyes. "We have so much farther to go in his company."

"That we have," said Ruthier, and moved out of the stream of pilgrims, slaves, and animals, making sure that Sandjer'min followed him.

As the riverbank fell into twilight, Sandjer'min felt much of his strength return, and by the time he reached the landing-master, his step was brisk and he was deciding how best to approach the man. He went to the front of the table where two torches had been stood in deep storage jars filled with sand, and made a formal gesture of greeting. "I am Sandjer'min, called Sidi by some. I am serving the leader of the pilgrims who have just landed as a translator, since he has no knowledge of the Coptic tongue. If you will provide me—"

"You are the physician," said the landing-master. "A monk known as Dinat told us you would be coming with the pilgrims, not two days ago. We had known of you before, but did not think to see you here." He scrutinized Sandjer'min's face, then, satisfied with what he had seen, he remarked, "Your eyes are dark but with sparks of blue. It identifies you as much as your European skin."

"So I have been told," said Sandjer'min, who had not seen his reflection in more than thirty-two centuries.

"Most unusual." He looked over at the pilgrims, his eyes narrowed in speculation. "Only one who is ill. Also most unusual."

"Why is it unusual?" Sandjer'min asked, as he knew he was expected to.

"Most pilgrims have those with them who are seeking healing. At the end of the last Inundation, there was one group of pilgrims numbering about fifty who came through on their way to the old Axum Empire, though it is now little more than a large oasis in a trade-route town. There are many churches there and pilgrims want to see them. These pilgrims want to seek out the holy sites there. One in four of the pilgrims had an injury or ailment they hoped to have cured by God."

"And did they receive their cures?" Sandjer'min inquired.

"I don't know. We have not yet seen them return." The landing-master paused again. "Why are you going across the desert now? The sun is growing stronger, and by the time you reach the Highlands of Ethiopia, the rains will have started, and travel will not be safe until the arrival of the planting season."

"It is Sieur Horembaud, the leader of this pilgrimage, who wishes it. I told him much the same thing, as have others, but he is determined." He paused. "Sieur Horembaud wants to know where these pilgrims are to find lodgings, where we are to stable our horses and asses, and where our belongings may be safely stored. In addition, we have an injured man among our numbers who needs special care and a place where he may lie undisturbed."

"There are inns and hostels in the travelers' quarter that will accommodate you and your animals, and the injured man. There are also storage cells in the town's counting-house. It is directly across from the main gates to the travelers' quarter." The landing-master gave a little cry of surprise as Frater Anteus came up to the table. "This man is one of the pilgrims?"

"He is Frater Anteus from Alexandria," said Sandjer'min, taking care not to sound troubled by the friar's arrival. "He has assisted Sieur Horembaud in many ways, and brings the comfort of religion to the pilgrims."

The landing-master subjected Frater Anteus to the same brief but intense perusal he had given Sandjer'min, then rubbed his chin. "Very well. If you need their assistance, I will authorize your company of travelers the use of four of our slaves to speed your settling for your stay. That should make your location of beds and meals less difficult. How many days will you be here?"

"Two, perhaps three," said Sandjer'min in Coptic and repeated it in Greek for Frater Anteus.

"That's what Sieur Horembaud has decided." Frater Anteus spoke with easy authority. "When we reach the First Cataract, we will travel overland. Tell him that."

Sandjer'min did as Frater Anteus ordered, then added, "There are slaves with us. What arrangements can you offer for them?"

"You may give them sleeping mats and post them with your animals and your goods; if anything is missing, you will know they are to blame for it. I will inform the town's guards to allow your slaves to be in those places. I assume they are from Egypt." The landing-master waited for Sandjer'min to relay this to Frater Anteus. "If you need more slaves than you have, then we can come to terms on allowing you to buy a day or two of our civic slaves to watch your animals and property."

Listening to Sandjer'min's translation, Frater Anteus began to frown. "We should have slaves enough, and we ought to be able to protect our property without needing to apply for help," he said. "It may be foolish of us, but we have good reason to be careful while traveling—I am sure the landing-master will concur." He motioned to Sandjer'min to translate while doing his best to make his expression more genial.

Sandjer'min softened Frater Anteus' remarks so that his refusal of the offered service would not be abruptly dismissed; so direct a response would be sufficient to make the landing-master look upon these pilgrims as rude and arrogant, which could lead to acrimony. He ended by adding, "We have been long on the river, and many of us are tired."

"And you must have your burned man moved," said the landing-master as if Torquil had escaped the official notice he deserved. "I will see it done at once. Why don't you and your man accompany your patient into the town?" Then he looked at Frater Anteus. "I wish you a pleasant meal and a good night's sleep. You may meet with the master of the foreign quarter in the morning, given that the hour is late."

Sandjer'min passed this on to the friar, adding, "It would be well to take him up on his offer, Frater. He still has to report on our arrival, and no doubt he wants to eat before he retires."

Frater Anteus bowed his head to the landing-master. "Thank him for us, and tell him we will meet with the master of the foreign quarter in the morning. Then let's walk into Edfu. There are things we must discuss."

"Not tonight, Frater Anteus," said Sandjer'min. "I am to see Torquil settled in the town, and dress his wounds. He will need water and as much food as he can be persuaded to eat." He inclined his head. "In the morning, I will wait upon you when I have completed taking care of Torquil, and will then attempt to conjure up a dream." He said nothing to explain his intention of seeking sustenance from a sleeping woman during the darkest hours, when everyone should be asleep.

Frater Anteus pressed his lips together to keep from making whatever remarks he had intended to make. "I will look forward to talking with you immediately after morning prayers," he said, dashed off a blessing, nodded to the landing-master, and hastened after the rest of the pilgrims.

"That man, religious or not, does not like you, Sidi. You would do well to be wary of him." The landing-master gave a signal to the slaves on the landing and called out orders to them. "Bring the ill man ashore on a pallet. Four of you should carry him as carefully as if he were fine perfume in delicate jars. If he utters one moan, you will all pay for his pain with your own." He watched while the leader of the slaves selected men for the job, sent them to get the pallet for moving Torquil. He said to Sandjer'min, "As soon as we have the hurt man inside the walls we will bring your belongings to the counting-house. You may assign those of your slaves you like to guard your chests and cases for tonight, and in the morning you may ask the master of the foreign quarter to permit them to continue at their task."

"I will inform Sieur Horembaud of this," said Sandjer'min.

"How good of you to do it," said the landing-master. "Wait here until the slaves bring your patient to you." With that he rose, gestured his farewell, and strode off toward the town gates.

Ruthier watched the landing-master go. "He's right about Frater

Anteus," he said thoughtfully in Imperial Latin. "Though I don't know why."

"And what have you discovered about the rest of the pilgrims? I haven't had a chance to do more than exchange a few words with most of them," Sandjer'min said. "Sorer Imogen speaks only of the care we need to provide to Torquil and to pray. She tells me little about herself: I know Bondame Margrethe is the nun's sister-in-law and that Heneri is her half-brother, but that is the extent of it; she tells me that to speak of oneself is a sign of vanity. Her faith is zealous and she does not like to have it questioned or slighted." He paused thoughtfully, trying to gather his impressions of the pilgrims, saying at last, "I have an impression of Sieur Horembaud, but the rest are something of a mystery to me. Occasionally I have wondered if he has decided to keep me apart from the rest, or if he is afraid that I may bring contagion, as if burns are contagious; he has certainly enforced his stricture that I keep to the barge."

"I think that was deliberate, that he wants to isolate you, which perturbs me. Sieur Horembaud seems to be worried that the pilgrims might prefer to follow you. He doesn't want to allow any temptations to change alliances." Ruthier looked up at the stars, like tiny, bright smudges on the darkness, fuzzed by a high, thin veil of sand. "You know Bondame Margrethe and Heneri."

"Yes," said Sandjer'min.

Ruthier ducked his head in agreement. "Sieur Horembaud has two servants with him, Florien, his squire, and Almeric, who serves the knight in much the same way that I serve you. Jiochim Menines is a Spanish knight, who has lived in Egypt since the start of the Fifth Crusade; he is a great gossip, and I think he's on this pilgrimage for some reason other than an expression of piety. Noreberht lo Avocat is a lawyer from Aquitaine here to do penance for forging wills and deeds; the law courts ordered him to pay recompense and then to do this pilgrimage to expiate his sin. He has an Italian slave, a young man named Baccomeo. There is a fellow who wears Egyptian dress but is English, Nicholas Howe, who has made it clear that his first reason for being with us is that he is interested in acquiring relics; religion is his business, not his belief. His comrade is a

Frater Giulianus, who shares his desire for relics, though for some-what different reasons. Beyond that, I know very little about either of them. Cristofo d'Urbineau is a defrocked priest who claims to be from Genova, though his accent sounds Corsican. There is a woman from Constantinople, whose family came there with the Latins, as menials. Her name is Lalagia and she is twenty-four. She is looking for the knight who has kept her for seven years and fathered her chil-dren. I gather that Sieur Arnoul, a knight from Brabant and her pro-tector, went on pilgrimage himself more than two years ago and has not been heard of since. She must find him so that her children by him may be made legitimate, which he vowed to do upon his return."

"Do you believe her?" Sandjer'min asked.

"I do. I don't know that I believe Perrin Bonnefiles, who has told everyone that he is a Vidame in Languedoc. There is something about him that doesn't ring true. But whether it is his title or his story I find questionable, I can't decide." He coughed and resumed his descriptions of the pilgrims. "A Venezian joined the pilgrimage four days after they set out, who claims to be an observer, but to what purpose, and for whom, who can say? His name—if it is his—is one of great respect: Viviano Loredan. He must be twenty-five or -six. He has a servant he hired in Alexandria, called Salvatore, who looks to be part Moorish and part European."

"There are many such since the Crusades began," said Sandjer'min. "They are a token of war as much as sacked towns and maimed sol-diers are."

"So they are." Ruthier went silent as four slaves came off the barge carefully bearing a pallet between them, on which Torquil lay in a painful haze. As soon as the slaves and their burden had passed, Ruthier continued. "I've been told that Torquil joined this pilgrim-age at the request of Richere Enzo, who is a learned goldsmith from Milano. He claims that Torquil has been his apprentice, although Frater Anteus says that Torquil is a Templar who cannot wear the mantle on a pilgrimage. Enzo has a slave, Ifar, who has told us all that he is an Egyptian, but he follows the Greeks in his religion."

"If he is an Alexandrian, this is quite possible," said Sandjer'min. "There are Roman and Greek churches there, and Coptic ones, as well. The Sultan permits it so long as there is no trouble from them."

A shrug of incertitude was Ruthier's only comment. He slowed his pace a little to allow him and Sandjer'min to keep behind the slaves carrying the pallet; he could hear Torquil moaning faintly with every breath.

"And the rest?" Sandjer'min adjusted his stride; he was no longer disoriented, though with the Nile so near, he was not entirely free of the vertigo that had possessed him.

"Methodus Temi; a blacksmith who makes iron gates and port-cullises. He has lost half his sight and seeks to be healed." He paused. "A very taciturn fellow."

"How do you mean, half his sight?" They were approaching the town gates, where a few curious guards lingered to admit them.

"He hasn't explained, not where I have been able to hear him."

"How many more?" Sandjer'min asked.

"Four: Micheu de Saunte-Foi, who is the branded penitent; a man nearing old age. You know the one I mean."

Something in Ruthier's voice prompted Sandjer'min to ask, "How penitent is he, do you think?"

"I can't say, but he hasn't the demeanor of one seeking to repent of his sins," said Ruthier, more bluntly than was his wont.

"There we agree." He thought for a few steps, trying to decide what else he might need to know of these pilgrims; for the time being, he was satisfied. "What of the last three?"

"Agnolus Raffaele dei Causi from Genova, a merchant dealing in linen and cotton; he says his wife hasn't given him children, and he hopes that this pilgrimage will give them some. His wife was deemed unable to travel, though I don't know why. Dei Causi has two servants, Carlus, and Vitalis." Ruthier glanced back toward the landing-master's table to discover it had been removed, and that one of the torches had been put out. "Aside from the rivermen's slaves, that is the company."

Sandjer'min went several paces in contemplative quiet, then, as they neared the gate, he said, "Have you spoken with Zekri and Olu'we?"

"Briefly," Ruthier told him. "We have been on the same boat most of the way."

"And what have they said?"

"Not as much as I would hope," Ruthier replied. "They are being very cautious, but whether it's because they are reticent among strangers or they have been ordered not to speak, I don't know."

"Zekri stammers, which might account for his silence," said Sandjer'min dubiously.

"True, but that doesn't account for Olu'we's muteness."

The gates of Edfu loomed ahead, thirty hands high, made of heavy planks of wood and fitted with four iron hinges. The walls were thick, made of rough-dressed stones recovered from the ancient monuments off to the side of the town itself, which lay between the monuments and the river; the fields were up-stream from the village and out of the shadows of the pillar-fronted building against the hills, and a second array of colossal, animal-headed figures half-buried in the sand. A group of three statues of a man with a bearded chin was placed so that the man faced the rising sun, the first thing the rays would touch; the three figures had identical faces and head-dresses.

One of the guards motioned to the slaves carrying Torquil to hurry, but got no results. "It's getting late. You must hasten; we can't keep the gate open all night," another guard shouted in heavily accented Arabic.

"The man is injured," one of the slaves replied in much better Arabic.

The guards moved to block the entrance to the town. "If he is ill, he must remain outside the gates," the first warned.

Sandjer'min listened to this exchange, and intervened. Stepping up to the front of the pallet the men carried, he said, "I am the pilgrims' physician, and I tell you that this man is suffering from burning by the sun. He is pale, as you can see by his yellow hair, and his burns have blistered and broken. He has no sickness that any need fear, but he requires regular treatment as if he had been kissed by fire."

"Why are his eyes covered?" the third guard asked, pointing to the strips of linen that circled Torquil's face, only the tip of his nose and the slit for his mouth showing.

"Because they are damaged," Sandjer'min said. "I hope to save him from blindness." For an instant he found himself wondering what the blacksmith meant by half-blind.

"Show us his burns," said the first guard. "We know what the burning you describe looks like, and will decide if you're telling the truth."

"Carry him up to the gate," Sandjer'min said, standing aside so that the slaves could obey. "Let me lift his sheet. I don't want him hurt," he told the guards.

One of the guards chuckled, saying, "Arrogant foreigner," in Coptic.

Sandjer'min turned to face him, and spoke in that language, "Not arrogant: protective. This man cannot speak for himself, so I must defend him." As he said this, he lifted the sheet up and held it, revealing Torquil's legs to the knees. "Take a look at him."

Three of the four guards gathered around, the second carrying a torch to illuminate Torquil's ruptured blisters. "By Saint Philip!" he exclaimed as he bent over the pallet. The other two blinked with shock.

"Those are burns," said the first. "How bad is his face?"

"Worse than his legs," Sandjer'min said somberly.

The third guard shook his head slowly. "Should he be traveling? Wouldn't it be better to find a place where he can recover?"

"And where would that be?" Sandjer'min asked. "I have been told he is pledged to go on, to seek out the shrines and holy places in the highlands far up-river."

The first guard moved back far enough to allow the slaves with their burden to pass through. "Keep him away from the old monuments. Who knows what manner of spirits would be drawn to him in this condition."

"He might end up with the head of an ibis," said the second, making a sign to ward off the Evil Eye.

"It might be better than how he'll look as a man, even if his blisters heal," said the first guard, trying to make a jest of his fright.

"Take him through. The foreigners' quarter is to your right, behind the fretwork gates," said the third guard.

"Thank you," said Sandjer'min in Coptic, then in Arabic, and went into the town of Edfu, Ruthier and the slaves behind him, walking in the shadows of the ancient monuments behind the town walls.

Text of a letter from Tsura'gar at the Monastery of the Visitation in Sese'metkra to Venerable Minseh at the Church of the Holy Apostles on the island of Elephantine, written on papyrus and delivered by the tertiary monk Kefrin nine days after it was written.

To the most reverend Venerable Minseh in this most sacred time of Our Lord's Passion in this, the 1225th year since His birth,

The greetings from the most humble monk, Tsura'gar, serving at the Monastery of the Visitation in Sese'metkra, who assures you of his devotion to the Coptic Christian Church and all its work, and in the cause of that work makes bold to send you this letter with the good offices of our tertiary Kefrin, with the prayer that what it contains will lead to the resolution of our plight in this place.

As you are doubtless aware, our leader, Aba'yam, is suffering from a damaged foot, and because of that has been unable to fulfill his duties during this holy period. It is increasingly obvious to most of us that what little progress has been made in his recovery, he is not going to be able to participate in our sacred celebration, and thus compromise our demonstration to our people and to God. Although the foreign physician and his manservant have left our monastery, Aba'yam has continued to follow the regimen of washing and bandaging that Sandjer'min recommended for him, but which I believe has contributed to Aba'yam's slow recovery. He prays for healing, as do we all, but he will not abandon the medicaments and potions that Sandjer'min prepared for him, which indicates that Aba'yam remains in

*the foreigner's thrall to the determent of all monks and the
people of Sese'metkra. He sets an example that does his position no good and spreads the belief that there are other
ways than God to regain health. Thus, I fear, there is much
that the foreigner has done to Aba'yam that is beyond med-
ication, and that more than his body may be affected, and
that his soul could be forfeit for his allegiance to Sandjer'min
instead of to God. This weakens us all at a time when we
must be steadfast.*

*With the men of Islam coming more and more fre-
quently to this village and others in the region, specifically
at the Sultan's behest to spread his religion, we must be especially careful to preserve our rites and rituals, or we may
lose our flock to the followers of the false prophet, a fate that
we must avoid, or consign our souls to the outer darkness
that is the destiny of those who refuse to honor God and His
Son in the practice of the true religion.*

*The Holy Days are upon us, and it is our duty as monks
in the service of God to uphold the promise that is the heart
of Christian faith and devotion. In all our days upon this
earth it is our calling to keep the sacrifice God made of His
Son before the eyes of the faithful, and to show our gratitude for what God gave us with Jesus' most precious blood
shed to redeem us. Aba'yam says that is his purpose, but he
cannot yet lead our solemn rites, nor can he reveal the
Grace of salvation so long as he remains unable to be whole
in body as well as in spirit.*

*Little as I wish to say this, I am growing ever more
certain that our present Aba'yam has reached the end of
his tenure as our leader, and that for the sake of all of us in
this Brotherhood, we must be allowed to elect a new leader
to be Aba'yam so that we may provide the prayers and service that it is our duty to offer all of our flock. Surely you
must be aware that the situation here is precarious through
the monks who send you regular reports of the monastery
and the village. You have been patient with Aba'yam, as is*

your nature and the obligation of your high office, but there are limits to patience if it allows laxness and self-indulgence to flourish. I ask you to pray and meditate on our situation, and to consider encouraging Aba'yam to do the same so that we may rightly uphold God's Glory here on Earth. You are the only one who can require Aba'yam to step down, which is why I have taken it upon myself to inform you of what is transpiring here, and to supplicate with you to guide us in this trying time.

May you reap the blessings of your holy office,

Tsura'gar

monk

6

"Sieur Horembaud," Sandjer'min said as the knight paused in his supervising the loading of the boats and barges to continue their journey, "may I have a word with you?" It was early morning and most of the pilgrims had not yet arrived at the landing at the town that had been called Ombos the last time Sandjer'min had been there, where the Priests of Imhotep had settled after the Christians had come to power.

Sieur Horembaud turned an exasperated face toward Sandjer'min. "Is it necessary? Can't it wait?"

"Yes, it is necessary, and no, it cannot wait," said Sandjer'min. "It is something that I would prefer not to discuss in front of the others." He waited while Sieur Horembaud sighed heavily, then gestured to him to speak. "I would like to ask you to remove Sorer Imogen from her work as Torquil's nurse, for his sake and for hers." He was wearing a black linen kalasiris instead of his cotehardie, and he had donned a square headdress such as many Egyptians wore; in the first flush of morning, he appeared to be one of the figures on the carved wall below Edfu brought to life.

"Why?" Sieur Horembaud asked, surprised by the request.

"She is not being helpful, and a few of the things she has done have been harmful—not that I believe she sees her actions as causing hurt, but she is not trained in treating the sick and injured; she lacks the . . . the temperament for nursing a man in Torquil's condition. She has told me that she is a weaver and seamstress and her faith is—"

"Would you take Bondame Margrethe in her stead?" Sieur Horembaud cut in. "It's the Bondame or Lalagia, and she's a camp-follower."

"I'd rather have Ruthier; he knows how to dispense medicaments and succor those who are suffering, but you wouldn't permit that," said Sandjer'min. "It would also keep me from falling into common discourse with those of your company."

"I will consider it. Frater Anteus has said that you are wise to keep apart from the rest of us, so long as you and your servant do not conspire together, which I agree. You told me you understood my decision in that regard from the first time I wrote to you; nothing has changed." Sieur Horembaud offered a quick, cynical smile. "Will you take Bondame Margrethe to assist you? She has been caring for her husband for four years or so. It will prevent any concerns regarding you and your servant."

"May I have a few days of her aid before I make a final determination?" Sandjer'min countered.

"If Bondame Margrethe is agreeable, then I will order it so."

"Must it be a woman?" Sandjer'min asked.

"Yes, it must. There are those who say you are a magician already, and if you have only your servant to assist you, they'll be sure of it, and then you will not be welcome to stay, and I have need of your abilities."

"Why should a woman prevent me from being a magician?" Sandjer'min asked, truly confused.

Sieur Horembaud opened his hands, then folded his arms and held his elbows. "The Pope believes that the Devil intrudes if men who have not taken holy vows are alone in their shared company, which leads them to deadly sins." He exhaled slowly. "If you were

Christian, things would be different, but, as it is—" He stared at Sandjer'min as if his eyes could drill the certainty of his words into the foreigner. "You may have three days to decide if Bondame Margrethe will do. If she is not what you require, then it must be Lalagia, in which case there will be gossip." He put his hand on his broad leather belt. "That will have to suffice; any greater concession would lead to unrest that would disrupt our journey, and that would result in danger to us all. You have more privileges now than many of this company: additional concessions would cause misgivings of the rest of this company to increase." He pulled at his short beard, at present in need of trimming. "What would you like me to say to Sorer Imogen and the rest of the company about this? The women are sisters-in-law, and everyone knows it."

Sandjer'min had anticipated this question and had a ready answer. "You may say that since Sorer Imogen would prefer not to devote herself to the work of one who is not a Christian, you are allowing her to resume her devotions without the problems of faith that have so distressed her. I think she will be grateful to be relieved of her duties here." He decided not to ask why the Pope thought the absence of women among pilgrims would lead men to sodomy and magic.

"I am doing her a kindness, in fact? as are you?" Sieur Horembaud asked, then regarded Sandjer'min with narrowed eyes. "Very astute, Sandjer'min. You cannot be thought a man against the pilgrimage if you put your position so charitably. You are more clever than you show yourself to be."

"My thanks," said Sandjer'min, and ducked his head respectfully; he would have gone aboard the barge to ready the shelter for Torquil's return but was stopped by Sieur Horembaud.

"The days are growing warmer, much warmer."

"And they will be hotter still, and the wind will come up; by high summer the Nile will begin to flood and the Inundation will restore the Egyptian lands," said Sandjer'min. "We will soon have to travel by night, or risk the kind of burns Torquil has."

"Up the river? It would mean changing boats in order to reach the Second Cataract, wouldn't it?" Sieur Horembaud asked with anxiety tinging his tone. "If it is going to flood—"

"No; as Gudjei told you when we left Edfu, we will arrive at the First Cataract and from there we will need to travel overland, first along the Nile, before the flooding begins, and then through the Nubian Desert: Gudjei has told you the same thing. It will save us many days on the river, even if we move quickly enough to avoid the start of the Inundation, and bring us closer to the junction of the Blue Nile." He hesitated, then said, "If you will permit me: I would suggest that you not be over-trusting toward Gudjei; I know Iri'ty recommended him to guide this company, but Gudjei is as yet an unknown among us, nor are we known to him. If the pilgrims are uneasy about me and my servant, spare a few doubts for Gudjei, though he is a Christian. He has been chary of revealing his thoughts or his plans for this journey, and that troubles me. I do not suspect him of any ill, but I have seen little virtue in him thus far." He saw Sieur Horembaud nod; he continued. "When a man is a guide, he should be generous with his knowledge, and Gudjei is not. For as long as we travel with him, it would be wise to observe him." He thought again of the road to Baghdad, and what had happened there; he had been too trusting of his guide then and was determined not to make a similar mistake now.

"So you want to divert suspicion from yourself," said Sieur Horembaud. "Not that I wouldn't do the same."

"No, I want to avoid any more problems than are necessary for this company," said Sandjer'min without heat.

"And you think that Gudjei may be a problem, because he tells us little." He tapped his foot impatiently.

"I think it is possible that he has intentions you know nothing of, and that he is in a position to take advanta—"

"I comprehend your meaning. He knows what lies ahead, and the rest of us do not, and yet he says little of what he knows. I agree this is vexing. You tell me that you have been along the Nile but not for some years, and you have admitted that the river is changeable. What you know may not be in accord with the river now, but it is more than the rest of us can say. Will your monks be able to help?"

"Zekri has knowledge of the river, and information from his father for what lies beyond in the green mountains, where we are bound. You may speak to him if it would reassure you to have a Christian second what I have recommended. He stammers, but he is willing to tell you what he knows." Sandjer'min shaded his eyes as the sun brightened in the east; the force of it sapped his energy and left him feeling enervated. "He has said he is willing to help as much as he is able. Ruthier can translate for you if you would rather I not do it."

"I want to avoid squabbles, if that is possible, and speaking to that monk of yours could offend Gudjei. It is a difficult problem. But I want no misdirection, deliberate or otherwise, to prolong our pilgrimage."

Sandjer'min met Sieur Horembaud's gaze. "Indeed."

"I will deliberate on what you say, and guard my tongue when I speak with Gudjei—and you," Sieur Horembaud conceded after a short moment of consideration. "You, being more widely traveled than most of us, would be more alert to certain kinds of dangers than we are."

Sandjer'min gave a single laugh. "If I have misjudged the man, you may blame me for any misunderstandings that may arise."

Sieur Horembaud did not share Sandjer'min's amusement. "You may be sure I will. Though Torquil suffer for it, I would not hesitate to expel you and your manservant from our numbers if you play me false or foolish." He swung around to summon the leader of his slaves and issued sharp orders in awkward Greek. When the slave bowed and moved away, the knight turned back to Sandjer'min. "Because I am willing to consider your advice, don't mistake that for an increase in trust. You are still a foreigner among this company, and will be so until you convert to the true faith."

"I won't forget," said Sandjer'min, and stepped aboard the barge, experiencing the queasiness that bothered him when he was over running water, for in spite of his native earth in the soles of his Persian boots, the activity of the water blocked the annealing power of the earth, and in sunlight he was made most uncomfortable. He went to the edge of the shelter and looked at the supports for Torquil's pallet, noticing that a little more water had accumulated in the bottom of the barge. He looked about for the bailing pail that had been stored at the first oarsmen's bench, but did not find it there. He was about to search elsewhere, but was interrupted by the arrival of Richere Enzo, the Milanese scholarly goldsmith who was hoping to find relics on this pilgrimage.

"They call you Sidi, don't they?" he said, resting his foot on the landing-rail and leaning his elbows on his knees to enable him to lean forward comfortably. His language was emphatically northern in its pronunciations.

"Some do, others don't," Sandjer'min said, curious why this man had suddenly decided to speak with him; he replied in the Venezian dialect, knowing that Enzo would be able to understand him but the slaves and rivermen would not.

"A great honor for someone who isn't a follower of Islam," Enzo remarked. "You must have gained an enviable reputation."

"So I understand." Sandjer'min waited a short while, and when Enzo said nothing more, asked, "Is there something you want of me?"

"Not exactly." For a brief moment, he squinted at the far bank of the Nile. "I want to offer you a proposal, if you're willing, of course, to advise me on any relics we may come upon. I have heard that some vendors have passed off simulated objects to those searching for relics; I would prefer not to be one of them. I am not looking to buy sheep's bones on the pledge that they are the relics of a martyr."

"What about Nicholas Howe?" Sandjer'min asked. "He is on this pilgrimage specifically to purchase relics. He must know more than I do."

Enzo gave a smile that was as much practiced charm as it was sincere. "You have lived in Egypt for two years, I'm told, and you know what the hazards are apt to be when we arrive in the land of the Holy Grail."

"You'd do better to ask Gudjei about that," said Sandjer'min. "He has lived here all his life and has been to the land of the Holy Grail six times: I have not been there before. He is more likely to know what to look for than I am." He did not add that he had no interest in relics, knowing such an admission would add to the doubts some of the pilgrims had about him.

"But he is one who may decide to help his countrymen, not one who is a Roman Christian, as most of us are. God has made you a man of steady character, I've heard." Enzo studied him. "Your man-servant has told me that you have a sharp eye for that which is not authentic, a skill which would be useful to my task."

Sandjer'min wondered why Ruthier had made such a claim, for although it was true, it was also more revealing than what Sandjer'min usually encouraged. "I have sometimes been able to tell which objects are originals and which are . . . copies."

"That's what interests me," Enzo enthused. "If you will be good enough to advise me, I will gladly pay you a portion of what I realize from any sales I might make."

Had Enzo been younger, Sandjer'min might have rebuffed him forcefully; as it was, he only said, "If you would like my opinion on any relic you have questions about, I will be pleased to provide it, but I cannot promise that that opinion will be accurate. If Sieur Horem-baud dislikes this arrangement, I will withdraw from it at once. If that is acceptable to you, I will do what I can for you."

"Understood. And that shows the steadiness of your character, that you admit the possibility of error." He stepped back and grinned. "You have eased my mind."

Sandjer'min resumed his search for the pail, and found it under the cargo platform; he bailed out the water he could reach, and was wiping down the supports for the pallet when the slaves carrying Torquil arrived and put him into his place under the shelter. "How is he?"

"He is restless, Sidi," said the leader of the four as he and his companions stepped away from the shelter. "He pulls at his covering, and that causes him pain."

"Then I'll have to provide him a calmative, and syrup of poppies for his pain," said Sandjer'min, and hoped Ruthier would arrive shortly with his chest of medicaments. He moved to his banded chest that was filled with his native earth; it stood next to the pallet in the shelter. He touched Torquil's neck, feeling the pulse which was too fast, and then bent to listen at his chest for the workings of his lungs; Torquil gave a bleat of pain, and Sandjer'min sat up at once, realizing that he had accidentally brushed the edge of his patient's jaw. "Do not fret," Sandjer'min said quietly. "I will give you something to make you more comfortable shortly."

"My master?" Ruthier said from the boarding-plank. "I have your chest."

"Thank you, old friend," said Sandjer'min, rising and going to help him aboard. He unbuckled the sling that held the red-lacquer chest on Ruthier's back.

"Sieur Horembaud is uneasy," Ruthier remarked in the dialect of Lo-Yang.

"That he is. I think this pilgrimage is proving more difficult than he thought it would be, and he hasn't decided how to deal with that," Sandjer'min said in the same tongue.

"Do you think he will turn back?" Ruthier raised his arms to help Sandjer'min finish the unfastening of the harness.

"I doubt it; he has too much riding on the completion of the journey. He wants to lead his troops again, and that will only be possible if he completes his pilgrimage." Sandjer'min glanced over his shoulder. "Are the pilgrims coming?" he asked in Imperial Latin.

"They'll be here soon. They have gone to pray at the shrine to Saunt Jerome." His voice was exquisitely neutral.

"I hadn't realized there was such a shrine here," said Sandjer'min, and caught the silent laughter in Ruthier's eyes.

"There is an ancient shrine to a man in a simple loincloth sitting cross-legged with a board balanced on his knees; he's writing, this man with close-trimmed hair and a smooth face," said Ruthier. "The pilgrims say it is Saunt Jerome."

"Ah. *That* shrine," said Sandjer'min, sharing Ruthier's amusement, and feeling an ancient pull to the shrines and statues to persons and gods that few recognized for what they were; his centuries in the Temple of Imhotep welled in his thoughts.

"The sculpture is preserved quite well."

Sandjer'min kept his recollections to himself. "If it pleases the pilgrims to honor that Saunt Jerome with prayers, so be it. There are worse gods and men they could pray to." He sat on the chest, taking strength from its contents, but still feeling the depletion the sun and water worked on him. "It will be hot in an hour."

"There is wind from the north." Ruthier knew that Sandjer'min was feeling the strain that traveling over water always gave him. "Perhaps you'll have a chance to rest during the worst of the heat." He placed the medicaments chest in its position for the day's travel. "Sieur Horembaud plans to travel at night tonight."

"If all goes well with Bondame Margrethe, then perhaps I may have a rest." He moved a bit so that the shadow of the shelter-cloth covered him.

"And you may be able to sustain yourself with something more than the blood of horses," Ruthier added.

"That would be risky, I fear," said Sandjer'min. "Our privacy is limited, and only one of the women is likely to be willing."

"But not wholly impossible, and night will give you cover. As to which is willing, that may change once we start across the desert. We have a long way to go; you would benefit far more from what a woman could offer than any creature." Then, satisfied that he had made his point, Ruthier asked as he unlocked the chest, "What do you need?" He looked down at Torquil. "He's not looking improved, is he?"

"To begin, pansy-and-willow-bark in solution with date-wine," said Sandjer'min at once. "It should provide relief for Torquil's fidgetiness."

"And syrup of poppies in his drinking water?"

"If you would, please." Sandjer'min was studying the burned man's face. "You're right. There is little improvement, but fewer of the blisters are opening, and his color is improved."

"Yes, and he is more restless, which means his vitality may be returning," said Ruthier. "He is beginning to itch in a few places."

"That's a sign of healing," Sandjer'min remarked. "But he mustn't be allowed to scratch, for it could bring putrescence."

A new voice spoke up. "Why should he not scratch?"

"Bondame Margrethe," said Ruthier, offering her a bow as she came across the boarding-plank.

Sandjer'min turned to her. "Bondame," he said, extending his hand into the sunlight to help her aboard. "I am most grateful to you for coming to assist me with Torquil."

"And why shouldn't he scratch?" she repeated.

"It could lead to putrescence in the open blisters, and then there would be more difficulty in treating him." He looked directly into her eyes. "We must guard against putrescence at all costs."

"Sidi—is that what I'm supposed to call you? It's what the Egyptians call you, isn't it?" she asked as she put her hand into his.

"Sidi, or Grofek, if you would prefer," said Sandjer'min, paying almost no attention to Ruthier's look of surprise.

"What manner of title is that?" she asked him. "If it is a title?"

"It is, and it is used in Hungary," said Sandjer'min.

She laughed to cover her confusion. "Sidi would probably be best. Everyone will understand it." Stepping down into the well of the barge, she said, "Thank you for explaining about the scratching. I am told I should take instruction from you in regard to Torquil and any others who may need your skills. You must tell me how I am to aid you."

"That is my understanding as well," said Sandjer'min, drawing her into the shadow of the tent-like shelter.

"It was good of you to relieve my sister-in-law; she would far rather keep watch on Heneri than have to tend to—" Her gesture in Torquil's direction completed her thought.

On the far bank, a trio of crocodiles began to slide toward the river as the increasing warmth wakened their hunger; a few of the slaves at the landing exchanged uneasy glances as they continued loading the barges while keeping a careful eye on the water. One of them made a series of gestures at the dark shapes in the river, only their eyes and snouts showing.

"Sieur Horembaud said you have tended your husband for some time." Sandjer'min was careful not to make this sound intrusive, or the sort of discussion that would gain Sieur Horembaud's disapproval.

"Not quite four years; he was struck on the helm in battle and lost that armor so that he had another blow to the head that cracked his skull; the Devil entered into him through the break, or so our priest told me. Sieur Dagoberht has been clumsy and forgetful and . . . and childish ever since, requiring as much attention as a baby," she answered without rancor. "It is for his sake that I am making this pilgrimage. If I return safely, we hope God will restore him to health. If he is not improved, his lands and titles must go to Heneri, for they need administration that my husband cannot give them. Sorer Imogen was chosen by the Bishop to accompany Heneri and me, since she is so truly dedicated to God." She moved to the narrow bench where Sorer Imogen had sat and sank down upon it, studying Torquil's bandaged face. "Poor man. He will be dreadfully scarred, won't he?"

"That he will," said Sandjer'min. "It is unfortunate. Did no one warn him of the risks with such a burn?"

"I believe Iri'ty said something to him, but Torquil dismissed it." Margrethe sighed. "He's a Templar, you know, but presently excommunicated, which is why he's on pilgrimage, so he cannot wear the mantle or use his title. He hadn't been in Egypt long when he was excommunicated; the Order made no allowances for his unfamiliarity with Alexandria. This pilgrimage is to restore him to the ranks of the Templars again."

"What did he do to deserve excommunication?" Sandjer'min asked, curious now why Sieur Horembaud had made no mention of it.

"Frater Anteus said that he had pillaged a Christian church, taking the sacred vessels from the altar," Margrethe replied, looking a bit ashamed for him. "If this burn is his punishment, then excommunication is a small matter."

"I wonder if Torquil thinks so," said Ruthier.

"We'll discover that in time," Sandjer'min said, deciding that he needed to know more about his patient. "For now, it is our duty to keep him alive and to save him from as much pain as we are able to."

"How much attention does he need?" Margrethe asked without any outward show of distress. "Is it more than watching him?"

"Didn't your sister-in-law tell you? For now he moves with difficulty and his vision is impaired. He is weak and his skin is . . . fragile." Sandjer'min took the ewer of water Ruthier handed him. "I supposed Sorer Imogen might have informed you."

"No; she only prayed for him. She said it was for God to heal him, not men." Margrethe hesitated, then asked, "What do we do with his urine and excrement?"

"We do with it as we all do: give them to the river." Sandjer'min turned to Ruthier. "The syrup of poppies is mixed in already?"

"Yes, my master," Ruthier said. "And I must go to my boat."

"So you must. The rest of the pilgrims are coming." He answered Ruthier's wave with one of his own as his servant left the barge.

"How long do you think it will take us to reach the land of the Holy Grail?" Margrethe asked after a brief silence; she watched Sandjer'min as he placed a fine cotton mesh over Torquil's half-open mouth, and then moistened it with water from the ewer Ruthier had given him. "Is this what you want me to do? give him water that way?" She watched Sandjer'min measure out another small amount of water onto the thin cotton.

"Yes. This will keep him from dying of thirst, and the anodyne in it will lessen his hurts and help him to rest," Sandjer'min told her.

"And the water has been boiled, or so Sorer Imogen told me?" Margrethe pursued.

"Yes. It kills animacules that can harm the guts. When we rest at mid-day, there is a gruel of peas and wheat you will offer Torquil for a meal. He may have figs if he is actually hungry, but otherwise, save the figs for another time. If we have fish to eat, see he has a little of it." He could see that she was paying close attention to his instructions, and would follow them. "Keep out of the sun yourself, Bondame. You are not as fair as he, but your skin might still blister if you remain in the sun."

"So Frater Anteus has warned us all," she said.

Most of the pilgrims were at the landing now, and half of them were boarding their boats. The horses and asses were being led aboard their barge, moving anxiously in anticipation of the handful of raisins and ground millet each of them would receive at the start of the day's travel; the slaves leading them watched the water for any sign of trouble. The landing was filled with activity as the loading of goods was completed, and the rowers and oarsmen took their places on the barges, while the rivermen raised the sails on their boats.

"God wills this!" Sieur Horembaud shouted as the pilgrims moved off into the morning breeze.

Their progress southward was steady, the wind not as high as most of the pilgrims would have liked. Waterbirds rose in noisy flocks as the vessels approached, and crocodiles swam nearer to inspect the boats and the barges, increasing the anxiety among the rowers, whose benches kept them uncomfortably near the water.

"Will the barge keep constant against the river? With those monsters coming near, shouldn't we move to avoid them?" Margrethe spoke up as the boats and barges reached the mid-stream of the Nile, where the current was steady. The sails on the boats were set to catch the wind from the north, and the rowers established a rhythm that provided progress against the current and could be maintained throughout the morning.

"You needn't worry. The rowers are strong and they know the Nile."

"Will they be with us all the way? I've never seen them come so close to our crafts." She crossed herself, still following the movements of the crocodiles. "They are like water-dragons; the Devil is in them."

"We'll have them for company until the First Cataract, where we will leave the river for the land. The boats and barges will be left behind, and when we reach the river once more, we will hire new boats and barges. We will purchase Dromedaries for crossing the desert." He paused, wondering how much Sieur Horembaud had told the pilgrims, then went on, "Haven't you noticed the nature of the river during your travel south?"

"Yes, but the boats are not the same as the barges." She dribbled a little water onto the cloth over Torquil's mouth. "How long will it take him to mend?"

"At least two months, perhaps three. If he were at home, he would recover more quickly. He could rest if he were at home." It was an optimistic estimate, including no further complications than the ones already addressed.

"Those burns are a great burden for him to carry," she said.

"They are," he agreed, and removed another small vial from the red chest. "There is an emulsion in this that can slow the burning of the sun if you will rub it on your face and arms. It will not stop the burn entirely but it will spare you the worst." He gave the vial to her. "Use it to protect yourself."

She hesitated as she took the vial. "If you give it to me, will you offer it to the others as well? What of the rowers and oarsmen? Are they not at greater risk than I am?"

"The rowers and oarsmen are born to this place, and they have their own ways of lessening the hurt from too much light and heat. I want to save this salve for those whose skins redden and peel. If the rowers and oarsmen are injured, I have an ointment that will aid their skin to mend." He stopped to listen to the shouts from the shore. "There is something in the river ahead."

"Do you know what it is?" Margrethe asked as she dripped a bit more water onto the fine linen. "He's swallowing."

"No. I don't think it's a boy or a man." He shielded his eyes. "It appears to be a young goat."

Two of the crocodiles increased their speed, closing in on the thrashing creature, now in full panic. One of the crocodiles seized the kid by the lower spine, and in the next instant, the second crocodile had the kid's front leg in its jaws. The kid gave a single, high shriek, then was pulled under the water by the crocodiles that were already starting to roll. A trickle of red in the water became a gush, and the crocodiles let the current carry them and their meal downstream as the pilgrims and their vessels continued southward. On the horses' and asses' barge the animals shifted and made low sounds of distress.

"That was quite horrid," Margrethe said after a long moment of silence.

"At least it was over quickly," said Sandjer'min.

Margrethe shuddered. "Poor wight," she said, and reached for the ewer. "I will use the emulsion when I have made sure he has swallowed the water."

"See that you do," said Sandjer'min. "It would help no one if you should become burned, as well."

She stared at him, startled at his concern. "Truly. It would help no one." Then she continued to drip water onto the linen over

Torquil's mouth, and would not look in his direction again for half
the morning.

Text of a letter from Frater Anteus at Syene Philae to Bishop
Heracletus of the Cathedral Church of the Resurrection in Alexandria, written in Greek on papyrus and entrusted to Maricopos
Pentablion, a Greek Orthodox monk, for delivery which did not
occur.

*To the revered Bishop Heracletus of the Cathedral Church
of the Resurrection at Alexandria, the greetings of your
most devoted servant, Frater Anteus, with Sieur Horembaud and his pilgrims at the ancient town of Syene Philae,
which the agents of the Sultan sometimes call Aswan, on
this, the morning of Christ's Rising in Glory, in the 1225th
year of Man's Salvation,*

*Most excellent Bishop Heracletus, we have arrived
here with only minor problems, and tomorrow morning
will visit the markets to buy camels for our journey across
the Nubian Desert, which we will begin in four days' time if
all goes well. Sieur Horembaud has appointed some of the
pilgrims to tend to the purchase of supplies so that we will
not be delayed by the necessity of securing them, but that
presupposes that the pilgrims will know how to conduct
business here, and on that point, I am not sanguine. I, myself, have been instructed to speak with the various guides,
if I can understand them, to learn what we will need for
this phase of our travels. Gudjei, our current guide, has
made his recommendations already, but Sieur Horembaud
has admitted his doubts on these to me, and wishes to have
other opinions before he commits himself to a course that
may lead to dangers once we pass into the desert. Sieur
Horembaud, to ensure his most complete understanding, has
ordered Sidi Sandjer'min—I mentioned him to you, as you*

may recall; the physician who joined us at Sese'metkra—to come with me, for he has a broader knowledge of the tongues of this region and will be able to assist me. We will have to report our findings tomorrow night, and then set about purchasing what we need. I applaud Sieur Horembaud's circumspection, but I am far from certain that it will bring about the degree of safety he seeks.

Torquil, our excommunicated Templar, continues to ail in spite of Sandjer'min's best efforts and the help of Bondame Margrethe of Rutland. I suggested to Sieur Horembaud that we might leave him here in Syene Philae, but without success. Sieur Horembaud insists that Torquil be given every chance for redemption, and has declared that were he in Torquil's place, he would want to go on, and offer up his pain as proof of penance; Sieur Horembaud believes that we would none of us consider abandoning him if he were a legitimate son and not the favored bastard he is, a policy that makes the Templars much more vulnerable than the Hospitallers are, admitting only legitimate sons to their numbers. Some of the pilgrims have said that they are worried that Torquil's presence will bring the Devil upon us, in that the Devil goes where he is welcome. I have tried to explain how the very act of pilgrimage provided protection from the Devil, for it is God's work for God's purpose and therefore is proof against evil. Cristofo d'Urbineau, the defrocked priest from Genova, has claimed that this is incorrect; he has been the most adamant in maintaining that we must leave Torquil behind, but thus far has only three supporters: Agnolus Raffaele dei Causi, the Genovese merchant; Noreberht lo Avocat from the Aquitaine; and Perrin Bonnefiles, the Vidame whose credentials seem questionable. I believe Torquil will be with us all the way to the land of the Holy Grail, assuming God gives him life enough to get there, which is far from certain. If he dies, I hope he can lie in consecrated ground, as Templars permit excommuni-

cants to do, for the pilgrimage should lift his excommunication by the holiness of his journey.

On the day before we leave here, we will purchase casks of water, there being none to be had until we reach the region of gold mines in the mountains to the southeast. There are springs there, which give pure water in great quantity, or so we have been assured by three guides, including our own. The assurance that we will not die of thirst has inclined the pilgrims to welcome this shorter route to the land of the Holy Grail. Sieur Horembaud has also required that we have tents large enough to hold our animals in case we encounter a storm or require protection from thieves and raiders. There are four tent-makers in the town market, where I will go as soon as I complete this report to you.

The days are growing steadily hotter, though I have thought it impossible that they could. Resting through the heat of the day is not a self-indulgent opportunity for the sin of sloth, but a necessity to keep from becoming wholly exhausted by the heat, which is why we will travel the desert at night. The traders who cross the desert have warned of sandstorms, and I am persuaded that we must take all precautions against them, as we will do to guard against attack, since we carry only hunting weapons, and they will not suffice to hold off more than a few outlaws. Beyond sandstorms, we have been told that it will rain in the mountains during the summer, and that that will refresh the Nile, but it will not make our time crossing the sands any less demanding. Once the Nile begins to flood it will be nearly impossible to navigate safely, and none of us want to be food for crocodiles and hippopotami, assuming we could stay afloat in the torrents. As you value your soul, I implore you to pray for us, since we have come so far already, and are sworn to complete the pilgrimage. In traveling such a great distance, I trust we will all gain what we seek in this journey.

If we do not, then there will be trouble on our return. May
God and His Angels keep us safe from robbers and slavers,
and may we all come to Grace.

Amen,
Frater Anteus, Ambrosian

7

"Who would have thought a camel could cost so much! And we have only hired them, not bought them!" Richere Enzo exclaimed as the pilgrims sat at their low dining table at the rear of the pilgrims' hostel they had discovered in the foreigners' quarter near the market-square in Syene Philae, a place the Sultan called Aswan. The sun was hanging at the edge of the steep hills across the river, its disk golden in a lavender sky. In front of the pilgrims was laid out a meal of broiled goat, fish-cakes, flatbread, dates, shredded duck-meat, a wheel of hard Italian cheese, peas and beans with onions and olive oil, peppers, wine and beer, and spiced figs in honey. At the next table over, the pilgrims' servants and slaves were enjoying a simpler but satisfying meal of broiled ducks, chick-peas with garlic, flatbread, and beer. "Could we not have paid for the use of thirteen instead of fourteen? And why did we have to engage the owner along with the camels?"

"Because the owner knows his animals, and he has charged us a fair price for his service. It is a sensible thing for him to do. He will escort more pilgrims back the way we came, and make his money that way, instead of having to rob us or betray us to slavers to gain his fee, or leave us with having to find a buyer for the animals before we move on," said Sieur Horembaud. "Gudjei told me so."

"And who is to say the two haven't colluded on this?" Noreberht lo Avocat demanded. "We should expect that among these people."

"Why are you complaining?" Nicholas Howe asked with a wide, insincere smile. "You didn't pay for any of them, did you? not so much as a groat. Sandjer'min covered the cost, and he isn't even one of us."

"We're on a holy mission," Noreberht declared.

"And Firouz is a follower of Islam, not a Christian, nor a pilgrim," said Sandjer'min at his most reasonable. "Why should he show you favor for your faith?" He had found a cushion in the corner next to the table and had taken his place there so that he could listen to what the pilgrims had to say without having to make it obvious that he would not eat with them.

Enzo coughed and muttered.

"If you would rather walk or ride an ass, or carry a tent on your back, I'll take one of the beasts back in the morning, before we're taught how to saddle and bridle them," Sieur Horembaud offered; he was weary of listening to complaints, and wanted to end the carping that had blighted their meal. "The day after tomorrow we set off at sunset. You will each have an animal to ride, and you will be responsible for that animal. No one is to walk once we're on the sands. Those who ride asses will have tack issued to you for the journey, and those of us riding horses will use our own tack for them. Firouz has saddles for all his camels. Each of you will be given a hunting spear, in case we have to fend off dangerous creatures, and, of course, we will use them to bring down food."

Viviano Loredan laughed. "Be most careful of the ones with two legs; they are the most treacherous of all," he advised, and was rewarded with a faint, sinister chuckle from Micheu de Saunte-Foi.

"Well-said," Noreberht lo Avocat declared as if appearing in court.

"And they're hard to clean and cook," said Agnolus dei Causi, his feeble attempt at a joke.

"Quiet," said Sieur Horembaud. "Let us meditate on this meal God has given us."

"The cooks certainly helped," said Howe.

"Remember: we will have to feed the camelman as well as the rest of our party," said Lalagia, daring to speak up. "If we give him short shrift, he may abandon us, with no one to care for the camels, or to show us the way to the Gold Camp." She sat between Methodus Temi and Frater Anteus, who made a point of leaning away from her.

"What about Gudjei? Doesn't he know about camels?" Richere Enzo asked. "Why do we have to rely on a Muslim?"

"He's a guide, not a drover," said dei Causi. "We need Firouz to manage the beasts. Best to accommodate him."

"I think Firouz has been good to us," said Heneri staunchly, and was immediately shushed by Sorer Imogen. "He has helped us so far."

"We're still at the Nile. Once we're on the desert, things may change," said Cristofo d'Urbineau.

"We must remember to collect the camels' dung so we will have something to burn once we start across the desert," Methodus Temi reminded the company.

"Trust a smith to think about fires," muttered Vidame Perrin Bonnefiles, and was rewarded with a giggle from Heneri.

"We can offer it up as humility," Heneri remarked with a grin.

Sorer Imogen crossed herself. "It is unfortunate that we lack charcoal for that purpose. To use dung is to make fire unclean."

Heneri sighed impatiently, looking up at his half-sister. "Imogen, think. Charcoal would have to be carried; dung only has to be picked up. The Templars are not above fueling their fires with dry camel dung."

"Can we talk about something else?" d'Urbineau demanded. "We have many things to consider before we leave here."

Jiochim Menines held up his hands. "True enough, Pater, and we will soon be out of time. We have tomorrow and most of the day after. We must look to the south in the next two days. This time, two nights from now, we will be departing to the southeast and we will leave the Nile behind for many days. We will be at the mercy of the desert, and that should warn us all to prepare while we can. What do you think we have neglected, that you believe we must consider?" When d'Urbineau said nothing, he leaned forward. "I advise all of you to go to the market in the morning and purchase whatever you do not have that you will need in the next thirty days. You have seen what we have bought thus far: is there anything you feel must be included that is not on our list?" He folded his hands. "God may lend us His help, but we would do well to prepare, in case God has other things on His mind."

Cristofo d'Urbineau shook his head. "If I weren't defrocked, I would have to accuse you of heresy."

There was a spurt of skittish laughter from the pilgrims; Sorer Imogen got up silently and left the rest of the pilgrims to their food; Margrethe motioned Heneri to come to her, and after an undecided moment, he did, squeezing in between his half-sister-in-law and Viviano Loredan, who was busy refilling cups with wine.

Sieur Horembaud got to his feet and waited to speak until he had everyone's attention. "Our order of march has been determined: when we leave, we will leave at sunset, as you know. Sandjer'min and I will be at the lead of our party, on horseback, and Vidame Bonnefiles will bring up the rear on a horse, with Jiochim Menines to accompany him on the fourth horse. The camels and the asses will be between us, you pilgrims will ride camels, your servants and slaves will be on asses, and our goods will also be carried by asses. Our guide Firouz has selected the camel he wishes to ride, and will have his choice of our numbers to ride with him, in the lead of the rest of this company."

To the general surprise, Heneri spoke up. "Firouz asked me to ride with him."

Sorer Imogen shook her head. "You must not. It is not fitting that one of your position should have such company."

"I've already said yes," said Heneri with a smug little smile.

Before this could turn into an argument, "What of Torquil des Lichiens?" asked Cristofo d'Urbineau. "How is he to get across the sands?"

"Lalagia is helping us to make a sling that will bear him between two camels—those set aside to carry chests, so that the pack-saddles can be used. She has seen this done before, and she says she will tend to him while we are on the move. During the day, when most of the company is resting, Sandjer'min will take care of him. This has been arranged. Lalagia and Bondame Margrethe will look after him at night, while we're traveling." Sieur Horembaud gave a disgusted huff. "Don't any of you speak against Lalagia. There are few nurses as good as camp followers. You may disdain her for her way of life, but any soldier who has fought in the Holy Land knows the value of the women who are with them."

Vidame Perrin Bonnefiles was less convinced than most. "We are devout Christians, yet we have a loose woman in our number, which speaks ill for our piety."

"Been on campaign often, have you? You know how to carry a wounded man between two camels?" Lalagia inquired with an edge in her tone; when Bonnefiles said nothing, she went on. "I thought so. You hear all the songs and stories, and you think you know what it is like, fighting for God in this hellish place. You see the knights as glorious beings needing only angels to assist them. My knight, like all knights, had sergeants and foot-soldiers and squires to support him, far greater in number than the knights. Slaves care for their comfort in their castles, and those like me do the same in the field. The knights could accomplish little without us. Look down on me and those like me if it suits you: but if you do, pray that you will never need my attention while we travel."

Sandjer'min spoke up before Bonnefiles could respond. "Lalagia is telling the truth. Without the camp followers, many Crusaders would be dead, some from wounds, some from hunger, some from mischance. Even the Templars and Hospitallers have such women in their companies, though they are sworn to chastity."

"Absurd," said Noreberht, his face eloquent of disgust.

"He's right," Sieur Horembaud said, his voice forceful. "Lalagia is searching for her man, who is missing from his own pilgrimage. Most of you know the story: Sieur Arnoul is from Brabant, and he has been gone for more than two years, so she is seeking him: they have children and she is trying to find him for their sakes."

"You're right—we know this," Nicholas Howe complained.

"It doesn't sound like it," Sieur Horembaud shot back, staring at Vidame Bonnefiles. "You have forgotten her reason for being with us."

"All right, all right," d'Urbineau soothed. "The Vidame has been less than charitable, but this arises from his zeal. A man in his position must be diligent in keeping his reputation as a zealous Christian unstained, or the Church could rescind his office in favor of another, more acceptable Vidame." He turned to the visibly annoyed camp-follower. "If you, Lalagia, can forgive him for Christ's sake, then the offense is mended."

"And it will fester, unless God has truly imbued her soul with compassion," said Micheu de Saunte-Foi in cynical satisfaction. "Forgiveness always does when there is no true compensation for it."

The rest said nothing. In the awkward silence, Sandjer'min got up, bowed slightly to Sieur Horembaud, and went toward the door; he was almost out of the room when Sieur Horembaud called out to him. "You're leaving us?"

"For now. I trust you will enjoy the meal. My manservant and I have matters to attend to before we leave here. Tonight we pack the medicaments."

"Go then, with our blessing," said d'Urbineau.

Howe forced a lascivious chuckle. "Make the most of the evening. It's a long way across the desert."

Sandjer'min went out, leaving the hostel and making his way to the stables, where he found Ruthier inspecting tack and ropes. He summarized the dinner conversation, adding, "Howe is right—I intend to make the most of the evening."

"Packing your chests and crates?" Ruthier suggested. "Or something more useful?"

"If it is possible, something more." His tone was deliberately ambiguous and his brows drew together in a frown.

Ruthier concealed his relief at this admission with a nod. "Are you in the stable for that purpose?"

"Not tonight. I need more . . . substantial nourishment with the desert ahead of us."

"Of course. There are women you can visit in their sleep here in the foreigners' quarter, but you will have to wait until past midnight to seek one out," Ruthier said in the Spanish of six hundred years ago. "From what I have discovered, there are many opportunities for amusements until midnight."

"No doubt you're correct," said Sandjer'min in the same tongue.

"In the meantime, what do we need to do?" Ruthier inquired.

"All the medicaments in the red-lacquer chest need to be readied for crossing the desert. I have a stack of rags. We can wrap each container in one, and that should keep them sealed and guarded against breakage." He looked out to a section of wall near the rear of the hostel; half of it was deeply buried in the sand, but the part above it showed a procession of ancient gods. "Horus, Thoth, Min," he said to himself. "Anubis, Maat, Isis, Osiris, Hapy, Bubastis, Sekmet. All good gods for a journey, with the exception of Sekmet."

"Forgotten gods," said Ruthier with sympathy.

"Not by me," Sandjer'min said with a trace of a smile; he picked up a rag and went to open the red-lacquer chest. "And not by those who see their images, little as they know which gods these are."

"No; they think the gods are demons that Moses banished to the wastelands." Ruthier shook his head. "Is it the animal heads, do you think?"

"In part," said Sandjer'min as he worked the lock and opened the door. "But Maat—she's the one with the wings—is also regarded as a demon, when you'd guess she were an angel."

"Probably one of the rebels cast out of Heaven, or Lilith," Ruthier said.

They set to work wrapping the medicament containers and putting them back in their places in the chest. The stable grew dark as the last of sunset faded, and after a while, Ruthier lit one of the rushlights so that they could be observed at their work; neither he nor Sandjer'min was visually hampered by darkness. The two men kept at their labors with the contents of the red-lacquer chest. Most of the time they maintained a companionable silence, though occasionally they exchanged minor remarks.

"The wind's coming up," Ruthier observed.

"It often does at night," said Sandjer'min, then changed his tone. "I'm not easy in my mind about the next stage of our journey; I apologize for being brusque."

Ruthier smiled. "You are not the only one. Sieur Horembaud only repeats himself when he is worried, and he's been doing that all day."

Later, when the unmusical clang of a gong announced the city gates were closing, Ruthier said, "Tomorrow night's the last time we'll hear that for a while."

Some time after that, after the noise level from the hostel had dropped, Carlus and Vitalis, dei Causi's two servants, came into the stable, both carrying heavy cases. They nodded to Sandjer'min and Ruthier, then lit a few more rush-lights; their wavering flames provided uneven illumination to their work.

"Are they still at table?" Ruthier asked in the common tongue of northern Italy as the two servants strove to put their burdens in a safe place.

"No," said Vitalis, the older of the two. "Noreberht has gone off with Menines, I suppose to a house of pleasure."

"And him so against Lalagia," scoffed Carlus.

"Do they have such a thing here?" Ruthier did his best to look surprised.

"Everywhere has such a thing if you know where to look for it," said Vitalis. "This place is no different."

Ruthier gave a diverted snort. "True enough. Well, I wish them joy of their evening; they'll find little such amusements in the Nubian Desert."

"Do you mean there really are pleasure palaces in the desert?" Carlus asked, wide-eyed.

"He's joking," Vitalis explained with exaggerated simplicity.

"Not entirely," said Ruthier. "After a few days on the sands, an oasis seems like Paradise."

"Then you have traveled the great desert?" Vitalis looked at Ruthier with real interest.

"I have traveled *a* great desert, but not this one." He saw the look on Vitalis' face. "I have crossed the Takla Makan, to the north and west of China, some years ago." Almost seven hundred years ago, he added to himself.

"He has; I was there," said Sandjer'min, giving the first indication that he was listening; he knew Sieur Horembaud and Frater Anteus would disapprove of this discourse, and gave a warning gesture toward Ruthier.

Vitalis laughed. "Travelers! They would have us believe all manner of tales. I have heard that there are ponies in the East that breathe fire, and that there are men as spotted as leopards in the forests of Russia."

"Since you are curious, my servant is answering your questions. Would you prefer he did not?" Sandjer'min's tone did not alter at all from its geniality, but there was something in his eyes that made Vitalis take a step back, and Carlus brush his hands on his femoralia as if to rid them of something unwelcome. "For the sake of the company, perhaps silence would be better—what do you think?"

A stillness came and passed: Vitalis shrugged. "It will be as it must."

Ruthier regarded the two men closely. "Are you worried about the crossing?" He wrapped the last jar in a linen rag, put it in place, and stepped back so that Sandjer'min could lock the chest once more.

"Yes," said Vitalis at the precise instant that Carlus said "No."

"You have crossed desert before," Ruthier said to Vitalis.

"Yes. Twice. Before dei Causi employed me." He coughed. "Not that one, the Syrian Desert. The second time we came as near to dying as I would ever want to again until God calls me." Vitalis gave Carlus a sharp look. "He believes that crossings are tests provided by God, that so long as his faith is strong, he will be able to make his way in safety. But he has never before faced the open sands."

"You're getting old," Carlus said as if that contravened any opinion Vitalis might express. "Your faith is faltering, like your legs."

"Young men always say that when we old men disagree with them." He laughed and aligned a long case next to the far wall. "Put the smaller cases on this for now."

Ruthier came up to Sandjer'min. "I'll test the water casks now and fill them for the journey shortly before we leave."

"Thank you; and be sure the water is boiled; this company cannot afford flux at this time." He took one of two bridles from his chest of tack, pulled it out, and began cleaning it, taking care to inspect it for signs of wear.

"Boiling, to be rid of the animacules," Ruthier said, ducking his head; he had been very careful to behave like the pilgrims' servants since their journey began, especially when the other servants were present.

"The casks are with our supplies," said Sandjer'min.

"Yes," Ruthier agreed, and went toward the four closed rooms at the end of the rows of stalls.

Sandjer'min worked steadily, finishing his inspection on the bridle and the spare set of reins he carried, then started on the halter-with-reins that Ruthier would use for the ass he rode; he paid little attention to the two servants: Carlus and Vitalis had almost completed stacking dei Causi's crates and chests and were both showing signs of fatigue. When Carlus yawned for the second time, Vitalis set down the crate of Egyptian pottery their master had already purchased on his journey south.

"Shove your crate out of the way for tonight," he recommended to Carlus. "We can deal with them in the morning."

"And have dei Causi deliver his thanks with a stick? No. We must finish this." Carlus attempted another step, nearly tripped, and let out a shriek of dismay. He stood still until he was steady on his feet once more, then shuffled to the wall and very charily set down his crate with a sigh. "Excuse us, Sidi," he said to Sandjer'min. "We are going to retire before we collapse into a stall for the night."

"Most wise of you," said Sandjer'min, evincing a hint of irony.

Carlus gave Sandjer'min an uncertain scowl, then made for the door; Vitalis lingered, dawdling over securing a cord around a box filled with cloth.

"Don't hold his youth against him, Sidi," he said.

"Certainly not," Sandjer'min said with an ironic smile. "All of us were young—once."

"Yes," said Vitalis, ducking his head respectfully before he left the stable.

Sandjer'min inspected a girth-buckle and decided he would have to make a new one; tomorrow would be time enough, since they would have the whole of that day and most of the next to make ready. He returned his tack to its chest and closed it, securing it with a lock he had carried from Lo-Yang. After taking a quick turn around the stable, checking stall doors, leaving ripe figs in the mangers, and topping off the water in the troughs, he blew out his rush-light and left by the rear door.

The streets were almost empty; only the torches at the intersections of streets were lit. Music came from the upper floor of a food-and-entertainment shop; Sandjer'min passed them by, going toward that part of the foreign quarter that was given over to more private pleasures, and to the foreigners who had decided not to move on, up or down the Nile. He had turned down an alleyway, planning to go toward the side-gate of the town, when his attention was caught by a boy of eight or nine, who stepped out of a doorway.

"You. Foreigner," he said in acceptable Arabic.

Sandjer'min realized that unless the youngster were addressing the two striped cats a half-dozen paces ahead of him, the boy was talking to him. "Yes?" he said in Arabic, looking around in case there should be more youths in the shadows, though his night-seeing eyes could make out none but the boy. "What do you want?" He moved a little to the left so that he could bolt from the passage if he had to.

"You. Are you looking for a woman?" The sensual smile he gave was at odds with his age, something he had been taught to do without being aware of its intent. "I know where women are. Pretty women. Women as fair as the full moon."

"Do you." Sandjer'min went up to him.

The boy moved back into the doorway, continuing with his rehearsed offer. "It is no trap. There are women. Pretty women. Waiting for men."

"But there is only one of me," said Sandjer'min in amused apology after giving the house a brief but thorough scrutiny; small as it was, there might be as many as three women living in it, but that did not seem likely. "What are all these pretty women to do?"

The boy took hold of Sandjer'min's sleeve. "You come with me. It's getting late. You come."

Without any sign of effort, Sandjer'min pulled his square, black-linen cotehardie's sleeve from the boy's determined grip. "Why should I believe you? You could be luring me off to a trap set by robbers."

"You must come," the boy said, a note of desperation in his plea. He tried to catch hold of Sandjer'min's clothing again.

"No trap? Why would you say that if you had no plans for a trap?" Sandjer'min took a step toward the youngster. The game, paltry as it was, was beginning to wear on him, so he added, "Very well. Show me where I will find these pretty women."

The boy gave a little scream and fled to the interior of the house; a moment later an attractive woman of about twenty appeared; sloe-eyed and olive-skinned, she wore a simple long deshba of sheer linen, and her face was partially veiled by a length of fine, pale silk. "Never mind Kayru. He hasn't learned how to approach strangers yet. He needs more practice." She gave him a brief appraisal in the dim light cast by a guttering lamp inside the doorway. "He may have been wise to stop you." There was a world of innuendo in her simple words. "It's been a slow night so far. You could change that."

Sandjer'min studied her, trying to decide what was best to do. Taking shared pleasure as something more than a dream was tempting, but if this woman were a practiced whore, she might have set her own satisfaction aside in favor of business: not all women in that profession were pleased with their work as much as Melidulci had been, or as gratified by it.

"See? Pretty woman. You go with her," said Kayru.

"Hush, you wretched boy," said the young woman, her eyes never wavering from Sandjer'min's.

"I am not wretched," Kayru declared, and winced in anticipation of a reprimand that never came.

To fill the silence growing between them, Sandjer'min asked, "What is your name?"

"Ruia," she answered. "Kayru is my brother."

"You live here, just the two of you?"

She smiled. "My family sent Kayru to me a year ago, to teach him. He is a very beautiful boy, and will be so until he has a beard."

"I see," said Sandjer'min.

"Would you prefer him?" The question was so direct that Sandjer'min was startled.

"No," he said, no change in his demeanor. "He is a beautiful boy, and doubtless will do you proud, but my tastes run to women, not boys."

Ruia shrugged. "Whatever you prefer."

Sandjer'min watched her watching him, seeing her trying to decide how to lure him in. "I am interested," he told her. "What do you expect, if I should accept your offer?" He did not know how to deal with this woman, but he was increasingly curious about her; over his long life, he had encountered many women, and a number of men, who earned their livings by selling sexual pleasure, but this woman was a puzzle to him.

"Tell me what *you* expect: that is what will matter." She regarded him speculatively. "I will not allow knives used on me, I won't be whipped, and I won't pray. And I will not do any of those things to you."

"That's acceptable to me," he said, making up his mind to make the most of the opportunity she presented. Ruia was a willing, awake partner, and that was more than he had hoped to find this night. "So this night will not end in rancor, what would you charge me for your company from now until dawn?" He waited while she made up her mind.

"You are a foreigner—don't deny it, I can tell by your accent, and your clothes." She calculated. "Ten silver denarii for that long."

"Why not a Venezian ducat?" Sandjer'min suggested, catching Ruia's surprised blink.

"That is more than twice as much as the denarii," she told him, maintaining her composure with an effort as her eyes glittered at the thought of the money. "Why would you pay more?"

"Why will you not accept it?" he rejoined, and once again waited while she thought.

She glanced over her shoulder at Kayru, then looked back at Sandjer'min. "I will take your ducat, but it will buy you no favor."

"Understood," he said, making no effort to hurry her inside. "I will abide by your terms."

"Oh. You're one who likes to be coaxed," she said with the world-weariness of an old woman. She stepped back. "Come in. The second chamber on the left is mine." She rounded on her brother. "Kayru, you can go to sleep now."

The boy kicked at a low stool. "Why should I?"

"Because I have told you," said Ruia with strong purpose in her voice. She closed the door and slid the bolt into place, then followed after Sandjer'min. Her chamber was surprisingly large, with a bed of ample proportions, two small tables, one with a ewer of water on it, the other with a jug of wine, an upholstered chair, two sconces with bound papyrus-stalk torches burning for light, and pegs for clothes. Coming into the room, she said, "You may put your clothes there, on the wall, on the end pegs. You need not fear darkness and treachery. One of the torches will keep burning."

"I won't be taking off more than my peri," he said, dropping into the chair and unlacing first his right pero, then his left.

She paused in closing the door. "Are you seeking to disguise some ill?"

"No. Would you like me to raise my hem to show you?" He made the offer calmly.

Nonplussed, Ruia shook her head. "Not for now. Do you want me to undress?"

"It would be more pleasant for the both of us," he said.

She stretched languidly and unfastened her deshba, letting it slither off her onto the floor, leaving her naked but for her veil, which she cast aside as she turned one of the torches upside down in its sconce, extinguishing it. Her body was lissom, and she moved smoothly, sliding onto her bed as if entering the river to swim. "It's warm enough not to use the coverlet," she said, and ran the tip of her tongue over her lips.

Sandjer'min held up his hands. "No need for so much display, Ruia, not for me. Let me rouse you."

Ruia stopped moving, then slowly pouted. "I don't please you?"

"You do, and because of that, I would rather please you, if you are willing," he said, coming to the side of the bed and looking down into her lovely, bored eyes. "You are everything a man could want, but you—"

She interrupted him with an exasperated sigh. "But you've changed your mind about the ducat."

His laughter was sad. "No." He reached into the sleeve of his cotehardie and drew out a small leather purse, removing a golden ducat from it before restoring the purse to its place. He held out the ducat. "Here."

"Gold," she said, a little surprised, after she bit it.

"That it is." He sat down on the side of her bed, resting his right hand on her hip. "Will you lie back and let me seek out those pleasures you may have missed? Haven't you a taste for pleasure?"

"So you're one of *those*," she said with heavy sarcasm. "One who has to believe that this is something more than a simple transaction."

A millennium ago, Sandjer'min might have given in to disappointment, but Sran's treachery had taught him a vital lesson. "For a ducat, indulge me in my illusion, then," he suggested gently.

Ruia considered this. "If you must have it, then I'll comply—but remember that it *is* an illusion, not your knightly vision of passion."

It was not a very promising beginning, but Sandjer'min nodded. "If you will lie back, and let me do what I can to give you pleasure."

Her sigh offered no encouragement, but she did as he asked, and closed her eyes. "If I fall asleep, I will apologize when you wake me."

For a short while, Sandjer'min did nothing, but then he began to massage Ruia's calves and feet, not seeking to stimulate her, but to provide relaxation; if this surprised her, she gave no sign of it, but allowed herself to ease into the pleasant sensations he was able to impart. Gradually, his ministrations became more sensual. "If you will turn over, I will massage your back," he said, his voice low and musical. "If you fall asleep, I will not be troubled." He waited while she rolled onto her stomach, squirmed a little to adjust the coverlet beneath her. "I'll start at your shoulders." His small hands kneaded and loosened her muscles until she was limp with satisfaction. Then he bent and very lightly kissed the nape of her neck.

"That's nice," she murmured.

He kissed her neck again, and as she arched into the delectation he gave her, his arms went around her and he cupped her breasts in his hands, lying lightly atop her, bolstered by his arms so as not to hamper any movement she might make. When she started to turn, he whispered, "Not yet."

Baffled, she lay still, and felt his languid, sensual caresses moving down her body between her flesh and the coverlet. Nothing she had anticipated prepared her for the intensity of her response, for the elation that rioted through her body, evoking ever more rapturous transports. She had neither the capacity nor the will to stop the ecstasy that claimed her as his hands slipped between her legs, into the sea-scented folds and the access to the core of her body. He did not hurry her, but tantalized and teased the bud there, until it tightened and quivered; his hands moved deeper. She had pushed herself up on her elbows, her head thrown back as her body prepared for release. For what seemed half the night, she held back the gratification that every fiber of her being sought, then, when she could contain herself no longer, she let out a little cry as her body spasmed, spasmed, and spasmed again, until she fell back onto the bed, her body replete. She lay for a short while, relishing her fading rapture, and only then was she aware of his lips on her neck. As she struggled to contain her thoughts, she felt him move away, which filled her with such unexpected desolation of spirit that she challenged him. "Why didn't you face me?"

He touched the edge of her cheek. "I didn't face you because you wanted your fulfillment for yourself."

She drew up her knees and turned to confront him, her mouth square with anger. "And you know what I want?"

"I have touched the soul of you," he said simply. "I want to give you what you sought, for myself as much as for you."

This was more than anything she was prepared to accept: she reached for the ewer of water and threw it at him, determined to make him pay for the pain of his leaving after he had so utterly exposed her.

Sandjer'min got off the bed as the ewer smashed into the wall. He picked up his peri and gave her a long, thoughtful look. "You probably won't believe me, but I am deeply grateful to you, Ruia."

Her glare seemed to have the power to set fires. "Get out. *Get out!*" she ordered, her voice rising. "And never come here again."

He knew better than to thank her again; he left her alone, wishing she had been willing to accept his gratitude for the nourishment she had provided to him. Why was it, he wondered, that she resented her apolaustic passion? Was it because of its brevity? Was it because she had abandoned herself to him? Whatever the cause, he knew that her delectation and her turmoil would be with him all across the Nubian Desert.

Text of a letter from Ernost of Briarie, notary of Norfolk, to Hassan-al-Yaasim in Alexandria, written on vellum and carried by Templar courier overland and by ship, delivered thirty-nine days after it was written.

> *To the merchant of cotton cloth, Hassan-al-Yaasim, the greetings of Ernost of Briarie, notary of Norfolk, on behalf of the Sailmakers' and Drapers' Guilds of Norfolk:*
>
> *This is to confirm the transfer of one hundred-fifty Venetian ducats to the treasury of the Poor Knights of the Temple in London, which amount will be held in credit by the Templars in Egypt, against which you may draw such payment as has been agreed in our contract of November 29th, 1224, and which has been received here on January 18th of this year. All parties now being signatory to the contract and the authorization of payment, I am pleased to inform you of the same and to ask that you provide an acknowledgment to the Templars of Alexandria. A bona fides copy of the contract itself is included with this confirmation.*
>
> *It is agreed that the Sailmakers' Guild will receive the first bales of cotton canvass from you, that the cloth will be free from flaws and of uniform width, that any inferior bales of cloth will be returned and any monies collected for it returned to the Templars, and that the Drapers' Guild will receive your basic cotton cloth, undyed, in the second shipment, that it, too, will have been inspected for flaws, that notification of the departure of the ordered cloth will be made through the Templars, which will have both the name of the ship, its owner, and the name of the Captain,*

which information is to be transferred to the Templars in England with all due haste. *The percent of the Templars' service fee will be borne by all parties equally, and to that end, the Sailmakers' Guild and the Drapers' Guild have provided their portion of that payment along with the deposit specified. When we receive your confirmation of the deposit monies being available to you, the Guilds will also expect to receive notification from the Templars that they have your portion of the service fee in hand, so that we may commence our most beneficial exchange.*

We, signers and witnesses, are all known to one another, all are men of good character, and have all consented without coercion to sign, seal, and witness this codicil to our existent contract.

Ernost of Briarie
Notary
(his seal)

The Great Seal of the Sailmakers' Guild

The Great Seal of the Drapers' Guild
Jeremy Sudcliffe, Master
Thomas Boyes, Master
sworn to and witnessed as shown
on this, the Monday after Easter
in the Lord's Year 1225

Matthias Rochiver
Joiner of Saint-Clement's

Andrew Creighton
Apothecary of Norfolk

Edmund Loche
Upholsterer of Norfolk

PART II

SIEUR HOREMBAUD DU LANGNOR
BARON DU CREISSE-EN-AQUITAINE
SIEUR OF THE FIEF SAUNT-DIDIER

Text of a letter from Frater Misericorde, physician, at Creisse in the Aquitaine, to Margrethe of Rutland, wife of Sieur Dagoberht Gosland, on pilgrimage in Egypt, written on linen with dye and carried by Hospitaller couriers as far as Alexandria, given to pilgrim monks to carry up-river, but never delivered.

To the good, pious, and devoted Bondame Margrethe of Rutland, wife to Sieur Dagoberht Gosland; knight and courtier to His Grace, King Henry, of that name the Third; Counselor to the Regent; Baron du Creisse-en-Aquitaine; and Sieur of the fief of Saunt-Didier, also in the Aquitaine, on this, the 27th day of April, in the Year of Our Lord, 1225:

Most illustrious Bondame,

It is my sad duty to inform you that your dearest, revered husband Sieur Dagoberht, Baron du Creisse, etc. has been called to the Right Hand of God, his bodily suffering finally at an end, his earthly burdens passed to others, his place in this world given over to his successor, and his soul ascended in glory. It was on Good Friday that Sieur Dagoberht was overcome by a fit during which he saw a vision of the New Jerusalem, as fine and golden as any painting has shown, and he remained in a rapt state from mid-day until near sunset, at which time, he fell to weeping for a goodly stretch of time, and could not be succored. The tears stopped as soon as the Angelus began, and so there were supplemental prayers offered for his recovery at the conclusion of the sunset service. He slept peacefully enough, but was distracted for most of the next day. On Resurrection Sunday, he was much improved, almost to a state of giddiness, and he sang and danced after the Paschal Mass, which everyone agreed was a sign of God's favor. By late afternoon, he grew tired, and seemed to fall into a lethargy that lasted until the afternoon the next day, when he wakened and said he would have to leave soon. He was able to swear it was his wish that his title and lands should pass to his half-brother, Sieur Heneri, who is presently in your company as you journey to the distant holy sites at the headwaters of the River Nile. Then he was taken with a great fit, in which his back bent like a bow and he shook and twitched as a stag will when brought down of a sudden by arrows; when it was over, Sieur Dagoberht's soul had departed his flesh. To spare you the necessity of explaining this to Sieur Heneri, I will send him a letter, as well, so that he will have his own proof of the change in his position in life. Because he is as young as he is, a regent is needed to be appointed in his place, and Sieur Dagoberht appointed you to fulfill that office until such time as Sieur Heneri is fully twenty-one years of age and deemed ready to assume the dignities of his heritage. Until your return, I will hold the estate in trust for you and your half-brother-in-law, and will submit my discharging of that office to annual inspection by the Bishop and the King's appointed officer who supervises these situations. King Henry, young as he is, is a minor still, as is Sieur Heneri, and will tend to regard his present situation with understanding, making allowances for Sieur Heneri's pilgrimage and the disorder to which his absence contributes. I have written to the London chapter of the Poor Knights of the Temple of Solomon to inform them that Sieur Heneri will not be joining them on his return from Egypt as had been arranged, since he will accede to his half-brother's duties and honors as soon as he is once again in Europe.

As to Sorer Imogen, Sieur Dagoberht has endowed her Order with an annual sum of ten pounds, a most generous amount, and one that is intended to be given in perpetuity. If you will impart this sad news to her and offer what comfort you can to her in this time of sorrow, it will demonstrate once again that magnanimity of character that has ever been your watchword. It is hard to lose a brother, especially for a nun, for it severs yet another link to the world outside the cloister, leaving her more completely in the care of Our Lady and the Sorer's Good Angel. All things happen as God wills, and say we all Amen, but it is hard for us to see His plan in this: dying while his wife and his heir were away, and in the company of his sister. With faith, there is hope, and with hope there is salvation, and in the prayers of holy virgins is there more Grace than in a mumbled Ave Maria in the dead of night. You, Bondame Margrethe, would be well-advised to seek Sorer Imogen out for the sanctity of her vocation, to preserve your reputation during your travels; one hears such tales of the conduct of pilgrims that, if all were true, the Holy Father in Rome must forbid women to venture beyond the limits of Christendom for the sake of their good names. It is fortunate that you have Sorer Imogen in your company, especially now that you must make your way back to English France in haste, without the protection of monks or knights. As a nun, Sorer Imogen will have the discipline of Hours and liturgy to lend her fortitude while you make your return to the Aquitaine, and certainly your good council will ease her grief, as well. Women know best what will bring surcease of suffering to other women; may God show you Mercy in these hard days.

I know you do not use titles of possessions on pilgrimages, so I will not address you or your husband's half-brother by the titles and honors to which you are made recipients by this most unfortunate death, but it is fitting that the Templars and Hospitallers observe the dignities with which you will be invested. I must reiterate that your return upon receiving this is necessary. It will not do for the heir of the estate to be away too long, especially since he is *not yet of age and there are members of his family who might make an acceptable claim upon the lands and titles should Heneri remain away too long. His seneschal, Guillaume des Grossierterres, and I will maintain the estates and fief until your return, provided it be by Christmas; after that, the law may demand proofs of your living or, if such are not provided within a year, dispose of the lands and titles to secondary heirs. There is already a submission to the judges to hear the case at the Nativity season, and the judges have no reason to deny such a request, since Sieur Heneri is not yet of age and has no living brother or uncle to speak for him. I do not say this as a threat, but as a warning, for you have undertaken so much that I know so swift a return may not be possible, but it must be begun as soon as this is in your hands, for time is pressing. If it is the case that you are too far to be able to ensure your arrival by Christmas, inform the Hospitallers that you are preparing to return—choose them over the Templars, who charge more for relaying messages than the Hospitallers do—and entrust them with such proofs of life that will ensure the judges that you are traveling toward Creisse, to present your claims in the law courts, which should buy you as much as another year to make your way back to English France. No matter how great a distance you have gone, the assurance you give of your efforts to return will be met with delight here, and with concessions from the judges.*

I am grieved that God did not bless you and Sieur Dagoberht with children, for all these problems would not exist if you had produced an heir; it has pleased God that you have no issue of your husband's body, and so you must face the demands made by your state. Your family must feel your failure most keenly, for if you had produced an heir, the line of succession would stay with the senior branch of the Gosland House, and not devolve to the junior, as it will; Sieur Heneri is a male heir, to be sure, but of his father's second wife. Had you given Sieur Dagoberht a son, the title and lands would be safely in the senior line. Then Sieur Heneri could have become a Templar, as has been planned since his birth, and you would not have had to make the pilgrimage upon which you are engaged, and all the confusion with which we now must deal would not exist. You would have remained here, with your son, had Sieur Dagoberht suffered the addling of his wits; it would have been Sorer Imogen, for her deep piety, who would have gone with Sieur Heneri to pray for their brother's restoration of health while you attended to him and his heir. But it is not for us to question what God sends us in this life; we are the sheep of His pastures, and He will shepherd us to His Glory.

May God's Angels guide and protect you and bring you safely back to the Aquitaine and Creisse, may your Saints guard you in the treacherous lands you travel, may you be consoled in your mourning by the knowledge that Sieur Dagoberht has come to the end of his earthly suffering and joined with his Gosland fathers at the Wedding Supper of Our Lord, and may your prayers be heard in Heaven with loving-kindness by your husband and the Hosts of God.

In the Name of Father, Son, and Holy Ghost
Amen
Frater Misericorde
Cistercian

1

Sieur Horembaud was the first one through the gates of Syene Philae, as he had intended to be; his horse, a neat bay Barb mare with a star on her forehead, a snip on her lip, and two white feet, was fresh and eager to run, but Sieur Horembaud knew better than to let her; they had a long way to go before sunrise, and he needed his mare to husband her strength. He allowed her to scamper a little, then pulled her to order as Sandjer'min came up to him, his dove-colored gelding behaving himself. Sunset turned the sands to ruddy gold, and the wind skittered along the ground, carrying a fine spume of sand with it. Behind them came the camels and asses with their riders and packs, and last, Jiochim Menines and Vidame Perrin Bonnefiles on horses. Sieur Horembaud, determined to make a good beginning, raised his arm to signal them all to continue forward.

"South, bearing slightly east," Sandjer'min reminded him; he felt the wind rising, making the cooling sands buzz.

"Yes, yes. If we must, we can ask Firouz if we get too far off track." He swung around in the saddle to make sure his people were following him. "We'll have some moonlight tonight, that's something."

"It will rise soon after we have gone the first league," said Sandjer'min, knowing that Sieur Horembaud was as appetent as he was excited.

"When do we stop to rest?" Sieur Horembaud asked, although he knew the answer; he had spent from noon until almost sunset yesterday going over all the plans with Sandjer'min and Firouz, so the question was more of a check to find out if Sandjer'min were still in agreement with his plans. He had to call out as if ordering soldiers in battle; Sandjer'min knew Sieur Horembaud would be hoarse by dawn.

"At midnight," said Sandjer'min, keeping his voice level, aware that despite his show of enthusiastic confidence, Sieur Horembaud was anxious about this phase of the journey. "We rest, we have food, we water the animals, and we travel until dawn." He could not keep from adding, "As we have agreed already."

"I wish we had met with the pilgrims bound north who came through Syene Philae ten days before we did—we could have learned so much from them. As it is . . ." The words trailed away in the hum of the cooling sands. "Well, we know our route, and Firouz knows the way. We'll do, if we keep to our plans."

"In general, I agree," said Sandjer'min carefully, "but I know too rigid a commitment to plans can end up creating its own trap. We must be prepared to accommodate the dangers we haven't anticipated." It had happened to him the first time when he was still breathing, and several times after that; the worst so far had been on the road to Baghdad.

Sieur Horembaud accepted this reprimand with the appearance of good grace. "I know you think this repetition is useless, but when you've commanded troops in battle, as I have, you learn that you cannot go over plans too often or too firmly. We are in strange territory that could be dangerous, and all of us need to know what is expected; what is true for soldiers is true of pilgrims, and they deserve the same instruction soldiers do, and for much the same reason: so that they can cover the distance with as little difficulty as possible. Like an army, our men will need to know what is planned for them, and they will have to remember accurately during the fight."

Sandjer'min did not mention that he had commanded troops in the past, and that he understood the need for repetition, saying only, "We face no army here, only the desert."

"And that is enough," said Sieur Horembaud, watching how his mare made her way through the sands. "That is why we hold to the walk and are strung out in this double line, which would be folly if there were enemies nearby."

A short distance on, they passed a pair of great heads emerging from the sands, carved by ancient hands and long neglected; the heads were no longer smooth, but pitted from the constant abrasion of sand, their mouths partially covered, the nose of one broken off. Sieur Horembaud stared at them as the band of pilgrims approached them. "What manner of people make such monuments and then bury them? How much more than the heads are there?"

"Probably a whole body for each head," replied Sandjer'min, knowing that there was. "And I doubt the ancient people buried their monuments: the wind and sand did that."

"Then the sand is deeper than I thought, to have covered so much." He looked about him, as if he expected the dunes to rise up and cover him.

"We have been climbing slowly since we left Syene Philae, and the dunes are stretching out ahead of us," Sandjer'min reminded him as calmly as he could. "Firouz told you that the ground rises gradually toward the hills south of here, where we will find the Gold Camp. You can see the edge of the hills ahead of us. They'll be plainer when the moon has risen." He patted his horse on the neck, aware by the angle of his ears that the gelding was listening to the conversation. "Nothing to trouble you, Melech," he said.

"You coddle your horse, Sandjer'min," said Sieur Horembaud, shaking his head. "He doesn't even belong to you."

"For this leg of our journey, he does," said Sandjer'min. "He is a strengthy animal, and for that I thank him."

"A mere convenience, nothing more. And yet you cater to him," said Sieur Horembaud, looking for some manner of dispute to rid him of his anxiety; now that he and his company were out in the vastness of the desert night, he was becoming uneasy.

"Of course; while I am able to, so he will remain loyal when I am not." Sandjer'min saw Sieur Horembaud try to stifle annoyed laughter. "I see no reason to argue over the matter."

Sieur Horembaud snorted in derision. "I'm not arguing: you are being unreasonable. That horse is your servant, as God made him to be. As master, you will enforce your authority; he will take what you give him and be grateful, for men are masters of beasts. And he will obey you if you keep a firm hand on him and use spurs to correct him—and I don't mean those coin rowels you use; you need spikes, to enforce your will."

Rather than argue with Sieur Horembaud, Sandjer'min said, "On that we must disagree," and rode on in silence.

A little later on, Sieur Horembaud said to the air, "You were right; we do need the extra asses we bought in Syene Philae."

Sandjer'min was wise enough to say nothing.

Some way back at the head of the main body of pilgrims, slaves, and servants, Firouz was trying to help Heneri to learn to ride his camel. "Rock with his movements; do not strive to remain fully upright. Your back will pain you if you do," he said in Arabic, and exaggerated his own motions to show what he meant. "Be like a flag in the breeze—let the air do the work. The camel is like the air; you are the flag."

"Like a flag? It's like being at sea in a tempest. I might be sick," said Heneri in schoolboy Church Latin as he clung to the saddle; he knew Firouz did not speak it beyond a few words, but he persisted in using it, as if by repetition, Firouz would gain understanding; he told himself that no matter what he had promised Pater Foulepiau back home, it would be best to learn more Arabic, and to improve his Greek, as well. He struggled to come up with an Arabic word that would convey the sensation he was experiencing on the camel, and settled for miming throwing up.

Firouz chuckled. "You are making it too hard," he said, and even as he said it, realized Heneri did not understand him, so he showed the boy a second time how to move with the camel, all the while resolving to teach Heneri—and any of the other pilgrims who wanted to learn—some basic Arabic so they would not constantly be caught in a mass of misunderstanding, requiring the help of Frater Anteus or Sandjer'min to explain what was being said. It had been hard enough on the boats, but riding compounded the problems. He decided to make his start now, and held up his finger, pointing the direction they were traveling. "South," he said in Arabic.

Heneri repeated the word, and pointed, asking in his woefully inadequate Arabic, "Aysh?" meaning *what*.

Realizing he was attempting too much, Firouz held up his finger again, and said, "Wahid," then raised a second finger and said, "iht-nane," and raised a third, saying, "tahlatah."

With a sudden smile, Heneri held up a single finger. "One—wahid," then a second, "two—ihtnane," then a third, "tahlatah—three."

Firouz echoed Heneri's smile with one of his own. "Yes," he said in Greek, nodding several times. "Ney."

Although Heneri did not understand the word, which sounded more like no than yes to him, he knew approval when he saw it, and settled down to learn a few more words of Arabic; only then did he realize that he had been riding the camel without difficulty since he had put his attention on words and not the animal's rolling gait. He glanced at Firouz, and saw him grin. "A fine beast, this camel."

"Yes," said Firouz, smiling and nodding to make his meaning clear.

At her own request, Margrethe rode astride on an ass, a thick, surcingled pad serving as a saddle and two lead-ropes tied to the noseband of the halter for reins. She was positioned behind the two pack-camels with Torquil's sling between them, where she could keep watch over him, waiting impatiently for the moon to rise so that she could see him more clearly, for now he was little more than a dim shape in a broad shadow. Behind her, she could hear Sorer Imogen praying, her cadences matching the sway of her camel, her eyes turned toward Heaven. "May God hear her prayers, and may we have no need of them," Margrethe said softly; she carried in the leather bag slung across her chest an array of medicaments Sandjer'min had provided her, in anticipation of need; for now, Torquil was heavily asleep, having been given some syrup of poppies shortly before they left Syene Philae. She decided that when they stopped at midnight, she must speak with Lalagia, who had experience with caring for wounded men while traveling, to learn how best to deal with Torquil if he should become restless.

From the back of his camel, Micheu de Saunte-Foi watched the group of servants and slaves ahead of him, all mounted on asses; be-hind him came the camels, but for the pack-camels, that were ahead of him, in the middle of the lot, in theory for protection of their goods, food, water, and Torquil des Lichiens. He shook his head, thinking how ill-prepared these pilgrims were, and how little they knew it. Why, he wondered, had the pilgrims not hired their servants from among the abandoned soldiers in Alexandria, instead of bringing their helpers from Europe with them? Those idle fighting men would have been grateful for work and for a chance to do something more than loiter around the waterfront, looking for someone to hire them. These servants might have their uses, but they would not be much good in a fight or some other crisis. Only Viviano Loredan's man, Salvatore, looked as if he might be able to hold his own, and Sandjer'min's Ruthier, if he were younger, had the bearing of a fellow capable of facing danger. For the rest, Micheu de Saunte-Foi was all but certain that at best they would cower and at worst would flee. How was it that God had made so many men to be cowards, since courage was a virtue? He wished now that he had accepted a prison cell in which to do his penance instead of this disastrous pilgrimage. Most distressing was Sieur Horembaud's insistence that they not leave Torquil des Lichiens behind. What was the advantage in having him with the pilgrims? How could an excommunicated Templar inspire the pilgrims to greater faith? Why burden everyone with a dying man? What would happen when Torquil died? The most likely result would be that several pilgrims would want to turn back, no matter what oaths they had taken. He began to contemplate the possibility of escape, some means to make it appear he was being heroic, not shaking off the legal chains that bound him to this group of ill-assorted travelers. What would arduous travel do to rid his soul of his crimes, he asked himself for the hundredth time. Yet he took satisfaction in his own preparedness. For the first time since they left their boats on the Nile, Micheu de Saunte-Foi, convicted assassin and spy, began to relax; he would not have to endure leagues and leagues and leagues of boredom and danger, after all. He could go to another part of Africa, or cross the Red Sea to Muslim lands, or take ship and travel over the sea to Hind. He turned these options over in his mind, wondering if it had been God or the Devil who had wakened such plans in him.

Riding to the right of Micheu de Saunte-Foi, Cristofo d'Urbineau watched the penitent as covertly as possible, taking care not to seem overly curious about the man. Studying Micheu, d'Urbineau puzzled again on what Micheu had done that required him to journey to such a distant outpost of the Christian religion in order to expiate his sins. He had made only vague references to being accused, and had resisted all of the attempts to convince him to speak. For his own case, d'Urbineau had broken the Seal of Confession, telling his fellow-priests that the merchant Davin Morcetroit had been kidnaping children and selling them to slavers from the County of Austria and from Leon and Castile in Spain. Most of the time Morcetroit blamed the gypsies while he pocketed large sums of money. This was such a great scandal that d'Urbineau had been unable to keep it to himself, and had informed the Console of Morcetroit's activities. D'Urbineau understood that his being reinstated as a priest was completely dependent on this pilgrimage, and once again, he studied Micheu, wishing he could see more clearly; the vast scattering of stars were not enough to reveal more than general shapes, and moonrise was still a short while away.

From his vantage point behind d'Urbineau, Noreberht lo Avocat fought the urge to sleep. The camel was the very devil to ride, and once he had become accustomed to rocking as if he were back on a boat, the inclination to doze was well nigh irresistible. He reproved himself for failing to stay awake and alert much as he might belabor an opponent in court. He prided himself on his style of delivery, and knew that his flair for the dramatic had won him cases in which the law, strictly enforced, would have held his client to account. The trouble was—and he was well-aware of it now—he was lazy. He had realized early in life that his charm and glib tongue made the profession of his father easy for him, and this knowledge ended by drawing him into what was described as collusion and corruption, though he was fairly sure he did not have such ignoble goals in mind, simply the inclination to take the facile way. He was beginning to see how real struggle had more value than the priests had ever convinced him of with their haranguing and castigation. Perhaps, he thought as he started to drift off again, the pilgrimage would improve his character after all.

A nacreous glow limned the angular eastern horizon, heralding the coming of the moon. Sorer Imogen stopped her prayers long enough to tell herself that the desert-dwelling hermits of long ago may have hit upon something in this fastness, for the emptiness lent a purpose to her prayers that no cloister could. She caught sight of Heneri on his camel at the head of the asses, riding beside Firouz. This troubled her, for she knew the camel-drover was a faithful Muslim and therefore likely to try to spread his evil teaching to her half-brother. Only the recollection that they had no more than a dozen words in common offered her any consolation. She resumed reciting the Psalms, which seemed more appropriate in the desert than *Pater Nosters* and *Ave Marias*.

By the time the moon, showing slightly more than half its face, was fully clear of the distant hills, Sieur Horembaud called for a short halt. "Camel dung to my servants, for our fire." He pointed out Florien and Almeric in case the pilgrims had forgotten which servants belonged to which pilgrims. "Human excrement is to be buried. Men will go behind that boulder, the big one with the hollow on the east side. The women will go to the next boulder on, the one with the overhang, and take care to stay well out of sight while their skirts are up. Remember to bury what you leave. And watch where you put your hands." He had noticed the massive stones as they approached, and was now pleased with how rapidly he had reached his decisions for the boulders; he had worried that he might not find so convenient a place for their short rest. "We will open one cask of water, but don't take it unless you are truly thirsty." He swung down off his mare. "Water for the horses and asses, not the camels. All will drink when we camp for the day." He trudged toward Frater Anteus, leading the mare by her reins. He was finding it difficult to move quickly in the deep sand, and he decided this was another thing he would have to make allowances for.

"Sieur Horembaud," the monk said, inclining his head gracefully. "This ass has a trot that could churn butter. He doesn't want to walk, but his trot is killing me. He'll make a eunuch of me if I have to endure much more of it."

"Our Lord rode an ass," said Sieur Horembaud, thinking as he did that he missed war: he knew how to handle himself in a war, but on this pilgrimage, with few useful weapons and an ill-assorted company around him, his confidence was badly shaken, a state he was committed to conceal from everyone.

Frater Anteus laughed; this seemed a little forced, but that could be as much because of fatigue as lack of amusement. "So He did. He must have had an Angel between Himself and the animal's spine. That pad we've been given isn't nearly enough."

"We haven't the time to break them all to saddles," Sieur Horembaud said, and deliberately changed the subject. "You still have made no progress with Sandjer'min."

Frater Anteus hung his head, abashed. "I've tried. He's . . . stand-offish. He's not a Christian, and makes no secret of it, but says little about whatever religion he follows. He has said that he has promised not to disrupt the company with tales of his travels or anything beyond what he is pledged to do for the company." He gave Sieur Horembaud a pointed glance. "I don't think he's going to open his heart to a monk like me." Seizing on the one positive sign, he added, "It appears to me that Sandjer'min is more likely to befriend you than me. I observed you talking shortly after we set out. You should be able to learn more about him while you ride." He could not keep from adding, "On horses."

"What we spoke of was nothing important." Sieur Horembaud cleared his throat and spat. "But you may be right; I'll see what he'll tell me in the next few days."

"May God lend you His aid," said Frater Anteus, and moved off toward the jutting boulder.

Richere Enzo came up to Sieur Horembaud, walking stiffly, his face looking remarkably pasty in the moonlight. "I need to have a word with my man Ifar."

"Then do so. He's with the servants and slaves." Sieur Horembaud told himself that God had given him a suspicious mind, and that it was not unusual for a warrior like himself to have little cause to admire men like Enzo, who earned their bread by procuring relics for the great churches in Europe.

"What he and I should discuss is private," Enzo said.

"Then wait until the women are done with their relieving themselves, and go to that second boulder. No one will disturb you." Sieur Horembaud wanted to urge Enzo to move on with a wave of his hand, but was certain that Enzo would be offended, and so cocked his head toward the nearer boulder. "I have my own needs to attend to."

Enzo blinked. "Why, yes. I won't detain you. I'll just go find Ifar and tell him what you have approved." With that said, he went off to where the asses were circled together, and quickly found Ifar with three lead-ropes in his hands. "When the women return, we may go speak privately in the curve of the farther boulder." He spoke in the Milanese dialect, his demeanor revealing nothing.

Ifar spoke the same, but more roughly. "I've been trying to learn more about the Apostle's Hand, but only Firouz knows anything about it, and my Arabic isn't very good, as you know. I haven't been able to find out anything useful."

A short distance away from Enzo and Ifar, Ruthier seemed not to be listening, although he was. He patted the flank of the nearest ass, and peered up at the moon.

"Do we know which church is said to have it?"

"Not yet," said Ifar, revealing his impatience with the situation. "Shouldn't we wait to talk about—"

"Probably not. And I have no wish to intrude on the women," said Enzo.

"We'll know more as we get nearer our goal," said Ifar as if speaking to a restless child. "Hold yourself in patience."

"But we know the Apostle's Hand is in Ethiopia? Ifar, you told me that's where we can find it, didn't you?"

"I know it is *rumored* to be there. But who's to say the rumors are reliable?" Ifar scratched at his scrawny beard. "I think it is possible the Hand is there, perhaps it is even likely, but it would help if we could find out where it is. Ethiopia is a large place. It would take years to visit all the churches there."

"To have come so far and not to have any useful information about it: this grows worse and worse. Do you think we should turn back, or continue? It's so hard to know what to do," Enzo complained.

"You could pray," Ifar suggested, and laughed quietly, then changed his tone, to one sounding much more certain than Enzo did. "Don't speak too much about it, for I'll wager that Nicholas Howe and Frater Giulianus are after the same relic."

"True enough. And it is possible that Howe can understand the Milanese dialect," said Enzo, glancing over his shoulder. "Well, when we reach the Gold Camp, we may find out something useful."

"And then we could turn back; once we have what we want, we can—" What they could do went unsaid; Ifar ducked his head respectfully, and he spoke, this time in Greek. "It would be a wonderful accomplishment to come upon three or four relics that can be carried with respect. I believe the ass would be better than the camel."

Enzo took his cue from Ifar. "God made the camel to express humility. Surely that makes it a better choice."

Behind them, Methodus Temi waded ankle-deep in sand toward the nearer boulder, making no effort to hide his curiosity about the conversations around him as he went; watching the smith eavesdrop brought Ruthier perilously close to laughter.

"It could, but relics must be packed in straw and cloth to prevent damage while on a camel's pack-saddle," Ifar said in a self-deprecating manner.

"I would do that in any case, out of reverence." Enzo glanced at Temi's retreating figure. "I think he's out of range."

"That doesn't mean he won't try again," said Ifar.

"Howe is the worst of them," said Enzo, once again in the common tongue of Milano. "He keeps trying to find out what I know, and he would call me a liar if I told him I don't know enough to lie."

"Don't be petulant. The rest will notice." Ifar shrugged.

"Oh, God, why did I let you talk me into this? We did well enough in Alexandria." Before Ifar could speak again, Enzo shook his head. "I know. If we could get the Apostle's Hand, we could make our fortune, and our reputations." He looked up as he saw Sieur Horembaud approaching. "Something is wrong, Sieur?"

"No; I'm about to open the first water-cask. Bring your cups and pails so we can get the horses and asses watered and be on our way." He went to the pack-camel carrying the water-casks and unfastened the net holding the highest of the casks. With a grunt, he tugged the cask free of its netting, moving it to his shoulder so that he could choose a place to stand where he could pour out the portions for men and equines. "You." He was addressing Zekri, who was standing a little apart with his ass's reins in his hand, and the lead-rope from a pack-ass.

The young monk jumped visibly. "Me, Sieur?"

"Water," he announced, repeating the word in Greek and a poor version of Coptic.

Zekri ducked his head, and reached into his saddle-pack for his pail and cup, pulling them out and going to Sieur Horembaud. As he and his animals moved, several of the pilgrims came up behind him, clustering the asses tightly around the servants and slaves who used them. One of the asses squealed and kicked out at another that was pressing against Vitalis' two asses. Carlus and Baccomeo moved quickly to separate the irritated animals, which put an end to the excitement. But now the men were jostling one another, and an occasional sharp word put the other pilgrims on notice that pilgrimage or not, there was rancor to be dealt with.

"It will go more quickly if you make a line," said Sandjer'min quietly to Sieur Horembaud. "And the women won't have to take the last drops from the cask." He held the reins of his gelding and Sieur Horembaud's mare, ready to lead them to drink.

Sieur Horembaud nodded. "Make a line," he said in a voice that would rally troops in a battle. "We must resume our travels."

Gradually the line was formed, and the appropriate ration of water was provided. The horses and asses drank last, each horse and ass being ridden getting three ladles in shallow pails; the remounts received two ladlesworth. It took a little longer than Sieur Horembaud had planned to get their company back into order to travel; when he mounted his feisty mare at last, he was feeling more harried than he had anticipated, and it made him cross.

"Are we ready?" Sieur Horembaud called back to Firouz, and Sandjer'min repeated the question in Arabic and Coptic.

"Not quite," Firouz said in Arabic.

"My sister-in-law is adjusting the covering on Torquil's sling," Heneri added, his Anglo-French needing no translation for Sieur Horembaud.

"Tell her to get on with it," Sieur Horembaud grumbled.

"Would you like me to assist her?" Sandjer'min volunteered.

"Yes," said Sieur Horembaud, jobbing the reins impatiently. "We're taking too long."

"A word of advice," Sandjer'min said quietly to Sieur Horembaud as he turned his gelding around to face the company. "Don't take your ill-temper out on your horse." Without waiting to hear whatever Sieur Horembaud might say, Sandjer'min tapped Melech with his heels and the dove-colored horse moved out at a brisk walk, going back along the line until they reached the pack-camels carrying not only chests and sacks, but a sling between them. Sandjer'min dismounted and signaled to Margrethe, who had not yet mounted her ass; she was bending over Torquil, her face worried. She straightened up and removed her veil to speak with Sandjer'min.

"He's doing poorly," she said bluntly.

"I can see that." He touched Torquil's neck. "His pulse is fast and he's hotter than he should be."

"I gave him the willow-bark tincture, but I don't think it's done much good." She offered a confused semi-smile to him; it was disturbing to have Sandjer'min so near. "He was moaning for a time, but I gave him more syrup of poppies when we stopped, and he's resting now."

Sandjer'min examined the blisters on Torquil's head and neck carefully, his eyes unimpeded by the dark. "When we make camp at dawn, I'll do what I can for him. What he needs now is to have his pain taken away, and the syrup of poppies should do that."

She laid her hand on his arm as he carefully replaced the coverlet over Torquil. "What if he becomes worse before then? What should I do?"

"Stop the company and let me see how he's doing." He saw dissatisfaction in her face. "What is it?"

"I'd have to scream to stop the company, and that would cause Torquil distress."

"Better distress than putrefaction," said Sandjer'min bluntly. "Get on your ass; we have a long way to go."

"I think he should have been sent back to Alexandria, excommunicant or not," she said, and before he could speak, she shook her head. "I know: the Templars will not take him back until the pilgrimage is complete, no matter how badly hurt he is."

"True enough," said Sandjer'min, and added, "I'll arrange to care for him while you sleep during the day."

"That's . . . very kind of you." Before she said something more, she motioned to him to leave. "You're right, we have a long way to go."

"We do," he said, walking away toward Melech. As he mounted he scanned the sands behind him, and wondered if he should inform Sieur Horembaud that they were being followed.

Text of a letter from Tsura'gar at the Monastery of the Visitation at Sese'metkra to the Venerable Minseh at Edfu, written on papyrus in fixed ink and carried by the monk Dinat; delivered nine days after it was written.

> *To the Venerable Minseh, august leader of our Christian community, and leader of eleven more such communities, the respectful greetings of Tsura'gar, monk and monitor of the treasury and charity for the Monastery of the Visitation at Sese'metkra, and the prayers for your long life and valiant faith on this, the 4ᵗʰ day of May in the 1225ᵗʰ year of Salvation.*
>
> *Most esteemed Minseh,*
>
> *It is with great reluctance that I write to you, but I believe no other course is now open to me, and I cannot, in good conscience, keep my concerns to myself, for that would only tend to let the rot spread. Thus it is with many misgivings and trepidations that I write to you on behalf of the monks of our community, seeking to preserve them from evil.*

As you know, two years ago, Aba'yam took into our monastery a foreigner and his servant, though the man said he was not a Christian, nor was he a follower of Islam, nor was he a Jew; he divulged nothing of his religion, though I made many attempts to learn what gods he worshiped. He declared that he did not serve the Devil, and Aba'yam took him at his word, giving him a place to make his medicinal salves and unguents, and allowing him access to the scriptorium, where his knowledge of many languages proved useful. He cared for the monks when they were ill and he set bones and dressed wounds, gaining the good opinion of the monks.

We know that the Devil has a pleasing face and that he presents himself as virtuous when his heart is black with sin. His followers are the same, and this Sidi Sandjer'min, as I came to realize, was one of them. I followed on three occasions when he left the monastery late at night, and under cover of darkness visited a woman in Sese'metkra, whom he abused most lasciviously; I myself heard her shrieks and moans, and when he left, he had blood on his mouth, as I saw by the light of her lamp. She was in a swoon and her face was not good to look upon, for she was in the throes of the lust he had wrought upon her.

Our Aba'yam has said that he does not believe any of this happened, and that Sandjer'min is a man of good character, an assertion that fills me with alarm, for it shows that he, too, has been deceived by this foreigner's manners and supposed acts of charity. How can we maintain our vows as monks if we continue to be led by a man who is in the thrall of one of the Devil's minions? I ask that you exert your authority and remove Aba'yam from his post and consign him to one of the hermits' cells back in the hills, where he may pray for forgiveness for his great error in bringing this terrible foreigner among us.

I volunteer myself to serve as Aba'yam until you select who shall succeed our present Aba'yam, and to work to eradicate all trace of Sandjer'min's influence and presence in this place, so that we might once again seek to live holy lives, unbesmirched by the ungodly nature of Sidi Sandjer'min.

If I have overstepped my position, I crave your forgiveness and in all humility tell you that it is my zeal that has caused me to speak of my dismay. If you decide to keep the present Aba'yam in his post, I ask that you release me from my monkish vows so that I may be free of the dire taint of diabolism that has come upon this place, and may seek other means to live in the embrace of sanctity.

Amen,
Tsura'gar
monk

2

Morning sunlight set the east wall of Sandjer'min's square pavilion-tent aglow, and the heat increased as the sun moved higher in the eastern sky; Sandjer'min sat on the woven-reed mat that served as a floor, dribbling water onto Torquil's swollen lips; the man was not improving, and Sandjer'min realized it was only a matter of time before the sun-scorched knight shed the life that had become such a torment to him. In the four days since Sieur Horembaud's party of pilgrims had started across the desert, Torquil had sunk into an ever deeper torpor.

"How much longer? He's beginning to stink," Ruthier said in Farsi, more bluntly than was his habit. It was the first time they had had to speak privately since the camp was set up, and would be the last until the brief evening meal; he stood by the closed tent-flap, ready to go out to take up his post with the animals.

"Do you mean how much longer do I think he will live?" Sandjer'min asked in the same language, and saw Ruthier nod. "Not long. Five, six days at most. He is losing flesh and is refusing almost all food, which weakens him still more. And he has stopped fighting his burns. There is putrefaction in his skin, and it has spread too much for my sovereign remedy to stop it. It won't be long."

"And we are what? five days from the Gold Camp?" This obvious display of anxiety was rare for Ruthier, and for that reason, Sandjer'min paid him close attention. "What will happen if he dies on the way?"

"Roughly five days, if the wind doesn't pick up, in which case it will take longer to get there, so he may not get that far." He lifted the bandage across Torquil's eyes and dampened it in the little bit of remaining water in the bowl, then put it back in place. "It will depend upon the weather; the winds are increasing, and that will slow our travel. We've come twenty leagues and have about thirty-two or thirty-three to go to the Gold Camp."

"What will Sieur Horembaud do when Torquil is dead?" He asked this quietly, in case Torquil should be able to hear them.

"With the body?" Sandjer'min thought about it briefly, understanding what Ruthier intended; would they have to transport his corpse, and if so, how far? "I don't know. He won't be able to take the time to boil the flesh off and send the bones back to English France, much as the family might approve, but Sieur Horembaud won't want to leave him in a desert grave, either."

"He won't have much time to make up his mind once Torquil is dead," Ruthier said. "In this heat . . ."

"Yes. In this heat." Sandjer'min sighed fatalistically. "Poor man."

"If there is a church in the Gold Camp, do you think they would bury him?"

"He has been excommunicated," Sandjer'min reminded Ruthier. "If the clerics at the church—which may or may not be there—knew about it, they would not be willing to take him, I suspect."

"Then why tell them? Why not say he is a Templar taken ill, who died while the pilgrims were traveling? It is true, up to a point. Wouldn't that guarantee his burial? Assuming there is a church?" Ruthier waited a long moment, but Sandjer'min remained silent. "You think Sieur Horembaud will tell of Torquil's disgrace, don't you?"

"The pilgrims may insist. It's in accord with their vows to do so: not to reveal Torquil's excommunication would be to bear false witness by omission, which is against—" Sandjer'min finished with a palms-up sign of futility. "They must lead virtuous lives as pilgrims or forsake the benefits of the pilgrimage."

"So they say. But what does it matter? Once the man is dead, the question of damnation or salvation is settled, isn't it? Why disdain the body?" Ruthier asked, his aggravation unabated. "Don't attempt to explain it. I wouldn't understand it now any better than I did seven hundred years ago."

Sandjer'min stopped moistening Torquil's lips and set the empty bowl aside. "Then we can both be puzzled, old friend."

Ruthier took a deep breath and let it out slowly. "I should go out to stand guard on the animals. We may have to put up the sail for shelter." He reached out and lifted the door-flap, asking as if it were a matter of minor curiosity, "Will you want to take some nourishment from one of the horses or asses this evening, before we move off? You look tired, and there is no one among the pilgrims you may safely visit in sleep."

"No, there is not." He ventured nothing more.

"So it must be horses or asses that provide blood for you," Ruthier said patiently, aware that Sandjer'min was once again feeling the weight of isolation. "I'll take you to the ass while the pilgrims have their meal."

"So you can ensure my privacy?" Sandjer'min asked with a suggestion of ironic amusement. "Or keep it from braying?"

"You'll probably require caution while you feed, and I can make it appear that you are tending to the animals rather than taking sustenance, which should not be difficult; most will have their minds on *their* supper, not yours," said Ruthier, unfazed by Sandjer'min's sardonic remarks. "Sieur Horembaud will want a full report on Torquil before we set out tonight, and you will not have long to take the little blood you need. And you do need it, my master."

"No doubt you are correct. I will join you at the pen as soon as I have taken down the tent and packed it. If I can obtain a little blood without risk, I will. Otherwise, I will wait." Sandjer'min made a gesture of acquiescence. "Thank you. I do appreciate your aid. To start with, you may choose the ass from which I will take blood. A dark-coated one is preferable, so the blood will be less noticeable on the coat."

"I'll select a strong one for you, and be sure it is among those that are remounts for tonight," said Ruthier, relieved that Sandjer'min had decided to feed. Then something occurred to him. "And I will let it be known that you will be treating the ass with the bothersome ear, so there will be no questions about your presence in the pen."

"Who is keeping watch with you?" Sandjer'min asked. "The duty has changed every day."

"Except for me," said Ruthier. "Yes, it has."

"Then who is guarding the animals this morning?" He paused, then added, "How will you distract them?"

"Olu'we and Baccomeo have that duty," Ruthier answered, glanced through the lifted flap to the refulgent sunlight. "We are allowed whips to keep the animals in check. I may think of some way to use mine."

"To keep the animals from straying; yes, I know. You may also use them to gather small game in one place—not that there is much small game to hunt in this stretch of the desert." Sandjer'min looked out at the shattering brilliance, then averted his eyes, for even with his native earth in the soles of his solers and in the nearby chest that served him for a bed, the force of the sun was painful for him. "Be alert."

"Is this company still being followed?" Much as it troubled him to think they might be, he wanted to know rather than guess.

"We are. Two men, one of them is Islamic, for he stops to pray five times a day. I saw him from the low ridge we crossed at day's end yesterday, as we were beginning our travel. His companion does not pray, but waits for the other man. They are about a league behind us, and keeping pace with us."

"Wouldn't that be the case whether they were following us or not?"

"If they hadn't made a point of staying at the limit of sight, I would agree, but as it is, I must assume they are watching us, since they are at such pains to keep their distance." Speaking of the two men gave him a sense of malaise. "They would be easily seen if they came closer, but at a league, they are largely beyond our sight; they can follow the prints of our animals, unless the wind is high enough to carry them away quickly."

"And you saw them this morning?"

"As we made camp. They were on the crest of the northerly dune, but dropped down onto the far side as soon as we began to raise our tents. The one man was doing his dawn prayers just before they moved out of sight." He got up from the mat and went to the large jar of water so that he could refill the bowl.

"Might they be travelers bound for the Gold Camp who do not want to travel with unknown persons? They may have some private purpose for keeping their distance." He had thought of all these possibilities, and hoped that one of them would persuade Sandjer'min that he was being overly circumspect.

Sandjer'min answered promptly, "No, I don't think so. If they were, they would be likely to make an effort to catch up with us so that they could have the safety of our numbers in their journey, but they have made every effort to stay behind us."

"If one of them follows Islam, perhaps he isn't eager to travel with Christian pilgrims?" Ruthier suggested.

"Perhaps." He paused thoughtfully. "They have a horse and two camels."

Ruthier nodded. "Yes, they might seek to join us, if they didn't wish to avoid Christians. That isn't very wise: we joined this company, and neither of us is Christian," he said, and stepped out of the tent, shielding his eyes with his hand. Wading through the sand that rose to his ankles, he passed through the cluster of tents to the improvised enclosure where the asses, camels, and horses were penned. He stopped at the sacks of fodder and picked up one of the whips lying beside the sacks, then looked for the two guards. As he approached the nearer one, Olu'we raised his hand in greeting; he did not raise his voice for fear of disturbing the sleep of the company of pilgrims. When he was near enough to be heard speaking quietly, Ruthier said in Coptic, "How are they, Olu'we?"

"They're brushed and they've been fed. We'll have to water them in a while, but so far, all is well." Olu'we lowered his voice. "A pity we haven't any shade."

"For all of us," Ruthier agreed. "We can put up the sail if the wind gets worse—give them some protection."

Olu'we held up his open hands in prayer. "May we be spared wind."

"Any sign of trouble?" Ruthier asked.

"Baccomeo killed a scorpion a little while ago, but nothing more than that. I think I heard a jackal just after sunrise, but I'm not certain."

"Who takes the afternoon watch?" In their days of travel, they had yet to find the most useful combination of guards.

"Almeric and Ifar," said Olu'we with a frown.

"A pair not to your liking?" Ruthier ventured.

"Almeric does well enough, but Ifar claims disinterest; he doesn't know much about camels and asses. Nor very much about horses. He won't wield a brush or a rake, and he is afraid to lift a hoof." Olu'we shrugged. "Vitalis doesn't know that much, either, but he does his best, and he doesn't complain."

"Then perhaps tomorrow, you should be on duty when Vitalis is and Ifar can do his watch with someone else, for the benefit of all." Ruthier stretched and stared out at the vast expanse of sand; in the distance, three columns of swirling sand undulated on the wind, like ghosts of long-vanished dancers, or djinns. He turned back to Olu'we. "I'll walk the edge of the pen, and then you may walk the tents."

Olu'we placed his hands over his heart and bowed enough to show respect. "As you command."

Ruthier made his way around the posts and ropes that marked the pen, taking time to examine the conditions of the posts and ropes for signs of wear or deep abrasions, as well as the behavior of the animals inside. One of the asses—the dark one he had mentioned to Sandjer'min—kept flicking one ear, and shaking his head; even if he did not need attention for his ear, Sandjer'min would have a look at him before they moved on in the evening. Pausing to take stock of their current location, Ruthier could not keep from looking back the way they had come the previous night, wondering if he might see the two men, two camels, and the horse that Sandjer'min had been able to make out; after a short while, he conceded to himself that vampires could see better than ghouls, especially in the dark. The air was dry and carried a faint odor of dust and dung; the sand was humming as it skimmed along on the low wind.

Watching Ruthier approaching, Baccomeo rose from where he had been seated next to a heavy post, saying, "Nothing has happened. There is no sign of other travelers. I will walk patrol again shortly."

"No need; I'll attend to it. You can use the time to clean tack." The suggestion was given sedately enough, but Baccomeo knew it was a necessary chore and one he was expected to do.

"Certainly." He looked toward the stack of goods lying under a taut tarpaulin.

Satisfied that he had done what he could, Ruthier nodded toward the make-shift pen. "The animals are resting and there is just enough wind to keep flies away."

"Most of them are dozing, as you see," said Baccomeo, doing his best to impress upon Ruthier his alert observation.

"That's probably a good thing, under the circumstances," said Ruthier, and resumed his walk along the fence.

The day was uneventful; the animals were watered before Olu'we and Baccomeo were relieved by Almeric and Ifar, who spent the afternoon idling at the edge of the pen while Ruthier patrolled the tents. Aside from hearing Sorer Imogen praying, there was no indication that all the occupants were not asleep. By the time afternoon faded to dusk, the animals had been fed and watered and the pilgrims were breaking camp, their tents taken down, packed, and loaded while Florien and Salvatore took their turn at making a quick meal to sustain the pilgrims through the night. It required only a little while for the fire to flare and the cauldron to be brought, along with a flat metal griddle.

Ruthier went back into the group of tents, now coming down and folded into great canvass sacks, he called out to Sandjer'min for the benefit of the pilgrims, "One of the asses is having trouble with his ear. You'll need to have a look at it."

"What kind of trouble?" He stopped his work to stand up.

"He flicks his ear and tosses his head."

"Ah. I will need to get into the red-lacquer chest. I have something that should ease the ass' discomfort." He stopped gathering his goods together and went to free the chest from its netting. Removing a jar of ointment, he said, "Which ass is suffering?"

"One of the dark ones. He is going onto the remount line tonight." He noticed that three of the pilgrims had stopped listening to their exchange, and was pleased.

"A good precaution. An insect has probably laid eggs in his ear," said Sandjer'min while he returned the red-lacquer chest to its netting and set it with the rest of his belongings to be loaded onto camels and asses.

"Are you ready, my master?" Ruthier asked as he watched Sandjer'min finish with his chests; he could see that some of the pilgrims were listening. "He's one of the larger asses, about twelve hands."

"I'll look for him." He followed Ruthier to the large pen, noticing that Salvatore was already putting pack-saddles and halters on the asses and saddling the horses; Sandjer'min stopped and glanced at Ruthier. "Now may not be a good time, after all. I'll try again at midnight when we stop. We can hope the wind drops before then. Show me the ass with the ear-trouble, and I'll remember him."

Ruthier frowned. "I can volunteer to help Salvatore, and you can have a little time to—"

"I think not, unless there is no one to observe what I do," said Sandjer'min. "Best to treat the ear for now."

"Very well, but if you can . . ." said Ruthier, and made his way through the animals to the dark-haired ass who was still shaking his head. "Shall I get you a rush-lamp?"

Although Sandjer'min did not need the lamp to see, he said, "It would be wise." He did a quick perusal of his surroundings, and allowed himself a little hope; so far no one he was aware of was watching him.

From the sacks and chests piled next to the tarpaulin-covered tack, among the containers of their animals' feed, Micheu de Saunte-Foi paused in his loading of the pack-camels' saddles and settled into the deepening shadows to watch what Sandjer'min was doing, his gaze speculative. He frowned as the sunset faded into night.

Ruthier trudged off toward Salvatore, who had half a dozen rush-lamps hanging from a rope strung between the two tallest poles. "My master is treating the dark mule with ear problems with one of his medicaments, and needs a lamp. Can you spare one?" He spoke in the Venezian dialect. "The night closes in quickly in these climes."

"That it does." Salvatore was adjusting the girth on Sieur Horembaud's frisky mare; he stepped back, and said, "Take one. The poor ass needs something to ease his discomfort." He watched as the girth seemed to loosen when the mare let out her breath. With a sudden, triumphant grin, he reached forward and tightened the girth. "There!"

"My master will saddle Melech when he's through with the ass," said Ruthier as he claimed the rush-light and went back through the misassorted herd.

"It is as I thought," Sandjer'min said. "I've cleaned out the eggs and I've put the ointment in; it has something to dull the pain, and that will relieve him. I've also taken about a cup of blood from him, enough to hold me for a day or two. Thank you for distracting Salvatore." He held out the jar. "You should probably keep this; the site of the infestation will need to be treated twice a day for the next three days."

Ruthier took the jar and slipped it into the large leather wallet on his belt. "Is there anything else?"

"Not just now. I want to see how Torquil is doing, and then I'll saddle Melech and prepare to begin our night's journey." He nodded to Ruthier and left the crowd of animals, going toward the place where the pilgrims were beginning to line up in their order of travel to make the final packing of animals easier and more rapid; an odor of cooking came from the campfire, where Sorer Imogen led the pilgrims in prayer. He saw that his chests and sacks were already on one of the pack-camels holding Torquil's sling, and that Bondame Margrethe stood next to it, attempting to get Torquil to take a little food. "How is he doing?"

She looked up at Sandjer'min, her face showing her distress, and something more disturbing; she breathed a little faster and struggled to answer his question. "He's hardly taken anything. I managed to get some water into him, and a little of the syrup of poppies, but he won't eat any of the flatbread, or the mashed figs you prepared this afternoon."

"Then don't force him. Water is more important than food just now. Did you try the salt-fish? He may need that because of the heat during the day. It depletes the body of salt."

"I haven't, but I will," she said, little hope in her tone; she took a sliver of fish from the small tray she held, and laid it across Torquil's lips; nothing happened.

"Leave it there for now, and give him a little more water; he may yet swallow."

"I'll do it," she said, doing her best to pour a few drops of water over the fish, but though Torquil swallowed the water, he would not open his lips for the fish.

"Wait a bit and try again," he recommended, and suddenly he felt the force of her despair; she had resigned herself to Torquil's death, and was waiting for him to give up his body's fight. "He is exhausted, and not eating is making him worse."

The shelter-flap rose, snapping, and then luffed like an ill-tautened sail, and the sling fluttered; both Sandjer'min and Margrethe stared at it, exchanging uneasy glances until the wind dropped as suddenly as it had risen, and the flap settled back in place.

"If you think it will make a difference for him to have so little," she said as if in a dream. "He does not want it, and I cannot make him want it." Again she turned her pale eyes on his. "I feel the life drain from him, and I can do nothing." It was a plea for approval, for support.

"You're doing all that can be done, Bondame," he said to her with all the gentleness he could summon. "There isn't much hope, but you can be assured that you have not failed in your care for him."

"Then you think he'll die, too," she said with guilty relief.

"I'm afraid so, as everything must. But that is not cause to ne-
glect him." He touched her shoulder, lightly, for reassurance.

"I'll try to watch him more closely tonight," she promised.
"You're right: he shouldn't be neglected."

"Are all your things ready?" Sandjer'min asked, not wanting to
say more about Torquil's worsening condition.

"Yes, I think so. Sorer Imogen hasn't finished her prayers yet,
and I don't think she has closed and strapped her chest, but Heneri
and I are ready to leave as soon as the order is given." She folded her
hands and said quietly, "Taking care of Torquil, knowing it is futile
without a miracle, I have come to wish I could believe our travels
will deliver my husband from his affliction, but the farther we go, the
less I have hope that it will." As soon as she had spoken, she wished
she had not: revealing such thoughts to a foreigner was against her
pilgrimage vows.

"Will you turn back?" Sandjer'min asked.

The kindness in his voice compelled her to answer him. "No.
Sorer Imogen would never agree, and when we returned to Creisse,
she would most certainly denounce me for failing in our mission; she
thinks me lax enough already for not praying whenever I can. She is
expected to report on Heneri as well, but she has said she will not
speak against him for the good of the family; she has no such com-
punction with me, for I have not produced a child for Creisse, and
have only my vows to Dagoberht to bind me to his House. She has
warned me that she will appeal to the Bishop to have me sent home
to England if I fail in this pilgrimage, and the Bishop will probably
do so." She turned to meet Sandjer'min's dark eyes, her anxiety returning. "Say nothing to Frater Anteus, will you."

"If that is your wish," he assured her.

"I don't plan to Confess my doubts." This was a bit more defiant,
and her gaze slid away from his.

"I would say nothing in any case, since I am not of your religion."
He said this dismissively, as if it were of little importance, yet he was
aware of Margrethe's precarious circumstances.

"But you were in a Coptic monastery when we came upon you,"

she said, implying a question she had wanted to ask since she had first met him.

"I was there to study and to share information with the monks in the scriptorium; Aba'yam encouraged me," he said with an attempt at tranquility. "I'll tell you more when we camp again; for now, I have duties to attend to."

"Yes." She blushed, and wondered why she had so forgotten her duty as to speak so candidly with him. "I'll do my best to get Torquil to take some food."

"I have no doubt of it, and I thank you for your diligence," he said, and walked away from the sling and the increasing activity to the gathered animals, where he found Melech, gave him a cursory brushing, then saddled and bridled him before leading him out to the right-hand head of the pilgrims' train.

A short while later, Sieur Horembaud rode up, his expression harried. "Vidame Bonnefiles is unhappy in his position, and asks to trade with you. He says it is demeaning to be led by a foreigner who isn't Christian."

"Is that what you want?" Sandjer'min inquired calmly.

"No, it isn't. But Vidame Bonnefiles has been complaining about our present arrangement, and some of the company are taking his part. He says that you might be taking us on the wrong road." He shook his head ferociously. "He's a fool, and of an envious character. No wonder he was sent on this pilgrimage."

"Would you like me to change places with him for tonight?" he offered, thinking being at the rear of the train would provide him an opportunity to watch for the two men following them. "You have Firouz to guide you, who knows the way better than I. I'll trade places with the Vidame."

Sieur Horembaud's breath hissed through his clenched teeth. "I would not like it at all—Vidame Bonnefiles would see it as capitulation, and who knows what he might demand next?—but it would probably be wise, for it would silence the rest in the company's complaints." He glared at the head of the line of animals. "If this were a company of soldiers and not pilgrims, problems like this would not arise. But since they are pilgrims . . ." He made an exasperated gesture as words failed him.

"Since they are, I will trade places with Vidame Bonnefiles," said Sandjer'min. "For tonight."

"Good. Frater Anteus warned me that Vidame Bonnefiles was displeased, and was stirring up trouble. I want to stop it while it can be done with little rancor." He brought his mare up to Sandjer'min. "What do you think of this concession?"

"It is more a question of what you think; you are the leader of this group and they have placed themselves in your hands," said Sandjer'min at his most neutral.

"If I can make Bonnefiles agree that this is not a permanent change . . ."

As Sieur Horembaud's voice trailed off, Sandjer'min added, "And when another pilgrim—Micheu de Saunte-Foi, or Nicholas Howe, perhaps—demands the same right, what then?"

"Then I will explain why it will slow us down," said Sieur Horembaud, enjoying his own cleverness. "Everyone wants to make good time, with good reason. I can ensure it that we don't travel as far tonight as we have previously, and in such a way that the cause for it belongs to Vidame Bonnefiles." He crossed himself suddenly, and said, "Saunt Michael between me and the Devil."

Sandjer'min studied Sieur Horembaud's face. "Amen: but why do you ask this?"

"Of Saunt Michael? Because I seek to do ill to a fellow-pilgrim, and knowing that, I am ashamed. To make it appear that any delay is Vidame Bonnefiles' fault is to bear false witness through omission, and a sin I will have to Confess. If this were the army, no one would be troubled by—" He rubbed his beard. "I cannot always abide by what I have vowed to do, and that will count against me when we Confess at the conclusion of the pilgrimage, when we are once again in Alexandria."

Sandjer'min took a little time to think about the implications of such a Confession, and finally said, "Do you think Vidame Bonnefiles will admit to vanity and envy when he offers his Confession upon your return?"

"I don't know." His expression was glum.

"Then do as you think would benefit the greatest number of your company, and apologize to those you must disappoint," Sandjer'min suggested.

"I have already given Vidame Bonnefiles my Word, so tonight he will occupy your place and you his." He straightened in the saddle. "Tomorrow night, you shall be back in your position." He tapped his mare with his heel and was about to turn away, but stopped. "How is Torquil?"

"Much the same."

"That's unfortunate," said Sieur Horembaud, looking as if he would like to say something else. "I will want a report when we make our midnight stop," and before Sandjer'min could respond, he was off to the head of the caravan-line.

Text of a letter from Chretien Ormerusge, Hospitaller clerk, in Alexandria, to Frater Wilges, Hieronymite monk at Saunt-Huon monastery in Genova, written in Church Latin on vellum and delivered two months after it was written.

To the most devoted Frater Wilges, keeper of pilgrimages for Saunt-Huon's, this report from Chretien Ormerusge, Hospitaller clerk in Alexandria, on this, the 10th day of May in the Lord's Year 1225.

Most pious Frater Wilges,

Allow me to present to you this record of pilgrimages originating in and returning to Alexandria in the last six months, as is our custom:

Since the Nativity, two bands of pilgrims have set out, both seeking the Chapel of the Holy Grail. The first had twenty-nine pilgrims led by Templar Drapier Teodosio da Rovigo, all men of military backgrounds, all pledged to bring the Holy Grail to the Pope for the Glory of the Church and Christendom; two reports from well up the Nile have marked their progress; as of the end of March, they had reached Edfu and had secured passage across the desert in the company of a large band of traders. The second was a smaller and more mixed group, led by Sieur Horembaud du Langnor, whose company includes merchants, various penitents, and three women. The last report on his progress indicates that four more have joined the pilgrims at Sese'metkra, a village far to the south where the Coptic Christians have a monastery, two of whom are monks from that monastery. The report does not indicate if they plan to cross the Nubian Desert or keep to the river all the way to the Land of the Grail; the river is longer but not so hot as the desert becomes under the summer sun.

Of those pilgrimages returning, seven have thus far reached us in Alexandria: the first, which set out in the middle of August, a company of thirty-six, mostly clerics, of whom eighteen have returned, two of whom are now blind; they reached the foothills of the Ethiopian Highlands and were advised to turn back by priests at the Chapel of the Book, and did so. The second company set out at the start of September, twenty-six in number, planning to travel on the Nile the whole of the distance, and turned back at the Third Cataract when they lost three boats to hippopotami attack, which reduced their number by eleven; the survivors traveled on foot as far as Anibe, where two of their number succumbed to Nile Fever, and a third was taken by slavers. The third company, of forty-one, left two days after the second, and was set upon by bandits, and only nine of the company were able to return; we have received ransom demands for two of those who were captured. The fourth company, of twenty-nine, left at the middle of the month, composed of tertiary monks and four novices; aside from the report received in February which placed them at the Gold Camp in the Nubian Desert, only two have returned, both novices, and neither has yet been able to speak of what happened to the company; for now we remember them in our prayers. The fifth company, thirty-eight in number, merchants and military men, set out at the end of September, reached the Land of the Holy Grail in the mountains of Ethiopia, and have reported to us on the amazing churches they saw being built into the ground; four of their number succumbed to sun and heat, two were the victims of snakebite, and another four stayed behind to join in the building of the great Church of Michael the Archangel. The sixth company, of forty-five, composed of twenty-nine men, and sixteen women, all penitents from Roman Church lands, left Alexandria in the third week of September, and returned only three days ago, so there is no account yet on what befell ten of the men and twelve of the women who are not with them, although there is some reason to think they were set upon by slavers; the ones who have returned are presently in the care of our physicians, and will make their reports in the next ten days. The seventh company, a group of thirty men of diverse heritage and place, set out in early October, and returned two months ago, having agreed to abandon their pilgrimage at Esna, where nine of their company were taken by bandits to be sold or to be held for ransom; three from that company have declared their intention to join a larger company of pilgrims and make a second attempt at reaching the Land of the Holy Grail, and are prepared to wait until companies of pilgrims are again making ready to travel southward.

Submitted with such letters and reports as are entrusted to us for family, business, and religious associates, which you are mandated to deliver to their intended recipients.

Chretien Ormerusge
Hospitaller clerk

3

Margrethe was shaking and she seemed unaware of the tears on her face. Very slowly and carefully she laid Torquil's hand by his side and reached out to take the bandage from his eyes. She crossed herself and wished there were a priest among the company to say the prayers for the dead over him, thinking as she did that he had wasted from hunger as much as he had been consumed by putrescent fever. But, she reminded herself, Torquil was an excommunicant, and could not receive such rites, a realization that made the gentle susurrus of Sorer Imogen's prayers from the other side of their pavillion seem oddly futile, a call to something that could not hear her over the wind. It was mid-morning and the pilgrims' camp was quiet; aside from the three servants watching the animals, Ruthier, and Sandjer'min, the others were inside their tents, trying to sleep in the rising heat. Margrethe occupied herself trying to decide how to inform Sandjer'min of Torquil's death when he returned from his tending to one of the horses' swollen pastern joint. She was worried that she felt so little emotion, and decided in a remote way that it was because she was being spared the distress of this loss by her Good Angel. "Such a lonely place to die," she whispered, remembering the vista of trackless sand interrupted by escarpments and outcropping rocks that she had seen at dawn, and again prayed that Torquil would not have to lie in such utter desolation.

The company of pilgrims was still a day away from the Gold Camp, according to Firouz; their tents were set up in the lee of a shoulder of rocks carved into fantastical shapes by the wind, which crooned over them now, continuing its sculpting. Crossing herself a second time, Margrethe got to her feet and went to the thin mattress that was laid down for Sandjer'min's use on a chest of about the same size; it was half-way between dawn and noon, and she wanted to rest before the company began what obsequies they could for Torquil. Just touching the rough cloth of the mattress brought Sandjer'min vividly to mind, almost as if he himself were there to comfort her. To her surprise, she found herself rapidly drifting into sleep; she made herself sit up, remembering that there was no one but herself to honor Torquil by keeping vigil; she continued to tremble as she tried to pray, listening to the rising wind and the hum of the flying sand.

A short while later, the tent-flap was raised and Sandjer'min stepped inside, taking care to close the flap against the drifting sand moved along by the wind. The first thing that caught his attention was that there was only one person breathing inside the tent. A swift glance in Torquil's direction told him that the former Templar had succumbed at last to the putrescence of his burns; he swung about and saw Margrethe seated on his bed, her face dazed and her eyes filled with banked despair. Wanting to provide her solace, he went to her, taking her hands. "My poor Bondame," he said quietly.

She stared up at him, her silent tears returning. "He just . . . left. There was no struggle."

"How long ago?" Sandjer'min asked; he released her hands and went to Torquil's pallet, leaned down and touched his neck. "Not very long, I gather?"

"No, not very," she said as if she were speaking of something in the distant past. "You were expecting it, I know."

"Yes: his flesh is still warm, and no longer from fever, or the heat of the day. The limbs are not yet rigid, so he cannot have been dead for more than the time it takes to recite a dozen Psalms," he said, and sat next to her on the hard mattress; he felt her shivering, and he took her hands again and this time he did not release them. "You cared for him well, Margrethe; now you will grieve for him."

"Grieve? He is not kith or kin of mine. I have only known him since we left Alexandria and most of the time he was . . . hurt."

"All the more reason to mourn," Sandjer'min told her. "To aid him and not to know him can bring terrible sorrow." A shadow passed over his face as he said this; she glimpsed something in it that made her tremble.

"I wonder if I did aid him; he died, didn't he?" She gave a very little shake to her head. "I wanted to—to see him healed; I did, but he was so . . ."

"He was too much injured to live," said Sandjer'min, the kindness of his manner lessening the brusqueness of his words.

"And yet you tried to save him, as well," she said as if trying to solve a riddle. "And you are not overcome by his death; you show no signs of sorrow." This last was nearly an accusation; she modified its impact. "Or you do not seem to."

He took a moment to respond; when he spoke it was in a soft, steady voice that had no trace of fear in it. "I have seen death often in my travels, in many forms, and it no longer is a failure to me that we should die; everything, everyone dies. In time all of us will be gone." He deliberately blocked the wave of memories of wars and famines and plagues and disasters that welled within him—for now, he put his whole attention on Margrethe. "I feel his death in the way those of my blood do."

His last remark struck her as strange, but he was a foreigner, she reminded herself. "You treated him. Didn't you intend to make him whole again?" Her voice was steady, but the stuporous shine was still in her eyes.

"I doubt anyone could have done that; I did what I could to lessen his agony, and you made him as comfortable as he could be. Had he recovered, he would probably have not been truly restored to health, and there would have been scars and some blindness." He had taken such a stance before, not just in this century, he added to himself; in all his years at the Temple of Imhotep he had never seen anyone, no matter how carefully tended, survive such burns as Torquil's.

She nodded, barely moving her head. "When we first set out from Alexandria," she said, "he was so fair and gallant. He had a laugh that rang. But the sun burned him for many days, and he . . . wilted. At first he said the red would pass because he had been burned before, but as the days went on, he became worse and worse—"

"It was reckless to ignore such burns, especially in one with light-colored hair and such fair skin—the burns go more deeply into the flesh than for those with darker skins." He wanted to offer her consolation, and felt his way cautiously; he could see that she was appalled by the finality of Torquil's death and was searching for some way to accept it without adding to the guilt that possessed her.

"God could have worked a miracle, even for an excommunicated Templar." Her fingers tightened on his, and she started to weep once more, just as silently as before. "Sorer Imogen prayed for him and is still praying. Surely God heard her, and refused her supplication."

There were a number of responses he considered and rejected, and finally said simply, "According to your priests, God has His reasons," though he had long since ceased to believe in deities of any kind, even his own forgotten gods.

"If he hadn't been excommunicated, he might be called a martyr, to remain on pilgrimage in spite of his burns," she muttered, thinking aloud.

"Surely God will judge Torquil mercifully; that's what your religion teaches you, isn't it? that God is merciful?"

She went on as if she had not heard him. "Unless Torquil is bound to Hell, where the reasons are the Devil's, and the judgment is cruel. Only Our Lord is proof against the Devil." She pulled at the broad cuff of her blue habit's sleeve. "If only we had a priest to pray for him, a real priest, not a defrocked one," she said, shuddering more noticeably.

"Sorer Imogen might pray for him now he's dead, don't you think?" Sandjer'min ventured, seeking to ease Margrethe's heartache.

Margrethe shrugged. "She might, but . . ." She made herself sit straighter. "It's so *sad* that he came all this way, and suffered so much, and wasn't able to reach the Chapel of the Holy Grail so that he could return to the Templars and his Church. The Devil has taken him for his own, and there is nothing more to do." She leaned against his shoulder. "You want to console me, and it is good of you, but you don't understand our religion and the purpose of a pilgrimage. For Torquil, he was sworn to pray at the Chapel of the Holy Grail, but he's dead and his excommunication cannot be lifted now. He is not restored to Grace. He must face eternal fire for . . . for . . ." The enormity of Torquil's expiration and its implications overwhelmed her, leaving her feeling as if she were the one abandoned in the desert, lost and unsought. In desperation, and before she could stop herself, she turned to Sandjer'min and pressed her mouth to his, sinking into the kiss as if into salvation itself.

Her passion, as unexpected as it was intense, awakened his, and he loosened her hands so that he could more fully embrace her, drawing her more closely against him; her pulse was loud in his ears. He could sense her need and her desolation in every lineament of her presence; both sharpened his loneliness, and desire stirred his esurience. "Margrethe," he murmured as she pulled back from him.

Her cheeks were reddened and she could not bring herself to look at him; she whispered as if she feared immediate discovery and castigation. "I didn't mean to . . . Not with Torquil . . . You must be disgusted . . ."

He took her face in his hands and turned her toward him, his voice low yet deeply melodic. "You do not disgust me, Bondame, you honor me." When he saw how startled she was to hear this, he kissed her, very lightly, on the lips. "I mean you no harm."

"Then you should chide me," she said somberly. "I deserve your rebuke for what I've done, and in the presence of the dead."

"Why? You want to do homage to life; I understand that." He held her eyes with his own.

"But this is not the way. I would have to Confess for a week, and beg my bread for a month if we were to do anything so grotesque as . . ."

"Nothing you could ask from me, or that I can offer you, would deserve such harsh condemnation," he said even as he released her. "I mean you no disrespect, I mean Torquil no dishonor."

"I must maintain my virtue. I cannot want you," she said in an undervoice, as if reciting an unwelcome lesson. "I should not have . . . Pilgrims must not tempt others to sin, and I have almost done so. I must beg you to forgive me."

"You are too severe with yourself, Margrethe."

"I want to forsake my marriage vows, and I want you to . . . to . . ." she said in a soft rush of words, her face darkening again.

"Nothing you can have from me will compromise your marriage vows: believe this," he said, aware that though she was fortunate enough to have a fondness for her invalid husband, theirs had been a political marriage, intended to seal alliances rather than confirm their mutual love.

She shook her head. "Not those vows alone; my vows as a pilgrim."

"How have you broken them?"

"I have yearned for . . . You have wrought such tempests in my soul, that I cannot think of my holy purpose without gladness that you will be with me—it makes me unworthy of my vows, any of them."

He started to move away from her, but she reached out and clung to him. "Margrethe," he said softly. "Then what do you want of me?"

The question surprised her. "I told you."

"You've told me what you don't want from me." He waited for her to decide what to do, saying only, "The wind is growing stronger; we may not be able to travel tonight."

Margrethe turned to him, her eyes alarmed. "Truly?"

"If the wind keeps rising, yes," said Sandjer'min; he laid his hand over hers. "It isn't safe to travel in a sandstorm."

"But Torquil . . . It would not be wise to leave him . . . where he is for a full day, let alone two days. "

"I'll speak with Sieur Horembaud about it," he assured her. "If we can travel on tonight, we should take him with us, if the company is willing. Otherwise, an arrangement of some kind must be made."

"You cannot mean to leave him to the sands," she declared, her voice raised. "He is a Christian, and must be protected."

"No, not in the sands," he said. "There are some broad shelves in the rocks above us. If we lay him out on one of them, he should be safe from sands and scavengers." There were vultures, he knew, and a few others, who could find the body in very little time, but he wouldn't be left to the caprice of the dunes.

"Do you think we should leave a cross for him? In case?"

"If you would be solaced by it, I will see it's done," he told her, and rose, pausing to kiss her hands, then going to the other side of the tent. "I should wrap the body. It will have to be done whether we stay here for the night or not."

She watched him as he went to one of his two smaller chests, from which he removed a linen winding-sheet, and went down on one knee to begin his task. "Shouldn't he be bathed? Aren't bodies washed before burial?"

"More of his blisters will rupture if they're washed, and we haven't water enough to spare," he said, going to a smaller chest to remove long, broad rolls of linen, then coming back to where Torquil lay.

"No, I suppose not," she said with growing doubt. "If we have to spend the night here, and the next day."

"Indeed," he said, and began the wrapping at Torquil's feet, working steadily, never needing to stop and undo his work.

"You've done this . . . before, haven't you?" Margrethe asked as she watched him.

"Yes. More times than I like to think."

"To watch you, one would think that he weighs nothing now that he's dead," she remarked, needing to say something.

He cursed himself inwardly for not being more circumspect. "He's barely more than skin and bones; Heneri could lift him without difficulty," he said, and saw that Margrethe accepted this without question.

"Poor man," she whispered.

"He ate little while his fever raged, and that burned the flesh away from him," said Sandjer'min, sounding more composed than he felt. "The body cannot sustain such demands for months on end."

"With God's aid, it can," she said, for the first time with an edge to her voice, and the line of a frown between her brows. "I have seen it for myself."

Sandjer'min realized she was speaking of her husband, and said nothing, busying himself with making the winding-sheet lie in flat, even turns across Torquil's chest; when all that was left to wrap was his head, Sandjer'min glanced up at Margrethe, saying, "I'll need Ruthier's help to set Torquil up high on the rocks."

"He's supervising the animals, isn't he?" she asked, grateful to have something ordinary to talk about.

"He is; they're often hard to manage in high winds," he said, then looked down again at Torquil's devastated face. "I should go waken Sieur Horembaud so that he can identify Torquil officially as deceased."

She nodded, trying to make herself tend to the duties that were now upon her. "I ought to go tell Sorer Imogen, but I'm . . ."

Silence like a gulf yawned between them; neither moved for twenty of Margrethe's heartbeats, then Sandjer'min got to his feet. "You may stay here with Torquil until Sieur Horembaud comes, to continue your vigil. Then, if you wish, you may tell Sorer Imogen of Torquil's death, or leave the task to Frater Anteus. But Torquil shouldn't be left alone." This last was for Margrethe's benefit; in his view the body was now an untenanted shell, deserving respect in order to provide comfort to the living, not the dead.

Her smile was brief, yet it conveyed a gratitude that was almost as vivid as her sudden kiss had been. "I'll do that. You're right; he should not be left alone, not yet."

"Would you like me to ask Sorer Imogen to join you now?" he asked, seeing her hesitation in her response; he wondered if Margrethe did not want to have to tell Sorer Imogen of Torquil's death.

"No; it's better she should pray for him as long as possible. I will stay with him." She waved him away. "Time enough to summon her when you return."

"This is kind of you, Bondame," he said, his compelling eyes on her face with all the force of a caress. "I will not be any longer than I must," he assured her as he went to unfasten the tent-flap; the wind caught it and snapped it vigorously. He lifted the hood of his black cotton coule froq and stepped out into the raging sun and the blowing sand; for a long moment he stood, his eyes shaded with both hands as he looked toward the horizon, his attention on the grayish haze that was approaching, confirming his worst fears. The wind battered at him as he made his way among the tents to Sieur Horembaud's, which was painted with his recumbent, crowned stag on a green field, and called out, "Sieur Horembaud!"

On his fourth shout, a very sleep-groggy Florien lifted the tent-flap. "Oh. It's you." He moved back, allowing Sandjer'min to enter. "Sieur Horembaud is laid down on his bed," he said, an obstinate angle to his jaw.

"Don't worry; I'll wake him. You won't be blamed." Sandjer'min went past the broad curtain that separated the sleeping portion of the tent from the meeting area; there he found Sieur Horembaud stretched out on a simple, straw-filled mattress, a single linen sheet pulled over most of his chest; a straw-filled pillow was stuffed under his neck. A large tankard lay, overturned, beside him, the last of its wine running from it like a rivulet of blood. Sandjer'min bent down and picked it up. "No wonder he rests so well," he said, loudly enough to disturb Sieur Horembaud's slumber.

The leader of the pilgrims wadded up the sheet and grasped it to his chest, his under-froq gathered up around his waist, showing legs and groin covered in a dense growth of ruddy curls. There was a sweaty shine on his face and shoulders. He grunted and flung out one arm as if to deliver a blow to anyone having the misfortune to be sleeping next to him. Finally he spat, pushing himself up, grumbling, "Have to piss," while reaching for his pot. As he relieved himself, he raised his voice. "Who the Devil woke me up?"

"I did," said Sandjer'min with unruffled imperturbability. "I regret to inform you that Torquil des Lichiens is dead. I've wrapped the body, all but the face, so that you may verify that this has happened."

"Why couldn't he wait until tomorrow?" He set his pot aside and scrabbled to his feet. "We could leave him in good hands."

"It would make no difference if he had lived another day—not in that sense," said Sandjer'min.

"We'll be at the Gold Camp tomorrow, won't we?" He tugged his under-froq down to his knees and reached for his pilgrim's habit, brushing off the front of the modified cotehardie where his heraldic device was displayed. "Sand gets into everything," he complained as he pulled the blue garment over his head.

"No, we won't. We will be here." Sandjer'min saw Sieur Horembaud scowl, and went on, "There is a large sandstorm coming, and we will need to stay where we are until it passes. Here we have some shelter from the wind and sand, gained by the rocks around us, and we have time enough to take more precautions."

"Are you sure of this? I don't want us to waste a day for no reason." He glared at the tent wall that was billowing inward under the force of the wind.

"Nor do I. Which is why I tell you now that to go out into this not only means risking our animals, it means we could become lost. Ask Firouz, if you doubt me; he knows this desert and I don't. We should plan to wait out the storm for the sake of the animals." He said this genially, not wanting to create unnecessary disputes. "But for now, I need your statement of Torquil's death so Ruthier and I may set about moving his body to a sheltered place high in the rocks."

"What are you talking about?" Sieur Horembaud exclaimed.

Sandjer'min outlined Margrethe's reservations about such a burial, knowing that most of the pilgrims would share them, and ended by saying, "The primary consideration here is that it is very hot, and his body is deeply corrupted. A day, and we will have vultures all around us if the wind drops."

"There is nothing you can do to preserve him until we reach the Gold Camp? You don't have anything in that chest of yours that will delay his rotting?" Sieur Horembaud asked, punctuating his question with a clicking of his tongue. "I'll talk to Frater Anteus, but I'm fairly sure he won't like it. Surely there must be some way to—"

"I have nothing that I can do here. And since, if Bondame Margrethe is right, he could not be buried in any churchyard, I believe finding him a place that is as permanent as anything in the desert is will be the best we can do for him. I am afraid that having his corpse with us could be cause for the men of the Gold Camp to turn us away. He smells now, and that will only get worse." Sandjer'min paused long enough to give Sieur Horembaud a little time to think, then said, "With Ruthier's help I can get him to a safe place before the heart of the storm hits."

Sieur Horembaud brightened a little at this. "You're going to take care of the burial, then?"

"If that's satisfactory to you. The monks and d'Urbineau might protest, for all he's defrocked."

"How soon will the storm arrive?"

"Mid-day, or a little after," said Sandjer'min. "From out of the southwest."

"Then you may have the best answer, no matter what the company thinks: if they won't bury him—and they won't—then they mustn't complain at what I authorize." He clapped his hands. "Almeric, come dress me. I have a duty that can't wait for evening." With a sigh of ill-usage, he turned to his servant as Almeric moved the curtain aside.

"What has happened?" He was dilatory in his manner, his glance going from Sieur Horembaud to Sandjer'min and back.

"Torquil died and as leader of this pilgrim company, I must verify it." Sieur Horembaud folded his arms. "The solers, I think, and the knitted braies. Then go waken Frater Anteus and tell him to bring his writing materials."

"Yes, Sieur Horembaud," said Almeric, opening Sieur Horembaud's clothes chest and pulling out the shoes and leggings that Sieur Horembaud had requested.

"We'll need black and red ribbons for Bondame Margrethe and Lalagia. Sorer Imogen shouldn't wear them, of course. You can find some at the bottom of the chest," Sieur Horembaud went on. "We'll be here through tonight and tomorrow-day, and resume our travels when the wind has ceased to howl."

"Very good, Sieur Horembaud," said Almeric, removing a stack of garments from the chest.

"I suppose we'll have to wake the camp after I've seen Torquil and Frater Anteus has recorded it. They will have to be told."

"I doubt you will have to do that," said Sandjer'min. "The servants guarding the animals will talk, and soon all the company will know."

"You sound certain of that," said Sieur Horembaud as he sat on a three-legged stool and waited for Almeric to bring his braies and solers.

"When servants learn a thing, everyone knows," said Sandjer'min, and went on more vigorously, "And speaking of servants, I am going to find Ruthier so that he may aid me in making the device that will allow us to lay Torquil to rest."

"Do you require his help?"

"I do. And Ruthier will need to put up more containing ropes for the animals, as well. We will try to move Torquil before mid-day, so I will have to make the arrangements quickly." He inclined his head. "I will return to my tent shortly, and will meet you and Frater Anteus there, if that suits you? You will find Bondame Margrethe keeping vigil over Torquil's body."

"Praying?" Sieur Horembaud asked nervously. "Not for Torquil?"

"Not for Torquil, for the pilgrims, yes," said Sandjer'min. "She will inform Sorer Imogen of Torquil's death once you have verified it, or you may ask Frater Anteus to deliver the news."

"You seem to have the matter in hand," said Sieur Horembaud readily enough, but with the suggestion of truculence.

"I am pleased to be able to help you at this difficult time," said Sandjer'min, making his way toward the tent-flap; he paused for Florien to open the flap for him, and went out into the whipping sands. He lifted his hood and drew a length of cotton over the lower part of his face as he went toward the L-shaped boulders where the animals had been penned, protected by the rocks and the sail which fluttered over the animals like a huge, ungainly bird.

Ruthier emerged from the shadow of the sail and approached Sandjer'min. "My master," he said in six-hundred-year-old Spanish. "We're going to have to stay here today and tonight?"

"We are," Sandjer'min agreed. "But this is a bit more pressing than having to make preparations for the storm."

"So. Torquil died." Ruthier looked down at his dusty hands. "It is over for him."

"Not quite," Sandjer'min said, squinting and peering up into the rocks above them. "He has to be put up there."

"And you have offered to do it," said Ruthier with some exasperation. "What do you need me to do?"

"Get the sling from the camels' saddles and rig it so that I can sink a rod for the block-and-tackle into the rock; it's in the fourth chest. The rope and a draw-line as well."

One end of the sail flailed as its stay-line came loose; Ruthier shouted for Salvatore to fetch a rake and come catch the sail's end, then turned back to Sandjer'min. "This must be done soon."

"Yes; it must," Sandjer'min agreed. "I don't want to be on that rock-face when the heart of the storm arrives."

"I will get to work on it," Ruthier said.

"Good. I need to see Sieur Horembaud, and as soon as the verification of death is done, I'll come back." He started to move away, but stopped as Ruthier called after him.

"I'll order the servants on duty to get as much of the food and tack that they can into the tents, so we won't have to try to dig them out when this is all over. We won't be able to move it all, but I should think that more than half can be sheltered."

Sandjer'min offered Ruthier a tired smile. "Thank you, old friend," he said, and resumed his trudge back around the end of the outcropping to the cluster of tents, his hand raised to shade his eyes from the blurry sun.

Sieur Horembaud was in Sandjer'min's tent with Frater Anteus beside him, his wax tablet and iron stylus in hand; Margrethe had sat down on one of the smaller chests, waiting patiently to see what the two men would do next. Sieur Horembaud looked up as Sandjer'min came in through the flap and inclined his head. "Are you ready to do it? To raise the body up into the rocks?"

"Yes. I'm going to take a mallet and an iron rod up with me and use his sling to pull him up."

Frater Anteus looked aghast. "How can you do that? It would take more strength than three men possess to pull him up so far."

"That is why I'll have a block-and-tackle; I have a very long rope with me, in case it might be needed." He did not add that there had been a number of times when he had needed such devices and did not have them.

"Will you be able to bring the block-and-tackle down with you?" Sieur Horembaud asked as if he had no particular interest in the answer.

"That is my intention," said Sandjer'min, and bowed slightly to Sieur Horembaud and more deeply to Margrethe, and for most of the rest of the morning, he pulled and climbed his way up the promontory that thrust out between the tents and the animals, while the wind grew louder and sand scoured his hands and the side of his face, so that when he at last reached a small plateau that included a shaded declivity, he readied himself for the more difficult part of his task: he set the rod, pulled his netted pack from his back, tugged on the feed-line, rigged the block-and-tackle, then signaled to Ruthier, from more than two hundred hands above the tents and pens. By the time he had moved Torquil's body into the trough-like declivity, it was almost mid-day and the air was buzzing loudly with wind-borne sand. Sandjer'min looped his rope around the iron rod, secured it with a releasing knot, and carefully let himself down, then tugged to loosen the knot that held the rope, motioning to Ruthier to collect the block-and-tackle as well as the rope before he stumbled toward his tent, his face aching from sunlight and scouring wind. The last thought that he could later recall was the realization that the sandstorm would keep the vultures away from Torquil's corpse until the company of pilgrims moved on.

Text of a letter from Esteven del Aquafuere in the Kingdom of Portugal in Oporto to Jiochim Menines in care of the Hieronymite monk Frater Duro, bound for Egypt to join a pilgrim company; written on parchment, and returned to Portugal without being delivered.

> To the distinguished traveler Jiochim Menines, the respectful greetings of Esteven del Aquafuere, on this, the 19th day of May in the 1225th year of Salvation,
>
> Most enterprising Jiochim Menines,
>
> It is my duty to inform you that word has come from the Kingdom of Navarre that you are on a mission in the distant Christian lands beyond Egypt, where you have been posted for Portuguese interests for eight years. The purpose of your residence there is to ascertain the extent of trade that exists in that part of the world. Given the difficult situation King Sancho II has with the clergy and the nobility here, I must ask you to abandon that Navarrese mission for the sake of your homeland, and to uphold the worth of all you have accomplished. Navarre is not as extensive in its range of trading as Portugal is, and therefore, we of the

Council of Merchants and Traders appeal to you to put our interests before those of Navarre; Portugal has supported you and your family since you went on the mission, and for this you pledged us fealty. We are aware that you have been in Egypt for eight years, and may believe that you need not honor the country of your birth in such affairs as you now conduct on our behalf, but I urge you to consider your situation: you have gained advancement in Egypt, it is true, but only because you deal with Portuguese merchants and traders. The contracts and other dealings you have done on Navarre's behalf in the last few years have compromised some of the negotiations of our Council, and this is not acceptable to us. If you do not mend your ways, you may find yourself banished to Egypt, living a life vastly different than the one our Guild has made possible for you. Should you attempt to return with this matter unresolved, you know that Navarre would not offer you a place within their borders for fear that you would act clandestinely for Portugal, and most other Kingdoms would share Navarre's doubts. Therefore, if you fail to give up this mission for Navarre, and do not return to Alexandria and your old post within three months, you will become an exile, one whom no Portuguese trader or merchant will call upon to assist in bargaining, or will rely upon for information. Surely you do not wish to place yourself in such an untenable position. As you value your homeland and the well-being of your kinsmen, and the repute of those who have served you, abjure your service to Navarre at once, or declare yourself a traitor to your people.

Esteven del Aquafuere
for the Council of Merchants and Traders

by the hand of Frater Duro, Hieronymite

4

"We must leave here tomorrow night," Sieur Horembaud declared, facing the pilgrims as they sat around a long table waiting for their supper to be served. Evening was closing in, and the travelers' inn had set braziers of camel dung alight to ward off the darkness. "Five days is sufficient rest. It is time we were underway once again. Our animals are getting fat and lazy." He gestured to take in the dining room. "It is easy to grow accustomed to this place, but we have vows to fulfill." This inn, located in the central part of the travelers' quarter, was still busy although the approaching summer would soon stop most of those on the road from continuing until autumn brought the end of the Inundation and the lessening of heat. Those who would spend the summer in the Gold Camp would retire to cabins located at the far edge of the travelers' quarter. This inn would soon close its doors until travel resumed when the worst of the heat was over.

The room they occupied was set up for diners of all sorts, some tables being low and having cushions, some, like the one where most of the pilgrims were sitting, was high and had benches; the women were relegated to a small, round table in the far corner of the room, and partially concealed by a carved screen. Six of the other tables were occupied with companies of merchants and pilgrims, about half of whom were foreigners to the Nubian Desert. A large open-pit fire at the other side of the room held a collection of various-sized spits, a few of which had animal carcasses turning on them slowly, worked by slaves of skin colors ranging from olive to black, and ages from six to ten. The landlord, a lanky fellow with tawny-dark skin and amber eyes, showed a heritage that was both Egyptian and African; he treated all his patrons with the same, slightly unctuous courtesy, and posted two slaves near the door to keep out roughians and beggars.

"You still haven't spoken to the Abyssinian merchants who

arrived yesterday, and you must; everyone says they're the last cara-van to come from the south until the flood is over," Noreberht lo Av-ocat protested in his native Anglo-French, which, with Church Latin and Greek, had become the most common languages for the pilgrims. "We are nearly into summer, and Firouz, and the Copts have said that it is in summer that the Nile floods, and the channel above the Second Cataract isn't safe for any boat. If you still intend that we will follow the river again once we cross the desert, what would be the use of—"

At the women's table, Sorer Imogen raised her voice in prayers of thanks for their coming meal; hearing her, the monks blessed them-selves.

Viviano Loredan started to speak, but stopped as Methodus Temi interrupted. "They say that it isn't safe to venture across the sands until the flooding is over."

"What *they* is that?" Sieur Horembaud demanded.

"That party of Arabian slavers, bound for the coast of the Red Sea," he said, pointing to a low table on the far side of the room. "I know enough Arabic to ask them about travel while I repaired one of their chains for them."

"When did you do that?" Sieur Horembaud asked stiffly.

"Earlier today. I told you they had asked for my help. Two of the men stayed with me while I used the travelers' forge." He folded his arms and laid them on the table, making it clear that he would stand by what he had said.

Sieur Horembaud tapped his fingers, and an ominous silence fell over the company of pilgrims.

Into that silence Sandjer'min came, returning from his daily in-spection of their animals. "The animals are bedded down for the night, but the ass with the bad ear is still having trouble and is off his feed."

"Does it hamper him beyond use?" Sieur Horembaud asked. "Will the putrescence damage him? Is he safe to ride?"

"No, his ear will not damage him, not yet. But you may want to trade him for another when we move on, so that he can have a chance to recover." Sandjer'min paused. "I'll leave an unguent to treat his ear, if you arrange such a trade." He did not mention that he had taken a cup of blood from the headstrong black Barb that Jio-chim Menines had been riding, or that he was beginning to long for the nourishment only human touching could provide.

"I'll consider it," Sieur Horembaud said. The tension lessened at once, but did not entirely vanish. "We will go on land, keeping to the bank of the river once we reach it again," he went on to the company in the tone of voice that did not encourage argument, paying no more attention to what Sandjer'min had said. "That way the river will guide us without harming us, and will provide some coolness." He drank carefully from his cup holding his daily portion of wine, savor-ing it in spite of its increasingly sour taste.

"We must get there first, before the flooding begins," Richere Enzo pointed out. "We have another twelve days at least until we reach the bend in the Nile between the Fourth and Fifth Cataracts; the village is called Baruta, isn't it."

"Where there are crocodiles and thieves of all sorts in equal por-tion, as well as jackals, scorpions, and serpents, each of which are not hampered by the heat, as we will be, and our animals," said Ifar, speaking with lackadaisical certainty. "When pilgrims are many, at least the human killers keep their distance. But when they are few, and the thieves are hungry for loot—"

"How can you know? You have said that you have never been beyond the Second Cataract," Agnolus dei Causi challenged; the ten-sion was rising again.

Sandjer'min caught sight of Ruthier at a small table near the kitchen, and went to join him. "They are still bickering," he said in Persian as he sat down.

Ruthier looked up from his haunch of young goat which he ate—as he ate everything—raw; he wagged his short knife. "They'll have to settle something soon if they intend to move on tomorrow night."

"Every day they wait, the crossing will grow harder; we are late into May, and by July the whole of the desert and the mountains will be furnaces," Sandjer'min said, reaching for the end of the bench; he was about to sit down when Sieur Horembaud raised his hand and motioned Sandjer'min to join them.

"Besides," Vidame Bonnefiles interjected loudly, interrupting Frater Anteus, "who is to say that the floods will come this summer? There were many boatmen who expressed fear of a dry season. What do you say to that?"

Ifar refused to be goaded into dispute. "True, we cannot know what is to come, but we do know what has come before. Egyptians always fear for a dry summer, for if the summer is dry they will starve by the end of winter. I have been as far as the Second Cataract, and I cannot believe that there is much of a change in the wildness of the flood until the Blue Nile is reached, and there are many leagues to go before we reach that branch of the river." He waved around the room. "Ask any traveler coming north and hear what they have to say. The Abyssinians, for example, can inform you—the ones at that table near the window; a few of them speak some Arabic. They will know how the summer is coming in the mountains, where the rains fall."

From the far end of the table where the servants and slaves sat, Olu'we spoke up. "The Inundation is not a time for boats to go against the current, if you were planning to travel by water again. You would need all the winds of the desert to blow against the raging of the Nile, and even then, you would not go far."

Sandjer'min, drawing a stool up to the table, translated this into Sieur Horembaud's Anglo-English and into the tongue of northern Italy, adding, "Regarding the Nile, I trust Olu'we to know more than anyone but Firouz."

"Do we have anyone who can speak with the Abyssinians?" Frater Anteus suggested. "Once we know what they have seen, then—"

"Why should they tell us the truth?" Sieur Horembaud demanded. "What are we to them, that they should—"

Viviano Loredan sighed audibly. "Why should they not?"

Nicholas Howe offered his thoughts. "We have sworn to go to the Chapel of the Holy Grail, and if we fail, our travels this far have been for nought. Think of poor Torquil."

"He's probably little more than scattered bones now that the vultures have sure got at him," said Micheu de Saunte-Foi.

Cristofo d'Urbineau coughed his disapproval and made the Sign of the Cross for all the pilgrims. "May God forgive him and bring him to Paradise."

"You're defrocked," Frater Anteus scoffed.

"I still retain the chrism: that cannot be taken from me," d'Urbineau reminded him. "And defrocked or not, we all could use God's Grace on this journey."

Firouz nodded. "Allah is Merciful," he said in Greek.

Heneri shocked everyone by echoing "Allah is Merciful," in Arabic. He smiled and added in Anglo-French, "Firouz has been teaching me."

D'Urbineau glared at Firouz. "This is a Christian pilgrimage," he declared in clumsy Greek.

"So it is," said Firouz in the same language. "But it may be useful to have one of your own numbers speak more Arabic than most do. I will not be with you in the mountains; I will take my camels and a few of the asses and wait for another caravan to go back to the First Cataract, but you will travel on." He took a sip of the strong mint tea he drank at meals. "You cannot always rely on the Sidi, can you? He speaks Arabic well enough, and Coptic, but the tongues of Abyssinia and Ethiopia he does not know. I have a little knowledge of a few of them, but you will find it useful if the young man learns enough Arabic to converse. I am told that many of the people in that region know Arabic. You should encourage Heneri to learn it, for your own sakes."

"Not if he uses the language to dishonor the Savior," said d'Urbineau.

Heneri stared at d'Urbineau. "I wouldn't do that."

"Well, see that you don't," said Frater Anteus.

Heneri drank some of his wine. "See? Still Christian."

Firouz wagged a finger at him. "Do not disrespect your people or your religion," he said in Arabic. "Your Jesus is a prophet of Islam."

"Yes, you told me," Heneri answered in the same language.

D'Urbineau glowered at Firouz. "You are mocking me."

"No," he said in Greek. "Ask Heneri if you doubt me."

"No mocking," Heneri said before d'Urbineau could speak; the pilgrims went quiet.

Frater Anteus got to his feet, prepared to intone the blessing on their meal. He waited until he had full attention, then pronounced the prayer in Church Latin; he watched the pilgrims cross themselves, then sat down to unusual silence.

Several heartbeats later, Loredan cleared his throat and said in his best Anglo-French, "After speaking to some of the other travelers here who have come from the south, Salvatore and I have decided to leave with one of the caravans going north in two days. There are six pilgrims in their company already, and they are willing to have us join them. Do not stare about: the group that has agreed to take us on has already dined. All our arrangements are made, and we will not continue with you. We have been willing to come this far, but we have no reason to risk our lives by crossing the sands with summer coming. It will be harsh enough going back the way we came."

Sandjer'min translated this into the northern Italian dialect, and into Greek, all the while thinking that Loredan's going was not a good sign for the pilgrims.

There was another silence at the table, this one of shock and dismay; Enzo muttered something that might have been a curse, Frater Anteus and Frater Giulianus crossed themselves, both looking away from Loredan. From the women's table came louder praying as Sorer Imogen realized what had been said.

Then Sieur Horembaud glared at the Venezian. "What sort of traitor are you, that you would abjure your pilgrims' oath and depart when faced with hardship?"

Loredan shook his head as if he were dealing with a temperamental child. "We've had hardship enough, and we are not sworn pilgrims as you are, we are observers, and we have seen as much as we need to; we swore to keep to your Rule while we traveled in your company, and we have done so, but we need not go on to the Chapel of the Holy Grail; we have learned all we need to know. We can now inform our Console, the Doge, and our Patriarch that this pilgrimage is too arduous for any but the most hardened sinners, and that the distances are greater than our merchants will want to travel." He paused, letting what he said be taken in by all the pilgrims. "We will need two camels, two asses from among the animals you have; since we provided money for their food and upkeep, we are entitled to them. And the monk Ze-kri will be coming with us, to guide us once we part from the caravan." His voice grew more confident as he spoke. "You knew that we re-served the right to turn back from the first. We do not ask any of the rest of you to do so; that would be contrary to our pledge to the pil-grimage. Now that you have been informed of our departure, Salva-tore will move our goods out of our chamber and out of the stable tonight, and we will join the caravan bound for Edfu, and will claim our animals in the morning. We will pray for your pilgrimage."

At the women's table, Margrethe hissed Sorer Imogen to whis-per; reluctantly the nun obeyed. "We need to listen," Margrethe ex-plained, and added, "Be sure you eat enough tonight, Sorer Imogen. This is no time to fast. Once we're underway again, the food will be rationed."

"As will the water and the wine, Sorer." Lalagia shook her head. "It's a bad business, having the Veneziani leave," she said in Greek-accented Anglo-French, which she had learned from Sieur Arnoul during the years they were together. "Some of the others are dissatis-fied with our travels, and they may decide to forswear their vows and go back the way we came. Devout as they wish to be, they want to remain alive."

"Why do that? After all the distance we have come, what is to be gained in turning back?" Margrethe asked. "Surely if they—who are not true pilgrims—have no desire to continue, it is our duty to re-lease them from their . . . pledge."

"They are experienced travelers, and they have a good supply of ducats with them, which we may need before we're done, not only for food and shelter, but for bribes. Everyone says that pilgrims are ex-pected to pay bribes." Lalagia looked around as if she feared being overheard, then went on quietly, "Temi says that there are more sla-vers about than the ones here in the Gold Camp, and they would not hesitate to capture a company of pilgrims to add to their wares."

"Mightn't they keep the money and the pilgrims?" Margrethe's tone was sharper, and she made no attempt to conceal the frisson of dread that the thought of capture and enslavement gave her.

"Those who trade with Veneziani know that any such chicanery could lead to warfare," said Lalagia. "Sieur Arnoul told me that. Or are you thinking about Sandjer'min? I have seen your face when you catch sight of him, which shuts out the rest of the world as if you were alone in all of Africa and only he could find you. I felt that way about Sieur Arnoul, two years ago, so I know how a man can become a fire in the blood."

Margrethe realized that challenging anything the missing Sieur Arnoul had said, or what Lalagia had confided in her, would be met with anger. "We're a long way from any port where Venezia trades," she said defensively, as if she had not heard what Lalagia had said. She tried to imagine where she might end up if she were captured and sold, but her mind balked at the notion. "It would take more than a year for a ransom to reach this place."

"Knights held for ransom have often waited five years and more to be delivered from their captors," said Lalagia, anxiety roughening her words. "I fear that Sieur Arnoul may be held captive, though there has been no demand for ransom."

"Would pilgrims be worth holding?" Margrethe asked before she could stop herself. "Would slavers even bother to try to collect a ransom?"

Lalagia shrugged. "They might hold you—you're a noblewoman. But me? Who would ransom a camp-follower?"

Sorer Imogen crossed herself, and continued to pray.

Margrethe could think of nothing to say, so she leaned a bit forward and strained to listen to what the men were saying.

"—serve no purpose to wait here for four months before going south into the mountains," Sieur Horembaud was proclaiming, his loud voice overwhelming all the others at the table.

"I agree," said Agnolus dei Causi. "I cannot afford to be so long away from my business and my family. I said I would be back in Genova by Easter next year, and that would mean I would have to abjure my vow, which would compromise me in the eyes of the Church even more than I am compromised now."

"Then we proceed as we planned," said Sieur Horembaud, smacking the table with the flat of his hand; his wine-cup tipped over and the red liquid ran out of it, staining the cuff of his broad blue sleeve.

A whisper passed among the pilgrims, all of whom knew that the omen was not a good one.

Sieur Horembaud forced himself to laugh. "There, you see? We're encouraged to keep to our purpose. We have been reminded that Communion at the Chapel of the Holy Grail is our goal. You need only look on my habit to garner up your resolve when it flags. Our bodies will endure our travail for the good of our souls."

Nicholas Howe nodded his support, saying, "We cannot allow ourselves to be tempted to laxness and melancholy."

"And say we all Amen," Vidame Bonnefiles declared at his most pious.

The rest of the pilgrims echoed the *Amen,* and the women repeated the *Amen* loudly enough to be heard by the men.

Jiochim Menines half-rose as three youthful scullions came toward the table, each holding a large platter of grilled meat: one carried goat, one carried sheep, and one carried speckled fowl, sliced and ready to eat. "Our meal is here," he announced. "Let us ask God's blessing on this bounty."

One of the cooks brought a tray of flatbread to the table, and a gruel of coarse-ground beans with garlic. He laid this in the center of the table and stood back to permit the scullions to set down their platters. The cook said something and withdrew to the kitchen.

"What did he say?" Sieur Horembaud asked.

"The same thing he's said every night since we came here," Sandjer'min told him patiently. "He will have his wife take bread to our women."

"And the women will have the meat we don't eat," Sieur Horembaud finished for him. "Of course. Yes. We know this." He reached out with his small knife and pronged a slab of goat, dropped it on the flatbread he had already seized, and then he added a wedge of fowl to the pile. "They put onions in the goat before they turn it on the spit," he went on, whetting his appetite with words. "Gives it a good flavor. You should really have some." Before Sandjer'min could speak, Sieur Horembaud held up both hands in a gesture of surrender. "I know. I know. Those of your blood dine in private by custom. You've told me that more than once. Why that should be your custom, you haven't told me. But it troubles me that you do not take your meals with us. It would be better if you did, for all of us."

This did not surprise Sandjer'min; he was aware of the suspicions several of the pilgrims had of him. "I follow the customs of those of my blood, as we agreed at the first. Enjoy your meal." He got up. "The next leg of the journey may not be so pleasant." His warning brought uneasy glances from others at the table.

"You've told me that before, as has Firouz. I think we're prepared to endure what God sends us." Sieur Horembaud hacked off a chunk of goat, stuck his knife-point into it, and began to eat it off the end of his knife.

Others at the table were scrambling for their shares of the flatbread and meat while the scullions brought bowls of chopped cucumbers, shredded herbs, mustard seeds in olive oil, mashed onions, honey with garlic, and fresh curds with pepper in them. A cry of approval went up from the pilgrims; two tables away, a pair of Greek monks with a flock of young men scowled in disapproval.

Sandjer'min stepped away from the table. "I will have a word with Ruthier: we were interrupted." He ducked his head respectfully, then turned away from the pilgrims and threaded his way back through the various groups and their drone of conversation to the small table near the kitchen; it was the hottest place in a very warm room; from the women's table behind the screen, Margrethe looked through a crack in the carving so she could watch his progress through the dining room.

Ruthier had almost finished his dinner; two bones were lying on the untouched flatbread, and he had already wiped his face. "My master," he said as Sandjer'min approached.

"The copper-dun mare may be casting a splint," said Sandjer'min, glancing back at the pilgrims as if he expected to be summoned again. "She shouldn't be ridden."

"No, she should not, particularly in this sand," said Ruthier. "She's a favorite of Sieur Horembaud's."

"I know. He considers her a bringer of good fortune." Sandjer'min took a long breath and let it out slowly.

"Should we take her with us as a remount, or do we leave her here?" Ruthier began to weigh the advantages to each solution in his mind.

"I don't know. I've done as much as I can, but if Sieur Horembaud insists that we depart tomorrow night, I won't yet know if she's improving."

"Can she keep up if she's not ridden?" Ruthier asked.

"It's possible, but I don't know," Sandjer'min said, sounding frustrated. He shook his head. "Perhaps Loredan will take her as a remount."

"Veneziani don't know much about horses," Ruthier pointed out.

"Zekri does, and I can give him instructions," said Sandjer'min, looking toward the kitchen as two of the cooks came out carrying the carcase of a calf on a spit, taking it to be turned by the scullions.

"You are hungry," said Ruthier in Persian.

"I have fed not long ago," Sandjer'min replied in the same language.

"Not truly fed; you are losing flesh, as always happens when you take too long to find a willing consort; you have been a dream for too long. It's time you seek a knowing woman," Ruthier said, and felt the distance between them widen. "You needn't deny yourself. The Bondame yearns for you."

"I know. When she looks at me, I can feel the power of her desire. She is like the heroine in an epic story, and a sworn wife at the same time. Yet I know she is determined to keep her pilgrims' vows, and that she is unable to admit to the emotions that have been stirred within her," he said slowly. "You know that there is no advantage to either her or me if I should press my suit with her."

"Lalagia might be willing, if you should ask her," Ruthier suggested.

"She is a pilgrim; she took the vow, though she's looking for her man, not the Chapel of the Holy Grail. She would be scorned by the rest if there were any suggestion that she had broken her vow; the others already regard her as tainted."

"I understand," Ruthier nodded, waiting until the cheering for the trussed calf died down. "The other pilgrims would not sanction—"

"No, they wouldn't," Sandjer'min agreed, cutting Ruthier short. "And pious or not, I do not want this to be another encounter like the road to Baghdad."

"It wouldn't come to that, surely," said Ruthier in alarm.

"I would hope not," said Sandjer'min. "But I cannot be . . . sanguine." His smile was quick and ironic.

Ruthier answered the smile with one of his own that exposed his worry. "You are clever, my master."

"I need cleverness with this company," Sandjer'min admitted.

Another cheer went up as another dressed-and-trussed goat was carried out from the kitchen, ready for basting over the fire-pits.

"Do you think we will leave tomorrow night?" Ruthier asked when the cooks withdrew.

"It is certainly Sieur Horembaud's plan," said Sandjer'min, in the Venezian dialect.

"But with Loredan leaving . . ." Ruthier's question trailed away.

"I'll make our chests and cases ready, in case."

"Thank you, old friend," said Sandjer'min. "I apologize for adding to your annoyances." He started to rise, but was stopped when Ruthier reached out and took hold of Sandjer'min's wrist; this was so uncharacteristic of the man, that Sandjer'min sat down again at once. "What is it?"

"You've continued to watch for our followers; I know you have," said Ruthier in a brisker tone.

"Yes."

"Are we still being followed?" Ruthier asked.

"There are three of them, on camels, now. I know they are somewhere in the Gold Camp, but not in the travelers' quarter, which suggests to me that they have associates here, or they have bribed the tax collector." Sandjer'min took a little time to stare around the room. "No one here resembles the two I have glimpsed from time to time, and I have yet to get a good look at the third."

"Have you told Sieur Horembaud?"

"No; I don't think we're in immediate danger—not if there are only three of them. We may have only hunting weapons, but there are enough of us to hold three men at bay." He stared down at his hands. "What troubles me is the possibility that they are scouts for robbers or slavers. I have only a guess that they might be, but I have just the guess, no proof, and if I should report this and be wrong, Sieur Horembaud could send us away."

"That might not be the worst that could happen," Ruthier remarked.

"Two men alone in the desert are at more risk than a party of pilgrims," Sandjer'min said. He heard a shout of approval go up from the slavers' table as pale-rinded melon was brought to their table.

"They're on their second jug of palm-wine," Ruthier said.

"I've been told it is strong and quite sweet," said Sandjer'min. "It will quickly go to their heads."

"I believe they want that; they have not tasted palm-wine, and it's that or beer."

"Then I hope the landlord is prepared to deal with their celebrations," said Sandjer'min dryly. "It sounds as if they are hoping to carouse."

"So it does," Ruthier said with a knowing nod; he released Sandjer'min's wrist. "I will plan to leave here shortly."

"And I will leave now. I have guard-duty on the animals tonight, with Olu'we." This time he got up unimpeded. "Carlus and Firouz will guard the tents."

"I thought it was Salvatore, not Firouz, who—" He pressed his lips together.

"Firouz is reserve; since Salvatore will be leaving with Loredan, he will be in no position to stand guard tonight," Sandjer'min reminded him. "They will have to move their tent and goods before morning."

"There is something you should know," Ruthier said in a rush.

"What is it?" Sandjer'min recognized the distress in Ruthier's outwardly calm demeanor.

"Frater Giulianus is going to stay here in Gold Camp. He says the village needs someone to tend to the sick."

"How do you come to know this?" Sandjer'min asked, glancing at the pilgrims' table where Nicholas Howe was deep in conversation with Frater Giulianus.

"I know it because he told all the servants, in case anyone should care to join him." Ruthier pressed his lips together as if to stop saying anything more.

"Sieur Horembaud won't be pleased," said Sandjer'min.

"Nor will Nicholas Howe," Ruthier said.

"When will Frater Giulianus tell the others that he is staying here?" Sandjer'min asked.

"After Loredan and Salvatore go to the other company of travelers." Ruthier nodded in Sieur Horembaud's direction. "Will Sieur Horembaud provide the animals Loredan and Salvatore need, do you think? or will he force them to buy others? He will have two asses free with Frater Giulianus remaining behind." Ruthier gazed in the direction of the pilgrims' table.

"He cannot abandon them because they are leaving: that would break his vow. He'll provide the camels, asses, and horse that is requested or his pilgrimage will be in vain; Frater Anteus will not be able to vouch for him to the Church." Sandjer'min nodded to Ruthier, then turned and moved through the dining room as quickly as the crowd of diners would allow. And all the way to the door, he felt Margrethe's eyes upon him, as hot as the fires that burned to cook the calf, and goats, and sheep, and fowl.

Text of a letter from Aba'yam Elshaday of the Coptic Christian Chapel of the Holy Spirit at the Gold Camp to Respected Bebe Moges, at the Coptic Church of Jesus the Redeemer in the ancient town of Anibe, carried by courier monks and delivered fifteen days after it was written.

To the most holy teacher and leader, the Respected Bebe Moges, at the Church of Jesus the Redeemer, the devoted salutation from Aba'yam Elshaday at the Chapel of the Holy Spirit at Gold Camp, on this, the third day of June in the Christian Year 1225.

Most holy Bebe Moges,

After long consideration, meditation, and prayer, the

monks of this church have agreed that it is our duty as Christians to continue to provide food for the leper colony, four Roman leagues distant from the Gold Camp, for another year. Their oasis is small and the heat of summer is severe, but they do have a spring to give them water, and so long as we bring them food, they will not starve. The caves around the spring provide them shelter, and we have given them blankets for when the nights are cold. We include them in our daily prayers, and we carry such messages as they entrust to us, all in the spirit of charity. I fear that if we have another summer this year as we did last that the lepers may have to find another location for their colony, for the heat has been greater than before, and at some point, their spring may prove insufficient. Already we have heard that many of the small springs that run along the flank of the hills are lower than they were last year, and may dry up entirely.

One of the lepers, a man from the County of Austria called Jaroslaw, has died and the leader of the colony asks that notification be sent to the Templars in Alexandria so that the dead man's family may know his fate. Four more of their number have shown a marked worsening of their affliction and neither we, nor their leader, expects them to sustain life much longer.

There are three new lepers in the colony: Gabra, a goldsmith, an Abyssinian; Simeon, a guide, the son of a Greek father and Egyptian mother, who has a wife and child in Abydos; and Sieur Arnoul, a Roman Christian knight fighting the armies of Islam, from a place called Brabant, who asks that no notification of his condition be made, for he would rather be thought lost or dead than have it known he has the White Disease.

We were also informed by the leader of a company of pilgrims, one Sieur Horembaud, bound for the Chapel of the Holy Grail, that one of their company died as a result of putrescent burns; he was put in a winding sheet and left

high in the rocks at what is probably the place called The
Sighing Stones, *where the wind blows almost constantly.
The dead man, Torquil des Lichiens, was an excommunicated Templar seeking redemption through penance. Sieur
Horembaud asked that we notify his Order; if you will
grant us permission, we will do so. We must also inform you
that one of Sieur Horembaud's company, Frater Giulianus,
has asked to join our numbers to assist us in tending the
sick. He understands that means treating lepers as well as
those with cough and broken bones and burns of all sorts,
and he says that he is willing.*

*You spoke recently of your desire to see our Chapel of
the Holy Spirit enlarged, with a greater number of monks
among us, and two or three more priests. I would welcome
such a change, that we might demonstrate our faith more
completely to those who work the mines here, and who cater to the travelers who pass this way. It is a great task for
us to provide the Christians who come here with the comforts of our shared faith. During the cooler half of the year,
there can be as many as one thousand men in the Gold
Camp, miners and travelers combined; had we more monks
to attend to them, we might increase the respect and dignity
of Christians who pass through our gates. The men of Islam
have established themselves in a most persuasive way, and
we have lost souls to them. If our chapel were a church, or
a monastery, those who have turned away from our religion may see the advantage of returning to it. I, and the
seventeen monks living here, thank God for your plan, and
we pray that the day is coming when your wish is made
manifest here in Gold Camp. We await your orders and we
thank God for your kindness and greatness of soul.*

Amen
Aba'yam Elshaday
The Chapel of the Holy Spirit
Gold Camp

5

If it had not been for the thorn-bushes growing out of the rocks, they would have missed the well completely, for the wind was coming from the southwest, bearing only the scents of the desert, not the tempting aroma of water hidden in the rocks to the northeast. They had left the Gold Camp six nights ago and had been making fairly good time along the sandy wastes for this time of year. The thorn-bushes, spiny, unwelcoming, and sparsely leaved, jutted out from the pile of boulders, and wreathed around the base of them, concealing the dark blot in the sand. It was well past midnight and the pilgrims had been following the ill-marked trade route for more than half the night, going along the hip of an escarpment that gradually sank into the sand, and now could be traced in rocky spurs and boulders lying along the same line as the ridge had done.

Sandjer'min rose in his stirrups and pointed off to the left, his night-seeing eyes fixed on the spindly plants. "There! The Daughter of Water!" he shouted, while behind him, the company straggled to a halt; it was nearer dawn than midnight and the demands of the night's travels were telling on the pilgrims. Everyone was tired, and most were thirsty, so that the promise of water was more tantalizing than the urge to continue on.

Two of the horses raised their heads and one of them whickered. "The spring! God be thanked!" Frater Anteus exclaimed.

Sieur Horembaud, who had taken the lead on the narrow track that forced the company to go single-file rather than in the safer two- and three-across formation they had used for most of their overland journey, pulled in sharply, and shouted, "Follow Sandjer'min!"

A few of the company had been dozing in their saddles, and now were jarred awake as their mounts hurried to get as close to the water as they could, for although the pilgrims' company still had two days' worth of water in their casks, by now it was brackish, and the spring was fresh and sweet.

The spring itself was in a deep recess in the tumbled rocks, the thorn-bushes sprouting out between the smaller boulders; as Melech bore him to the base of the cluster of rocks, Sandjer'min swung out of the saddle and began to climb up toward the spring, following the damp patches on the rocks; the gelding stood expectantly at the foot of the rocks while the rest of the company came up, Sieur Horembaud in the lead, on the copper-dun mare he regarded as lucky, and whom he rode in spite of her occasionally favoring her leg.

"Get me some pails," Sandjer'min called out, and held up his hands to catch the first one to be tossed to him.

Carlus flung one up, missed, and grabbed it as it clanked down the flank of the rock.

Ruthier took some mid-weight rope, tied it in a knot, and flung it upward to Sandjer'min. "You'll need this!"

"I will," Sandjer'min agreed, snatching the rope out of the air, and immediately after grabbing Carlus' pail. He tied the rope to the pail, lowered it down through the gaps in the rocks to the spring, wriggled the rope so that the pail would turn on its side and sink. As soon as he felt the pail drifting downward, he pulled it up and lowered it down to the waiting pilgrims and their animals. "Tie on another pail!" he called down. "Keep them coming. The Daughter of Water is deep enough to fill all our casks five times over."

The pails tied to Sandjer'min's rope made twenty-nine trips up the rocks and into the spring before the casks were all once again filled with fresh water and each one of the animals had had sufficient water to drink. Sandjer'min tossed down the rope with the last pail and made his way down to the ground, brushing off the front of his black cotehardie before gathering up the rope. He stood for a few moments in silence, then said, "The next water is four days away, according to what we were told. Firouz, what do you think?"

"Four, perhaps five," he replied with remarkable calm.

"Then we ration for six, or seven," said Sieur Horembaud, striding purposefully up to Sandjer'min. "You did well. We would have had a hard time of it had we not restocked our casks."

"Firouz would have seen the spring if I had not," said Sandjer'min.

"Do you think so?" Sieur Horembaud asked, his dubiety un-apologetic. "Why would he?"

"Because he is part of this company, and he, too, is thirsty," said Sandjer'min. "He has been this way before."

"He would have seen it," Heneri interrupted, having overheard this exchange. "He was watching for it, too."

"Be quiet, whelp," Sieur Horembaud told the young man.

Heneri said something in Arabic that did not sound flattering.

"Amend your tone," Sieur Horembaud barked out, adding, "Perhaps you should not study Arabic any longer."

Heneri shook his head and took a step back. "I meant no disrespect," he said in exaggeratedly proper Anglo-French.

Most of the pilgrims had not yet remounted their animals, and a few of them began to offer their opinions, only to be cut short by Sieur Horembaud. "Dawn comes early these nights, and the days are long. Spare your words until we have stopped to rest at dawn," he declared. "We need to go another two leagues before we make our camp for the day. So you pilgrims and your servants and slaves, prepare to move on."

Everyone complied; before he mounted his camel, Micheu de Saunte-Foi stopped beside Sandjer'min, saying very quietly, "Be on your guard, Sidi. Sieur Horembaud is jealous of you."

Sandjer'min nodded and vaulted into Melech's saddle, gathering up his reins and taking his place in the line of march. In the last few days, he had wondered if this might be the cause for the tension growing between him and Sieur Horembaud. He had thought it unlikely; Sieur Horembaud had no reason to be jealous of a foreigner. His opinion had been that Sieur Horembaud was worried at their slow progress and expressed his concerns by fixing the blame on someone in his company who was not a pilgrim, or a Christian. Now, in his second-in-line position in the pilgrims' caravan, he let himself think again of the possibility of jealousy as he listened to the faint whistle of the desert wind; he began to realize that he might have been wrong before, and Micheu de Saunte-Foi right, a perception that troubled him for all the last of the night's march.

When they made their camp in a flat stretch of hardened earth, the eastern horizon was paling, a high, thin haze making the edge of the rising sun shine like a polished metal shield in the east; there was little sand drifting over the baked ground. The track of the trade route they were following was readily discernable in the long-shadowed sunlight, a shallow rut running almost due south, and lost in the sands about half a league ahead. The animals were weary, so Ruthier ordered the men assigned to guard them for the first half of the day to feed them well, providing them with a handful of grain for the horses and asses, and three or four dried figs for the camels. He, himself, undertook the task of grooming the horses and asses, assigning the camels to Baccomeo, who glowered but consented. While Ruthier, Olu'we, and Baccomeo attended to the animals, the tents were set up by Ifar, Vitalis, and Carlus; as soon as the pilgrims' goods had been properly stowed in the lee of the tents, there was a general rush to get to bed before the day grew any hotter and made sleep impossible. Frater Anteus led them in brief morning prayers, reminded them of their pilgrims' vows, and made his way to his place in the tent he had shared with Frater Giulianus and now shared with Vidame Bonnefiles. Agnolus dei Causi was given the command of the first watch, and Jiochim Menines would be wakened at mid-day to command the second. All the rest sought slumber just as the sun heaved itself into the eastern sky.

The camp drowsed through the morning and into the afternoon, the animals keeping under the shadow of their sail-tent as much as they could, the pilgrims in their pavilion-tents, the servants and slaves keeping to the shade of the stacked chests. The sun rose higher, the sands grew hotter, even the wind was reduced to nothing more than a low, slow breath; the pilgrims' company lay suspended in the heat.

At mid-afternoon, the peace of their rest was shattered by a loud cry from Sorer Imogen's tent, the one she shared with Margrethe. It tore at the stillness; when it came the second time, it was more distressing than before.

Everyone came awake, a few of the pilgrims looking about for anything they could use as weapons to defend themselves. Sieur Horembaud came roaring out of his pavilion, his bow and three arrows in one hand; his hair was mussed from sleep and he was not yet wholly awake. "What is going on!" he bawled; his camisa was damp and clung to his chest and shoulders, revealing his profusion of coppery hair.

Sandjer'min, who had been grinding herbs in a pestle, emerged from his tent, his light-olive skin lighter than usual, his cheeks a bit hollower; only Ruthier noticed, and it bothered him. "It sounds as if someone has had a bad dream," Sandjer'min said as the shrieks gave way to hysterical weeping. "No one is approaching the camp, and the wind hasn't got stronger."

The pilgrims remained wide-eyed and edgy; Sieur Horembaud looked around, trying to discern who, among his company, was missing.

The shriek came again, at a higher pitch, this time with a new element of gagging horror in it. There was a short silence for a breath, and the keening resumed.

Olu'we began to pray in a soft, steady murmur.

"Sounds like one of the women; men don't cry like that," said Micheu de Saunte-Foi as the scream got louder. He looked about at the faces around him. "Only Lalagia is with us. The other two women are not."

"Sandjer'min, go to their tent and make sure all is well," Sieur Horembaud ordered, who then gave his full attention to his company. "All of you: stay out of the direct sun. We don't want another of us dying as Torquil did. Get into the shadow of your tents if you don't want to go into them."

Vidame Bonnefiles muttered something under his breath, and faced Sieur Horembaud. "We must prepare for danger," he announced. "A scream like that means trouble. There could be a beast stalking us, on four or two legs."

"The guards didn't see either," Sieur Horembaud told the Vidame.

"Perhaps the stalker is keeping its distance," Vidame Bonnefiles said, undeterred from his purpose. "We should make ready to defend ourselves."

"Not yet, I think," said Firouz, watching Sandjer'min walk toward the two women's tent. "Only the woman has trouble. The animals are calm. This is dangerous to just the woman."

"Unless God is working to command us," said Frater Anteus, his handsome features made less attractive by the repellant turn of his mouth. "I wouldn't want to have to deal with any woman who screamed like this."

The nearer Sandjer'min got to the flap, the more he worried that Margrethe had had a nightmare in the heat of the day; it had happened to him more times than he cared to remember, in those long-ago centuries at the Temple of Imhotep. He paused before he raised the flap, calling out, "Bondame Margrethe? Are you well?"

Almost at once, the flap was lifted and Margrethe motioned him to come inside. "It's Sorer Imogen," she said. "I think she's had a vision."

"A vision?" Sandjer'min repeated. "May I come in?" he asked for form's sake. "What kind of vision?"

The howling was growing rougher, a sign that Sorer Imogen was getting tired.

"If you would, please," said Margrethe, relief making the words rush. She took two steps up to him, and indicated the sheet that divided the interior of the tent down the middle. "Sorer Imogen is . . . lying down on her pallet, all in a knot, and you can hear how she is weeping."

"Indeed," he said, for the wailing was loud enough to require both Sandjer'min and Margrethe to raise their voices to be heard over Sorer Imogen's sobs. "Have you any thoughts on why she is so distrait? Has she told you anything of her vision?" He could feel her pulse, and it distracted him; he forced himself to ignore his esurience and her burgeoning passion.

"Not directly, no," Margrethe said, not meeting his eyes, aware she should not be in his company for the danger of his presence. "How could she, when she is so overcome with horror?"

"Then we must pursue our answers without her. You are closest to her," he said, speaking as sensibly as he could, trying to find a way to diminish Margrethe's dread. "How has she been of late? I have seen her praying at all hours of the day, when the rest of the camp was sleeping. Has she exhausted her strength in her praying?"

Margrethe laid her hand on his arm and started to lean on him, then pulled away as if she had been burned; she was sorry now that she had not taken the time to pull on her pilgrim's habit, for in his company, she felt vulnerable to things she knew it was a sin to think on. "I have told her that her constant prayers have been too zealous for our travels, that she would do well to curtail her observances," she explained, speaking more loudly as the wailing from the other side of the tent grew louder again. "Since Torquil died, she has become increasingly despondent. She has said that all of us have failed to honor our pilgrims' vows and are getting a foretaste of Hell for our sins. I tried to tell her that this place is always hot through the summer, but she . . . she . . . doesn't believe it." Margrethe took his arm, and this time did not release it. "She will strike out at you if you approach her. She has slapped me once, and attempted to bite my hand." She held out her right hand, which bore the beginnings of a formidable U-shaped bruise from the base of the thumb to the middle of her palm.

Sandjer'min looked at it quickly. "Such a bite can be dangerous; I will dress it for you later," he said with far less anxiety than he felt; at least, he thought, the skin is unbroken. "Can you move your fingers and your wrist?" he asked.

Margrethe demonstrated that she could, saying impatiently, "Go through to her, but be wary."

"I will," he said, as much to reassure her as to show he was prepared for Sorer Imogen's distressed state. "It was good of you to warn me."

"I want to help her—I tried—but there's nothing I can do," she said, condemnation for her own fear making her explanation harsh.

"Will you get a cup of water, Margrethe? And hold yourself ready for my call to bring it to Sorer Imogen?" he asked, wanting to provide her something to do other than to listen and worry. "Her throat will be dry, and water will help calm her." It was not entirely true, but the very act of drinking it would impose its own relief.

"Yes," Margrethe said, and moved away from him.

Sandjer'min went around the sheet, taking stock of what he saw: Sorer Imogen was, as Margrethe had said, curled into a ball at the foot of the pallet that served as her bed, her rosary wound around her hands; her eyes were closed tightly. Pale strands of close-cropped hair stuck out from her head at odd angles, testimony to her hot, troubled sleep; there were bruises on her face and hand where she had struck herself with her rosary beads, and her sweat soaked most of her rumpled night-rail, smelling bitter and civet-like. Her light coverlet had been flung off her during her slumber, and now lay in a tumble at the side of her pallet. She continued to screech, as if in the throes of an appalling dream that held her more completely than the reality of their journey could.

"*Salva me. Salva me. Salva me,*" she screamed, and let out another agonized cry.

Going down on one knee beside the distraught nun, Sandjer'min touched her shoulder very lightly, noticing as he did that she was hot even for this place. He moved his hand near her mouth, and felt the heat of her breath as she screamed. When she took her next breath, Sandjer'min spoke her name, quietly but with enough authority to demand attention. "Sorer Imogen, the day is ending. We must be on our way."

Sorer Imogen blinked, then struck out with her hands, now made into fists with the added power of rosary beads that were still in her hands. "*Apage, Satanas!*" Her second blow caught him on the shoulder; the third struck the edge of his jaw.

He did not attempt to move away. "I am not Satan. I am Sandjer'min," he said in the same steady voice. "You are sleeping, Sorer Imogen, and it is now time to waken. You are making yourself ill."

"No, no, no," she whimpered, drawing herself into an even smaller ball, her knees jammed against her chest and under her chin. "No, no, no, no."

"You must. As a nun, you must turn to God," he said, hoping it would break the grip fear had upon her. "Come. Open your eyes. I will help you to your feet, and Bondame Margrethe will bring water to soothe you."

"Go away, Demon!" she yelled, and hit him on the nose with her rosary's crucifix. "Be gone, in the Name of the Savior."

"I am Sandjer'min," he repeated, doing all he could to spare her more abrupt measures. "I am here to wake you. It is late in the afternoon and we must soon have our supper, break camp, and continue southward. You have pledged to travel to the Chapel of the Holy Grail."

She went limp and silent, then she began to strike herself in the face with the heavy beads of her rosary. "It is all doomed. We are bound to Hell," she said, sounding half-asleep and disoriented. "Our pilgrimage is hopeless."

"How could that be?" Sandjer'min asked, to keep her talking.

"Vanity, vanity," she murmured. "It is an unforgivable sin. Vanity. All is vanity . . ." Her voice began to trail off.

Sandjer'min knew it was dangerous to allow her to drift back into her dream; he spoke a bit louder. "Your sister-in-law is waiting for you to rise, so that the servants can make ready to depart. You, yourself, need to rise and dress yourself so that the servants may attend to their chores." He gave her a little time to pull herself out of whatever part of her dream still held her.

From her place by the curtain Margrethe said, "If it would help, I will send for Frater Anteus."

Sorer Imogen blinked, and faced Sandjer'min without truly seeing him. "Spare me that," she pleaded, as if aware of his presence for the first time.

"Spare you from what, Sorer?" he asked, coaxing her into wakefulness.

"The visions. God has shown me Hell, that it is all around us." She shuddered, her face set in a rictus of horror.

"Then Frater Anteus will help you to be free of—"

"No. No. Not that one," she said, for the first time opening her eyes without the dazed look of lingering sleep.

"Then who among the clergy?" he inquired.

"None of them. Not the monks in the company. Not them. Not them. No. The unfrocked one. D'Urbineau. I will tell him what has been revealed to me. He may hear my Confession." She now sounded slightly drunk, which Sandjer'min knew was impossible; the dream had not yet released her.

"If you will rise, I will leave you, or send in Bondame Margrethe to assist you. It isn't fitting that you should face a man, even one in holy Orders, in your bedclothes." His manner was unflustered, but it concealed his growing alarm; it was more than illness that had brought about her daytime nightmare. Soft words and quiet persuasion would not diminish the power of Sorer Imogen's dream, he realized, and so he got up from where he was kneeling and said, "I shall send Bondame Margrethe to you, and then I'll ask Cristofo d'Urbineau to come to listen to what you have to tell him."

Sorer Imogen had made it as far as her knees, where she remained, praying softly; she seemed wholly unaware of Sandjer'min's presence.

Margrethe was waiting as he came around the end of the sheet. "She is awake?"

"Not fully, no, but I suspect she will be in a little while. She wants to talk to Cristofo d'Urbineau."

"Why? The man is defrocked. It would be heresy to—"

"Do not fret, Bondame," Sandjer'min said as gently as he could.

"But how can I not? She is here for the purpose of restoring my husband—"

"Her brother," he reminded her.

"Whatever the matter, she would not be here but with me. She is suffering because I have brought her here." She wiped away her tears, not willing to sob. "Were she still in her convent, she would be spared all this."

"You don't know this, Margrethe. Bad dreams know no limits, neither in place, nor in persons." He took her chin in his hand and turned her head so that she would have to look directly at him; he could sense her yearning for succor and the solace of his kindness, and something more she refused to contemplate. "Whatever has happened to her, you are in no way to blame for it: believe this."

"If it were not for me, she would not be here. How can this not be my fault?" Now she pressed her lips together to keep from sobbing.

"If it were not for your husband's injuries, she would not be here, nor would you, nor would Heneri," he reminded her with as little harshness as he could. "You three came for the same intent."

She gave him a look of tentative hope. "Then perhaps God is testing us? Perhaps this is for the good of our souls."

"Perhaps," he said, keeping his doubt from his tone. "I have to fetch d'Urbineau. Give her the water if you will while I find him."

"Shall I dress her? It would not be right for her to receive d'Urbineau in her night-rail."

Sandjer'min shook his head. "You might try to gather her coverlet around her, but she might fight you about clothes, and she has bitten you once already." He took her free hand and kissed it. "I will be back as quickly as I can."

Margrethe did her best to smile, wanting him to stay near her and knowing he should not. "Thank you, Sidi. I knew you would help us."

Outside the women's tent, Sandjer'min paused long enough to scan the group of pilgrims gathered in the middle of the tents. A few of them milled about, but most just stood still in whatever shade they had found; only Sieur Horembaud spoke, his voice uncharacteristically low. Sandjer'min saw d'Urbineau standing with Frater Anteus, not far from Nicholas Howe, and he made for him, trying not to be distracted by the questions called out to him.

"I said, is she going to improve?" Sieur Horembaud bawled.

Sandjer'min stopped walking. "I don't know. She is quiet for now, and that's all to the good."

Sieur Horembaud came toward him. "If she is going to continue to shriek about devils, I must know."

"I don't know that, not yet. Right now she wants to talk to d'Urbineau. I think it best that she be allowed to do so, although the Church would not approve," Sandjer'min said quickly, hoping to forestall any on-going disputes about d'Urbineau's defrocked status. "It may teach both of them humility."

Sieur Horembaud scratched the stubble of his beard. "Do you think she would object if Frater Anteus goes with d'Urbineau? Then we could say he ministered to her, not d'Urbineau, and he could be a witness."

"She won't have Frater Anteus, and, before you ask, I have no idea why. In her present state I doubt she could explain it to anyone," Sandjer'min said. "For now, I think it best that she see only d'Urbineau, as she requested. When she is more herself, she may agree to seeing Frater Anteus."

"Is she possessed? Is that why she's asked for a defrocked priest?" Sieur Horembaud asked, and nearly held his breath for the answer.

"No, I don't think so; I think she feels safer with him than with Frater Anteus. She is overwrought and it will be better for her if we accommodate her. I believe she will abandon her terrors sooner if we provide what she asks for," Sandjer'min said quickly. "Furthermore, I think she has practiced too many austerities—she has fasted too long and slept too little—and it has left her prey to her worst fears; in her weakened state she has become prey to unwholesome dreams." He could see that Sieur Horembaud was not convinced, so he added, "She is also taken with a fever, so that may also account for her unhappy condition."

"A fever? What manner of fever?" Sieur Horembaud was now seriously alarmed. "What of the rest of us?"

"I doubt any of you will take the fever from her," said Sandjer'min. "I have an unguent your company may use to keep from taking the fever. I will see that all the company has some when I have finished with Sorer Imogen."

"Will you use it before you return to the women's tent?" There was an accusation of sorts in the question.

"It's more important that the rest of the company have the unguent than that I do," he said, and realized he had put it badly.

"But you will not use it?" Sieur Horembaud asked, his suspicions fully roused. "Why is that?"

"Because I am convinced the fever is not dangerous to me; those of my blood are rarely ill; you pilgrims have more use for it than I," said Sandjer'min in utter candor; since he had wakened from his unsuccessful death more than thirty-two centuries ago, no disease, no matter how deadly to the living, had the power to touch him.

"God will protect you?" Sieur Horembaud persisted.

Sandjer'min met his eyes. "We can discuss this later, if you insist.

For now, Sorer Imogen will need to speak with Cristofo d'Urbineau before we can travel on; night is coming, and we must make the most of it: this camp must be packed, the evening meal prepared and eaten, and all the animals watered before we—"

"Yes, yes," Sieur Horembaud agreed impatiently. "Have d'Urbineau attend to the nun. I'll get the servants to build the fire we will need to cook our supper, and then I'll have them start to break up the camp. You're right: we need to be ready to move out at dusk." He all but shoved Sandjer'min away from him. "Get d'Urbineau. I'll explain to Frater Anteus."

Sandjer'min nodded and went to find the former priest, trying to decide how best to present Sorer Imogen's requirement. He wished he knew how d'Urbineau had come to break the seal of Confession when he had explained the reason for his defrocking and this pilgrimage, for that would provide him with the means to approach the penitent priest.

"How did you get the woman to quit screeching?" d'Urbineau asked as he stopped rubbing sand out of the saddles set up atop their water-casks.

"I gave her my Word I would bring you to her," Sandjer'min said.

"What does she want with me?" d'Urbineau asked in patent disbelief.

"I can't tell you; she is still not recovered. Yet it seems that she wants you to be with her." He shrugged, not in indifference but to show his helplessness.

"All right, I'll come," d'Urbineau said, setting down the saddle he had been cleaning. "If she Confesses, I can say nothing of what I hear," he added. "I know the perils that attend on such lapses."

"So I understand," said Sandjer'min, taking the saddle from him and putting it with the others, tipped onto the front end on a wide cotton ground-cloth where all the tack was laid. "You will know how best to deal with her."

D'Urbineau crossed himself. "If she starts to scream again, I will not remain."

"I should think not," said Sandjer'min, and led the way back to the two women's tent, telling d'Urbineau what Sorer Imogen had said to him.

"Visions. Hah!" d'Urbineau exclaimed as they reached the tent. "Well, I'll do what I can, but it may not help."

"It is better to make the attempt, though," said Sandjer'min, and lifted the flap so they could enter.

Margrethe had dressed herself, and was just securing her simple belt around her waist when she saw Sandjer'min return, closely followed by Cristofo d'Urbineau. She smoothed the front of her blue habit and lowered her eyes. "Thank you for coming," she said to the defrocked priest.

"It is what a man of my calling is expected to do," said d'Urbineau with a sigh. "She has become quiet—that's something."

"Sandjer'min calmed her." Margrethe glanced at him as she said this, then quickly looked away. "I have said I will leave you alone with her: she has asked that."

"Does she also wish I leave?" Sandjer'min asked.

"Yes," she said, and began to apologize.

"There is no need to find excuses for her, Bondame," Sandjer'min said to her. "Come. I will give you a task to do so that the rest of the company will not pepper you with questions. We will not disturb Ruthier, who has laid down to rest." He lifted the tent-flap for her. "Keep to the shade for now."

"Where will you take me?" She sounded breathless.

"To the animals and their tack. Since d'Urbineau was cleaning it, and it must be finished, it would be fitting that you and I attend to it. The rest of the company is busy with their tasks already." He stepped out into the sunlight, and winced at the force of it; the hand he offered to Margrethe was steady enough.

"I'll finish here, then find you," said d'Urbineau, making for the sheet as the tent-flap closed between them.

Text of a letter from Pendibe of Dongola, a translator working Nilotic towns and villages from the Third to the Fifth Cataract, to Yemuti,

Coptic priest at the Third Cataract, written on papyrus in Nubian Coptic, and carried by a series of boatmen; delivered seventeen days after it was written.

> *Pendibe of Dongola to Yemuti at the Third Cataract, my report on the river:*
>
> I and my comrades have gone all the way to the place where the River Atbara joins the Nile, and everywhere people of the river are saying that the Inundation will begin sooner this year than last. Already the clouds in the south at night are filled with soundless lightning, and that means that the Nile will soon be high on its banks and racing. I, myself, have seen birds that fish at the water's edge make nests higher up the bank than is their habit, and so we must surmise that the Inundation is not only coming early, it will be a heavier Inundation than usual. Docks and landings may suffer if they are not properly cared-for, and those who hope to fish through the Inundation will be disappointed, for even nets may not be enough to catch anything. Boats may not be able to withstand the flood at its height, and should be pulled out of the water.
>
> The Blue Nile is likely to be more flooded than the White, at least at the beginning, so passage into the highlands of Ethiopia will be more difficult than usual. Some say that the Burning Mountains are creating the storms that flood the river, and it may be so, but I have heard nothing of eruptions, and as those mountains smoke often, I put little store by that belief.
>
> Traders in Nuri and in Baruta have declared that they will not venture into the mountains until the Inundation is over; they fear not only the floodwaters, but those things that often come with floods: landslides and collapsing roads. I take their concerns most seriously, for any trader who is willing to be slow to market must be certain that the risk of trying to go there is greater than the risk of lower

prices for their goods, and disadvantages in trade. Once the traders decide to move on, then there will be opportunities again to venture into the highlands.

If I should learn more, I will dispatch another report to you, but otherwise, this will be my last message to you until the floods recede and it is safe for fishermen and merchants to take to the river again.

In the Name of the Most Holy, may you abide in His favor.

6

"When you reach the foothills, you will need to have horses and asses only; you will not require camels, so I will take them, as we agreed, and I will find horses and asses for you to go on," said Firouz as he paced around the campfire, lit equally by the fading sunset and the flames, his attenuated shadow undulating over the rippled sands as he made his way from the fire-pit to the gathering company, and back again. "I will go to Nuri and wait for those seeking to cross the desert to the south."

Sieur Horembaud glared thunderously at their guide and translator as he heard Sandjer'min repeat in Anglo-French what Firouz had said. "Yes. Yes. We had an agreement, and it didn't include you leaving us," he said at last. "Now that we're a night's journey out from Baruta, you have decided to amend our terms?" Baruta was the market-village on the bank of the Nile between the Fourth and Fifth Cataracts where the river bent from its southwestern running current to a north-northwestern one; from Baruta, the Nile stretched up to the foothills of the jagged, green peaks of the Ethiopian Highlands. "All of you, keep your distance," he ordered the pilgrims.

"Circumstances change," said Firouz, unmoved by the fury in Sieur Horembaud's eyes. "The Inundation is coming."

"I would listen to him, Sieur Horembaud," Sandjer'min told him when he had translated what Firouz had said.

"You knew that when we started out; so did we, for the Inundation comes every year. There is nothing new in it," Sieur Horembaud reminded Firouz.

"Not quite every year; there are variations that are known to those who live on the rise and fall of the Nile," said Firouz and added to Sandjer'min, "Why not tell him what the monks at the Visitation Monastery in Sese'metkra recorded in their accounts? They go back centuries, or so I'm told by Olu'we."

"Do you think he would believe me?" Sandjer'min asked in rapid Arabic.

"He would, if Olu'we also—"

Sieur Horembaud interrupted. "What are you nattering on about?"

"Nothing to our immediate circumstances, Sieur Horembaud," said Sandjer'min, then added to Firouz, "Tell him what he wants to know. I'll make it intelligible to him."

"What difference does it make?" Firouz asked petulantly.

"Tell him, or we'll be here all night."

Firouz sighed profoundly. "Yes, I knew the Inundation was coming, but I thought we would have three weeks more to reach the separation of the Blue and the White Nile before the water rose, and it appears that we do not; the signs are for heavy rains, and early. As it is, you may have to delay going up the Blue Nile if the Inundation is increasing to full force in the next month, and will remain so through your July. This is not a matter of negotiated terms, it is a matter of nature. The route is perilous when the waters are rising." The guide lifted his right hand to show it was impossible for him to change the Inundation.

"And why do you believe that the Inundation will change so much, coming early? Do you understand God's Will, that you are certain? Well? What convinces you that the Inundation can—"

"Because I listened to the slavers we encountered yesterday, who told us what they had seen and heard at Khemra, ten days since; you didn't want any of your pilgrims dealing with them," said Firouz as if the answer were obvious. "But I will tell you now what I learned from them. They crossed the Nile at Nuri, and were warned there as well that the signs are for an early start to the flooding. They said they had decided to make for the coast at once and not wait for more trade on the river."

"More fools they," Sieur Horembaud muttered, which Sandjer'min did not translate. "And you believed them, did you?" he asked, fixing Firouz with a hard stare.

"Yes. I have seen them myself: there were lights in the southern sky for the last two weeks, in the clouds at night, at the edge of sight. You must have seen them, the flickers on the southern horizon?" Firouz stretched, craning his neck while he extended his arms. "So I will not risk my animals and my life to take you farther up-river. I will stop at Baruta."

"But if the Inundation is truly coming soon, you will have no travelers going north for many weeks. If you remain with us, there will be money in it for you. Isn't staying with my company a wiser course to take than staying at Baruta?" Sieur Horembaud protested.

Sandjer'min saw that Sieur Horembaud was more frightened than angry, but would never admit it; he realized he would have to proceed with care. He turned to Firouz, speaking before Sieur Horembaud could frame another question. "Is there no way a compromise can be reached? Surely you realize that you are putting the pilgrims in danger if you are not with this company. You will receive the full measure of pay that was agreed upon for your services. If you remain in Baruta, you will not be paid for the last part of the journey. No one but you knows the way into the mountains."

"There is the river. Any fool can follow it," Firouz said bluntly, then went on more reasonably. "You knew I would leave you at the division of the Blue and White Nile. I am going to do what is sensible and leave when we reach the trading station at Baruta," said Firouz, sounding more stubborn than before.

"But this is intolerable," Sieur Horembaud burst out when Sandjer'min translated for him. "You must go with us to that division of the Nile."

"I'm afraid I cannot take such a risk, not with early floods. You are facing a delay in travel, and you cannot get into the mountains without following the river. The course of the Nile is narrower here than in Egypt, and narrower still in the mountains. Where the river is contained in steep banks, it flows very fast, and will do so in short order. Allah has provided a warning, and I must heed it." He turned from Sandjer'min to Sieur Horembaud. "I have a family to support, and Allah does not require that I assume the hazards of others, especially not on behalf of infidel foreigners." He waited while Sandjer'min translated this, then added, "I am willing to help you to try to find a guide, one who will not rob you, or sell you."

Hearing this last from Sandjer'min, Sieur Horembaud had to struggle to contain his wrath. At last, when he could trust himself to speak, he said, "Gudjei told me you are an honorable man. Yet you are going to—"

Firouz nodded. "And so I am an honorable man. I have told you my plans, rather than simply desert you. I could take my camels and leave you during the day, while you sleep, but I haven't done that. I am willing to assist you to continue your pilgrimage, as I agreed to do at the first. And do not think to set your servants and slaves to guard me: I will not be constrained by men of that order."

"What do you call your departure? It is desertion, nothing less," Sieur Horembaud asked, his temper beginning to fray.

"I am helping you so that when I go, you will not be stranded; if I were to leave you now, taking my camels, you would very likely perish," said Firouz, adding to Sandjer'min, "Can't you make him understand?"

"I am trying," Sandjer'min said in Arabic, then translated Firouz's remark for Sieur Horembaud, adding, "It would not be prudent to depend upon a reluctant guide. If Firouz is unwilling, he may also be unreliable. You should be able to find another to lead your company. One who is trustworthy, perhaps even one who is Christian."

"Truly? And yet he"—he pointed at Firouz as if his finger were a sword—"is preparing to abandon us here at the edge of the Nile. I cannot permit him to do that. Tell him that he is abjuring his pledge."

When Sandjer'min had translated this for Firouz, he said, "I have offered to find you a guide, and I will. Others might leave you to your own devices, but you are entitled to my help, as I am entitled to reclaim my camels."

"Do you think any of this is acceptable to me? to us? You are a scoundrel, a caitiff." Sieur Horembaud's choleric visage warned Firouz to answer carefully.

"It does not matter if it is acceptable or is not." Firouz was doing his utmost not to challenge Sieur Horembaud. "You do not rule here."

"Neither do you, Firouz," Sieur Horembaud warned.

"No, but I have relatives and friends who ply the river, who know the lands to the south, and they have taught me much about its ways," Firouz said flatly. "And I do not harbor a madwoman, as you do, who will call all the demons of the desert to her before you can reach the mountains."

"It is our duty to care for the afflicted," Sieur Horembaud said. "Our oaths as pilgrims require us to minister to her."

"A woman who has lost her wits? A woman who speaks only to pray constantly, without understanding, and will do nothing more? She is a servant of God, or so she says when spoken to. If that is so, why does God not care for her by allowing her to say what she requires? Has He turned His Face from her? Or does He seek a sacrifice from her? Could it be that she is a harbinger of disaster?" Firouz watched Sieur Horembaud as Sandjer'min explained what had been said.

"Sorer Imogen has faith beyond most. She prays for our salvation, and her own." Sieur Horembaud spoke stiffly. "She has exhausted her body in the ardor of her faith."

Firouz laughed as he heard Sandjer'min's careful translation of Sieur Horembaud's words. "But what good will her prayers do you? She cannot guide you. You are strangers here; I am at home. She is a chain around your company, and may yet drag you to your death, if Allah so wills it." He sala'amed to Sieur Horembaud, then turned and walked away.

"Go after him!" Sieur Horembaud ordered Sandjer'min.

"And do what?" Sandjer'min asked, keeping his tone as neutral as possible.

"I don't know." Sieur Horembaud pulled at his beard, scowling. "Talk to him. He respects you. He'll listen to you. Persuade him to remain. Show him it is his duty to guide us all the way, as he agreed."

Sandjer'min glanced at Firouz, who was now at the improvised pen where their animals were milling about, making ready to start on their way; Firouz was talking to Heneri, their voices too low to be overheard. Sandjer'min shook his head. "I doubt that will work. He has already made up his mind, and pressing him is apt to make him more obdurate, not less."

"But we need him," said Sieur Horembaud, putting his big, square hands on Sandjer'min's shoulders. "You have a glib tongue, and you have the man's respect. You must know some way to bring him around to—"

"He has pledged to find us a guide, and I will hold him to it." He moved back a step. "Firouz isn't being unreasonable, for all you think he is. He knows Egypt and Nubia with the familiarity of home and years. If he says there is danger, I believe him." He shook off the jumble of memories he had acquired during his centuries at the Temple of Imhotep, and the occasional droughts that blighted all Egypt, and the occasional years of terrible floods that swept away villages, fields, livestock, and human beings; the Inundation was a gift of Hapy, the Nile's hermaphroditic deity, but it was a gift that was not always welcome. "Neither you nor I know what lies in Ethiopia, other than mountains and the Chapel of the Holy Grail. It is not just the roads we must travel, it is the people with whom we must deal. Firouz is right: any fool can follow the river, but a guide will know what to do among the people encountered, what is safe, what is dangerous, how to behave to win the good opinion of the people, and that is more valuable than camels and slaves and horses."

Sieur Horembaud glared at him. "If you will not do as I ask, Firouz isn't the only one who may leave us at Baruta."

Sandjer'min shrugged Sieur Horembaud's hands off his shoulders without effort. "That is your frustration talking, Sieur, not your good sense. You asked me to come with you, though you knew I had never traveled into the mountains to the south. You needed my command of languages to help you, and you need my medicaments to keep your company in good health. Send me away, and where will you find the soporific to calm Sorer Imogen. Or do you plan to leave her in Baruta, too, as Firouz thinks you will?" He inclined his head respectfully. "I must pack my chests and tent onto our beasts of burden, and I still haven't treated the pastern on the copper-dun for tonight's travel."

Sieur Horembaud scowled. "Say you will talk with Firouz again before we reach Baruta, that you will make him understand."

"You mean sometime tonight?" Sandjer'min inquired.

"Of course sometime tonight. We will have our night-time meal around the usual hour, and that will make it possible for you to seek Firouz out. God's Nails, man, whenelse should I mean?" Sieur Horembaud swore in French, his whole manner expressive of his disdain.

"I will talk with him—if he will talk with me—after we stop at midnight for our meal; I cannot promise you that his mind will change, but I will do what I can to explain what the company requires, and guarantee him better pay if he stays with us," said Sandjer'min, knowing whatever extra sums were to be set aside for Firouz would have to come from his own supply of gold; he walked away toward his tent, now lying flat on the sand as Ruthier busied himself folding and rolling it for packing. Two camels and two asses waited patiently to be loaded up for the night's journey.

"More unrest," said Ruthier in the language of Poland five hundred years before.

"And likely to increase," said Sandjer'min heavily; he made an attempt at shifting the subject. "What do you hear from Lalagia or Bondame Margrethe? They are sharing the burden of Sorer Imogen now, and I believe they have some degree of assessment of her condition they may offer? Do they think that Sorer Imogen is any better? I have only seen her once today, and that was early this morning, and neither Lalagia nor Margrethe could take time to speak with me." He paused. "Margrethe feels guilty for her desires, and has kept clear of me, to rid herself of the shame." His face, for a moment, revealed deep sadness.

"I have seen that," said Ruthier.

"So has the rest of the company," said Sandjer'min wryly. "I'm afraid I have to rely on your reports: has there been any change in Sorer Imogen's condition?"

"Yes," said Ruthier. "It was wise to provide a second dose of the tincture; it allowed all three of them to get some rest." He cocked his head. "Do you want to see the nun now, before we move on?"

"If she is unchanged, I will wait until we stop at dawn." He hesitated. "It is disconcerting to have days and nights vary so little in length through the year."

"It is," Ruthier concurred. "It makes it difficult to sort out the days and the seasons, there being so little variation." He was silent, then asked, "Is that why the men of Islam measure their time by the moon, do you think?"

"Possibly; the stars wheel overhead as the moon waxes and wanes—the sky reveals the time of year, not the desert," said Sandjer'min, and resumed his inquiry. "At mid-day, when you visited the women's tent, how did Sorer Imogen behave?"

"As I mentioned, she slept through most of the morning, thanks to your tincture of poppies. She has been groggy when she wakes, but that is the nature of the tincture. She may yet resume her prayers once she is fully awake again, but with the tincture to calm her, and without the passion that distresses the rest of the company. The last time Heneri came to see her, two days ago, she denounced him for terrible sins, including gluttony and apostasy." Ruthier glanced in the direction of the women's tent, one of the two still standing. "The problem this evening will be to get her onto her camel and belted in place."

"We've managed so far," Sandjer'min said, aware that there was more in Ruthier's words than a simple complaint. "Why the unease, old friend?"

Ruthier took a long breath. "Bondame Margrethe is worried about Sorer Imogen; the nun frets and curses in her sleep."

"Those who have struggled with the fumes of madness often do those things—you know this from Rakhel."

Ruthier nodded. "I remember her well; it was not so long ago— hardly more than four centuries. But Bondame Margrethe says that there has been a change in Sorer Imogen. Nothing so obvious as her first distress, but still worrisome." He lowered his voice, for he noticed Jiochim Menines lingering nearby. "She told me that Sorer Imogen is still not herself, that she is not as meek as she appears. It is not just her outrage at her half-brother, who she says is becoming an apostate, that troubles the Bondame, it is the things Sorer Imogen says along with all her prayers, things that are worse than curses. During the day, she chafes in her sleep, and does things that are unlike her. The Bondame wants to ask your advice, if you will speak to her when we stop at midnight. She does not want to cause gossip, but she needs to talk to you."

"I will try to do as she wishes," said Sandjer'min, seeming apprehensive; now there were two members of the company he would have to speak with when the company stopped to refresh themselves.

"She'll be most grateful," said Ruthier.

"Will she," Sandjer'min wondered aloud.

Ruthier paused in his gathering up of belongings. "What troubles Sieur Horembaud?"

If anyone but Ruthier had asked him, Sandjer'min would have fobbed him off with a facile phrase or two, but Ruthier received a direct answer. "Sieur Horembaud is not as capable as he would like to believe, and that is catching up with him; he is beyond his skills, though he cannot admit it, and that is a problem for all of us. Since he has been told that God is protecting him, he is sure that he cannot err." He helped to roll the tent into the heavy net that would keep the tent in place on the pack-saddle.

"How could he be the master he wants to be? He's a soldier, not a leader of religious; he wants to do his penance and return to battle, doesn't he?" Ruthier asked. "He knows very little of the desert, and almost nothing about the people who live in it."

"And nothing about Nubia or the lands to the south," Sandjer'min agreed. "He may still succeed in this pilgrimage if he keeps in mind what has to be done, and doesn't allow himself to be distracted by every minor problem confronting his pilgrims. As it is, he jumps at every petty inconvenience and pays no heed to greater difficulties." He picked up his red-lacquer chest and secured the bands around it. As he lifted it, he touched the concealed scabbard of his katana. "We may still need this."

"I hope it will not come to that," said Ruthier. He took the chest of Sandjer'min's clothes and tied it to the second camel's saddle. "They say we will be in Baruta tomorrow."

"The chances are good."

"Some of the servants think that Richere Enzo and his man will leave us there, as Loredan and Salvatore have done. And with Frater Giulianus staying in the Gold Camp, we cannot continue on if our numbers decrease much more." There was no emotion in his voice, just a simple recitation of information.

"Which of the servants think this will happen? Do they have guesses or are they actually informed?" Sandjer'min asked in the same level tone.

"Vitalis and Florien are certain, at least they're the ones talking about it," said Ruthier. "They are persuaded that Enzo will leave, and that he will take Ifar with him."

"How very awkward," said Sandjer'min in Imperial Latin.

"For all of us," Ruthier agreed.

"They'll want asses and camels, I suppose."

"No," was Ruthier's surprising answer. "Florien says that Enzo wants to remain in Baruta now that the water is rising, and then, when the flood is over, to ride the Nile down to Alexandria. It would not be difficult to find a Genovese galley to carry him home. Milano and Genova are at peace just now, or they were when we joined this company. Enzo believes it will save him time to go down-river, and entail less hazard than another crossing of the Nubian Desert. Enzo has lost his interest in what lies in the mountains. Ifar admits that to the other servants. Enzo wishes to return to Milano and his family. He has enough experience now to do a work on travel up the Nile, and that will enhance his reputation as a scholar; he need not depend on goldsmithing. It isn't necessary that he complete his pilgrimage to have enough material to produce a useful volume for other Christian travelers. His Bishop will accept his efforts, and grant him the position he is seeking, or so he claims, and Ifar says that he is convinced of it. He will gain the post of Episcopal Librarian and be an instructor at the cathedral school." His Imperial Latin was less precise than Sandjer'min's, having a suggestion of his Iberian origins in its cadences.

"It could be a dangerous voyage; the crocodiles at the First Cataract are hungry after the Inundation," said Sandjer'min, balancing one of the smaller chests on the off-side of the larger mule's pack-saddle while Ruthier did the same on the on-side.

"Yes, it could be a dangerous voyage," said Ruthier, "for more reasons than crocodiles."

"Well, worry won't change it, and it may be that Enzo will elect to continue on with the company, once he understands about the Nile in flood," Sandjer'min said, a small inclination of his head warning Ruthier that they were being overheard. "We must hope that there will be no more resignations among the pilgrims. It would be dangerous for all of us."

"Yes, it would," said Ruthier. "I haven't heard Ifar say anything about the possibility, and that keeps me from being wholly convinced." He adjusted the girth on the pack-ass. "The animals are thirsty."

"There will be some water tonight. By morning we should reach Baruta, and our casks will be refilled again," Sandjer'min said.

"Do you think that Firouz will leave the pilgrims?" Ruthier asked suddenly.

"Yes," said Sandjer'min. "Unless something changes."

"How do you mean, changes? What sort of changes could there be?" The question was unusually blunt for Ruthier, and the shine in his faded-blue eyes indicated he was not inclined to accept a simple assurance.

"The weather is starting to shift again, and could bring us another sandstorm; Firouz knows it, and Jiochim Menines senses it, too; both of them know the temperament of the weather here. As for Richere Enzo, he has discovered we are being followed. He's afraid that robbers or slavers are hunting us, and will come after us once we're beyond the Fifth Cataract." Sandjer'min had explained the last in the old Polish tongue. "Thank all the forgotten gods for the chatter of servants."

"What else can they do?" Ruthier asked. "The desert is usually silent but for the wind on the sand and the bells on the camels. After a night spent in silence, and a day of chores and exhausted rest, they speak to one another to keep from being overcome by the emptiness."

Sandjer'min studied Ruthier's composed features. "I ask your pardon; I had thought that they spoke out of boredom and to hear their own languages," said Sandjer'min, sympathy in his compelling eyes.

Unable to think of what to say, Ruthier asked, "Do you think the followers will attack?"

"Three men with three camels and two asses? No, I don't think so," Sandjer'min said ironically. "But if they are scouts for others, or vultures, hoping that we will die and they can pick over our belongings and take our animals if they're worth saving, well, that is another matter." He looked up at the darkening sky. "If our followers were captured, then he might change his mind, but otherwise, I wouldn't think so."

"How did Enzo find out about the followers?" Ruthier asked. "Do you think anyone else has seen them?"

"I expect Enzo saw them as we broke camp night before last. He kept looking over his shoulder as we moved south; he hadn't done that before. You say the servants don't talk about it, and no one of the pilgrims, other than Enzo, seems vexed. If anyone else is aware of them, I haven't seen anything to suggest it."

"That's unfortunate," said Ruthier, and went on with the last of their packing, adding only, "It's another cause for dispute."

"If it becomes a matter of discussion, you're right. I should make ready to travel." Sandjer'min said. He checked the buckles on the asses' pack-saddles, then asked, "Does it ever bother you, watching and listening to the servants?"

"No; I, too, am a stranger in this company, and I must use all the information I can garner if we are not to become more pawn-like than we already are, my master."

"That is a very disconcerting thought," Sandjer'min observed, and when Ruthier said nothing more, went to find Melech; the gelding had proven to have stamina as well as steady gaits, and a steady disposition so that he was alert without being skittish. Sandjer'min was planning to buy him from Sieur Horembaud when they reached Baruta.

The sands were thrumming by the time the company stopped for their midnight meal; fine sprays skittered off the crests of dunes, like spume from the tops of waves. Huddled around the small fire that Methodus Temi had built, Frater Anteus and Almeric supervised the preparation of chick-pea oil-cakes and wedges of firm, pale-yellow cheese taken from Sieur Horembaud's own supplies, the pilgrims strove to keep their meals free of the encroaching sand. Lalagia measured out water into their cups.

"This is not His Body," Sorer Imogen protested as Bondame Margrethe handed her a wide bowl of oil-cakes and a wedge of cheese; she let her spoon drop into the sand and began to weep softly, her head bowed, her hands resting on her knees as if they were numb.

"But you must eat," said Margrethe, a suggestion of temper in her voice.

"Not this, not this." Her quiet weeping suddenly became a scream, long and filled with agony and rage.

The rest of the company shifted about; Sieur Horembaud got up and went over to where Sorer Imogen was sitting on the sand, her legs folded under her, her bowl lying at a precarious angle on her knees.

"You must not do this. God will not reward you for this," she yelled.

"Sieur Horembaud," Frater Anteus cautioned; Vidame Bonnefiles and Cristofo d'Urbineau exchanged troubled glances.

Sieur Horembaud slewed around and glared at the monk. "You! Stay out of this." Then he turned back and slapped Sorer Imogen across the face with the full force of the back of his hand.

Shocked and appalled, Sorer Imogen went silent.

"Sieur Horembaud," Margrethe began, "she isn't clear in her—"

He rounded on her, lifting his hand. "Do you want the same?" he yelled at her.

The rest of the company had stopped eating and sat staring at the two women and Sieur Horembaud; Lalagia put down her water-cask and moved toward Sorer Imogen.

From his place by the fire, Frater Anteus said, "Think of your pilgrim's oath, Sieur Horembaud. You must guard against the sin of wrath."

Sieur Horembaud slowly lowered his hand and once again turned back to Sorer Imogen. "You will pick up your bowl and your spoon and you will eat. Then you will take your tincture and get back on your camel. We need to be at Baruta before sunrise, and by Mary's Tits, we will be." He rocked back on his heels, nearly oversetting himself. "Then you," he said, pointing at Margrethe, "and you,"—he singled out Lalagia, now only a few paces away from him—"will see to it that she remains meek and submissive while you get your tent and chests packed. Olu'we and Temi will help you." He glowered and walked away toward where two camels were being loaded with his belongings, including his crates of foodstuffs.

"We'd best obey him," said Noreberht lo Avocat, picking up his cheese in his fingers. "It's almost midnight now."

Olu'we began to eat steadily, saying through his full mouth, "I will rise to help you, women. You should eat now, too."

Temi mumbled something to indicate his agreement.

"Everyone should eat, and eat quickly," Sieur Horembaud shouted. "We have a long way to go."

"He says that every night," Heneri said, not quite loudly enough for Sieur Horembaud to hear.

The company took up their positions once more and resumed their meal. As if she were a wooden puppet, Sorer Imogen picked up her spoon and balanced her bowl more carefully as she began to eat.

Text of a letter from Kerem-al-Gamil, factor for the Eclipse Trading Company in Alexandria, to Atta Olivia Clemens at Lecco, written on vellum in Church Latin, carried by the ship *Starry Crown*, and delivered forty-two days after it was written.

> *To the most excellent widow, Atta Olivia Clemens, the respectful greetings of Kerem-al-Gamil, factor to Sidi Sandjer'min's Eclipse Trading Company at Alexandria on this, the 11th day of June in the Christian year 1225,*
>
>   *Esteemed Bonadonna Clemens,*
>
>   *I regret to inform you that I have had no word from Sidi Sandjer'min since he left the Monastery of the Visitation at Sese'metkra, bound for the mountains of Ethiopia. It may be that he has written and the letters have failed to reach*

me, or it may be that he has written and found no safe messenger to whom to entrust them.

I, too, share your concerns for the Sidi's safety, and at another time of year I might dispatch one of the couriers we have used to try to trace the band of pilgrims he has joined. But the Inundation is beginning in a short while, and that will make travel against the current difficult at best. Overland travel often ceases for the three months of summer due to the extreme heat, or those who do travel are compelled to do so at night, which may be what the Sidi is doing.

If I should hear anything of the Sidi, I assure you I will send you word at once, no matter whether the news is good or bad. And I will tender your greetings to him in the way you have asked by giving him your letter, which I will keep in my office in my closed chest. It is humbling to see such affectionate consideration expressed so clearly, and by a woman. But then, women are more perceptive in these matters than men can be, judging by the conduct of the European knights we see in Alexandria.

May God bless and guard you, and may you and the Sidi be reunited as soon as God wills it.

> *Kerem-al-Gamil*
> *factor, the Eclipse Trading Company*
> *Alexandria*

7

Baruta was a green frill at the northern edge of the bend in the Nile, the residents' part of the town running along the low bluffs that rose thirty-five hands above the river that was already two hands above its usual level, leaving the slip at the base of the cliffs half under water, and the barge that ferried goods and people across the river was secured to a pair of cedar columns anchored in the soil at the top of the bluff. In the western two-thirds of the town, palm trees and small plots of fodder, papyrus, flax, and vegetables spread out along the bluffs watered by a system of irrigation ditches that were kept filled by Archimedes screws located at regular intervals along the river-front. Back from the river where the farmlands gave way to desert, there was a travelers' quarter that included markets and inns. This was where the Coptic Church of the Nativity and a monastery housing twelve monks was located; on the other side of the travelers' quarter was a small mosque.

It was mid-morning when Sieur Horembaud's company arrived at Baruta, weary, hot, and hungry. A drowsy wind carried the scent of the fields to them, and made their animals restless.

"There," said Firouz, pointing to the gate in the high walls. "We go in there."

Sandjer'min started to translate, but Sieur Horembaud waved him to silence. "I got his meaning." He swung his arm, directing the company to follow him into the town.

The guard at the gate was a Nubian man with dark skin and well-defined muscles. A Coptic cross hanging from a thong around his neck, he stepped out to meet them; he inclined his head slightly, holding up a placard that showed an exchange of coins. In the full glare of the sun, his elaborate loincloth was rust-colored linen and he carried two spears and a wide-bladed knife. There was an exchange of greetings which Firouz spoke in Arabic, and then Sandjer'min repeated in inexpert but adequate Nubian Coptic, which was the guard's native tongue. After some general haggling, they finally arrived at an entry sum to be paid for the pilgrims to spend up to ten days inside the walls, money changed hands, the guard suggested the Waterbird Inn on the livestock square to Sieur Horembaud, pointing out which of three streets to take to reach the foreigners' quarter.

"Is there another inn you could recommend for Richere Enzo and his slave? He will be staying here until the Inundation is over, when he will take a boat down-stream. Since he is no longer of our company, I believe it is best that we part here." Sieur Horembaud waited for Sandjer'min to translate for him.

The guard spoke quickly, and Sandjer'min told Sieur Horembaud,

"There is a small inn, the Old Grain-House, that should suit him. It is near the monastery. You follow the second street to reach it."

"Thank him for me," Sieur Horembaud said.

"It is my duty," the guard said, then stepped aside to admit the pilgrims, remarking as he did in Nubian Coptic, "You are into the beginning of the Inundation; you will have to use much caution when you travel on."

"We will; we still have a long way to go," said Sieur Horembaud through Sandjer'min, who added, "Thank you."

"You show great faith, keeping to your pilgrimage despite the Inundation," the guard told Sieur Horembaud. "Most pilgrims abandon their quest once the water rises, or remain here until the river drops; they would rather face winter in the Ethiopian Highlands than the Inundation on the Nile. May God bless you for your piety, that you place your trust in Him to protect you. May He keep you safe."

"God bless you, too," said Sieur Horembaud, signaling his company to follow him into the town. "Caution!" he muttered as soon as he was beyond the guard-station.

"I think it was good advice," said Sandjer'min. The sun was beginning to hurt him, giving him a headache and increasing vertigo; his native earth in the soles of his boots could not completely block the enervating impact of the summer sun. "The Nile in flood is ferocious; it is best not to underestimate its strength."

"So everyone keeps telling me," Sieur Horembaud grumbled.

"Then it may be wise to listen to them," Sandjer'min suggested. "Even that guard thought you will be taking a great chance."

"He may have reasons of his own to do that."

"And if he hasn't?" Sandjer'min asked lightly. "You would do well to consider his warning, or at least make your own inquiries while we stay here." He saw the shadow of figures in the upper rooms of the houses that lined the street. "We are being watched," he remarked.

"Of course we are," Sieur Horembaud said. "In market-towns like this, everyone watches strangers when they come."

Sandjer'min nodded, and said again, "Will you find out what you can about the Inundation and the road south? This may be your last chance to do that before we face the Nile's flood, once we set out, we may well be at the mercy of the river."

Sieur Horembaud thought that over, and concluded aloud, "He did seem a sensible guard; I'll ask around, if you will assist me." He drew up at the Waterbird Inn; he raised his heavy brows. "Enzo, you and your man go on to the Old Grain-House. I think it's that way. They'll take care of you until the Inundation is over."

Enzo, who was riding at the rear of the company, started to say something, then drooped in his saddle. "Should we leave our camel and ass here?"

"You have belongings on each, which you will want to unload yourself," said Sieur Horembaud. "Firouz will collect the camel and the ass from you before sunset." He turned to Sandjer'min. "If you will come with me, we will have a word with the innkeeper. We'll see if that guard steered us right."

"As you wish," said Sandjer'min.

"That guard—he probably gets a doucement from the innkeeper at this place."

"He is as reliable as anyone in his position is," said Sandjer'min with supreme neutrality. "And what man in his position doesn't expect doucements? Or commissions?" He had a brief, unpleasant memory of Telemachus Batsho, whose avarice, eight hundred years ago in Roma, knew no limits, and who invented taxes and fees for the sole purpose of filling his own purse. "This guard seems fair enough. He has no reason to discourage Christian pilgrims, being a Christian himself."

"Why do you say it that way?" Sieur Horembaud asked as he watched the first few camels sink down to allow their riders to dismount; Richere Enzo and Ifar moved off in the direction Sieur Horembaud had pointed. "You're suspicious of him? Why? The amount we're giving him is reasonable."

"Because we haven't left yet. Who knows what costs we may have to meet when we depart. He has no vows to fulfill." Knowing that he had blundered in giving voice to his concerns, and eager to correct his error, Sandjer'min swung out of the saddle and lifted Melech's reins over his head. "Is there a stable?"

"There must be; what inn lacks a stable? I'll want the copper-dun sound by the time we leave, if you have to treat her in a pasture," said Sieur Horembaud, clicking his tongue as he watched the camels Bondame Margrethe and Lalagia rode kneel down; the women dismounted and went to get Sorer Imogen off her camel. "What are we going to do about her? The nun? She's not getting any better, and you've told me you haven't very much of your calming tincture left."

"We will care for her," said Sandjer'min, looking around as two young men bustled out of the inn. "As your vows require you to do."

"My vows. Yes." He stared at the ground, and when he raised his head, it was to yell at Firouz. "Come here, you rascally rogue. You and I must talk."

Sandjer'min stepped aside so that one of the grooms could take Melech and the red-roan mare Sieur Horembaud had been riding to the stable. As the horses walked off, Sandjer'min translated Sieur Horembaud's orders, noticing as he did that Firouz appeared to have understood a large part of what the leader of the pilgrimage had said. Perhaps, he thought, it isn't only Heneri who is learning a new language. "We will go speak to the innkeeper, to see what he has to offer," he said to the rest of the company as they began to get off their animals. Olu'we and Methodus Temi gathered up the reins of the horses and asses as their riders relinquished them.

The Waterbird was a large hostelry built around a courtyard, and boasted a pond in the middle where reeds and other water-plants grew; fish swam among the stalks, feeding on the insects and scraps that landed in the pool.

"I didn't realize how dry I am," said Sieur Horembaud as he hesitated at the pool's side. "I think I will ask for a ewer of water for each of us, once we've arranged for our lodging. Some tea would be welcome, too. And perhaps a bath, if they have such a thing here." He looked around, taking stock of what he saw.

"Water, tea, and baths for everyone? including servants and slaves?" Sandjer'min inquired.

"Um." He went through the open arch into the central room of the place and shouted, "Guests have come."

Sandjer'min repeated this in Coptic, his voice at a much lower level than Sieur Horembaud's was. "Pilgrims bound for Ethiopia."

The landlord appeared, a middle-aged man with a skin of dark bronze, with short, curly hair that was graying at the temples, dark-gold eyes, and wearing a tan-linen garment that looked like a long smock, being pleated at the shoulder and tending to billow around his portly body when he moved. He bowed in the Coptic fashion. "You are most welcome. I see you have a company of pilgrims with you, but not so many that we cannot house you all. You are most fortunate. We have only a few guests at present, so room is no problem until the end of summer, when the caravans will come again. How long do you expect to stay? all through the summer, perhaps?"

When Sandjer'min had translated this to Sieur Horembaud, his response was, "Tell him no. We'll leave as soon as we find a trustworthy guide. Firouz! Come in here and tell this fellow what we require."

Firouz appeared in the doorway. "What is it you want me to say?" he asked, and waited while Sandjer'min translated. "Rooms for each of us, or shared rooms for all?"

"We need to allocate space as we do with the tents, assigning our comrades to rooms in pairs or more," Sieur Horembaud said when he heard the translation. "So, most of the pilgrims in pairs, the three women together, the servants and slaves three or four to a room, all in the same part of the inn, for our safety's sake. If the innkeeper can accommodate us." This last was sarcastic, since the Waterbird was conspicuously short of patrons.

Firouz explained this to the innkeeper when Sandjer'min finished relaying the message. "They will pay; they have paid me as we agreed, and have kept to the purpose of their pilgrimage; they will cause you no harm," he assured the innkeeper. "I have been with them for many leagues and many days, and I can tell you they will not withhold your money. It would be wise to offer them a low rate. The company is large enough that you can do that without any disadvantage to you."

The innkeeper smiled, and asked, "The man who translates, why doesn't he bargain with me instead of you? He speaks the language well enough."

"Because he is a foreigner, and I am not," said Firouz.

"Ahh," said the innkeeper with a wise nod. "An excellent reason."

Sandjer'min translated that exchange for Sieur Horembaud's benefit; he laughed and clapped Sandjer'min on the back. "You're a foreigner to all of us," he enthused. "For which I thank God. Keeps you from playing favorites." He nodded to Firouz. "But he's right. In a place like this, being a stranger has no benefit."

Firouz did not wait for the translation, making Sandjer'min think that he had indeed improved his understanding of Anglo-French. He leaned forward and spoke rapidly to the innkeeper, then listened intently to the innkeeper's answer. Then he turned to Sieur Horembaud, leaving Sandjer'min to translate. "The innkeeper will provide five rooms with two beds for a ducat for each room per night, or its equivalent in gold; he will also have two rooms with four beds for slaves and servants and monks. Your smith can sleep in the stable with your animals. The two rooms and the pallet in the stable will be another ducat. Food for the company can be negotiated later, as can feed for your animals. That would be six ducats a day, as things stand now. "

"Can you get him to go any lower?" Sieur Horembaud asked, and waited for Sandjer'min to relay his question. "I could get luxury in Alexandria for such a sum."

"But you are not in Alexandria," the innkeeper said through Firouz in Arabic. "If you cannot afford it, there is always the grounds of the monastery; they permit pilgrims to camp there for a small donation."

"It is a high price," Sieur Horembaud insisted.

"Alas," said the innkeeper.

Sieur Horembaud rubbed at his beard, then addressed Firouz through Sandjer'min. "Do you think he will go lower, or is this his price?"

"I doubt he will let you have the rooms for less. Business is slow now, so he is offering good value, considering the time of year and where we are. He would rather have you here than elsewhere." Firouz turned to Sandjer'min. "You will share your room with your manservant. The rest of the servants and slaves will sleep in one of two rooms."

"Thank you," said Sandjer'min, nodding once, then asked defer-
entially, "What about the women? That room for three?"

Now Firouz frowned. "It will take some arranging. He"—he
nodded to the innkeeper—"is not comfortable having women without husbands or fathers staying here."

"There is Heneri," Sandjer'min reminded Firouz. "He is young,
but he is half-brother to Sorer Imogen and half-brother-in-law to
Bondame Margrethe."

"He is too young," Firouz explained, a bit too quickly. "Were he
a year or two older, he might suffice, but fifteen and unmarried?
That would ensure nothing. In this place Heneri's presence would not
be deemed sufficient, not with Sorer Imogen in such travail." He
hitched up one shoulder.

"Then the women must stay together," Sieur Horembaud declared when Sandjer'min explained the problem to him. "That way,
none of our pilgrims' vows will be compromised, including Heneri's."

Sandjer'min spoke to the landlord in Coptic. "Give the women
your best room; they will need three beds; you will post a servant at
their door. I will pay for the room and the servant—would two ducats a night be acceptable?"

The innkeeper boggled at the sum. "Yes. Yes. Most acceptable,
Sidi," he was able to say as his eyes remained fixed on Sandjer'min's
face.

"They will need to walk in your courtyard in the evening, if that
can be arranged?" He studied the innkeeper's demeanor. "If you have
a female servant to wait upon them, I will pay for that service also." He
did not reveal that he had seen Sieur Horembaud's grimace of distaste.

"I have two female slaves. One of them will tend to your women."
The innkeeper put slight emphasis on *your*, then shook his head.

Sandjer'min chuckled. "Hardly mine. One of them is . . . unwell,
and I have been treating her. None of us wants to see her become
worse."

The innkeeper drew back in alarm. "I want no disease in this
place," he began, but Sandjer'min interrupted.

"Her affliction cannot be given to others, or I would ask her to
be housed apart from the rest of the company." He slipped his hand

inside the capacious sleeve of his black cotehardie and brought out a good-sized purse from which he removed thirty ducats and set them on the table between them. "Here. This should take care of the room for the women."

Sieur Horembaud was staring openly at the gold coins. "What's going on, Sandjer'min? What are you doing?"

"I am ensuring that the women have suitable lodging," he said in Anglo-French, and turned back to the innkeeper, speaking again in Nubian Coptic. "We will want water to drink, baths if you have them, then a large meal at mid-day, with tea as well as wine. I will pay for that. If you have ducks you can prepare, and eggs as well, they would be welcome; cook them with onions or garlic. Green beans, if you grow them in your fields, or peas. Do you have a young sheep or goat you could serve?" He saw the innkeeper's smile widen. "Very good. Then after the meal, we'll rest until late afternoon. All of us, including the servants and slaves. If your grooms will see to our animals, I will cover that cost as well."

"It is an honor to have so gracious a guest as you are," said the innkeeper, sliding the ducats Sandjer'min had paid him into a metal box set on a shelf behind him.

"Tell me what you have arranged," Sieur Horembaud demanded. "This is my company and I have to know."

Sandjer'min explained about the arrangements he and the innkeeper had agreed upon, then turned to the innkeeper once more. "Do you have baths? Simple ones would be fine."

"We do, and more extensive ones; pilgrims prefer them. They have a warm pool and a cool one, and couches for relaxing between the two," he said. "I will send servants to make them ready. In the meantime, I will show your company to your rooms, if you will have them come into the courtyard." He bowed and called out for three men, rattling off orders to them as they came into the reception room.

"What do we do now?" Sieur Horembaud asked Sandjer'min.

"Have your company meet in here. The servants will show them where they are to sleep once you decide how the men shall be divided up." He inclined his head respectfully, then went out into the courtyard and motioned to the seven pilgrims who had come into that part of the inn. "Rooms are being readied," he said, first in Anglo-French, then in the northern Italian dialect. "Sieur Horembaud will assign you as he thinks appropriate. The women will share a separate room."

Agnolus dei Causi frowned. "What about our servants?"

"That, too, is being settled." Sandjer'min waited while most of the company wandered into the courtyard, then told them, "There will be baths ready in a while. And after mid-day, a meal for all of us."

"Except you," Heneri interjected.

Sandjer'min paid him no heed. "When that is done, we can retire to our rooms to rest through the heat of the day."

Sieur Horembaud appeared in the door. "Come inside. We have worked out the arrangement for rooms. Firouz will assist you if you require it." He watched Sandjer'min through narrowed eyes.

"He doesn't speak our language," Vidame Bonnefiles complained.

Sieur Horembaud made an effort to control his temper, forcing himself to speak calmly. "Then talk to Sandjer'min. He should be able to handle all your questions." In spite of his intention, there was an edge of annoyance in this admission; he saw Bondame Margrethe and Lalagia leading a languid Sorer Imogen into the courtyard. "There's something being done for the three of you."

"God be thanked," said Noreberht lo Avocat.

"This woman needs your help, not your scorn," Cristofo d'Urbineau told Noreberht.

"Be quiet, the both of you," Sieur Horembaud snapped.

"It isn't good to keep the afflicted too close to the rest of us," d'Urbineau said.

"Then what do we do for the women?" Vidame Bonnefiles asked. "Find an empty house in the village they can occupy?"

"The women will keep to their quarters for most of the day, except to go to church if they desire to," Sieur Horembaud announced. "They will have their own servant to wait upon them, and their room will be guarded at night. They will be permitted to walk in the courtyard every day at sundown for as long as we are here."

Frater Anteus looked troubled by this. "For Bondame Margrethe and even Lalagia there is no difficulty, but Sorer Imogen? She cannot be left alone in their room, and it would not be wise to permit her into the courtyard. Who knows when another fit will come upon her?"

Vidame Bonnefiles said, "Frater Anteus makes a good point. Sorer Imogen must never be alone."

"Then I will sit with her, with a guard, if it is necessary," said Jiochim Menines.

"Do you realize you may be putting yourself in danger?" asked Sieur Horembaud. "And that she may accuse you of outrages on her person?"

"I have vowed to maintain my virtue on this pilgrimage," Menines said, unusually unflustered by the implications in Sieur Horembaud's questions. "I will continue to do so. You may have the servant watch her while I am with her, if you have any reservations about my conduct."

"For now, this will do," Sieur Horembaud decided. "All but the women, go inside and have your rooms assigned to you. Noreberht and Howe will have the same room. D'Urbineau and dei Causi will have the same room. De Saunte-Foi will share with me. Vidame Bonnefiles and Menines will share. Methodus Temi will sleep in the stable in order to guard our animals. Firouz will tell our slaves and servants where they are to sleep; he is making arrangements for himself and Heneri."

The pilgrims moved slowly inside, except for the three women; Sorer Imogen had dropped to her knees beneath a Coptic cross fitted into the wall, and was almost at once lost in prayer. Margrethe approached Sandjer'min carefully. "You are very good to my sister-in-law," she said, not quite looking at him. "I don't know how we could have got her so far without your help." How much his nearness unsettled her!

"Sorer Imogen needs care," he said, and touched her hand. "You have done well by her."

Now she looked at him with grateful eyes. "I hope I have. I'm at a loss where she is concerned. Nothing I do seems to ease her distress." Abruptly she seized his hand and kissed it. "I cannot thank you enough. Without your tincture, and all your help with her, I don't know what we would do."

He lowered his hand. "The servants are watching."

"Then they know that this is my expression of gratitude," Margrethe said with more force than she realized. "I am much obliged to you."

"You needn't be," he said, sensing her attraction to him more strongly than he had before, and her shame at her desire. "I have done what Sieur Horembaud has required of me." He saw dejection in her features, and a kind of hopelessness that troubled him. "But I thank you for your kindness, Bondame Margrethe. I am only sorry I can do so little for Sorer Imogen."

She moved an arm's-length away from him, color rising in her cheeks. "She is in God's Hands."

"Then we must hope He will be kind to her." He was about to move away when he heard Margrethe speak and turned back.

"I thought it would be different," she said, staring out the gate into the market-square. "I thought the pilgrimage would be . . . I don't know . . . *freeing* somehow, that if I observed the Commandments and maintained my virtue, I would be able to deliver my husband from his affliction. But it isn't freeing, or inspiring, and hasn't been from the first." She sat down on a simple bench built on the edge of the pond, her eyes still fixed in the distance. "The galley we boarded at Genova stank, the quarters were cramped, the seas were rough, and when we reached Alexandria, we were charged far more than we had expected for our lodging and food. Several of the Alexandrians said we were fools to go all the way to Ethiopia, that there were shrines and chapels in plenty in Egypt that would be sufficient to our needs. Frater Anteus, who joined us at Alexandria, was tasked to accompany us, to monitor us for the Church. He swore the same oath the rest of us did, but he also vowed to speak truth of our conduct when we returned."

"That is not uncommon," said Sandjer'min.

"It was just the beginning. Oh, Sandjer'min, how much I disliked it when we took boats up-river. We saw wonderful sights, but Sieur Horembaud would not stop to look at them because they were made by pagans as idols, and we could be accused of heresy or apostasy for our interest in them." She sighed wistfully. "I thought the Nile would be beautiful, like the Thames and the Gwash, framed by trees and faced by villages, but I didn't understand about Egypt, nor did I consider the dangers. Crocodiles and hippopotami in the water, and vultures and jackals out of it. Horrible beasts, all of them. Many, many cats everywhere, all of them capable of being possessed by devils, and lions near the river. Seeing Torquil burn slowly to death made me dread the sunlight on the water. Then, when we left the river to travel by night, other trials awaited us." She took a deep breath, trying to keep from talking, but unable to do so. "Journeying through the wastes was nothing like what our priests promised, who likened our pilgrimage to the Holy Family's escape into Egypt, not what we have endured, though it is supposed to benefit us, for those whom God loves most He tests most, therefore we should welcome our hardships and praise Him for His favor. It is enough to make one want to shout and scream, those hours of silence going through the night, only the wind and the sand making noise."

"But for Sorer Imogen," he said.

"Do you mean you think the emptiness and silence have driven her mad? Is that why she screams?" She turned to him at last. "Can such a thing happen?"

"It is possible," he said, pursuing the matter. "Has she always been very devout?"

"How do you mean?"

"She prays constantly for God to forgive her sins; are there really so many of them?" His voice was kind, but still Margrethe winced.

"Since I married her brother, she has been in Orders, and credited with true zeal," she said.

"Can you tell me something of her life before she entered the convent? Do you know why she took up the pious life?" Again, he spoke gently, and this time she rested her hand over his, saying nothing for a short while, then nodded.

"I'll tell you what I have been told." Margrethe spoke as if dazed, with little inflection in her words, as if saying them gave her relief beyond what she imparted to him. "Before he suffered his injury, my husband said to me that she had been a fervent girl, single-minded and disciplined more than most young women were; she supervised the maintenance of her chamber, she also insisted on learning to read, and was taught her numbers. She scorned religion when she was a child, according to Dagoberht, so much so that the priest said she could well be an agent of Satan, sent to put all of her family in peril. But then a new priest—one of the ardent preachers, who captivated her—urged her to seek for truth in God, to repent her unruliness and devote herself to acts of piety." She stared off into the distance, recalling those times as if she could see them before her. "For two years she resisted him, and then, when her step-mother died, she saw it was her sins that had brought it about. She professed her vocation when she was fifteen and entered the convent a year later after refusing two handsome offers of marriage, which the family had sought for her, saying she had much to expiate and would not drag a husband into her errors and wickedness. From that time on, she was a model novice and a highly regarded nun; many called her a living saint. I . . . I have thought, now and again, that her—" She broke off as Firouz came into the courtyard again. "I am saying too much."

Firouz sala'amed. "Your room is being made ready. It is beyond the kitchen. You will be guarded by the slave who sleeps in the storeroom." He glanced at Sorer Imogen. "She will need a slave to tend her."

"Choose a woman of steady temperament who will not be distressed or angry with her behavior," Sandjer'min recommended.

"I'll do what I can," Firouz promised, noticing the confusion Margrethe was attempting to conceal. "The baths will be ready shortly." He gave a quick glance in Sorer Imogen's direction, then stepped back into the reception room.

Margrethe hung her head. "I'm sorry, I shouldn't—"

He turned his hand over and held hers before she could pull it away from him. "I'm not. You speak what you feel, which is an honor to me, a sign of friendship."

She turned to him, the brightness returning to her pale-blue eyes. "Is that what it is?"

He did not quite smile, but he nodded. "If friendship is what you want it to be," he said softly.

Margrethe was about to speak when Sorer Imogen began to scream. With a little shake of her head, Margrethe rose and went to try to calm her overwrought sister-in-law, leaving Sandjer'min to ponder what he would use to quieten Sorer Imogen when he ran out of tincture of poppies.

Text of a letter from Heneri Gosland to Guillaume des Grossierterres, Seneschal to Sieur Dagoberht Gosland, Baron du Creisse-en-Aquitaine, Sieur of the fief of Saunt-Didier, written with ink on papyrus in Church Latin on June 17, 1225, delivered ten months later by Hospitaller courier.

> *To Guillaume des Grossierterres, Seneschal to my half-brother, Sieur Dagoberht Gosland, may God improve his capacity to think, on this last day that I am a Christian;*
> *Seneschal,*
> *In my travels, I have come to accept the teachings of Mohammed as more holy than those of Jesus, and I will profess my faith in the mosque in this town, Baruta, on the River Nile in the Nubian Desert, and then Firouz will take all the camels that are part of Sieur Horembaud's animals, replace them with horses and asses, which Sieur Horembaud's company will need for their climb into the Ethiopian Highland, whither they are bound; we will purchase our own animals.*
> *Sieur Horembaud's company has lain here at Baruta now for fifteen days, unable to continue due to Sorer Imogen's fits. I begin to fear that such afflictions are likely to occur in the children of my father's first wife, Elinor de Saunt-Norme of Brittany, for first my brother is incapacitated by a blow to the head ending in a fall, and now Sorer Imogen is reduced to praying constantly for all her sins, though what sins those might be, none of us can know. Firouz, who has been the company's guide and my instructor, and I will go to the oasis of the Three Djinni two days to the*

northeast, where I will finally study Arabic and the Qran, and will remain there until the Inundation ends, at which time we will travel back to Baruta to take up other travelers to guide them across the Nubian Desert to reach the Nile at Abu Simbel, a town of great antiquity and the crossroad for merchants from Darfur bound to Alexandria, and pilgrims returning from places to the south.

I ask you do not attempt to find me to dissuade me from my decision, for I am content that Allah has shown me the way. I had the same dream on five nights, when I bowed on a prayer-rug and was allowed to have a look at Paradise, at the gardens and the beautiful virgins who will serve me through eternity. I will take a Muslim name and live as they live. If I speak Church Latin or my native tongue again, it will be to translate for Muslim travelers dealing with Christians, as Firouz has done for Sieur Horembaud's company. I think it will be a good life, if Allah wills.

Tell my brother and Frater Misericorde what I have done and tell them that I do not do this to shame my House, but to follow where my faith leads me. The pilgrims may be distressed when they discover what I have done, but they may look upon it as God's test of the strength of their love for Him. I have no wish to harm any of them through my actions, but I cannot continue on this mission without betraying my beliefs, which would offend both Christ and Allah, for Jesus is a prophet of Islam, and regarded highly by the faithful, who venerate his memory and honor his teaching. I hope Sieur Dagoberht understands what I do, and remembers me with Christian charity.

I have written a letter to Bondame Margrethe, explaining what I am doing by declaring myself a follower of Islam to her, so that she will not worry for me, or imagine anything dreadful has happened to me. I have asked her to do what she can to inform Sorer Imogen of my conversion and my reasons for not remaining with the company, which she will do, if only to help contain Sorer Imogen's worries, for *she is apt to decide that I have been possessed or bewitched or some other malign influence has left me a victim of the wiles of Satan. She may add me to her constant prayers, for which the pilgrims will have to forgive me. Since Sieur Horembaud does not read well, I have also prepared a letter for the company's translator, Sandjer'min, who will be able to comprehend what I have set down and will perhaps be able to convince Sieur Horembaud of my sincerity in my decision, for Sieur Horembaud regards me as a youth, not a young man. With Sandjer'min's help there is a chance that he will convince Sieur Horembaud that I mean him and his company of pilgrims no disrespect.*

May Allah, the All-Merciful, open your eyes and your heart.

He who was Heneri Gosland

8

"Damn their pernicious souls to Hell!" Sieur Horembaud raged as he paced in the shade of the Waterbird's stable's mid-day shadow, his brow shining, and his pilgrim's cotehardie spotted with sweat on back and chest and underarms; his femoralia were wrinkled above the tops of his boots. He glowered at Frater Anteus, daring him to castigate him for swearing; it was two days since Firouz and Heneri had vanished, and Sieur Horembaud had not yet steadied his temper. "The Devil take all Goslands, root, stem, and branch! It's bad enough that Sorer Imogen is out of her wits, but Heneri departing to become a follower of Mohammed! No prayers will save him from Hell, not even Sorer Imogen's. What manner of House is theirs, that they have such creatures in it? All that's lacking now is for dire misfortune to befall Bondame Margrethe! She has been sighing after Sandjer'min for weeks. If she should allow more than that to happen, all the pilgrims will be suspected of breaking their vows, in their hearts if not in the flesh." He kicked at a barrel, almost knocking it over; an ass, tied up a short distance away, brayed in alarm. "Silence!" The ass brayed again.

"The boy should not have been put in Firouz's company," Frater Anteus declared. "There are reasons we pledged to limit our dealings with strangers."

"I'll do penance for allowing it to happen," Sieur Horembaud said, "I have to—the company is rife with gossip, and I must bear the brunt of it."

"Heneri is a feckless youth," Frater Anteus stated. "He was willing to be taken in by Firouz, and must answer for his laxness before God at the End of Days. I agree with the Vidame: Heneri should be disowned by his kin, and *Anathema* pronounced against him when our pilgrimage is over." He saw Sandjer'min enter the stable. "Had you done your duty and kept up your translating, not spent time weakening our mistrust of foreigners, this would not have occurred. You see what comes of encouraging conversation with strangers."

Sandjer'min knelt down in the straw, wrapping the on-side foreleg of the copper-dun; he looked up at Sieur Horembaud. "Yelling will not bring them back, either the Gosland heir, or the camels, but it will lead to more gossip in the town than there has already been," he said levelly. "If you can contain yourself, the rumors will cease."

"Let them gossip. What harm can it do us?" Sieur Horembaud exclaimed. "I am responsible for failing to require Heneri to ignore Firouz, not to accept instruction from him. I allowed myself to be blinded by your suggestions, Sidi," he accused.

"This turmoil can make it more difficult to find a new guide," Sandjer'min told him without heat or rancor. "That could lead to harm for the company, for which you are also responsible. The Nile has risen in the time we've been here, more than three hands, and it will rise at least ten more. The longer we must wait to leave, the more hazards are we going to face." He saw the obdurate thrust of Sieur Horembaud's jaw, and went on in less stringent tones. "Do as Frater Anteus recommends: declare your penitence and ask forgiveness. Trust your God to settle the matter for you. There is no cause for you to become choleric, and many reasons for you to seek a sanguine state of mind."

"So you would preach to me? You? Do you purport to embrace

this pilgrimage, take our vows? It's all very well to advise tranquility, but you're not a Christian, are you? How can you grasp what these turns of events mean to us? It does not strike at the heart of your faith to see a youth like Heneri turn away from the Church to embrace its enemy." Sieur Horembaud shuddered in disgust, then sat down on a simple plank bench. "Firouz deceived us, and there is nothing we can do to claim redress of wrongs, not while the followers of Mohammed rule in Egypt."

"We are not in Egypt, and will not be until we complete this pilgrimage. There are Christian churches throughout this country," Sandjer'min reminded him. "There is one a few streets away, with a monastery. The Coptic Church is still predominant in southern Nubia."

"Oh, yes. Islam is only just arrived in Nubia, and it moves cautiously; in Egypt, Christians may only live in Christian districts, and must allow their male children to be soldiers for the Sultan. What family would not be upset at this inequity? It is the task of Christian chivalry to contain the spread of Islam, and to preserve our faith." Sieur Horembaud shook his head, staring out at the horses and asses drowsing in the shade of a stand of palm trees. "To take our camels!"

"He provided excellent replacements in the six horses and seven asses he left us, and he was right to say that the camels would not help us when we climb up into Ethiopia. He has been fair to us according to his own lights. We would have to sell them and buy horses," Sandjer'min said before Frater Anteus could speak.

"The Devil lurks in soft words," Frater Anteus muttered.

Sieur Horembaud flung up his hands. "Another one of your facile answers. Tell me, Sidi," he said with overwhelming derision, "do you have any faith in our pilgrimage or is this all an amusement for you? Something to get you out of the monastery?"

"I rarely find travel in the desert entertaining," Sandjer'min said more sharply than he expected, remembering his journey across the Takla Makan, nearly seven hundred years ago. "I left the Monastery of the Visitation because it was becoming unsafe to remain."

"Then you do have faith?" Sieur Horembaud raised his thick eyebrows, looking now like a startled bear.

"When I was hardly more than a child, I was initiated into the priesthood of my people. I had faith then." He did not add that this had happened almost thirty-three centuries ago.

Sieur Horembaud shook his head. "So you were a novice. What ruined your faith?"

"I was captured by our enemies." He did not mention his execution by disemboweling, nor the centuries afterward when he exacted vengeance on all those who had contributed to or descended from those who had betrayed his family.

For once, Sieur Horembaud did not scoff. "That was hard. But perhaps God is giving you this pilgrimage to restore your faith, to learn from those in the company what faith can achieve."

"Twice blessed is he who repents his sins before God," Frater Anteus announced.

Sandjer'min weighed his answers carefully. "I know some of your company are sincere in their purpose, but you also have dangerous rascals in your numbers; they all, rogues and virtuous alike, deserve more than lambasting for keeping to their vows thus far." He knew Sieur Horembaud assumed he had been Christian, and that his captors had been Islamic, and had no intention of correcting this impression.

"Very worthy sentiments," said Sieur Horembaud with a prolonged, angry sigh that ended on a snort. "Foreigners!"

"Here in Nubia, I am not the only foreigner in your company." He said it easily enough, having grown accustomed to being a perpetual stranger. "Every one of us is in a strange land, except for Olu'we, and he is well beyond his . . . native earth." A quick, ironic smile tweaked his lips and was gone.

Sieur Horembaud muttered something under his breath, then folded his arms and glared into the distance. "All right, Sandjer'min, I take your point. We are in a bad position. Getting a guide is essential to our travels and no one in the company can fill that post at present. We must find a guide."

"Not an Islamic one," Frater Anteus interjected.

Sandjer'min was tempted to tell Sieur Horembaud that this had not been his meaning, but decided it was best to accept Sieur Horembaud's interpretation for the time being. He changed the subject. "I am going to the Master of the Market as soon as I am done with trimming the hooves of the new horses; I'll do what I can to arrange the feed for our next part of our journey."

"Tell me what you decide upon," Sieur Horembaud ordered. "We will have to be more prudent in how we load our pack-animals now the camels are gone."

"Of course. With a little foresight and good fortune we should be away from here in less than five days."

A sudden, impertinent breeze tossed dust into the air around them, bringing the scent of the fields to them; the horses whuffled and one of the mules huffed.

"How do you reckon that? Are you going to find us a guide?" Sieur Horembaud asked sarcastically; he rocked back on his heels and gave Sandjer'min an appraising look. "You're still losing flesh. Not getting enough of whatever it is you eat?"

"It is not a question of quantity, but of quality," Sandjer'min replied accurately but obliquely. "Unfortunately, what provides the most sustenance for me is not to be had on pilgrimage."

"How inauspicious for you, then, to be among us; I am surprised that you choose to remain with the company," Sieur Horembaud said with no indication of sympathy before he turned and walked back toward the Waterbird Inn, Frater Anteus following him as if guarding him from Sandjer'min's gaze.

The copper-dun tossed her head, fussing out of boredom.

"Quiet, girl." Sandjer'min watched the two men go, more aware than ever that Sieur Horembaud was losing the capacity to lead his pilgrims safely. The company would have to leave Baruta as soon as possible or face disintegration. With Richere Enzo and Ifar officially no longer part of the group, but lodging a short distance from the Waterbird Inn, there was a constant reminder that turning back could occur. With these discomfiting thoughts for company, he took his nippers and rasps and set about his farrier's chores.

By the time he was finished, the mid-day meal was over and most of the inhabitants of Baruta were napping through the worst of the day's heat. Sandjer'min felt a bit queasy, the brilliant sun and the enveloping heat having taken their toll upon him; he knew it was useless to go to the market until the sun was lower in the western sky.

He put his tools away and returned to the inn and went along to the room he shared with Ruthier. Although Ruthier was not in the chamber, Sandjer'min decided to rest while he had the opportunity. He removed his black-linen cotehardie, and his underclothes, then pulled on an old-fashioned black cotton tunica, turned back the fine linen sheet that lay over a thin mattress set atop an iron-banded chest, got into this austere bed, lay back, and quickly fell into a stupor that served as sleep for his kind.

He was wakened by Ruthier speaking to him. "Would you say that again?" he asked as he sat up, fully alert.

"I believe I have found a guide," he said in Imperial Latin. "He is from Ethiopia. He has been staying at the monastery, helping the monks draw up some maps, which makes me believe him, or why would he be instructing the monks?" He smiled. "He might be willing to show us the way to his homeland, in spite of the Inundation."

Sandjer'min got off his bed and pulled up the sheet, and spoke in the same tongue. "Sieur Horembaud will be most pleased to hear this, if I present the matter carefully. Just now, Frater Anteus is warning him off of strangers, so Sieur Horembaud is frustrated now: he's like a porcupine, all prickles. Having a guide will let him resume his plans. What languages does this possible guide speak?" For he was certain that Ruthier had ascertained that.

"He speaks Coptic, but nothing more than his own tongue, and those of the peoples living around his people. No Greek, no Arabic, no Latin, Church or otherwise. But he has a few phrases in Hebrew that he learned from the Jews in the old city of Axum." Ruthier dropped down on a low hassock, and absent-mindedly brushed sand off the open sleeves of his cotehardie.

"At least a few of us can communicate with him. And he will be able to speak with peoples none of the rest of us can understand; he sounds very promising," said Sandjer'min, hoping he could convince Sieur Horembaud that this guide would be an asset to the company. "Is there another black cotehardie in our clothes chest? The one I've been wearing is developing thin patches that will shortly be holes, and if I am going to speak with this guide, I had better present an appropriate appearance."

"I think there is a paragaudion in cotton. I could cut the sleeves at the elbow, if you like."

"You needn't cut the sleeves quite yet."

"Then I will wait until you make up your mind." Ruthier got out the dark-red Anatolian wool femoralia from the smaller clothes chest. "These are still in good condition."

"The sand has worn out two pair already. How many more pairs of femoralia do I have?"

"Three more pair you haven't worn yet, another four you have not worn through at any point," Ruthier told him, and came back to the more pressing matter. "Will you recommend the Ethiopian to Sieur Horembaud?"

"If the guide is willing and I am satisfied that he will be acceptable to the company," Sandjer'min said. "If it seems the man will suit, I will notify Sieur Horembaud. Until then, I'll say nothing to him. There is no use in getting his hopes up unnecessarily."

"True enough," said Ruthier. "Do you want to dress now?"

"Shortly." He stretched slowly, then went through a series of moves that he had learned in China a decade ago. "Tell me what you can about this man. How did he seem to you?"

Ruthier nodded as he got up and went to open the clothes chest. "He's very dark of skin, I would guess him to be twenty-five or a little older. Tall, well-muscled but lean. Clever features, but not rascally. He is thoughtful in his questions, not intrusive but more than cursory. He carries himself with the dignity most of the people of this region possess, reserved but not arrogant. His voice is not loud, but it is low, and it carries well. He says he has guided pilgrims before, both going toward Ethiopia and going toward Egypt. I liked his manner; I think he will be a good choice if he can be persuaded." He tossed the paragaudion onto Sandjer'min's bed. "I'll fix the sleeves later, if you wish it."

"Did you learn his name?" Sandjer'min pulled off his tunica, turning his back to Ruthier so that he would not have to look upon the wide swath of scar tissue that covered his torso from the base of his ribs to his pubic bone.

"I did. He is Gulema Pendibe."

"Gulema Pendibe," Sandjer'min repeated, opening the neck-frog, then tugging the Greek garment over his head, letting its hem fall to his knees, a wide pleat in the back made for comfort when in the saddle taking a little time to settle in place. He reached for a belt of black leather, set it around his hips while notching it two holes more tightly than the wear on the leather marked as usual.

"You need to find a woman to visit in her sleep; you're thin," said Ruthier.

"So Sieur Horembaud told me earlier, about being thin, not about visiting a sleeping woman." He took a deep breath, banishing his attempt at levity. "You're right, of course. But where am I to find such a woman in Baruta? It's not as if I can starve. Most women keep to their quarters at night, wives sleep with their husbands, and widows usually enter religious houses as tertiaries. I would not be able to find a woman alone unless she is ill, and then—"

"I know your scruples, my master," said Ruthier.

"One Csimenae is enough." He took his boots from the larger clothes chest, removing the heavy cotton cloth that was wrapped around them. "Sharing blood might strengthen someone with a disease, but she would not be prepared to come to my life, and I would not be able to teach her what she would have to know before we go on southward."

"You needn't share blood with her, only take enough to nourish you." As he said this, he knew it was useless.

"Ruthier, old friend, you know how I am inclined to want to heal those who are ill, and there are only two women abed with illness in this quarter of the town that I know of: one of them has an infestation of water animacules that causes her fever, the other has bloody flux. Even if I were to visit one of them in sleep, how could I have intimacy with her if I do nothing to ameliorate her suffering." He went to a small wooden box with his eclipse device carved on the top, unfastened the elaborate catch on the side, and removed a heavy silver chain from which a black-sapphire pectoral depended. He put the chain around his neck, centered the pectoral, and turned to Ruthier. "Will this do?"

"You're going to the monastery? Now?"

"The monks are at meditation at this time of day; Gulema

Pendibe and I may talk privately. Best not to put this off. Am I dignified enough for his company?"

"Once you put on your femoralia and your boots you are: you look impressive but not imposing," said Ruthier.

"That was what I was hoping to achieve, but lacking a reflection . . . What would I do without you? You protect me from myself," Sandjer'min said. "I will arrange for more feed for our animals when I am done with Pendibe. And you?"

"I have a pair of ducks for a meal. If you want their blood, I'll wait until you return; otherwise I'll dine now."

"Dine now. I will visit the horses and asses tonight. The new spotted mare looks to be a hearty animal, able to spare what little I will take. That will hold me over for a day or so." He studied Ruthier's face. "There is no reason for you to fret. I have managed on less than I have now."

"But need you do it again? Bondame Margrethe yearns for you. You could—" He stopped. "No, you couldn't. Not with Lalagia and Sorer Imogen in the same chamber. And if you were to meet clandestinely, everyone in the company—everyone in Baruta—would know of it."

"Truly," Sandjer'min said, pausing thoughtfully before going to their chamber door. "Having a guide would lessen the distress in the company."

"Sieur Horembaud might get resentful if he thinks you have usurped his authority in choosing a guide," Ruthier reminded him.

"He might, but he all but challenged me to do it." Sandjer'min nodded to Ruthier and went out into the heat of the day; with no one about to watch him, he crossed the market-square in front of the inn with long, surprisingly rapid strides, the sun leaching him of energy as he went. He would shortly have to replace his native earth in the soles of his boots with fresh, he thought, and went through the monastery gate.

A tired monk who sat next to the hospice door asked Sandjer'min what his business was, and having been told, he said that Gulema Pendibe was in the scriptorium, and gave directions to find it. "Do not speak while walking the halls; this is the monks' meditation time. They commune with God."

"Yes, Frater. I will take notice." He inclined his head and went along to the scriptorium, where he found a tall, lean African bent over a wide sheet of papyrus, making marks on it with a stick of charcoal. Sandjer'min paused just over the threshold, saying, "I am seeking Gulema Pendibe? Are you he?"

"I am," he said in heavily accented Coptic. "Are you the serving-man Ruthier's master?"

"Yes. Rakoczy, Sidi Sandjer'min. I am from the Carpathian Mountains at the edge of the Kingdom of Hungary," he said to be polite, knowing that Pendibe had no way to comprehend this information. He put his right hand over his heart and offered a little bow; he realized that Pendibe was head-and-shoulders taller than he, and hoped this advantage in height would not annoy Sieur Horembaud. "I gather Ruthier told you that our company of pilgrims stands in need of a guide and translator? Our leader, Sieur Horembaud du Langnor, wishes to visit the Chapel of the Holy Grail, as do several of our numbers."

Pendibe smiled, his large white teeth luminous as pearls in his dark face. "As many pilgrims of the Roman Church wish to do. So your man told me, when he informed me that you have served the pilgrims as a translator."

"He indicated that you might be willing to undertake that task, taking us into the mountains in safety," Sandjer'min said.

Pendibe considered this, and after a short silence, he said, "I was planning to set out on my own in a few days, but I would rather travel with companions. Inundation or not, a man alone is a target, isn't he?"

"That has been my experience many times, even when my serving-man is with me," Sandjer'min agreed, thinking back to the Year of Yellow Snow and the Polish marshes. "Perhaps we should sit down?"

"There are upholstered benches at the other end of the room," said Pendibe, and led the way to a large window shuttered against the sunlight. "Do be seated, Sidi."

Sandjer'min did as Pendibe bade him. "You have traveled the route before, you say? How many times?"

"I have made the full journey nine times. When I reach my

home, it will be ten times." He sat on the bench at right angles to the one occupied by Sandjer'min. "I miss my family when I am away from them."

"As do many of the pilgrims," said Sandjer'min, and added, "Ten times tells me you must have been quite young the first time."

"I was. Not quite fifteen when we started out. I was astonished at all I saw, yet I learned quickly."

"How far have you gone beyond Baruta?" Sandjer'min inquired, showing his interest by leaning slightly forward on his bench.

"I have been to Nuri, and once to the Third Cataract, but no farther. Perhaps, one day, I will see the monuments at Edfu, but that must be later, when my children are a bit older. As it is, I spend two-thirds of the year journeying." Pendibe looked at Sandjer'min. "And you? Have you ever traveled into Ethiopia?"

"No," said Sandjer'min. "This will be my first time."

"Have you heard about the country at all?" For the first time there was a note of doubt in his voice.

"I have heard it is mountainous, with plateaus, numerous peaks, some jagged, all very green, many valleys at different elevations, and one deep, broad canyon—the lowland region is called Abyssinia, I understand; Ethiopia is the north side of the canyon, particularly the plateaus. There are cities and towns on most of the trade routes, all the way to the sea in the east." Sandjer'min offered Pendibe an encouraging half-smile. "The people are mostly Coptic Christians, although there are many pagans in isolated places, and some Jews as well. There are profusions of animals, many birds, and at the northeast end of the canyon, there are volcanos and unwholesome lakes of sulphur-water."

"You've studied my country?" Pendibe asked. "How?"

"In the last few years, yes, I have studied the lands lying south of Egypt. I was staying at the Monastery of the Visitation in Sese'metkra, and had an opportunity to peruse their accounts and maps." Sandjer'min got up. "But studying is not the same as seeing. With one of your maps"—he nodded in the direction of the papyrus on the table—"I might be able to find the way beyond the division of the White and Blue Nile, but I am no guide in your homeland, only an informed traveler."

"Do any of the other pilgrims know as much as you do about Ethiopia?" Pendibe's attitude relaxed a little.

"I doubt it. Frater Anteus knows more than he admits, I believe, and Jiochim Menines, who has lived in Egypt for some years, probably has learned something from the returning pilgrims he has seen in Alexandria. Sieur Horembaud—"

"He is the leader you spoke of?"

"Yes. He listens to Frater Anteus, and occasionally to me in matters of travel; we need someone who knows what lies ahead, not who has studied what lies ahead," said Sandjer'min, giving slight emphasis to *knows*.

Pendibe put the tips of the fingers of his right hand together to show he comprehended Sandjer'min's remark. "Most foresightful."

"I hope so," said Sandjer'min. "Most of the pilgrims have no understanding of the demands that could be made upon us on our climb into the mountains. The desert has been beyond their expectations; Ethiopia is still more a dream to them than a place."

"As is often the case in an unknown land," Pendibe said, continuing as if from idle curiosity, "This Sieur Horembaud: do you have any impression as to why he is on this pilgrimage?"

"As I understand it, he is a knight who unknowingly killed a number of Christians, and has been given a penance to visit the Chapel of the Holy Grail before he will be allowed to lead troops in battle. He is a valiant fighter, and a man of position. He has estates in English territory in France—" He broke off, then said, "I will make an agreement with you, Gulema Pendibe. If you are willing to guide this company of pilgrims, I will be glad to provide you with maps and other information of the countries from which the pilgrims come. You may find such information useful if you continue to guide pilgrims."

"Isn't that disloyal?" Pendibe spoke cautiously, as if he expected an angry response. "How can you reveal so much and not betray them all?"

"It might be treacherous if their lands were not so very far away. As it is, the greater your understanding of the origins of the Roman Christians you guide, the fewer instances of confusion you and those you guide will have. They are not likely to tell you very much on their own, though you are a Christian."

Pendibe seemed much struck by Sandjer'min's answer. "A good point, Sidi." He pulled at his lower lip.

"I would appreciate your instruction." Sandjer'min walked slowly down the scriptorium, his demeanor calm.

"As I would yours," said Pendibe. "Shall I plan to visit the Water-bird Inn after the foreigners' quarter is once again awake?"

"That would be fine; I'll tell Sieur Horembaud that you may be the very man he is seeking." Sandjer'min hesitated, then added, "You may want to know that the company is being followed, and has been since we left the Nile to cross the Nubian Desert."

"Followed?" Pendibe managed not to reveal his alarm. "How do you mean?"

"There are two, and occasionally three men keeping far enough behind us not to be readily seen. So far they have only followed us, but I cannot tell if they pose any threat to us; I can only say that they have done nothing to warrant such an assumption yet."

"What does your leader say?" Pendibe asked, a frown gathering on his brow.

"Nothing. I am not sure he's aware of the followers, but if he is, he has put them from his mind." Sandjer'min waited for another question; when one did not come, he continued. "Our numbers are reduced from what they were when my serving-man and I joined the company at Sese'metkra. The followers may be hoping there will be fewer of us soon, and may then take us captive, which I have come to believe is their plan."

"Then you are wise to be cautious," Pendibe said with careful approval. "Many robbers deal in more than abandoned goods."

"I have surmised that."

Pendibe nodded. "In this region, there are men who follow foreigners—pilgrims for the most part—crossing the Nubian Des-ert, men who wait for the unprepared to be overcome by the heat, or to get fatally lost, and then, as they die, take any living animals and the pilgrim's chests and other belongings. It may be that you have those scavengers keeping pace with you. Slavers would be more distrustful, and of greater numbers."

"I thought it might be something like that for many days. You have shown me a vulnerability in our company. Hazards like that, that are unknown to us, leave us exposed to dangers. If you undertake to guide us, I will thank you, and provide payment for any service beyond guiding that you may perform for Sieur Horembaud's company." Sandjer'min saw the doubt in Pendibe's face. "What troubles you?"

"I . . . I have no wish to refuse you, but there must be limits on where we go." Pendibe took a short time to think. "I will see you as far as Lalibela. If you wish to go farther, you will need to find another guide if you don't return the way you came."

"Your family is in Lalibela?"

"Not far from it," said Pendibe; Sandjer'min sensed that Pendibe was being deliberately evasive. "When you return, you may well be going north to Axum when most travelers are going south and west, and that may make finding a guide more difficult, assuming you'll need one." He lapsed into silence again, his frown deepening. "I will speak with this Sieur Horembaud, and then decide what I should do," he said.

"That is satisfactory," said Sandjer'min, "at least to me. I'll inform Sieur Horembaud that you will speak to him this afternoon." He came back to where Pendibe was sitting. "Until then, you have my thanks for hearing me out." He put his right hand over his heart and nodded once.

"I hope Sieur Horembaud is willing to engage me." Pendibe rose. "Your serving-man has done me a good turn. I will remember him for it."

"I'll tell him." Without waiting for another exchange of pleasantries, Sandjer'min turned and left the scriptorium, and dropped a ducat in the donation tray beside the hospice door before he went across the forecourt to the outer gate; he thanked the novice who opened the gate for him, and went on toward the market-square where sacks of grain and rolled hay were sold. After arranging for grain and hay for the next leg of the pilgrims' journey, Sandjer'min returned to the Waterbird Inn, arriving just as the pilgrims were beginning to stir; he saw Olu'we and Carlus emerge from their chambers, and a few paces on, Lalagia coming out of the kitchen, a covered bowl in her hands. Something for Sorer Imogen to eat, he decided. As Sandjer'min reached his own room, he noticed Methodus Temi coming in the side-door. The blacksmith nodded and went on toward the room Cristofo d'Urbineau shared with Micheu de Saunte-Foi.

"Did your meeting with Pendibe go well?" Ruthier asked as Sandjer'min came through the door.

"I think so," said Sandjer'min. "I'll know after I talk to Sieur Horembaud." As he heard his own words, he was troubled by the realization that he would have to present strong reasons for the leader of the pilgrimage to accept his recommendation in order to keep from giving Sieur Horembaud cause to resent his success in finding a guide for the company. "Perhaps, old friend, you will join me when I do."

Text of a letter from the tenth Aba'yam for the Monastery of the Visitation at Sese'metkra, to Venerable Demetrios at the Coptic Church of the Archangel Rafaele in Alexandria, written in Coptic on papyrus and carried by Dinat, the monastery's courier, delivered twenty-nine days after it was written.

> *To the most Venerable Demetrios at the Church of the Archangel Rafaele in the city of Alexandria, the most respectful greetings of Aba'yam at the Monastery of the Visitation at Sese'metkra, on this, the 9th day of July, in the year of Our Lord, 1225.*
>
> *Blessed Demetrios,*
>
> *To answer your inquiry, yes, the Inundation has come earlier than usual, and the waters are rising rapidly. Two fields on the south side of this place were partially washed away when the Nile broached its banks, four days ago. There have been make-shift repairs, but for now we must*

rely on the Mercy of God to spare us any greater losses. I would advise any village on the river to reinforce as much of their waterside supports as they can, or risk having a more destructive Inundation than we have seen in many years.

We have taken your notice to heart and from now until you or your successor lifts the ban on succoring those who are not Christians, we will turn away all travelers who seek our hospitality but those who worship Christ. It is apparent that there are many worshipers of Allah coming into the south with the purpose of suborning those faithful to Christ, and for His Glory, we must stand against the swelling forces of Islam, or lose our communicants and energumens to the underlings of the Sultan. To that end, we have encouraged our congregation to undertake the rapture of spirit that the energumens pursue, embracing the angelic possession and zeal that are proof against all malign persuasion that Islam may offer for any falling-away from the only true faith.

It is my sad duty to inform you that my predecessor, who had withdrawn to a hermit's cave in the hills behind this village, was found dead three days ago, apparently from the bite of a venomous serpent, for there was a bite on his hand, and his lower arm was swollen and discolored, as was his hand and fingers. His face was also affected, being bloated. We have said Mass for the repose of his soul each day since his body was discovered by one of our novices, whose task it was to take food to him. I spoke to him a few days before his death, and discussed the new policy toward non-Christians, which much distressed him. He reminded me what a benefit the foreigner Rakoczy, Sidi Sandjer'min, had been while he and his servant stayed here, but I told him your order was firm, and I regret to say, we parted with hard words.

I have instituted a new policy that I hope will meet with your approval: I have let it be known that we will accept young men from the district as novices who might otherwise be seized by the Sultan's men to be soldiers in his army. I have, for the time being, suspended the test for monastic vocation, for I see it as God's work to keep Christians away from the Sultan, and not even Malik-al-Kamil would require a young man in Orders to go to war on the Sultan's behalf. May God preserve us all from the machinations of Satan and its embodiment, the servants of Mohammed.

Rest assured, I will promote Christian zeal for as long as I am Aba'yam, as I did when I was Tsura'gar, a simple monk devoted to our faith and our cause.

Obediently,
Aba'yam
the Monastery of the Visitation
Sese'metkra

PART III

Bondame Margrethe de la Poele of Rutland

Text of a letter from Regimus di Marcellus dei Ruschelinus, Seneschal of the Knights of the Rose, the Neapolis chapter, to Janarius Conradin da Rimini, Treasurer of the Knights of the Rose, the Tyre chapter, written in coded Church Latin on vellum and delivered by Templar courier thirty-nine days after it was written.

To my most honorable colleague, Janarius Conradin da Rimini, Treasurer of the Tyre chapter of the Knights of the Rose, the respectful greetings of Regimus di Marcellus dei Ruschenlinus, Seneschal of the Neapolis chapter of the Knights of the Rose, on this, the 22nd day of July, in the 1225th Year of Grace,

Most worthy cousin,

I hope this finds you in God's favor in that most ruthless climate, and that the members of our Order are persevering in their missions. In regard to expanding your chapter: Cardinal della Rovere has recently been granted audience with the Pontiff, and will receive authorization for a chapter in Egypt before the end of the year, at which time some of your knights will be sent to Alexandria to establish a Rosine church near one of the Roman churches near the Christian district of the city. As the time nears, I will inform you of what the Pope intends to achieve with the expansion of your Order, and define those missions that will be given you. Presently in that regard, there is one of your chapter's number who will need to be notified that he is no longer assigned to remove Vidame Perrin Bonnefiles from his pilgrimage; the Vidame's

uncle, Bishop Godeswain de Saunt-Felicien, has presented a
defense of the Vidame's actions that the Archbishop has accepted on behalf of the Pope. Your man is relieved of his task.
Vidame Bonnefiles is no longer under suspicion of heresy,
nor is he considered to have pilfered funds from the rents
owed to the Church; the obligation to complete the pilgrimage is lifted from him, as are your man's instructions to kill
him before they reach Ethiopia and the Chapel of the Holy
Grail.

I realize that it will take time for new orders to reach
Micheu de Saunte-Foi, and so I urge you to dispatch a courier to follow the company of pilgrims as rapidly as possible.
With the Vidame exonerated of all irreligious activities, his
death would be a sin for your Order. It would not be appropriate to kill the Vidame now that the charge of heresy has
been lifted from Bonnefiles. Micheu de Saunte-Foi is dedicated to his work, and must have sufficient proof that his orders are rescinded before he sets his duty aside, so I would
advise you to send a bona fides copy of this letter along with
the message from you with the courier, so that Micheu de
Saunte-Foi will have confirmation of the order.

As we take our name from the Rose beneath which all is
secret, we honor the members of our Order by keeping
their work closeted. I will make no official report of this
notification, nor will I record the mission given to Micheu
de Saunte-Foi. Only upon instruction from His Holiness
will any part of our Order's activities be made known to
anyone beyond the officers of the Order and the Pope. I
pledge my silence by the Rule of our Order and my vows.
You, cousin, will certainly do the same, in the Name of the
God Whom we both serve, even unto the end of the world.

                    Regimus di Marcellus dei Ruschelinus
                    Seneschal, the Knights of the Rose
                    Neapolis

1

Six nights after the pilgrims left Baruta, and one night since they had passed the Fifth Cataract, Gulema Pendibe suggested they move back from the banks of the Nile. "The water is nearly over the sands, and will soon spread up the ground." He pointed to a swath in the dust. "That is as high as the river rose last year, and this year it will be higher. The tops of the reeds are almost under water. With the river rising, many animals come down to drink, some of them hunters. If we withdraw from the river's edge yet keep in sight of the water, we will be beyond where most animals will come after us, and beyond the high water mark."

Sieur Horembaud drew in his bronze-grulla gelding—the most impressive of the horses Firouz had provided—while he considered this suggestion; the stars overhead showed that it was nearing midnight and their stop for supper. "I think it might be wise to do as he recommends; he's right, the river is getting higher, and we don't want our tents or supplies washed away," he said, then added, "It is probably better to take the eastern track, provided there are no other hunters waiting to stop us, to rob or capture us." He slewed around in the saddle and gave Sandjer'min a hard look that was visible in the darkness.

"I would not be concerned about such matters at this time; very few travelers are abroad, and because of that, there are fewer hunters; there must always be more antelope than lions or the lions starve. These men are not hunters or they would have done something before now, and at night. The days are too hot for fighting, so traders and robbers are waiting out the summer in towns and oases, not searching for foreigners to prey upon. On your return there might be cause for worry, but not now," Pendibe explained, watching Sieur Horembaud as Sandjer'min translated. "The men following us are few, and could not attack us if they have no comrades to join them. Two or three men are insufficient to challenge all of your company, whether or not you have swords with you. That would be foolhardy."

"What men following us?" Sieur Horembaud inquired with ill-disguised fury. He pointed to Sandjer'min as the rest of the company straggled to a halt around them. "Did you know about this?" he exclaimed. "Did you?"

"Yes, I knew; they were clumsy at first, but they have improved in their skills for concealing themselves—not beyond my ability to find them," Sandjer'min said calmly; his night-seeing eyes were unhampered by darkness. "There were two; for a time there were three men, but there are two again; one must have stayed in Baruta."

"You were aware they were in Baruta?" His outrage stifled his outburst. "And you said nothing to me?"

"I thought they must be inside the walls. They probably had relatives in the town, which is why I did not see them in the foreigners' quarter; I haven't seen their faces clearly, and it would be dishonorable to accuse someone I didn't recognize of following us, which is, in itself, not a crime." Sandjer'min gave Sieur Horembaud a long moment to consider what he had said, then went on. "Had their numbers increased, I planned to inform you, but as it is, so long as the men—whoever they are—stay well behind us, I saw no reason to add to your burdens."

"Oh, didn't you?" Sieur Horembaud was yelling now.

Pendibe reached over to tug on Sieur Horembaud's sleeve, and received a vitriolic glare for his trouble. He spoke in a reasonable tone. "Please tell Sieur Horembaud that yelling will only alert the followers to animosity in this company, and that could be troublesome. If they intend to do us mischief, they will try when there is discord among the pilgrims, when we will be too busy fighting amongst ourselves to see the danger from outside."

Sandjer'min relayed Pendibe's warning, adding, "The followers are likely to be followers of Islam, sent to watch us so that the Sultan may know what we have been doing." He repeated this in Coptic for Pendibe's benefit.

"There is a lesser route that won't be hard to reach; it moves toward the foothills most directly." He pointed to the bluish haze on the southern horizon. "That is the way it goes. It will keep us back from the river for two or three days, but with the water still rising, it would not be wise to remain too close, for as it rises, so also does it move faster." Pendibe watched Sandjer'min as he translated this into Church Latin, and then into Anglo-French.

"What lesser route?" Sieur Horembaud asked petulantly.

"It is a short way to the east, it follows the Nile beyond flood level, and it will bring us to the Atbara River as the riverside track will do." Pendibe paused, as if expecting something to be asked.

"The Atbara River?" Sandjer'min inquired. "I've heard its name but little more, and not from anyone who has actually seen it."

"It is a tributary of the Nile. It dries up in the spring, and is hardly more than a trickle until the rains come, and then it is a torrent," Pendibe told him. "Now, it will be filled to overflowing," he said, smiling. "It is a difficult climb, but you will reach Ethiopia more quickly taking it, provided you do it before the end of summer. There is a monastery near where it joins the Nile, and there we might be allowed to stay for a few days before going on. The monks there should be able to advise us if there are problems up-river."

"What, by God's Nails, is he saying?" Sieur Horembaud growled.

Sandjer'min translated for him, and added, "It might be a good choice, Sieur Horembaud. You have said you want to return as quickly as possible once you have prayed at the Chapel of the Holy Grail. Shortening our journey into Ethiopia contributes to that end. If we arrive at your destination more quickly, then we should be able to return before winter begins; otherwise it will be spring, or summer, before you are in Alexandria again." He translated his last remarks for Pendibe's benefit.

The wind was picking up, making playful gusts that sent sprays of sand into the air, like the elaborate scrolls and ornaments that all the company had seen set in mosaic designs around Arabic texts on floors and walls; Frater Anteus crossed himself, and after a few heartbeats, so did the rest of the pilgrims.

Sieur Horembaud swore comprehensively. "This is no place to wrangle, Pendibe's right about that. We must move on, and quickly. When we stop to eat, then we may have a proper discussion regarding the river. Or we could wait until evening tomorrow, when we are rested." He exchanged a quick glance with Frater Anteus. "The Church informed me, when I was entrusted with this company of pilgrims, that the Blue Nile was the proper way up the mountains. Though we haven't reached the mountains yet."

"We were told at the Monastery of the Visitation that the Blue Nile is the way into the Ethiopian Highlands, as well. How far is the Blue Nile's end from Lalibela and Gonder?" Sandjer'min asked before Sieur Horembaud could speak again.

"Both are nearer the Atbara than Lake Tana, where the Blue Nile begins. The last three days of travel is demanding, but not impossible." Pendibe shrugged. "It is your decision, but were I traveling alone, at this time of year, I would follow the Atbara."

"Do you know the way?" Sieur Horembaud challenged him. "The whole way?"

"Most of it. There is a stretch on the north face of the mountain I have not traveled, but the lower and upper ends, yes. It will allow us to go to the Church and Monastery of the Redeemer, for many of us, a place nearly as sacred as the Chapel of the Holy Grail."

Sieur Horembaud heard Sandjer'min's translation and answered with a scornful laugh. "Is it? Then why have I never heard of it?" He made a sharp gesture. "We will move on now, and stop to eat when we come upon a sheltered place. For now, we will say nothing more about the Atbara." He tapped his horse's side and turned away to take the on-side lead point, swinging his arm to the company to fall into double line behind him, and Sandjer'min to take up his place opposite him on the off-side. As they moved off, the wind capered along the sands.

Midnight had come and gone before they reached a low ridge of weathered rocks with thorn-bushes at the base, where Sieur Horembaud ordered the company to halt, and set everyone to their tasks. By now, all of the company knew what was required, and set about making remuda-lines for the horses and asses while others started building a fire or preparing food. No one paid any attention to Sandjer'min as he walked away from their camp, for he and Ruthier never ate with them, and often checked the condition of their ani-/mals while the rest of the company were at supper.

The fire was guttering by the time Sandjer'min returned, and the company was breaking camp. He went directly to the remuda, located Melech, and began brushing his coat with a boar-bristle brush. A bit later, Ruthier joined him, accepted the brush, and went to do a cursory grooming on the ass he had been riding for the last two nights.

"Did you find the followers?" Ruthier asked Sandjer'min in the language of the Wends; he handed Sandjer'min the brush.

"Yes." He put the saddle-pad in place, then lifted the saddle onto Melech's back, answering in Wendish, "Two men, three horses. No sign of any others."

"Did you recognize either of the men?" Ruthier pursued; he was keenly aware that Sandjer'min was putting a plan together, and Ruthier wanted to be part of it, whatever it was.

"No. I didn't get close enough to make out features. I watched them from a half-a-league distance; even in sunlight, that isn't close enough for features." He sighed. "They seemed more Egyptian than African. I can say nothing more specific than that."

"Then that would confirm that they are keeping watch on this company, keeping their distance so rigorously. That's strange," Ruthier remarked, still trying to draw Sandjer'min out.

"That it is." Sandjer'min reached under his gelding's belly, grabbing the girth and pulling it to the saddle-buckle on his side of the horse. "The two are not as well-supplied as we are, which suggests they may be expecting help of some sort along the way, or they aren't going all the way into the Ethiopian Highlands."

"Do you still believe that they mean no harm?" Ruthier shook his head slowly.

"Not as such, no, I don't think they intend to harm us as an end in itself, but they may be willing to tolerate harm as a secondary problem, which worries me." He swung the stirrup-leather back into place.

"You are convinced they are only watching us?"

"More than ever," Sandjer'min answered.

Ruthier uttered an obscenity in Chinese which translated to *five hundred one.* "Then why would they not approach us? What would be the danger in traveling with us, if all they are seeking is information? They have not fallen behind, nor sped up to pass us, nor turned away from the track we follow, and I can only think that we are the objects of their journey. If they prefer to travel separately, they are seeking to avoid us while we travel, which cannot bode well for us. What else would explain their behavior? Why are they are watching us, and for whom."

"I fear I will have to find out before too many days pass, for now the company is aware that our followers are out there, our companions will feel compelled to act. And now that Sieur Horembaud knows they're there, he will want to know their reasons for their surveillance; he may come up with a scheme to capture or trap them, which would be provoking at the least, and could bring about such a confrontation that our comrades may be seen as martyrs—assuming they are acting with others." He picked up the bridle, released Melech's halter, and slipped the snaffle into the gelding's mouth before guiding the headstall over his ears. He buckled the throat-latch, pausing to pat Melech's neck. "You're a good horse."

"Are you planning to do anything about the followers?" Ruthier asked directly, his gaze flicking around the company, now gathering with their horses, asses, and pack-asses, to resume their travels.

"Not tonight," Sandjer'min told him. "I see Temi is saddling horses for the women. I'll go assist him."

"Sieur Horembaud is growing more uneasy, my master," Ruthier persisted.

"That is hardly surprising," Sandjer'min said. He took hold of Melech's reins below the bit and went off through the company. "Master smith," he addressed Methodus Temi in French, "would you permit me to help with the saddling?"

"With gratitude, Sidi," Temi responded. "If you would saddle the Bondame's gelding—she calls him Westron Wind—I will attend to the Sorer's jenny-ass—she won't ride a male animal of any kind, not even clipped ones. And I'll saddle Lalagia's, as well."

"So I have been told; nuns' Orders often have strictures against male creatures of all sorts," Sandjer'min said, pointing to the saddle he had seen Margrethe ride. "Is this the one?"

"Yes, and the sheepskin saddle-pad. The Bondame rides the blood bay, and will for two more days, when she will get back on the white mare with the dark speckles. That gelding you ride has more stamina than most. You have an eye for horseflesh."

"Travel encourages that," Sandjer'min said levelly. "Melech is a good match for me."

Temi nodded at the blood bay. "What do you make of that horse?"

"A steady creature, this Westron Wind," Sandjer'min approved, taking a proffered brush from Temi. "You keep these horses' coats in good condition."

"Sieur Horembaud expects it of me," said Temi, setting the thick-woven cotton saddle-pad on the jenny-ass before placing the high-pommeled nun's saddle in the proper position and buckling the girth. "We have a way to go, and Sorer Imogen needs to be held in place from time to time; Lalagia doesn't bother with a saddle, not on an ass. All those years Crusading, she's learned how to manage the asses. A most admirable woman." To emphasize his point, he cocked his head in the direction of Sorer Imogen, standing with Lalagia, the nun's lips moving in relentless prayer.

"She will need something more than a saddle-pad and a surcingle when we start to climb into the mountains," Sandjer'min observed.

"I have a pair of Turkish saddles that will do well enough for those on asses who have no saddles of their own." Temi adjusted the nose-band on the bitless bridle. "The Sorer is not very skilled at riding."

"I wouldn't have thought she could be," Sandjer'min said, and led Margrethe's horse, along with Melech, over to the rear of the remuda where Olu'we had the saddled animals in order, and all eight of the company were waiting to mount.

"That is for me," Margrethe said, stepping forward. "Thank

you for bringing him, Sidi." She glanced at him from the tail of her eye, and quickly looked away, a slight flush rising in her neck and face; he felt her desire as he felt the intensity of the sun during the day.

"If you will let me lift you into the saddle?" He did not wait for her to speak, reading her answer in her features; he took her by the waist and swung her up and over her horse's back, setting her in the saddle with as much ease as if she had weighed no more than a child; a few of the company goggled at him, and Margrethe's face went from pink to crimson. Aware that he had overstepped himself, Sandjer'min said, "The movement permits it, the swing makes you easy to lift."

Carlus nodded. "Like the swing of the pitchfork when moving hay. You can carry much more on the tines if you swing the pitchfork first."

Sandjer'min looked over at Agnolus dei Causi's servant, relieved he had used such a commonplace example. "Much the same thing," he agreed with a slight smile, though it was not the same at all; he could hear Margrethe's rapid pulse and her deepened breathing as he stepped away from her horse, whom she had named after an old, passionate love song from her native England.

Margrethe stared at him, gathering up Westron Wind's reins and fitting her feet into the stirrups. "Thank you, Sidi," she said tonelessly, averting her face with an effort; then, tapping her heels to the gelding's sides, she moved away from the remuda to join with the others already mounted.

"Your servant is coming for you," said Temi, his attention fixed on Margrethe. "A remarkable woman, the Bondame."

"Indeed." Sandjer'min looked around to see where Ruthier was, and signaled him to join him, saying quietly when Ruthier reached him, leading three pack-asses, "I shouldn't have done that. It was her fancy, not what she expected."

"But she must be pleased that you did, or will be, when she gets over her discomfiture," Ruthier told him, his voice lowered to slightly more than a whisper.

"I would like to think she will be," said Sandjer'min, and moved off to take up his position in their line of march.

Sieur Horembaud went up and down the line twice, hectoring the company to get in order and move out, that the night was fading toward morning and they needed to reach the oasis Pendibe had assured them lay ahead.

By morning they had covered more than five leagues for the night, and found themselves in a small defile, at the back of which a spring burbled; its water soaked into the ground before all but a trickle ran out from the rocks. The place provided the pilgrim company not only fresh water but a fair amount of shelter. The land was rising gradually, and was not quite so arid as most of their route had been for more than five weeks. Not that there was not plenty of sand and hard earth around them still: there was, but now they also saw small clumps of scrub, stands of low-growing palms, and thickets of thorn-bushes along the course of a stream beneath the sand; there were small antelopes about, and more lions as well as jackals; Sieur Horembaud ordered Micheu de Saunte-Foi and Jiochim Menines to hunt for something to eat later that night. The secondary track they had been following was a short distance away from the underground stream, and Pendibe suggested cutting a few of the thorn-bushes and putting them at the entrance to the defile.

"If we should encounter anyone while we are here, we will know they are coming and we will be ready to meet them," Pendibe said, giving Sandjer'min time to translate before adding, "There are other travelers that might be on this trail than the followers, not all of them well-intentioned."

"You have said that there is little travel at this time," Sieur Horembaud said.

"That is the case, yes," Pendibe said, choosing his words carefully. "Which is why, if we encounter travelers, it is wise to be wary; this place provides protection."

Sandjer'min finished his translating, and added, "Why not be cautious? Where is the error?"

"Yes. A good point," Sieur Horembaud allowed.

"And the advantages of the location are real," Sandjer'min went on. "The pilgrims, the animals, all your company—"

"This is a fine place for us to rest. You've done well," Sieur Horembaud reluctantly admitted to Pendibe. "So far." They were at the end of the remuda-lines, near the pile of tack. "I guess you've been here before."

"Enough times to know that we should be careful of scorpions and snakes. Mind you shake the pads out before you put them on the animals," Pendibe said with a tight little smile.

Sandjer'min translated this without comment, certain that Pendibe recognized the tone in his voice. When he finished, he squinted toward the eastern horizon. "Once the animals have been fed, you could permit the company to bathe in the larger pool. It appears that it has been used for that purpose before."

Florien and Baccomeo went by, carrying rolled tents on their backs, the poles used like walking-staves of unknown gods; they ducked their heads in habitual respect, their pace unbroken, their heavy breathing revealing the weight of the tents they bore.

"I'll ask Frater Anteus if it would be vanity to do so," Sieur Horembaud said, paying no attention to the servants.

"How could it be vanity?" Sandjer'min asked, perplexed.

"It is not much more than a week since the company bathed. To bathe again so soon shows a preoccupation with matters of the flesh." Sieur Horembaud folded his arms. "Best to avoid the occasion for sin."

"But the sand chafes, and the heat can cause rashes," Sandjer'min objected. "That would require paying more attention to the body, not less."

"Pain and illness may be offered up," Sieur Horembaud said, dismissing this notion with a wave of his hand. "They may wash their hands and faces, of course, but—"

Sandjer'min dared to cut him off. "Howe has an open sore on his hip, and Vitalis has heat ulcers on his ankles. Both men must bathe before I can treat them."

"Oh, if you must," Sieur Horembaud conceded. "The rest will want to bathe if they see Howe and dei Causi's servant do it." He called out, "Frater Anteus! Attend me. There is something we must discuss." He motioned Sandjer'min away. "I'll tell you if I change my mind about the baths."

Sandjer'min went back to where Ruthier and Almeric were putting up the tent; two large stacks of chests and sacks lay on the ground; the red-lacquer chest was next to the sacks. The two servants were shadowed still by the defile, although the sky overhead was bright as polished brass.

"We'll be done shortly, my master," said Ruthier as he saw Sandjer'min come toward him.

"Do you suppose you could pitch this a bit farther back in the shade?" Sandjer'min asked politely in Anglo-French.

"I was going to do so," Ruthier said, "but Pendibe pointed out a number of snakes in the rocks. They like the cooler places."

"That they do," Sandjer'min agreed. "This will be in direct sunlight for less than half a day, which is far better than some of the camps we have made. Thank you for reminding me of the snakes." Like all of his blood, he was immune to their venom, as he was to all poisons, but a bite could be agonizing, and take many weeks to heal.

"The camp guards will need long-handled mallets to keep snakes and scorpions away from the company and the animals," said Almeric, rushing through the words as if to make sure he would finish his words before his nerve deserted him; he was unused to initiating talk.

"That is a careful suggestion. You may take my long-handled mallet for that purpose once the tent is up." Sandjer'min was aware that Noreberht lo Avocat was standing a short distance away, listening to every word, so he added, "I have a tincture that will keep snakes away from the tents. I'll make sure the guards have it. That should afford us some protection."

"Sieur Horembaud will be grateful," said Almeric.

"Will he," Sandjer'min said, and went to unfasten the bands around his red-lacquer chest.

But surprisingly, Sieur Horembaud sought out Sandjer'min as he was spreading an unguent of primrose and powdered malachite on the raw place on the side of Nicholas Howe's hip; it was time for the company to sleep, and most of the pilgrims hurried to finish their

prayers. Howe was in his small clothes, the waist-band untied to ex-
pose the injury. "There you are, Sandjer'min," Sieur Horembaud said
with an attempt at geniality. "Pray forgive my intrusion: I understand
from Noreberht that I have you to thank for the tincture that keeps
away snakes."

"I provided Carlus and Ruthier with vials of the formula,"
Sandjer'min told him as he rose from the stool next to Howe, and
pulled down the hem of his tunica. "I am pleased they found it useful."

"One of those things you learned to make in your foreign travels?" Sieur Horembaud prompted.

"Yes, it is." He turned to Howe. "If you can, try not to sleep on
that side. Less pressure will help it to heal."

Howe offered Sandjer'min a little bow. "You're most kind, Sidi."

Sieur Horembaud nudged Sandjer'min's arm. "I want to ask your
opinion on something that puzzles me," he explained as he guided
Sandjer'min out of Howe's tent.

Sandjer'min put his jar of unguent into his sleeve and stopped
still. "If you will tell me what it is, I'll give you my opinion, if I have
one."

"Come with me," said Sieur Horembaud, striding along the irregular avenue of newly erected tents, then out to the mouth of the
defile where Baccomeo and Vitalis were cutting the limbs from the
shrubbery and setting them across the opening. Sieur Horembaud
shoved some of the branches aside and went out into the full blaze of
the sun, where he stopped and turned south, pointing as he did.
"You and Pendibe say that those shapes are mountains."

"Yes," said Sandjer'min, the light as painful as shards of glass in
his eyes.

"Then what is happening to them?" Sieur Horembaud asked,
pointing to the distant smudge of obscured peaks.

Sandjer'min shaded his eyes with his hands, and squinted into
the distance, trying to discern what Sieur Horembaud meant. Gradually the horizon became visible. "Ah. I believe what you are seeing
are rain-clouds. You should have Pendibe look at them to be sure,
for that is his homeland and he knows its humors, but I have seen

similar sights in other mountains, and they always meant rain was falling."

"How long does it rain? This is July, not the season for it," Sieur Horembaud complained. "Rain should fall in winter, and only occasionally in summer."

"It rains in the summer in those mountains to the south; you were warned that the Nile would be in flood through part of this pilgrimage, and now you see the reason," said Sandjer'min. "All the itineraries at the Monastery of the Visitation said that from the end of June until the middle of September, there are long and heavy rains in the Ethiopian Highlands." He stepped back into the shadow of the defile. "The Nile will continue to rise through the middle of August."

"The Inundation; I reached Alexandria shortly after the last one had ended," said Sieur Horembaud. "And it comes from such a distant place." He stared at the southern horizon for a long moment, then he turned and came back to where Sandjer'min was standing. "How long will that storm last?"

"That is something to ask Pendibe."

Sieur Horembaud was thoughtfully silent, though he said nothing. Finally he motioned to Vitalis. "Move those boughs."

Vitalis and Baccomeo did as he ordered, and when Sieur Horembaud and Sandjer'min passed through, replaced them before cutting more of them.

"Will you be out of your tent this afternoon?" Sieur Horembaud asked as they went back through the camp.

"If there is enough shadow from the walls of the defile, yes." He waited a long moment. "Is there something you would like me to do if I am?"

"I want you to keep an eye on the rim of the defile. This is a protected place, no doubt, but we are vulnerable from above. If the men following us are seeking an opportunity to attack us with impunity, it would be in this place." Sieur Horembaud pointed out the high walls; as if to underscore his anxiety, he swept his arms wide to take in all the sky they could see. "Look there, Sandjer'min." A pair of vultures were slowly circling, not directly overhead, but a distance away, so that a third of their circle passed over the defile. "Something is dying out there in the desert. The birds are a warning, or are they an omen?"

"Perhaps they are simply hungry birds, looking for something to eat," Sandjer'min suggested, all the while remembering his centuries at the Temple of Imhotep at a time when the vulture goddess Maat was the embodiment of truth, the goddess who held the whole account of a person's life in the balance of one of her feathers.

Text of a writ of detention from the Master of the Gold Camp regarding the foreign monk, Frater Giulianus, written on papyrus in Nubian Coptic and placed in the Gold Camp archives on the 29th day of July, 1225.

The Council of the Gold Camp has met to determine the possible fates of Frater Giulianus, a Roman monk who volunteered to work among the lepers some weeks ago, and who has been discovered to have been using the lepers in the old quarry beyond the Camp as miners; for so long as they are capable of lifting the tools of that trade, they have been ordered by Frater Giulianus to labor on his behalf. He has accumulated a goodly amount of treasure: we have discovered two large baskets such as farmers use to bring crops to market that were near to full of nuggets and pouches of gold dust. He admitted that he had arranged with a few of the traders waiting here for the end of the Inundation to carry as much gold as he can accumulate to send down-river, entrusted to the Poor Knights of the Temple, for the benefit it may provide to Mother Church. What such a donation would be worth to the Templars we have yet to determine, but it is most certainly a large amount, and one that must be factored in our final decision. One of the lepers, another Roman Christian, has made himself Frater Giulianus' assistant, and he must also bear some of the blame for what happened at the quarry.

We of the Council have settled upon three possible sentences for the transgressions that have been defined. First: Frater Giulianus would have his right hand struck off, and be sent away to beg his bread until God claims him. Second: both hands would be struck off and his eyelids removed and he would remain in a penitent's cell until he departs this life. Third: that he be turned out from the Gold Camp with only a begging bowl and a small cask of water. These choices are fixed, and which one will be his fate will be voted upon when next we meet. Until then, Frater Giulianus will remain in his cell.

As to Sieur Arnoul, God has already sentenced him to the destruction of leprosy. He will be left among the lepers he has misused, where he may come to value those who suffer with him. Once he has lost his fingers and his feet rot, he will be wholly at their mercy, and say we all Amen.

2

In the last four nights, Sieur Horembaud's company had passed from a vast expanse of sand to dry, gritty ground punctuated occasionally by small clusters and tussocks of low-growing plants scattered over the rocky soil; there were more animals now, some that Sieur Horembaud planned to hunt once they came to the Atbara, to offer his company an occasion to celebrate before they reached the steeper, higher mountains, and the more demanding climb. The pilgrims had already ascended to a plateau about two hundred paces above the rising Nile that was roiling in the narrowing canyon below, its constant roar echoing up toward the broad ledge on which their tents were pitched at the edge of a cluster of stunted trees. Far to the south the wind was beginning to stir; lenticular clouds lay clustered in the sky, the line of the highest mountain ridges stretching up as if to hook them like vast, celestial fish.

The servants had set up a small fire for cooking their morning meal, and were almost finished serving the company; three servants were waiting for their bowl of breakfast. From the cooking-pot there arose the odor of wheat porridge that gained more interest from the animals than the pilgrims, most of whom were more eager for sleep than for such tasteless food. Sieur Horembaud was taking time to pray with Frater Anteus, having spent part of the midnight supper castigating his company for becoming lax in their religious observances, and swearing to amend his conduct to provide an example for the rest of them. Jiochim Menines and Agnolus dei Causi lingered at the cooking-pot, not out of hunger, but to have a little exchange of gossip. Methodus Temi was making his way along the remuda-lines, giving each horse and ass a quick examination before making a bed in the shade of the piled baggage. Though the sun was barely up, its long, slanting rays promised another grueling day.

Before all the company had retired for the day, Sieur Horembaud bawled out to them from the flap of his tent, "Each of you: six penitential Psalms before you sleep. I want to hear your voices! Servants, attend to your duties. No frivolous talk, no slacking of work. This is God's mission we are on, and we must show our devotion in all things."

Menines glanced at dei Causi, speaking in the northern Italian dialect, but with a pronounced Spanish accent. "We'd best do as he says," he remarked as he got to his feet. "He's determined to restore piety to the company. One Heneri is enough."

"Out here?" dei Causi asked incredulously. "Where would an apostate go? What faith can be found in such wild places?"

"It worked for the Desert Fathers," said Menines, brushing off the backs of his thighs.

"Amen to that," dei Causi agreed, stood up, and reached for a cloth to wipe his bowl clean. "I will look for you at sunset." With cordial nods, they parted; the camp was preparing for a day of sleep, with the pilgrims bound for their beds, the servants and slaves attending to the last of their chores.

Pendibe was in the shade of the sail put up to keep direct sun off the animals, where he went about his morning prayers in the privacy the remuda-lines provided him. As he completed his orisons, he nodded to Sandjer'min, who was finishing his tasks before retiring. "Sleep well, Sidi," Pendibe called out to him. "The wind is changing."

"I'll be abed in a little while. May you sleep well." Having treated Howe's abrasion and provided a new dressing for it, Sandjer'min now went toward the women's tent, his bag of medicaments slung across his chest, noticing as he moved that his black paragaudion was beginning to show wear from the sand; he would have to choose another garment from his dwindling supply, or go about in worn and tattered clothing. He paused at the edge of the flap. "This is Sandjer'min. May I come in?"

"She's had a bad night," Margrethe said to Sandjer'min as she raised the flap to admit him. "Thank you for coming to tend her."

"More praying?" Sandjer'min asked, knowing the answer.

"That, and exhorting us—Lalagia and me—about our sins. She is certain that Heneri left us because she sinned, and I did not stop her. She says that Sieur Horembaud was right to rebuke us, and Frater Anteus. She keeps saying to me that if I break my oath to keep sacred my chastity, the company would have to stone me."

Sandjer'min kept his face impassive. "Does that apply to Lalagia, or to Sorer Imogen herself?"

"Only to Sorer Imogen; Lalagia is in the company of pilgrims searching for Sieur Arnoul, and as his woman has taken no such oath. She would probably be made to leave the company, for setting her virtue aside, but she would be alive." She lifted her hand to touch him, but changed her mind; her face became as impassive as his. "She is not getting better, is she?—Sorer Imogen?"

As kindly as he was able to, he said, "No."

"She isn't being guided by angels, is she?" Margrethe held her breath for the answer, trying not to touch him for reassurance.

"It doesn't seem so," he said gently.

"Then she is prey to sins and evil," Margrethe said with terrible fatality. "Dear God, what is to become of her?" For an instant there was something wild in her pale eyes, then, once again, her features went mask-like.

Lalagia, who had been rolling out two beds on the floor of the tent, paused in her work. "She is in God's Hands now, for all she is not receiving visions from Him; it is within His power to turn her visions to Heaven. I pray He is merciful with her. All we can do is keep her from hurting herself."

"Has she done that?" Sandjer'min did his best to minimize the alarm he felt. "In what way? When?"

Margrethe gave a sigh of chagrin. "Yesterday morning, as we were making camp, she managed to find a hatchet that had been used to cut new tent-stakes, and she used it to score the palms of her hands."

Sandjer'min's memory of Gynethe Mehaut's bleeding palms was shocking in its intensity; her unexplainable wounds in the hands and forehead ended in her being confined in a cell in her convent's foundation for the temerity of having Christ's wounds on her unworthy body. In the centuries since the reign of Karl-lo-Magne, the Church had changed its position on the stigmata and no longer saw it as diabolism and heresy, but as a sign of holiness. He steadied himself mentally. "Why didn't you tell me? Have you cleaned the wounds, or dressed them?" He looked from Margrethe to Lalagia.

"You were busy talking with Sieur Horembaud and Vidame Bonnefiles," Margrethe said. "I wrapped her hands in linen strips."

"A good beginning, but I should see them for myself, to determine how serious her cuts are," he said. "Is she on the other side of the sheet?"

"On her bed." Lalagia stood up. "She didn't want us to remove the bandages, because the blood, coming from her palms, was sacred."

"I will try to persuade her to let me wash her hands, at the least," said Sandjer'min, preparing to go through to the other side of the tent. "I have a medicament that can reduce the pain from the cuts."

"She won't want that," Margrethe warned him, taking care not to brush him with her arm as she moved nearer to Sorer Imogen. "She thinks it will keep her from more sins, if she embraces her pain. Having cuts in her hands will help her to remember how Christ died for us. She says the cuts aren't very painful."

"All cuts to the hands are painful," Sandjer'min said, casting his thoughts back over nearly two thousand years of treating injuries, and all the damage done to human flesh that he had repaired. "If she claims otherwise, she is dissembling."

Lalagia laughed. "See if she'll let you."

"She will do as you request," said Margrethe, casting a sharp glance at Lalagia. "She is being very stubborn. She sees the Devil working in us to turn her from her prayers, so you may not be welcome."

"She is not willing to allow any man to touch her; she won't let Vitalis assist her onto her ass. She is afraid that any contact with a man will contaminate her so that she will be empregnated by demons in punishment. We must have a small chest left out for her so she can mount on her own," Lalagia reminded Margrethe. "She says she would dishonor her pilgrim's vows if a man were to touch her."

Margrethe shook her head. "I have been unable to change her mind."

"When did that start?" Sandjer'min asked.

"Just after she scored her hands," Margrethe said in a disheartened voice. "That's one of the reasons I didn't send for you. She was already distracted and I didn't want to make it worse. I thought it was more important to calm her. Zealous she may have been before we started our pilgrimage, but never anything so absolute as she is now. Something must be done, and neither Lalagia nor I know what she needs."

"Did anything happen to her yesterday or the day before? anything unusual, something that might cause her to be worried about her safety?" He saw Margrethe and Lalagia exchange a quick glance. "What was it?"

Lalagia sighed in exasperation. "All right; it wasn't her safety, exactly, but it upset her. If you must know, she saw me kiss Temi, day before yesterday, when we finished making camp. It was about this time of day. We were outside the tent, and our shadows fell on the side of her sleeping area. She became outraged, calling me by names that I found cruel and insulting. It was such a little sin, you would think no one would mind."

"She recognized you?" Sandjer'min asked, then nodded. "Of course she did."

Margrethe said, "Lalagia doesn't cover her hair."

"I'm not supposed to; I'm not married," Lalagia said. "And neither you, Bondame, nor the Sorer has breasts like mine."

Sandjer'min held up his hand. "What did Sorer Imogen say to you?"

"She said I was unchaste and would bring God's Wrath on all of us for kissing Temi. She called me harlot, trollop, whore, and worse," Lalagia told him, her voice low in order to keep Sorer Imogen from denouncing her again.

"That was before she cut her palms?" he asked to be sure.

"Yes." Margrethe and Lalagia answered at the same time.

"So she is paying attention to what's going on around her at least some of the time," Sandjer'min mused aloud.

"Her attention . . . shifts," said Margrethe. "There are times she dwells on what she says are the angels who pray with her. When she's like that, she pays no heed to anything else."

"And other times, she watches us, very narrowly. She spends much time concentrating on little things, minor things. Once in a while she allows a shock to distract her." Lalagia dropped small pillows onto each of the two beds she had laid out. "Seeing me kiss Temi shocked her, I guess."

"Yes, you've said so," Sandjer'min said, feeling Margrethe's eyes on him as he spoke to Lalagia; the passion that lit them was as bright as a fire. "That may be a difficulty if you're watching her during the day."

"I'm watching her in the afternoon; the Bondame has the morning." Lalagia yawned. "I should be asleep shortly."

"You should," he agreed. "Well, I will do what I can for Sorer Imogen. Bondame, if you'll come with me, you may ease her with your presence."

"Yes. Yes, I will," Margrethe nodded, but her eyes held a stricken glaze; Lalagia reached out and lifted the hanging sheet aside. "The Bondame had best go first," she said.

Margrethe swallowed once, then went toward the crouching figure on the bed. "Sorer Imogen," she began in a soft, reassuring tone, "here is Sidi Sandjer'min come to see you and to take care of your injuries."

"No-o-o-o-o," Sorer Imogen wailed, pressing her palms together and shoving her hands between her legs.

"Please, Sorer Imogen, for the sake of your body and soul," Margrethe appealed to her, taking two steps nearer her bed.

"No," Sorer Imogen said, rocking back and forth.

"But you must," Margrethe beseeched her. "Don't you see that you need to sleep? You are exhausted. Don't you know that you need to have the wounds on your hands treated? You remember how important it was for Torquil des Lichiens to sleep, and to keep his sores clean: put your faith in God's Goodness, and let Him comfort you."

"I do not deserve such from Him; Heneri has forsaken the True Church and for his depravity, we must pay the toll," said Sorer Imogen. "I must bear my wounds for the sake of my House and God's Son, or I am damned."

Sandjer'min moved a little nearer to the unrolled bed. "Then sleep to gather your thoughts, that you may address the Mercy Seat with understanding."

Sorer Imogen let out a shriek and pulled herself into a ball, praying loudly.

"She's been like this through the night," Lalagia said bluntly. "She held on to the high pommel of her saddle and let the ass rock her while she prayed."

"We need her to rest," Margrethe said as firmly as she could. "Another night like last night and I will be too exhausted to care for her." She crossed herself. "If I could stay awake, it would be different, but . . ."

"But," he repeated for her, showing he understood her predicament. "I will try to give her something to help her to sleep, and I have a combination of herbs that will help you to rest, but not so deeply that you cannot attend to Sorer Imogen if she should require help."

Margrethe did her best to smile, and nearly succeeded but for a trembling lower lip. "You are very good to us, Sidi."

He very nearly said he would do more if he could, but he was aware that Sorer Imogen, for all her distress, was listening, and might want to upbraid him for speaking suggestively to her sister-in-law, so he bowed slightly, and turned his attention to Sorer Imogen, "You will be the better for sleep, and your hands will be the better for being treated." He glanced at Margrethe. "Bondame, will you bring a basin of water, so Sorer Imogen may wash her hands?"

"At once," Margrethe said. "I have a ewer . . ." and she withdrew to the other side of the sheet.

"Sorer Imogen," Sandjer'min said, his tone musical and soothing, "you do not want to have your hands putrefy, which they may do if they are not washed and salved." He had learned the virtue of cleaning injuries from the Romans and the Persians, and continued to wash open injuries, often in the face of concerted opposition.

"Go away," she said with abrupt vehemence. "You must go away!"

"I cannot leave you in such a state as you now are, for I would fail my oaths as a physician if I did," he said as if she had addressed him politely.

"You are with the Devil. You are not a Christian. My soul is in danger with you here. Go now! Get away from me!" With that, she began to convulse, her whole body shaking and thrashing, her head strained back and her teeth showing.

Sandjer'min went down on one knee next to her, and reached to remove a broad oval of leather from his supply bag; this he worked to thrust atop her tongue, using more strength than he usually revealed to those around him. "At least we can save your tongue," he said in Imperial Latin.

Her seizure grew stronger, her paroxysms more violent. She kicked at him, drubbing at his torso with her heels, and as he slipped away from her, she struck out at him with her fists, and scraped his face with her nails; he drew back, but only to get beyond the reach of her arms. Her flailing became worse, her movements so dissilient that it was nearly impossible for him to contain all her limbs at the same time. Through all her distraint, he did all he could to contain her fury, and keep her from injuring herself. As her spasms diminished, he was able to move behind her and work his arms around her waist, from where he was able to get hold of her hands and confine them in his. Gradually her body relaxed, succumbing to a lassitude that was as torpid as her seizure had been maniacal. Her head dropped, her breathing softened, and the fixity of her muscles slackened.

Sandjer'min slid away from her far enough to reach around her shoulder and remove the leather disk from her mouth. "Lie back, Sorer Imogen. Let me attend to your hands." He got up from her side. "It's safe now, Bondame," he said, a bit more loudly than he had planned.

Sorer Imogen looked up at him, then away. "Damned thing."

"It was another fit, wasn't it?" Margrethe asked as she came around the sheet and stopped to take stock of what she saw.

"That suggests that she has had them before," Sandjer'min remarked, and waited for what would come next.

"She has, but . . . it was some time ago. When she entered Holy Sepulchre as a novice, she had two or three, and there was some talk of confining her, but her father would not permit it, and in the end, the matter passed. Her Superior hoped that this pilgrimage would ease her rigor, which was causing agitation among the Sorers at her convent." She bent to put the basin of water on the floor of the tent. "I have sometimes thought that she has prayed so constantly to keep from having another such fit."

Sandjer'min sat cross-legged next to Sorer Imogen, and carefully reached for her hand, touching it lightly before drawing it toward him. "Don't fret, Sorer. I am going to wash your hands and spread a medicament upon them."

"No. No." Sorer Imogen struggled weakly to pull her hand away. "The blood is sacred when it comes from the palms."

"But not if you cut the wounds yourself, according to your Church," Sandjer'min said patiently, distantly aware that hungry as he was, her encaramined palms were no temptation to him. "If your God should send them, it is another matter, but creating the injuries is for Him, not for you to do." He waited until she gave up her fight, then unwound the linen from her left hand and lowered it into the basin. Slowly the dry, crusted blood sloughed off and started to dissolve, turning the water a rusty pink.

Sorer Imogen began to weep, making a sound like a frightened puppy.

"What will you do with her?" Margrethe asked, anxiety in every aspect of her demeanor.

"As I've told you. I'll medicate and bandage her hands, and give her an anodyne and soporific drink, and then will make up a medicament for you." He could feel her awakening passion, and he took a step back. "The longer she sleeps, the better. If she doesn't rise until sundown, she will have an easier time during our night travels."

"I know I shall," Margrethe said with shaky laughter, looking at him with longing in her eyes.

He resisted the impulse to take her in his arms, as much as he perceived she ached for him to do so. "You need rest. You're worn to the bone."

"Sorer Imogen would say that is a good thing," Margrethe said, and saw Sorer Imogen languidly nod her head.

"It isn't," Sandjer'min told her flatly. "Travel like this demands every particle of strength possessed by each one of us. We must husband what we have. In this place, to deliberately weaken oneself is beyond foolish." He took his medicament bag off his shoulder and set it down at his feet. "I'm going to finish tending to her hands, and then I'll attend to you. If you would be willing to stay here while I work on the Sorer?"

"Oh, yes," she said, with more enthusiasm than she felt; she wanted to be away from Sorer Imogen until she was restored to good sense; the thought of seeing another such seizure troubled her deeply, and yet she could not ask Sandjer'min to attend to her alone without risking the kinds of gossip that could bring misfortune on them both.

He went down on one knee and removed a few more items from

the leather sack, and set them on the edge of Sorer Imogen's bed; the nun tried to pick up the vial filled with opalescent liquid, which Sandjer'min reclaimed from her without effort. He set to washing her right hand, taking care to inspect the wounds closely. He sensed more than saw Margrethe kneel next to and slightly behind him. "I'm going to give Lalagia something to help her rest, too. All three of you are in need of revivification, and sleep will be the most reliable source."

"But Sorer Imogen doesn't sleep long," Margrethe said, her anxiety returning. "One of us must be awake to tend to her, or she might . . . might do anything."

"What do you mean?"

Margrethe did her best not to sigh. "When we were preparing for this journey, when we were still at Creisse-en-Aquitaine, she had a fit, and afterwards, she had the same sort of lassitude she has now. The priest was sent for, and blessed her, and in time she fell into a profound sleep. When she had slept for a day and half a night, she entered a kind of ecstasy, and in that state, she attempted to strangle the serving girl—a child of eight—who had been set to watch her. She was unable to speak, and there was such vehemence in her attack— Afterward she said the Devil had possessed her, and used a scourge on her back when she prayed." She leaned her head against his shoulder. "It took two servants and a priest to hold her off. When she went to Confess, she said it had been a demon who took hold of her; she would not and could not do anything so profane. The Bishop said the pilgrimage might aid her as much as it could my husband." Even as she said this last word, it seemed hollow and without meaning.

While she spoke, Sandjer'min dried and dressed Sorer Imogen's injuries. He made sure the linen bandages were snug and the knots that kept them so were tucked in and could not easily be untied. He put the ointment jar back in his case, and opened the vial, saying to Sorer Imogen, "I want you to drink this. It will reduce any putrescence in the blood. Then I will give you a little olive oil mixed with blossoms from the edge of the Nile. It is not easily swallowed, but it will enable you to sleep soundly." He held the vial to her lips and tilted the vial so that a little of the liquid ran into her mouth.

"It's disgusting," Sorer Imogen said in a distant way.

"The next is as bad," Sandjer'min warned her.

Lalagia appeared at the edge of the sheet. "Make sure there's enough to keep her down for the day."

"I will give her sufficient to ensure her sleeping until evening," Sandjer'min said over his shoulder, and saw Margrethe pull away from him. "But what she will have now must suffice for the day: soporifics, like anodynes, must be administered carefully. Too much, and they become a poison, not a medicine."

"Poison," Sorer Imogen repeated, and attempted to spit out the liquid in her mouth.

"You must swallow," Sandjer'min said to her quietly, confidently, and was rewarded when she took more. "There is not enough in what I have given you to do more than let you sleep."

"That might be no bad thing," Lalagia said, and immediately held up her hands. "I speak in jest only. But you will allow, Sidi, that there are times when living is punishment and death a kind deliverance."

"Anyone who has treated the injured and the sick knows that, whether or not they will admit it," he said, and heard Margrethe's quick intake of breath. "No one can claim that there are not those for whom living is a brutal burden, more like a prison or a battlefield than the world your God gave to men."

Lalagia made a sound between an oath and a laugh. "And everything dies."

"Yes," he agreed. "Eventually everything dies."

"Can we not speak of life?" Margrethe pleaded.

Sandjer'min put the empty vial down and reached for the alabaster bottle that smelled of olives and something else. He picked up a ceramic Chinese spoon from the few unused remaining items, and poured it half-full of the greenish oil. "The color isn't pleasant. It doesn't taste very good, either, but it will do you much good."

Sorer Imogen drank dutifully, lay back, and offered a dreadful smile. "I will tell God not to blame you. You are only doing the will of others, and they must bear the burden for what becomes of me."

"Very good," said Sandjer'min, realizing that Sorer Imogen had assumed he had poisoned her. "This evening, be sure you drink much water." He put the last of his things but one bottle back in his sack.

"Will she be herself tonight?" Margrethe asked in an under-voice, getting to her feet as Sandjer'min rose.

"She should be calmer," he said. "You and Lalagia need not hover over her. I'll send Ruthier to come by your tent frequently today."

"Oh. Thank you." This time she actually took her hand in his, and impulsively kissed it. "I am so grateful."

He disengaged his hand and touched her cheek before slinging the strap of his sack over his shoulder. "You needn't effuse for my benefit, Margrethe," he said, trying to restrain his impulse to answer her passion with his own.

"It's not that," she said, looking confused as she stepped away from him. "I often fear I can do nothing to help my sister-in-law, so when you lessen her travail, I am thankful not only for your care of her, but for sparing me from helplessness."

His dark eyes were enigmatic. "Then I am honored to serve you, Bondame."

"Is it really safe for both Lalagia and me to sleep? Shouldn't one of us stand guard?" she asked, her face pale. "I'm so sorry she scored your cheek. You'll be scarred."

He touched her again, his fingers light as thistledown. "There will be no marks," he said. "And you did nothing to cause them."

The south side of the tent bellied inward, then flattened once more.

She seemed to master herself. "Then give me the mixture you spoke of, so that we may make the most of the day."

"This will let you rest until sunset." He opened a small box and removed two round pills. "Drink a cup of water with them, and when you wake."

She took the pills. "Thank you, Sidi," she said, turning back to pull a thin coverlet over Sorer Imogen.

He gave two more pills and the same instructions to Lalagia, and left the women's tent; he walked a short way to his own, and called for Ruthier as he entered through the flap.

"Yes, my master?" he said, checking on the tension of the tent on

the four upright poles and cross-poles. "With the wind rising, I want
to be sure we will not lose our poles' footing. The tent could be torn
away from its tethers."

"Do you think there is a risk of that happening?" Sandjer'min
asked, cocking his head to listen more closely to the skittering sands.

"Pendibe is trying to persuade Sieur Horembaud to remain here
for the night; he says it will rain before nightfall, and this is no time
to be traveling in the dark."

"Ah," said Sandjer'min, "Sieur Horembaud is not likely to agree to
remain here. He wants to press on to show faith that God will spare
him a soaking."

"How like him," said Ruthier at his driest.

Sandjer'min coughed diplomatically. "In the meantime, I have a
favor to ask of you: would you be willing to go by the women's tent
five or six times between now and sunset? Sorer Imogen has had a
difficult time of it, and may need extra help to sleep." He paused. "I
gave her olive oil with syrup of poppies mixed into ground valerian,
hemp-blossoms, and hyssop, which I should hope would keep her
asleep for some hours." He rubbed his eyes. "The solution was a
strong one, but her case is extreme."

"Even Sorer Imogen should sleep with such a mixture in her,"
Ruthier observed. "You've set broken bones on that formulation."

"Let us hope it is adequate," said Sandjer'min. "After such a day
as she has had."

"It sounded as if she were distraught," Ruthier said, admitting
that he had been listening while Sandjer'min was in the ladies' tent.

"She had convulsions," said Sandjer'min quietly.

Ruthier said nothing for a long moment, then, "What of Bondame
Margrethe? What of Lalagia?" he asked. "Is there any danger to
them?"

"I gave them something for sleeping as well. And I assured them
that you will go past their tent with some frequency." Ruthier bowed.
"Yes, old friend; I know. Neither of us bargained for this when we left
the Monastery of the Visitation, but remaining there was not possible, so— Fetch me if there is any sign of trouble. With what they
have taken, any tossing or talking in sleep is going to mean more

problems." He stretched. "I'll visit the remuda-lines come evening. I'm feeling . . . depleted, and a day on my native earth isn't going to be enough to revitalize me. The dark-bay Barb will provide sustenance." This admission bothered him, so he added, "I'll have to tend that copper-dun mare, since Sieur Horembaud is determined to ride her again."

"But the splint—" Ruthier protested.

"I've attempted to explain several times, without success," said Sandjer'min. "It was bad enough in deep sands, but with all the sharp pebbles underfoot, more animals than the mare may suffer because of them." He pulled off his paragaudion and reached for the black cotton Roman dalmatica Ruthier handed him. "Thank you."

"I'll visit the women's tent as you asked," Ruthier said. "Do you want me to wake you, or let you rise when you like?"

"If I'm asleep beyond sunset, then wake me," Sandjer'min said as he made for his thin mattress that lay across the chest of his native earth. He stopped, and looked up at the top of the tent. "Odd," he mused. "Look; the sunlight is fading."

"A cloud passing over the sun, perhaps," said Ruthier. "I noticed a great gathering of them in the southeast, and the wind is blowing from that quarter."

Sandjer'min nodded and got atop his bed. "Wake me if there's any trou—"

"Trouble. Yes; I will," said Ruthier, and went to pluck the crane that waited for him at the rear of the tent while the wind snapped about the camp and clouds thickened and darkened overhead, making the asses and horses restless and the pilgrims uneasy.

About mid-afternoon, the rain began; fat drops of warm water pelted the mountainside, and brought the Nile to a state that made it appear its water was boiling. Sleeping pilgrims were splashed awake as seams in the tops of the tents became saturated and leaked. Occasionally thunder trundled through the sky as the rain continued to fall.

Sieur Horembaud's two servants, Florien and Almeric, went about the camp informing all of the company that they would not be moving on that night, and that their dinner—such as it was—would be served under the latine sail that usually protected the animals from the direct sun. Almeric stopped Ruthier on his way back from the women's tent to pass on this information and to ask if the women needed any help.

"They're still asleep. I think it might be wise to send someone in to be sure they aren't getting wet."

"Is your master still asleep?" Almeric asked. "Since he is treating Sorer Imogen, shouldn't he be the one to care for her?"

Ruthier knew that Sieur Horembaud would expect Sandjer'min to care for Sorer Imogen, and the women who shared the tent with her, so he said, "I will speak to him as soon as I return to the tent."

"I will explain to Sieur Horembaud that you will take responsibility for the women." Almeric bowed his head, saying emphatically, "For the benefit of the company," accompanied by a fortuitous mutter of thunder.

"Certainly," said Ruthier as politely as he could. "For the benefit of the company," then turned on his heel and continued on to their tent, water running off his cotehardie and slicking his hair to his head as the wind continued to rise.

Text of a letter from Annis de Santo Andreas, secretary to the Spanish mission in Roma, to Pater Ruiz de la Sangre Sagrada with the Poor Knights of the Temple at Alexandria; written on vellum in Church Latin and delivered by Papal courier to Pater Ruiz twenty-six days after it was written.

> *To the most revered priest, Pater Ruiz de la Sangre Sagrada presently serving with the Poor Knights of the Temple in Alexandria, with the Spanish Templars, for the Glory of God and Christ, the most sincere greetings and blessing from Annis de Santo Andreas with the Spanish mission in Roma, on this, the 4th day of August in the 1225th Year of Redemption,*
>
> > *Most honored Pater,*
> > *Recent news from Hungary confirms what your letter of February 12th of this year told us: that the devilish*

armies of the Mongols are continuing toward Europe and Christendom, although some of the followers of Mohammed have attempted to arrest the Great Khan's progress, but if the rumors are right, without success. Those who have survived to flee the Mongols speak of numbers beyond reckoning, moving at astonishing speed; they are rumored to be able to cover more than twenty-five Roman leagues in a day, which is a number that amazes us all, for how can they move their cavalry mounted on squat little ponies so much farther than the Templars can move their armies in a day? It speaks of the Devil's work, and sorcery. Some say their horses are not horses at all, but demons, and that the riders take the fury from them. It therefore appears that we must prepare to face these heathenish fighters, and to keep a strong front against them, or risk losing much of our eastern territories to barbarians more savage than anything the Sultan may command.

You intimate that the recent increase in forced enlistment in the Egyptian Sultan's armies has been due not to the presence of European chivalry in the Holy Land, but to the dread of the coming of the Mongols, and upon prayer and reflection, it is apparent that this is a pressing situation. If it becomes necessary for our soldiers to join with the Sultan's for the purpose of sparing both them and us from the Great Khan, then you are not to acquiesce in any plan until you have the approval and support of the Church behind you. The Devil works in the Sultan's causes, and we must not allow ourselves to be misled by the illusion of a threat that conceals some stratagem that is truly pernicious. No matter how piously presented, any scheme to defend our faith and our territory must be acknowledged by the Pope before you or any other servant of the Church may act upon it. If the Orthodox Church decides to side with the Sultan, then we must consider posting our fighting men to other sites than the ones they presently occupy.

His Holiness has declared that since Jenghiz Khan has

ravaged so much of Russia, if our reports are to be believed, it is not just the Holy Land that is in danger, it is Poland and Bohemia and Moravia and Austria and Hungary, as well. We have received requests from the Hungarian Poor Knights of the Temple to be permitted to leave the Holy Land in order to return to their homeland to participate in its defense. This is a matter of some gravity, and a final decision has not yet been made, but it may be necessary to divert more than Hungarians if we are to preserve Europe for God. If that should be the case, you will be informed as quickly as Papal couriers may bring you instructions, but without such confirmation, it is your duty to stand against all those who would pull our Christian troops into wars that aid our nearest enemies.

Any news you have for the Pope, we ask that you provide a bona fides copy of the same to this mission. Speed is of the essence in these rapidly changing times, and secrecy is vital. Who knows where the Devil may have his servants waiting to misguide and befuddle the armies of Christendom? I am sending a warning similar to this one to our Spanish mission in Constantinople, with the same information and requests, and recommend you be in contact with them, for only in sharing what we have learned in the most timely manner we may can we hope to defeat this scourge which is being visited upon us. We do not seek to obstruct the Pope, the Poor Knights of the Temple, or any other Christian force, but we ask that you, in your capacity as priest to the Alexandrian Templars, keep us informed so that we will not be unprepared to do our part to defend our Roman faith.

In the Name of the Father, the Son, and the Holy Spirit, Amen

Annis de Santo Andreas
Secretary to the Spanish mission in Roma

3

As the second night of rain got underway, Sandjer'min was interrupted in his treating of Nicholas Howe's abrasion by Micheu de Saunte-Foi, who stepped inside Howe's tent, his garments sodden, and with a polite bow said, "A word, when you're through?"

"Of course; as soon as I've completed this," said Sandjer'min, as much out of curiosity as courtesy. "I will not be long."

Micheu withdrew, and trod heavily away toward the tent he shared with Cristofo d'Urbineau, the sound of his splashing footsteps marking his retreat.

Howe twisted on his bed, now set atop two planks laid across Howe's four chests, for the ground beneath the tent floor was soggy, and the seams of the tent were dripping. "Strange fellow," he remarked as Sandjer'min spread a thin film of honey over the ointment he was using to treat Howe's wound, then covered it with a pad of loose-woven cotton and secured it with a wide band of linen.

"He is doing penance," Sandjer'min reminded Howe, "as some others are as well."

"I think he used to be a fighter. He doesn't look like he's spent his life in contemplation and prayer," said Howe firmly. "He's got much the same bearing as Sieur Horembaud. Pity he's illegitimate."

Sandjer'min handed Howe the end of the linen band. "If you will pass this under your hips."

The brazier in the middle of the tent that provided both heat and light in the fading day spat a trail of sparks into the air; neither Howe nor Sandjer'min paid much attention to it as Howe complied with Sandjer'min's request.

"He says little about the reason for his penance," said Howe, a speculative lift in his voice. "He may have done something sinful as a former soldier; that's what Noreberht thinks."

"He may have," said Sandjer'min, gathering up his supplies and standing up. "Whatever he was before, he is a pilgrim now."

"True, true, as are we all, or almost all," said Howe, a little too eagerly. "How much longer until I may be rid of this treatment?"

"Not very long. The skin is growing back, and there is no sign of putrescence. The wound should close in a handful of days, provided no further hurt is done," Sandjer'min told him.

"And the ointment you treat me with: do you use it on your own injuries? Those gouges Sorer Imogen gave you are likely to leave scars, or worse." He indicated the three deep marks on his cheek.

"They won't," Sandjer'min said simply; since his death and awakening more than thirty-two centuries ago, no wound, no matter how grievous, had left any lasting mark on his body. "Those of my blood have few scars."

"You treat yourself with your potions and balms?" Howe inquired.

"When it is necessary," he said truthfully enough; he had never had reason to serve as his own physician. "The rain is beginning to slack off; if tomorrow is clear, we can dry our tents and our clothes, and be on the road again by tomorrow evening. I'll have a look at your scrape at the dawn of the following day."

Howe did not quite sigh. "Very well. Frater Anteus is not convinced that this constant remedication is not a sign of vanity."

"If he had such a wound on his hip as you have on yours, he would think otherwise," Sandjer'min assured him as he stepped out into the rain, and started toward his own tent, wondering as he did if Sieur Horembaud would order another attempt at building a cooking-fire for the sunset meal; the one that had been assayed at dawn had been drowned before any porridge could be cooked, and so the company had made do with dry lentil-and-bean cakes.

"Sandjer'min," said a voice at his elbow.

"Micheu?" Sandjer'min replied, turning to peer into the dripping shadows between Vidame Bonnefiles' and dei Causi's tent and Sieur Horembaud's.

"If I may step into your tent so we can talk?" He was a bigger man than Sandjer'min: taller and with a breadth of shoulder that spoke of many years of demanding labor, for although Sandjer'min was stocky and of average height, he lacked the knotted masses of muscle that marked Micheu de Saunte-Foi as a man accustomed to hard work and the disciplines of combat. For all his pilgrim's habit and a formidable crucifix on a brass chain around his neck, there was an air of violence about him. To emphasize his determination, Micheu leaned in Sandjer'min's direction.

There was a subtle change in Sandjer'min's posture; his compelling eyes met Micheu's, his attention sharpened, his stance seemed to increase his height, and then, somehow, without a challenge or a threat, Sandjer'min became master of their encounter. "Certainly," he said cordially, and led the rest of the way, raising the flap to give Micheu the chance to enter ahead of him. "What do you want to discuss?"

Micheu, still flummoxed by his loss of mastery of their situation, stammered, "I . . . I have a t-task to perform. I wondered if you would be willing to accompany me?" He was appalled at how he sounded, like a servant or a vassal.

"What task might that be?" Sandjer'min took flint-and-steel and set a spark to the lumps and peelings of wood in the brazier next to his bed. As Micheu collected his thoughts, Sandjer'min raised his voice a little. "Ruthier, is there any of the plum wine left?"

Ruthier emerged from among their stacked chests and said, "Two or three bottles, my master."

"Will you give a large cup of it to Micheu and take the rest to the women's tent?" Sandjer'min asked; he pulled a tall stool out from the stack of chests and crates and sacks. "Micheu?" he offered.

"At once," said Ruthier, and went back into the stack to open a medium-sized chest of light-colored wood with Sandjer'min's eclipse device carved in its lid.

"Most gracious," said Micheu, determined to recover his conversational footing. He sat down, perching warily on the stool as if he expected some trick or mishap could befall him at any moment.

"It is cool tonight, and a little wine will serve to warm as well as a fire." Sandjer'min sat on the edge of his bed.

"I have missed rain. I hadn't realized how much until this storm," Micheu admitted. "I knew I would miss cool days."

Sandjer'min studied Micheu's demeanor. "Tell me: what it is you propose in coming to me."

"It is not my choice; I would prefer to do this alone. Sieur Horembaud would like me to go and capture the two men who have been behind us for so long; as a protector of the company, I am bound to follow his orders, and he has forbade me to act alone," Micheu said, doing what he could to regain his control of their discourse. "Since the company will not travel tonight, this is the time he would like to have them caught."

"I see." Sandjer'min waited for Micheu to continue.

"I agree this is probably the best opportunity we will have for some days," Micheu said. "I told Sieur Horembaud that since he does not want me to go alone on this task, I wanted you to come with me."

"And why is that," Sandjer'min inquired, no sign of discomfiture about him; it did not surprise him that Sieur Horembaud had brought along a protector for the company, nor that that protector was Micheu de Saunte-Foi.

"Because you're calm in tight situations, as we've seen, and you speak more languages than I do; depending upon what we find, I may have more need of your translation skills than another sword," Micheu said with unusual candor. "And, unless I have you wrong, you must carry at least one fighting weapon with you somewhere, as Sieur Horembaud does, and I would wager a few of the other men do. Torquil did, and I suspect Bonnefiles does. I need a comrade who is not afraid of a fight."

"I believe I may be able to arm myself," Sandjer'min said, suppressing his amusement at Micheu's bellicose attitude.

"With a sword, I would hope."

"When would you want to go after these men?" Sandjer'min asked, saying nothing about the kind of weapon he had with him.

"Soon after it's full dark. It would be sensible to go on foot. We'll attract less notice that way, and we'll be able to approach their camp with less disturbance than horses or asses would afford us."

"That is a judicious notion. Do you plan to bring a lanthorn?"

"Possibly a dark one, with the light directed down, or a hooded torch," Micheu said, thinking that Sandjer'min had more fighting sense than Micheu had credited to him. "I have one, and so does Sieur Horembaud, as you must know from riding opposite his point."

"You prefer dark lanthorns to light ones?" Sandjer'min asked.

"For a chore like this, yes. Open lanthorns are all very well for lighting the road ahead at night; they cast their beams a long way. In this instance, that is not wanted, though the company has many of them, and few dark lanthorns."

"Vidame Bonnefiles has one, as well," Sandjer'min reminded Micheu. "You might ask him to join us, since you think he has weapons with him."

Micheu stiffened. "The man's a heretic. There's no saying what he would do if he had a sword in his hand."

"Then why is he on this pilgrimage?" Sandjer'min asked. "Strange behavior for a heretic, is it not?"

"He said he repents his error, but not everyone is fooled. Those of us who have escorted companies of pilgrims have learned to question the sincerity of penitents. For Bonnefiles, I believe this pilgrimage is a way to disguise his true intentions. No, Sidi, I would rather let those followers remain free than attempt to arrest them with Bonnefiles for a companion. Who knows what he is capable of."

Sandjer'min was spared the need to answer; Ruthier appeared with a large wooden cup on a simple brass tray, which he presented to Micheu. "It is sweet," he said, bowing.

Micheu hesitated before picking up the cup. "What about you?" he said, looking squarely at Sandjer'min.

"Oh, you must forgive me not joining you; I do not drink wine— none of my blood do."

"A weakness?" Micheu asked with a sly smile.

"Some would say so," Sandjer'min conceded.

"Mohammedans are forbidden to drink," Micheu said speculatively.

"So they are, but many do in spite of the prohibition," Sandjer'min pointed out. "And there are many Christians who abstain from drinking except at Communion."

"You have the right of it. Most unfortunate, you not being able to enjoy your own hospitality," said Micheu; he lifted the cup and made the Sign of the Cross over it before taking a long draught of the dark-pink liquid. "I hope the women will appreciate the quality of what you're providing them."

"I hope it is useful to them," said Sandjer'min, and motioned to Ruthier. "They will have cups of their own."

Ruthier lowered his head as he put the cork plug back in the neck of the small amphora. "I will return shortly."

"Many thanks." Sandjer'min pulled the flap back into place as Ruthier left his tent.

"A good servant," Micheu remarked. "You're fortunate to have him."

"Yes," said Sandjer'min. "I know." He looked away from Micheu.

Micheu took another swallow of the plum wine. "Where did you come upon this?"

"It was sent to me by a trading company in Alexandria," he said, not mentioning that the company was his, as well as the winery that produced the wine. "I had ten bottles of Tuscan wine from them, four years ago, but nothing so fine recently. The wine you're drinking is from Anatolia."

Micheu gazed into the middle distance. "I used to think I'd like to be a vintner, but bastards, without recognition, are not often accorded that privilege in France. God has deemed otherwise for me, and I am bound, as a faithful Christian, to serve His Will." He finished the wine. "Mother Church has places I'm needed."

"But not in one of the vineyards, I take it," said Sandjer'min.

"No," Micheu chuckled. "At least, not yet." He got up and handed the large cup to Sandjer'min. "I'll see you later."

"Where do you want to meet?"

"At the north edge of our camp, near the four squat palms," he said decisively. "As soon as the cooking-fire is put out."

"Assuming it is lit," said Sandjer'min. "In this rain, it may not be possible."

"No, it might not. Let us say we will meet after Frater Anteus completes his evening prayers." Micheu took a deep breath. "You do have a sword with you, don't you."

"I do," Sandjer'min said. "I'll bring it with me." He would also have a pair of franciscas tucked into the back of his belt, but this he kept to himself.

"Very good," said Micheu, feeling as if he had recovered a portion of his authority. "I will see you later."

"You will," Sandjer'min said, and went to lift the flap for him.

When Ruthier returned, Sandjer'min explained what had been decided, adding, "I wish I knew what Order he belongs to—he isn't a Templar or a Hospitaller."

"Are you sure of that?" Ruthier asked.

"Oh, yes," said Sandjer'min. "He hasn't the manner of either. No, I suspect he's with one of the clandestine Orders."

"Why?" Ruthier asked.

"He's too . . . self-possessed." He hesitated. "No, that's not quite it. He is calculating and observant."

Ruthier considered this. "Do you think he may be seeking to entrap you in some way?"

"For what reason?" Sandjer'min asked, but with a tingle of apprehension in his question. "But he might have a private purpose."

"You're not a Christian. You're not from France. You know more than he does." He flapped his hands in frustration. "I don't know."

"I doubt it, but I'm not certain." Sandjer'min looked toward the top of the tent. "It's unfortunate that we didn't treat the seams with tar."

"We'd still get wet," said Ruthier.

"That we would." Sandjer'min sat down again. "A pity I no longer have that boiled-wool pluvial for tonight's business."

"It's too hot for this place. You'd swelter, wearing it, if you still had it," Ruthier said.

"And this is terrible weather to go after our followers," said Sandjer'min. "But our attack will certainly be unexpected."

"Do you think you'll have to fight?"

Sandjer'min shrugged. "Perhaps."

"Then you'll want what the red-lacquer chest holds," Ruthier said, and moved into the stack of baggage once again to set the old chest upright. "Under the strap in the back," he said as he loosed the wide leather band and brought out a slightly curved scabbard, which he held out to Sandjer'min.

"Thank you," he said as he took it. "Masashige gave me a treasure when he presented me with this sword."

"That he did," Ruthier said. "You're going on foot?"

"It's what Micheu wants." He stood up, tightened his belt, and slipped the scabbard through it, then shifted it so it sat more comfortably on his hip. He tapped the pommel of the katana. "It is a beautiful weapon."

Ruthier said nothing more; he busied himself with rigging a number of vessels to catch the drips that came through the heavy canvass of the tent, then went to help Carlus and Vitalis set up for the evening meal; when that was done, he went to the remuda-lines to make sure the horses and asses were properly fed. By the time he returned to the tent, Sandjer'min had left.

Micheu was waiting by the low-growing palm trees, a dark lanthorn in his hand casting a small circle of wavering light on the puddle near his feet. "I was beginning to wonder if you would come," he said quietly as Sandjer'min came up to him.

"I'm ready to go," said Sandjer'min.

"You have a sword?"

"I do." He indicated the katana. "It's an eastern one."

"So long as it will cut, the rest hardly matters." Micheu touched his belt. "Two short swords. Almost as good as a broadsword and a shield."

"You're a tall man, and that makes the short swords good weapons for you, since you have a long reach." Sandjer'min squinted up at the rain. "It's lighter than it was."

"I think so." Micheu began to walk, trudging steadily.

Sandjer'min fell in beside him. "Do you know where the followers are camped?"

"Last night they were about half a league away, in a little cluster of desert plants. I doubt they moved today." He did his best not to swing the lanthorn. "Moving lights attract attention," he remarked.

"Yes, they do," said Sandjer'min, who had no need for the lanthorn; his night-seeing eyes saw the gentle slope ahead of them as if it were in half-light rather than full dark. Already his paragaudion and femoralia were damp and would soon be drenched. The rain made him uncomfortable, but not incapacitated.

"They have a single tent, and we can take them both at once." There was a note of pleasant anticipation in his voice. "We have the element of surprise in our favor; we must be careful not to lose it."

They went along in silence for a bit, then Sandjer'min asked, "You said we are to capture the followers. Does Sieur Horembaud want to question these men?"

"Of course. He wants to know why they are following us, who they work for if not for themselves, and he is eager to mete out punishment to them."

"Punishment? For what reason?" Sandjer'min was not surprised at this, but it troubled him.

"As a warning to others, if nothing else," said Micheu. "Sieur Horembaud knows his duty."

"Then he plans to kill them, or maim them."

They were nearing the place where the followers were camped. Micheu motioned to Sandjer'min to stop. When he spoke again, it was in a whisper. "Their animals are on the east side of the thicket. We will approach from the west. With the wind out of the south, they shouldn't catch our scent until we're in the camp." He pointed off to his left. "Less chance for the animals to make a fuss that way. Use your sword to open the side of the tent so we may enter unexpectedly. Make as little noise as you can."

"All right," said Sandjer'min, catching sight of the tent in the middle of the brush.

They were almost at the stand of bushes, and now slowed their pace. "Be careful not to break any branches. That could wake them and warn them. It would be sure to make their animals fret."

"I'll bear that in mind," Sandjer'min said quietly.

Big though he was, Micheu moved lightly as he sped up to a jog. "You keep to my right."

Sandjer'min matched his pace. "As you wish."

"Draw your sword," Micheu ordered.

The katana came out of the scabbard with a soft, metallic snick.

"Cut the tent up to down, and step inside as soon as the cut is made." They were less than ten paces from the tent now, and they were almost running. "I'll make a double-cut with my swords. See you keep away from me once we're inside. We'll be fighting at close quarters and we might inadvertently injure—"

"That I will," said Sandjer'min, and lifted his sword to thrust it into the heavy goats'-wool cloth; the side of the tent yawned open as three rents broadened. Sandjer'min went through into the interior, noticing that two figures on unrolled beds were coming quickly awake, one of them reaching for a Damascus blade lying on the ground next to him. Stepping over to him, Sandjer'min pulled back the upper coverlet and moved the point of his sword to a hairsbreadth above his throat. "Stay still," he said first in Coptic, then in Arabic.

The man swore comprehensively in Coptic but remained where he was, his eyes fixed on the rippled elegance of the Japanese blade.

An instant later, the man in the other bed reached out for his companion's sword, and took a swipe at the backs of Sandjer'min's legs with it, whooping as he felt the steel encounter cloth and flesh.

Sandjer'min yelled, the pain coming quickly. Both his calves ached and he could feel the muscles strain. He was so taken aback that he let his katana slip; the superb blade slid through the man's throat and spine as if passing through fresh cultured milk. The man gave a hideous gargling sound, jerked twice, and lay still. Appalled at what he had done, Sandjer'min tried to take a step back so as not to damage the body. The cuts he had received began to bleed in the steady, pulseless manner of his kind, and he had to steady himself to allow a moment of vertigo to pass that promised a hard recovery. "My legs. Are cut," said Sandjer'min, and fell back, pinning the second man to the ground. He raised his sword and, using the hem of his paragaudion, wiped the blade clean, then returned it to the scabbard; he noticed that his hands were shaking slightly. So much blood and all of it useless, he thought, for the man is dead. More than twenty-five centuries ago he had tried to restore himself tasting the dregs of battle among the fallen, but without life, the blood had provided nothing; that had been the last time when he had resorted to such desperate measures. He moved a little to hold his captive in place.

The second man twisted under Sandjer'min, trying to free himself, but Sandjer'min would not budge. Micheu lifted his dark lanthorn, directing the small circle of light down at the second man, and then at the dead man. "I underestimated you," he said to Sandjer'min.

Sandjer'min rolled a little but not enough to allow the man he was sprawled upon to move enough to reach his weapon. "Find this one's sword." The pain in the back of his legs had settled into a steady, acidic ache.

"Let me kill him and be done with it," Micheu said.

But Sandjer'min was staring at the second man. "Gudjei?" he said at last.

"Sidi," he said resentfully. "Why did you kill my brother-in-law?"

Outside the tent, one of the asses brayed, which started the horses and the second ass to fretting.

"What the Devil?" Micheu exclaimed. "What is he saying? Do you know this churl?"

"You should recognize him," said Sandjer'min, addressing Micheu. "He was the company's guide for a time, before Firouz," Sandjer'min said in French. "His beard is longer, but he is not much changed."

Micheu turned the lanthorn on Gudjei's face. "Lord Jesus!" He crossed himself.

Gudjei whispered something in Coptic.

"Why have you been following us?" Micheu demanded, moving a step closer to Gudjei and holding crossed short swords over his face.

"We were ordered to," said Gudjei, glaring at Micheu as he repeated, "Why did you kill my brother-in-law?"

Sandjer'min translated for Gudjei, and managed to sit up in spite of a persistent dizziness, and to slowly lever himself to his feet; once he was upright, he took hold of a tent-pole while he regained his balance.

"Your brother-in-law, was he?" Micheu said, pointing to the dead man, and let Sandjer'min translate. "Why were the two of you following Sieur Horembaud's company of pilgrims? Did Firouz threaten you, or pay you?"

Gudjei started to move, only to find Micheu standing over him, straddling his chest, both short swords pointed downward. "Stay still, you worthless pile of dung. It would give me great pleasure to kill you now."

Again Sandjer'min translated, then said to Micheu as calmly as he could, "You say Sieur Horembaud wants to question—"

"That he does," Micheu interrupted. "How badly are you cut? Will I have to leave you here and send others to bring you back to camp?"

"There are horses and asses; all three of us can ride," Sandjer'min reminded him. "The sooner we leave here, the sooner Sieur Horembaud will have his answers."

Suddenly Gudjei struck out with his legs, kicking Micheu on the knees with as much force as he could summon up; Micheu roared with fury and pain, going down heavily. One of his swords cut into Gudjei's shoulder, and then Micheu lunged at him, reaching for Gudjei's throat. "Lame me, will you!"

Sandjer'min lurched forward, reaching out to stop Micheu from throttling Gudjei. "No!" he shouted. "He must stay alive. For Sieur Horembaud."

Micheu tried to shake Sandjer'min off him, growling like an angry bear, his hands showing blood as he tried to squeeze above the slice he had made. To his astonishment, this was difficult to do; Sandjer'min was much stronger than Micheu had assumed he was, and his tenacity was formidable. "He tried to *kill* me!"

"And you're trying to kill him. Neither one of you is dead yet. Let go of him, let him up and secure him, then we'll work out how to use the horses and asses." Sandjer'min felt himself weakening and knew he could not reveal this to Micheu. "Come, Micheu. Release him."

The three men remained locked together for several breaths as the rage drained out of Micheu and Sandjer'min continued to hold him back from his captive. Then Micheu let go of Gudjei with a gesture of disgust, and pushed back from him, dislodging Sandjer'min in the process. "He's not worth the penance." He got up, then bent down and hauled Gudjei to his feet. "Where's your rope? And don't tell me you don't have any."

Sandjer'min translated this, and relayed Gudjei's response. "The rope is with the animals except for those lengths holding up the tent."

"We will need a length sufficient to hold this man's hands and to allow his animal to be led. I think he should ride an ass." Micheu fixed Sandjer'min with a hard stare. "You're still bleeding, are you? Then you should ride."

"What of you?" asked Sandjer'min when he had finished translating for Gudjei's benefit. "Wouldn't you prefer to ride, as well?"

Gudjei shook his head, not declining, but meaning he had no opinion. "It would be best to bring all the animals. Otherwise they will be bait for hungry creatures."

"I'm not one to waste good riding animals," Micheu told Gudjei through Sandjer'min.

"You'd best see what other things we have that you want."

"Don't be insolent with me," Micheu warned Gudjei, and added to Sandjer'min, "And don't you soften or lessen what I've told you."

"I have not done so," Sandjer'min assured him. He was growing weaker; the cuts would have to be sewn closed, and sooner rather than later. "Let's take what we need and leave."

"But what about Besim?" Gudjei exclaimed, realizing what was happening.

"That's his name? Hm. Leave him here. There's no time to bury him properly." Micheu was peering around the tent, turning a chest over to find the lock to open it. He stopped and wiped his bloody hands on his damp pilgrim's habit. "Wrap him up in a blanket to slow down the rot, but that's all we can do."

Gudjei turned stricken eyes on Micheu, but mumbled some kind of thanks, then knelt awkwardly, his shoulder still bleeding, to work the body, still mostly in his bed-roll, into his own bed-roll for additional protection.

After a short time, Sandjer'min went to help him. "You're hurting yourself," he said in Coptic, and helped to hold the open end of the bed-roll as wide as possible; Besim's blood was beginning to dry, and the coverlet was stiffening with it.

"Hurry it up. We must return to our camp," Micheu ordered. "Tell me about your animals."

"Two asses and three horses," said Gudjei without any trace of emotion. "We had more when my uncle was with us, but—"

"As to what this was about and why he was with you, Sieur Horembaud will determine," Micheu said, cutting Gudjei off as Sandjer'min began his translation.

They put Gudjei on one of the asses, and Micheu and Sandjer'min clambered aboard two of the horses bareback. Bridles and halters were taken as well as a large sack of grain, and they headed off into the night at a walk, the rain washing away much of the blood on all of them, and the lanthorn dimming as the flame guttered inside it. They picked their way through the low scrub, each man terribly alert as well as exhausted.

Sieur Horembaud was awake and pacing the path between the tents when the three men came into the pilgrims' camp. "God on the Cross! What took you so long. What happened to you?" The second question came more quietly as he saw that neither Sandjer'min nor Gudjei was very well-seated on their mounts.

"There was a fight," said Micheu. "One of the two men following us was killed. Couldn't be helped. That one got in a lucky hack at Sandjer'min." He slid off his horse and held out the reins and two lead-ropes for one of the servants to take. "Better get his servant. He's going to need help."

"But . . ." Sieur Horembaud saw Sandjer'min sway on his horse. "Ruthier!" he yelled. "Come!"

There was a surge of confusion as most of the pilgrims ran out of their tents to see what was going on. Shouts and other outbursts mixed with jostling and shoving; Sieur Horembaud castigated those nearest him, ordering them to return to their tents, and Vitalis was able to take the leads from Micheu's hand. Methodus Temi stepped forward to help take the prisoner off his ass, and a few moments later, Ruthier was able to reach Sandjer'min.

"My master," he said with alarm.

"My legs are cut," he said weakly, then slid off the horse; Ruthier caught him under the shoulders and half-dragged him away to their tent.

❖   ❖   ❖

Transcript of the questioning of Gudjei at the pilgrims' camp, conducted by Sieur Horembaud, recorded by Jiochim Menines in Church Latin from the translations provided by Rakoczy Sandjer'min, written on vellum, also provided by Rakoczy Sandjer'min, witnessed by Frater Anteus and Noreberht lo Avocat on the night and morning of the 11th or 12th of August, 1225.

I swear by Almighty God and His Angels that this is a full and complete transcription of the questioning of the guide Gudjei, the questioning being done by Sieur Horembaud du Langnor, at his camp in the desert between the Fifth Cataract of the River Nile and its junction with the Atbara River on the night of the 11th or 12th of August in the 1225th Year of Our Lord. May God blast my wits and make me blind if I report inaccurately. Amen.

Each question and answer is translated by Sandjer'min from Coptic to Anglo-French, or from Anglo-French to Coptic, and those questions and answers are translated by Frater Anteus and Noreberht lo Avocat. This record will be presented to the first Roman church where we arrive on our return journey.

Sieur Horembaud: *Gudjei, you have been our guide, but left that post before we left the banks of the Nile. Why did you do so, if you wanted to know where we are bound?*
Gudjei: *My uncle, who is the head of my family, ordered me to do so.*
Sieur Horembaud: *To what purpose did he do this? What did he expect to gain from this?*
Gudjei: *I did not ask him. It is not my place to know.*
Sieur Horembaud: *What did your uncle ask you to learn for him?*
Gudjei: *Where you were going and how long you took to get there.*
Sieur Horembaud: *But we discussed this when you first agreed to guide us.*

Gudjei: I knew where you intended to go, but I could not swear that you would actually go there.

Sieur Horembaud: You advised us, you found us a man you described as a suitable guide in Firouz, who deserted us, taking young Heneri with him. Did you think that would happen? Did you encourage him to do it?

Gudjei: I would not have recommended Firouz if I thought he would do so despicable a thing, upon my soul's salvation. I am telling you the truth, before God.

Sieur Horembaud: So you have sworn to do. Any lie condemns you to Hell.

Gudjei: That is my oath.

Sieur Horembaud: You tell me that though you stopped leading the company, you did follow us, on your uncle's orders.

Gudjei: I haven't denied it.

Sieur Horembaud: And you don't know why he ordered you to do this?

Gudjei: No.

(*Frater Anteus and Sieur Horembaud conferred with Noreberht lo Avocat on what avenue to explore next, for the answers that Gudjei supplied to this point were not useful*)

Sieur Horembaud: Has your uncle ever given you such orders in the past?

Gudjei: Yes.

Sieur Horembaud: And what happened to the pilgrims you followed at that time?

Gudjei: Various things.

Sieur Horembaud: Describe the most recent: what happened to the band of pilgrims before mine you were told to follow.

Gudjei: They were traveling at a better time of the year, and came as far as Baruta on the river, with another company of pilgrims. At Baruta, they took horses and asses and began the long, slow climb into the mountains of Ethiopia. Twice they met other travelers, and once they fought as best they could with marauders, where some of their men were

taken captive by slavers who bore them off to the east. I do
not know what became of them. If a ransom was demanded,
I heard nothing of it. The rest of the company abandoned
their pilgrimage and went back to Baruta. There four of
their remaining number became ill, and two of them died
of Bleeding Fever. The other two had to wait until another
company of pilgrims arrived; the two begged a place with
the other company. They left going down-river. What happened to them I do not know.

Sieur Horembaud: *Did you inform the slavers about the
company of pilgrims?*

Gudjei: *I warned the leader of the company that slavers
had many spies, but I did not inform the slavers in any way.
I did not have to.*

Sieur Horembaud: *Did you tell any slaver, or any slaver's
spy, about this company?*

Gudjei: *No.*

Sieur Horembaud: *On your soul's salvation?*

Gudjei: *On my soul's salvation.*

Sieur Horembaud: *Would you say the same thing if your
feet were to the fire?*

Gudjei: *Yes.*

Sieur Horembaud: *Shall we put that to the test?*

Frater Anteus: *He is a Christian, Sieur Horembaud. You
would have to defend such methods and it might require
more penance of you.*

Sieur Horembaud: *God have mercy on us! If you insist I
believe him . . .*

Sandjer'min: *I doubt he's lying,*

Sieur Horembaud: *You can say that, when he's the one who
cut your calves? How can you think he has any truth in him
at all? Almeric, bring a stool for Sandjer'min, his cuts are
bleeding again.*

(Almeric comes into the tent and sets down a stool)

Sieur Horembaud: *Your manservant must have done a
poor job of stitching you up.*

Sandjer'min: He did well enough.

Gudjei: He did my shoulder properly.

Sieur Horembaud: Little as you deserved it. You should have to go through the remainder of your life with a damaged arm.

Gudjei: God knows I have done nothing wrong.

(Gudjei slumps)

Sandjer'min: He can't stay awake much longer, Sieur Horembaud. For that matter, neither can I. My injuries are sapping my attention.

Sieur Horembaud: I want him to Confess his sins.

Frater Anteus: Prick his feet with the points of arrows, and he'll be awake.

Sandjer'min: What does that matter, if he cannot understand what he is saying? How much more do you intend to ask him tonight, Sieur Horembaud? Both he and I need to rest, and dawn is coming quickly.

Sieur Horembaud: All of us are tired. All right. If the rain has stopped by mid-day, we will move on come nightfall. I will need to know as much as I can learn from this turd before we break camp. And it must be the truth.

Frater Anteus: He is a Christian, Sieur Horembaud. Lying now will send him to Hell.

Sieur Horembaud: He has a strange way of showing his faith.

Sandjer'min: He's worn out. So am I.

Sieur Horembaud: Micheu will take you in hand, Gudjei, and he will guard you through the day. I will question you again at mid-afternoon, and you will answer every question I put to you or you will suffer for it. Do you understand me?

Gudjei: I understand.

(Gudjei is taken in charge by Micheu and Vidame Bonnefiles. Sieur Horembaud orders everyone to go to sleep if they are not assigned to guard-duty. The examination will resume at mid-afternoon)

This is the whole of the questions and answers asked by Sieur Horembaud of the guide Gudjei, to which I have set my hand in testimony before the following witnesses. May God lead us to see aright.

Jiochim Menines, recorder

Frater Anteus, witness
Noreberht lo Avocat

4

Five nights after the rain stopped, as they continued along the plateau, Sieur Horembaud's company came upon another company of pilgrims; they were traveling southwest on the trade route from the distant and ancient city of Axum, and were bound for the Church and Monastery of the Redeemer, as Sieur Horembaud's company was, in preparation for the next leg of their journey up the Blue Nile. The two parties met at a small oasis—the other group had made camp by the time Sieur Horembaud's company arrived—where the trade route and the pilgrims' trail came together in the shade of the palm trees around a rocky spring that provided water all year around; just at present, it was feeding a brook that would dry up to a trickle by the end of the year. This oasis was on a shoulder of the foothills, the Nile now three hundred hands beneath them, tumbling and roiling, and sounding like the water was waging war with the land.

When informed that Sieur Horembaud's company would be traveling up the Atbara, the leader of the other company scoffed at the notion, but two of his guides expressed cautious approval of the idea. "The Atbara floods, as the Nile does; it will fade away to a dry canyon in your winter," said Pendibe, and was seconded by the guides of the other company.

It was not yet midnight, but Sieur Horembaud called a halt for their night-time meal, and ordered Sandjer'min to keep at his side. "This is a good place to spend the rest of the night, according to Pendibe."

"For both companies," Sandjer'min said when Sieur Horembaud looked about doubtfully. "Our animals need rest, and we may be able to learn useful things from Pater Venformir's pilgrims."

"That old priest is a cagey one: Poles and Bohemians are like that—eager to suborn others for their purposes. I'm not convinced that he is as devout as he claims to be, or that his pilgrims are here for piety," Sieur Horembaud said. "If I were a more suspicious man, I might believe he and his pilgrims had been waiting for us."

"How would he know to wait for you? Who would have told him? And why?" Sandjer'min saw the annoyance in Sieur Horembaud's eyes, and went on, "For all you know, he is wondering the same about you and your pilgrims."

Sieur Horembaud took a little time to form his answer. "He's a priest: God or His Angel might have told Pater Venformir in a dream or a vision of our coming—which is why I want you to observe these pilgrims and tell me what you think of them. You can speak their language, can't you? We must know what they have been doing, and what they plan to do. I am unwilling to embrace their assurances that their motives are truly Christian." He stood a little apart from his company of pilgrims, watching the servants and slaves from both companies working to set up a cooking-fire, and struggling to work together, with limited success.

"They are as much strangers here as we are. Wouldn't you rather I ask Pendibe to watch their guides and their three escorts, to talk to them? Wouldn't they know more about the pilgrims' travels than the pilgrims themselves? The pilgrims know very little of this land." Sandjer'min stood with Sieur Horembaud, holding Melech's reins and leaning on the gelding's flank to keep his calves from aching too much. The threads holding his wounds shut were pulling, making any flexing of his calves painful.

"It is our fellow Roman Christians who concern me, not the Copts—I make allowances for your unknown faith; there is just you and your manservant to uphold it, and neither of you has shown disdain for Christians," said Sieur Horembaud. "We must know how we stand in the other pilgrims' eyes, and what their plans may be. Those from distant reaches of the German States and the lands of the Bohemians and Slavs and the Poles have greater bearing on our journey than any other Christians; it is their testimony that will honor or condemn us for what we have done here in this wild place. Their report will be the linchpin of our chronicle. We will be gone back to our homelands and when we are, the accounts carried by them will determine how our pilgrimage is understood."

"Well enough," Sandjer'min said, having recognized the language of the County of Austria, and a few other dialects from Bohemia and Moravia. "I can speak with some of them for you, but not all. That would rouse misgiving within that company. There are Lithuanians among them, and I don't know very much of their tongue; I will do the best I can and will tell you if I cannot comprehend what they say."

"Good enough." He patted the copper-dun's neck. "You've done well by me so far. This mare is much improved."

Sandjer'min shook his head. "It would be better if you would hold off riding her for another few days. She is improved, but not wholly mended."

"These little horses are tough; she'll manage, so long as you keep the leg bandaged," said Sieur Horembaud. "Tell me what you think of Magister Clothwig: he is unlike the rest," he said in another tone, pointing to the man in question among the pilgrims.

"A scholar, as he said he is," Sandjer'min summed up after giving the man a thorough perusal. "Seeking knowledge in the ends of the earth. He is preparing a book on the Christians here, or so he told Menines."

"A scholar? Not a heretic? They are often one in the same."

"Not a heretic, at least not so far as I understand it, although neither he nor I said anything about religion when I spoke to him; I asked him about Axum. He told me there are new churches being built, as well as a good number of Jews there, and some still in Meroe, which are much diminished from what they were; he was provided introductions to the scholars remaining there," said Sandjer'min. "Since I am not one of your faith, I may not know enough about heresy to be certain if he has that taint, but I feel no cause for alarm." He disliked making this admission, but he realized that Sieur Horembaud would expect a full and careful answer.

"You are being indirect, Sandjer'min, and that makes me uneasy."

"I haven't enough information to be more direct," Sandjer'min told him, then fell silent as Pendibe came up to them.

"They have been traveling for thirty-seven days without more than two days' rest during that time," he said. "The horses and asses are worn to the bone."

"I thought they looked thin," said Sieur Horembaud. "Do you know why they went to Axum?"

Sandjer'min relayed the question, and added, "Did they mention any other place they saw?"

"They had planned to go to the coast and turn southeast along it. There is said to be a great port to the southeast. I've heard mention of it myself from traders."

"What port?" Sieur Horembaud demanded as he heard Sandjer'min's translation.

"Ask their guides; they have seen it, or so they claim," said Pendibe. "They say it smells of sulphur these days, coming on the wind from the east."

"Why sulphur?" Sieur Horembaud asked anxiously. "Is there a gate into Hell in that place?"

"No," Sandjer'min answered directly. "From what I have learned, there are volcanos."

"Some say that they are windows into Hell," Sieur Horembaud persisted. "Perpetual fire in the earth: what else can they be?"

This time Sandjer'min spoke to Pendibe. "Do you know if there are fire-mountains near the port the other guides spoke of?"

"I have not seen them for myself, but I have been told by many who know these things, and have seen them, that there are a good number of fire-mountains between the sea and the high mountain lakes. If the port they speak of is real, it may well be near a volcano." Pendibe stopped to let Sandjer'min explain this to Sieur Horembaud.

"I have been talking to their head guide, Tsega is his name, and we are thinking that with a little planning, we will reach the Church and Monastery of the Redeemer by sunrise the day after tomorrow, assuming we stay here for the night and the day ahead. We have"—he thought a long moment, then said—"a bit more than six leagues to go. The climb is moderate and the road should be in good repair if the heavy rains haven't brought landslides. We will have to use the Inundation bridge over the Atbara, and it will allow only one beast or three men to cross at one time."

"Why not use boats?" Sieur Horembaud asked.

"Because the water is too high and wild. In the spring, that would be a good choice, but not now." Pendibe looked directly at Sandjer'min. "Make him understand: crossing the river in a boat is too dangerous."

"Three men or one beast? Does that mean the beast is unburdened or unridden? Or will the bridge take a beast if someone is riding it? I have seen horses balk crossing bridges, and that can lose the bridge and the horse together." Sieur Horembaud returned Pendibe's stare. "Or does the other guide have a better idea for getting over the Atbara? Another crossing, perhaps?"

"I have not asked him," Pendibe said stiffly. "I know of no such crossing. In the winter, you can step over the Atbara in the bottom of the canyon, no bridge is needed. But now? It is the bridge we must use, or we must find a way to cling to the walls of the canyon that the Atbara makes; the path we have been following stops at the bridge. We must cross there, whether we are traveling up the Atbara or the Nile."

"A bridge," Sieur Horembaud said, tossing his head with scorn. "But I suppose if we must use it, we must. God tests us in all things."

"Do you want to press on tonight, then, or wait until tomorrow afternoon?" Pendibe asked. "It is almost midnight, and the tents have just gone up."

Sieur Horembaud swung round to confront him. "Were it my choice, I would press on, but the rest of the company is eager for guests and an easy night. I pray they have not given the others our trust too quickly."

"They are your fellow Roman Christians. Why should you not trust them?" Pendibe added to Sandjer'min, "In the winter, we would have seen many more pilgrims than we have on this journey."

Sandjer'min translated, telling Sieur Horembaud, "You seem to think there's trouble ahead."

"One must always be alert to trouble; in such a strange land, we might easily be deceived by those who appear familiar but are not," Sieur Horembaud said. "Many a rogue has hidden his sins in a monk's habit or a pilgrim's blue cotehardie."

"There could be trouble, I suppose; there can always be trouble if you look for it," said Pendibe when Sandjer'min finished his translation. "But I find it hard to . . . to hold other Christians in such low opinion."

Sieur Horembaud audibly ground his teeth, then said, "There are reasons some of us do not embrace other Christians without hesitation; we have witnessed a few of those for ourselves already." He gave a vindictive little snort. "Many say they are Christians but in truth are sent of the Devil to lure us from our faith."

Sandjer'min translated this reluctantly, not wanting to give Pendibe or the other Copts any reason to resent the presence of Sieur Horembaud's company.

Pendibe sighed. "So you Romans say."

"And who is to blame us?" Sieur Horembaud asked truculently.

Before Sandjer'min could translate this, there was a wail that came from the edge of the camp, where tents had just been erected; it was underscored by a single bark of laughter and the sudden sounds of a scuffle. This was followed by a deluge of shouted prayers and more keening; a few of the other company of pilgrims looked about in consternation.

"Sorer Imogen," said Sieur Horembaud, turning to Sandjer'min. "You'd better attend to her before she frightens Pater Venformir's pilgrims away. I'll try to explain what I can to Pater Venformir."

"I will speak with the other pilgrims when Sorer Imogen is calmer, so that they can comprehend her circumstances; the sound of her outburst may distress all of us," Sandjer'min said as he waved to Baccomeo to take Melech's reins. "Brush him well, and note any rubbed places on his coat; give him a small amount of water now, and more after you have fed him," he said in the northern Italian dialect, then hurried off toward the disturbance.

Margrethe met him at the door-flap. "She is overwrought, which you must know. These strangers frighten her," she said, ushering him inside, her eyes shining at the sight of him. "Lalagia is with her."

"Very good." He hesitated long enough to make note of her condition; he saw the dark circles around her eyes. "You haven't been sleeping well, have you?"

"No," she admitted. "I have used the medicaments to keep Sorer Imogen more at ease during our travels." She held the sheet aside and allowed Sandjer'min to step into the side of the tent that was Sorer Imogen's.

The nun shrieked and resumed praying swiftly and loudly.

"If you'll remain beside her, Lalagia? I have some calmatives I can provide for now, and another soporific, as well, for after she eats." He felt more than saw Lalagia's glare as he took off his sack of medicaments and set it next to Sorer Imogen. Quickly he removed a small bottle containing a bluish tincture. "This will restore her composure for now." He unstopped the bottle and held it out, pressing it to her lower lip. "Good Sorer Imogen," he said quietly. "This drink will quieten your fears. Drink half the bottle and you will shortly be less anxious, and will be able to pray with more dignity."

As he hoped, his choice of words met with some approval. Obediently Sorer Imogen drank, then resumed her hectic prayers; Sandjer'min nodded to Lalagia. "Thank you. You did well."

Lalagia pushed up on her elbow. "You're going to need more of that drink before many days are out."

"I agree," he said, his worry revealed by the fine vertical line between his brows; he would have to find an herb-woman or someone well-versed in the lore of plants in order to make more of the calmative. As it was, he was nearly out of this medicament.

"What about water? Shall I get her some?" Lalagia asked; she was getting to her feet, her features pale, her face damp.

"Are you feeling unwell, Lalagia?" Sandjer'min asked as he took stock of her condition.

"Not unwell, just pregnant," she said in Byzantine Greek.

"Pregnant?" Sandjer'min echoed her.

"Only just. It may not catch. No use in being in a state because of it until it's certain." She watched him rise. "The cuts still bothering you? You're straining."

"Yes, they are, and they will for a while longer." He returned to the more pressing matter. "Who is the father."

"Methodus Temi, of course. Whoelse could it be?" She gave him a defiant stare. "I am not a whore, I'm a camp-follower, and loyal to the man who supports me. Methodus has been kind to me, and although he may not dote upon me as the Bondame does on you, he is truly fond of me, and minded to keep me with him."

"If your pregnancy is discovered, you will not be allowed to remain with the company," Sandjer'min warned, paying no attention to her remark about Margrethe's attraction to him.

"I have time, and they won't stone me, as they would the Bondame in a similar situation," she said sharply.

Sandjer'min moved a few steps away from Sorer Imogen, who was now completely caught up in her recitation of prayers. "Are you not seeking Sieur Arnoul?"

"I am; for the sake of his children. But I have looked for him a long time—more than two years—and I know I may not find him. I went up the Nile, as I was told he had done, and I made inquiries where I could, but after Edfu, any mention of him ceased. One of the priests I spoke to said there was nothing he could tell me." She wiped her face with the flat of her hand, but whether to be rid of sweat or tears, even she did not know. "I was not meant to be alone. Methodus has been with the Crusaders: he understands, and he wants me." She paused. "We may not go much farther with the company. We've been talking about waiting out the end of the Inundation, and then joining with travelers going down-river toward Alexandria. Sieur Horembaud will not want me to remain once he sees my state, which he will do in two months, when we will be at the limits of our travels."

"Just you, or you and Methodus?"

"Methodus and I, of course," she answered with a little more heat. "If he comes with me, I can make a report to the Bishop who sent me on this pilgrimage, and deliver a claim so that my children may have their father's protection. Methodus is my witness. The Church cannot refuse me. I have followed all I have learned about Sieur Arnoul to the edges of the Christian world and God has not brought us together." She pressed her lips together, and when she was certain she could go on, she said, "Methodus is a good man. More than that, as a blacksmith, he has a fine skill, one that will gain him employment anywhere, and he treats me well. I am not young, but I will not be old for a while yet, and he and I can have good years together. He says he will raise my children if the Church will release them to me."

"Have you said anything of this to Bondame Margrethe?" The question hung between them like an invisible web.

"No. That is one thing that gives me pause. Telling her is bound to upset her, and I am reluctant to do that. I like the Bondame; she has been good to me. She treats me better than the rest of the company. I don't want to leave the Bondame without any help. Sorer Imogen might well have another fit, no matter what medicaments you give her, and if she does, the Bondame will be hard-put to contain her, with your help or without it." She glanced at Sorer Imogen, who was now praying less frantically.

"I understand you," said Sandjer'min, and added, "I will do what I can to ease as many of Bondame Margrethe's burdens as I am able, so long as I do not compromise her, or Sorer Imogen," he said.

Lalagia smiled. "Good. I knew you wouldn't make me explain. The Bondame will be pleased to know that you will guard her." She went back to Sorer Imogen and said, "You should rest, Sorer," in her best Anglo-French. "You do yourself no good exhausting yourself this way. Ask God to bring you some peace, for all our sakes."

Lalagia said nothing more; she went to the other side of the sheet, had a few words with Margrethe, and left the tent.

Margrethe came to the end of the sheet and looked at Sorer Imogen lying on her side, her knees drawn up to her joined hands. "How is she?"

"Much less excited," said Sandjer'min, feeling her attraction as if it were the sun's full mid-day intensity.

"God hasn't sent this upon her, has He? as a punishment or a test?" she asked in a rush, frightened by her own thoughts.

"I am not a Christian, Bondame, but I would say no, your God has not visited the Falling Sickness upon her, any more than the desert has singled you out for suffering." He waited for her to speak, and when she blushed and looked away, he said, "She may be asleep before midnight supper is ready. In which case, I think you should have a handful of raisins for her, and one or two oil-cakes for when she wakes. She'll be famished by morning."

"I will arrange it with Lalagia." She watched him for a long moment. "The new company of pilgrims—there are no women with them, I'm told."

"I haven't seen any," Sandjer'min said quietly.

"Then it may be best that Lalagia and I stay in the tent while we are camped with them." She took a step toward him.

"I believe Sieur Horembaud would approve," said Sandjer'min. "He is wary of these pilgrims."

"He is wary of everyone." She yawned deeply. "I'm sorry," she told him. "I'm tired, though the night is only half over." Her face grew somber. "It seems so . . . strange to have other pilgrims with us. I hadn't realized how much the world has shrunk, as if we are the only people in it."

"I think that is a great fear in Sorer Imogen, though she dreads being alone." He said it gently, feeling her isolation as keenly as he felt her desire.

"Then, of course, I shall not go out unless I must." She studied Sorer Imogen. "What am I to do with her, to get her back to her convent? Heneri has gone, and I know of no man of our family who would come into Egypt to fetch us home, not even if Guillaume des Grossierterres should send them on my husband's behalf."

"The Hospitallers will send you with an escort, since you and your husband come from noble Houses," said Sandjer'min. "You will not be stranded here."

"That takes time, arranging an escort and securing passage. I will have been gone more than a year in a few days; who knows what waits, either for me or Sorer Imogen, in the Aquitaine? After so long, there could be many changes. The war between England and France may have finally ended, or it might have become much worse; the markets may be busy, or there could be no markets worth attending; illness or other suffering among the people could have spread, or ended. Frater Anteüs says we must all trust in God, and pray to the Virgin to still our doubts." She gazed at him, forlorn and filled with barely understood longings, then moved away from him. "If Sorer Imogen has the Falling Sickness, might not Sieur Dagoberht have it, as well? Might that be the cause of his condition? The physician who treated him said that males have it more often than females, who have the pains of childbirth in its place. Yet there may be a curse on all Goslands."

Sandjer'min spoke with gentle certainty. "Sieur Dagoberht might have the Falling Sickness, but I doubt it."

"Why?" She touched his hand, let go, then took it again. "You have never seen him."

"Because nothing you have told me suggests he had any of his troubles before his injury. From what I've been told, Sieur Dagoberht took a severe blow to his head, and that can cause many problems," Sandjer'min said. "I once treated a man who had been hale and strong until the beam of a lifting-rig struck him on the side of the head, after which he was without any sense of those around him, friend or foe. He jumbled words and could not remember the faces and names of his own children." He did not tell her that this had happened at dockside in Hippo Regia almost six hundred years ago.

"Then perhaps God gave us no children out of kindness, so the affliction would leave the House." Margrethe turned away from him. "I never did anything to harm him, and I did nothing to cause him to regret our marriage, and yet he treated me as if I were a servant of the Devil, sent to torment him." She broke away from him. "I'll stay with Sorer Imogen; she will not be alone while we are in the company of other pilgrims."

At another time, Sandjer'min might have tried to explain what he thought happened to those who received severe injuries to the head, but now, he knew, such theorizing would not be welcome, and might add to Margrethe's distress. "You and Lalagia can divide your time with her, so that each of you has a chance to rest. You cannot afford to let yourself be fatigued, not while she is so unpredictable in her reactions." He was about to go on when Lalagia called out, "Sidi, Sieur Horembaud wants you to join him and Pater Venformir at the cooking-fire."

Margrethe gave him a gesture of release. "Go. We will speak again before we break camp tomorrow evening."

"If you need my help, I will come," he said as he left her with the softly praying Sorer Imogen. He went through the cluster of tents to the center of the camp, where a number of Pater Venformir's pilgrims were already lining up to receive the simple stew of onions, herbs, and salted pork that was beginning to boil in the largest cauldron in the camp; pilgrims from Sieur Horembaud's company stood in ones and twos around the camp center, keeping careful watch on the others.

"Over here, Sandjer'min," Sieur Horembaud called, waving Sandjer'min toward him; he was sitting on a stack of chests, trying to appear at ease. Beside him stood Pater Venformir, and for the first time, Sandjer'min took stock of him; he was a forty-two-year-old man of remarkable ugliness: his face was sagging like an old hound's, with deep grooves in the cheeks, a lantern jaw that hung like flews, and heavy furrows across his forehead. His nose was large and lumpy, and his mouth turned down at the corners. But his clear blue-green eyes were bright as a youngster's and his voice was rich and sonorous as a pedal-note on an organ. His pilgrim's cotehardie had faded to a grayish-white, and the brass chain that held his pectoral cross was so dulled by long exposure to blowing sand that it looked as if it had been made of glazed ceramic links instead of metal. Frater Anteus stood with them, recounting their crossing of the Nubian Desert in Church Latin for Pater Venformir's benefit.

Sandjer'min made his way through the cluster of pilgrims, hearing a buzz of talk about him in the Moravian dialect; he wondered if they would say the same things if they knew he could understand them. "Sieur Horembaud," he said as he came up to the three men. "Frater Anteus. Pater Venformir."

"You are needed, I'm afraid," said Sieur Horembaud.

"For what tongue?" Sandjer'min asked with a half-smile.

"It is not that: these two manage well enough with Church Latin." Sieur Horembaud indicated the two clerics. "You are widely traveled. Can you tell us something of this Jenghiz Khan? in Church Latin."

Pater Venformir answered him. "When we left Venezia, we were told that his forces had conquered Persia and would be likely to stay there. Now I hear that it is believed that his troops are in the Russias."

"We had heard this in Alexandria, shortly before we set out on this pilgrimage," said Frater Anteus. "The Sultan was afraid that the Khan's armies would be set against his own as the Khan sets his eyes on Christendom."

"And Islam." Sandjer'min winced inwardly at the memory of Jenghiz Khan's troops in their fight against T'en Chi-Yu's soldiers, more than a decade ago. He coughed, and said, "I have been at the Monastery of the Visitation for a few years, and know only what I have been told by merchants and other travelers, but from these various accounts"—which included reports from the captains of his ships, and the factors in the ports they served—"I believe Jenghiz Khan is striking north of Egypt, at Samothrace and the Romanian region, and Hungary." A similar path to the one Attila and his armies had followed nine hundred years earlier. "He can move his army with great rapidity. At this time of year, his men can cover more than twenty-eight leagues in a day."

Pater Venformir crossed himself. "Then our homes could be in danger from them at least as much as Egypt is."

Frater Anteus muttered a prayer while Sieur Horembaud laughed. "Twenty-eight leagues in a day? Why not say thirty, or fifty? That is a tale, not a report, made to frighten those without faith."

"It is what I have been told, by those who have seen for themselves," Sandjer'min said, a bit stiffly; he was tempted to describe what he had witnessed of the Mongols a little more than a decade ago, but knew it would be folly.

"If half of that is their speed, then God protect the Russias," said Sieur Horembaud.

"Is it possible that they would attack Russia and the Holy Land at the same time? Are there enough men in the Khan's army to do that?" Pater Venformir asked Sandjer'min. "One of my sons has gone for a soldier, and my wife was so deeply troubled by it that she passed into the sin of melancholy and died."

Sandjer'min nodded. "If things continue as they are, it is more likely that your son will see the men of Jenghiz Khan before Egypt does."

Pater Venformir crossed himself. "God between him and danger," he said.

"Why should such misfortune come to Christendom?" Sieur Horembaud demanded.

"That is for God to know," said Pater Venformir in quelling accents.

"It is the battle of Armageddon that is coming," said Frater Anteus. "The battle at the end of the world."

"Christ have mercy on us," said Sieur Horembaud with an anticipatory grin. "Now that is a battle worth fighting."

From a way off a long, eerie wail cut through the darkness, a sound taken up by others of its kind.

"Demons," whispered Frater Anteus.

Sandjer'min shook his head. "No," he corrected. "Wolves."

Text of a letter from Basilios Vlamis, Eclipse Trading factor at Constantinople, to Paolus Bencord, Eclipse Trading factor at Ragusa, written in Byzantine Greek on vellum, carried by the Eclipse Trading ship *Sagittarius,* never delivered: the ship went down after a skirmish with pirates and was looted by villagers.

> *To the factor Paolus Bencord, Eclipse Trading factor at Ragusa, the greetings of your fellow–Eclipse Trading factor at Constantinople, Basilios Vlamis, on this, the 19th day of August in the 1225th year of Salvation,*
>
> *My good comrade in trade,*
> *I have recently received a number of warnings about increased pirate activities in the Cyclades Islands, and I*

wish to warn you of them so that you may order more arms for all such ships that set out from Ragusa may be prepared, and escorted as needed to keep the crew and cargo safe. In the last three months we have lost six ships to pirates, and that is the highest number we have recorded in nearly a century. It is a most lamentable development. We are not the only ones complaining about this: two other companies I know have had similar trouble, and they are asking all ships' captains to report any incidents of pirates, whether or not they are attacked. Last month, a Genovese galley, the Saunt Michele il Vittorio, *limped into port here, sails in tatters, half their oarsmen injured or dead. She listed heavily to larboard, and showed all signs of a dreadful fight. You are in a region where pirates hold their distance, but once into the Aegean Sea, the pirates have the advantage, as this incident shows. The Doge of Genova has ordered escorts for all the ships leaving Genova until the pirates are brought under control.*

To answer your question of your letter sent last April, no, there have been no messages from Santo Germanno to this office, not from Egypt or anywhere else. As far as I know, he is still in Egypt, well up the Nile, and has not sent any of his factors news of a change. I can send a letter to Alexandria again, and ask if there has been any news of him. It seems to me that there are many explanations for his silence, including the understanding that he might not have been silent, but that something has happened to his messages. There may be more fighting in Egypt, and that could account for his long stillness. I agree there is reason for concern, but I would not recommend sending men into Egypt to search for him. If another year should pass with no information on him, then it might be advisable to send two or three groups of trained men to find him, but it was just over a decade ago that he returned from China and India after a long absence and only occasional messages reaching us through Bondamma Clemens. If the other factors wish to institute such a search now, I will not protest, but I believe our employer would not approve of such action. He travels widely, and does not require us to search for him.

With the Mongols advancing again, we in Constantinople are seeing an increase in refugees from the northeast. The belief is that the Mongols want the grasslands of Crimea for their herds of horses, but some say they will press farther than that: into Polovtsy and Pereslavl and Kiev. There is talk of deploying some of the mercenary Legions to the eastern edges of Byzantine land, but little has been done so far. If the refugees continue to come, then it will be essential that we do something, but until that happens, we shall trust that soldiers and money will keep them away.

The Storm Cloud *is still missing, and none of the Captains who have stopped here have seen her in over three months, which does not bode well. In answer to your questions, the* Zephyrus *has been reported sunk off the western coast of Sardinia. The crew for the most part escaped, and half the oarsmen, but the cargo was lost, and the ship itself. The report is that there was a sudden gale and it drove the ship onto an underwater reef where it broke apart. As to the* Semiramis, *she is laid up at Tunis with damage to her hull. The repairs are expected to be complete by September; she should be able to make for Venezia before the winter storms begin, assuming Captain Morellus can assemble a crew in time, including men to fight off pirates.*

Speaking of pirates, the Sultan in Egypt is raising his customs fees again, at least for Christian vessels, and we must be prepared to meet those additional charges of markets we have traded with for well over a century. I believe Grofek Rakoczy will not begrudge us the money for those charges, for he rarely haggles over such things, but he does expect us to be prudent in how we deal with the officers of the Sultan when we must pay. Remember what happened to Captain van Hooten who refused to pay the extra: it is not worth losing an eye over money. Rakoczy has often told us that he does not expect us to put ourselves in greater danger than our professions demand. I found it difficult to understand that when I was younger, but now that I have reached thirty-five, I am in complete agreement with our employer. Age does lend us discretion if we permit it. Be advised by me and instruct all those negotiating with the Sultan's customs officials, to be willing to accept terms that are not as reasonable as they once were, for the benefit of us all.

God and the Hagios protect you and yours,
Basilios Vlamis
Eclipse Trading factor
Constantinople

5

As they neared the bridge over the turbulent Atbara they were forced to go in single-file, their lanthorns casting shafts of light onto the striated rock face on their left, still warm from the day's sun, as the road narrowed and the way steepened; across the river there was a rising, broad plateau that looked increasingly inviting to the travelers. As vexing as the need for crossing had seemed at first, now it was obvious why it would be ineluctable. It was not yet midnight, and so far they had made good progress since breaking camp at sundown. In the last furlong before the bridge the road widened again, broad enough to permit those using the bridge to dismount, reload, and change order of crossing without endangering themselves. The bridge was fronted by a level platform large enough to accommodate up to four animals and ten men, and it was becoming crowded; it angled downward from the eastern side of the river, the platform at the western end being almost four cloth-yards lower than the one on the eastern; not a tremendous drop but enough to be daunting for some travelers.

Sieur Horembaud pulled in his copper-dun mare and motioned to Pater Venformir and Sandjer'min to come up to him. "Pater Venformir," he said, "as we agreed, you shall go first, and ten of your company and twenty animals, then six of mine and twelve animals, another ten of yours and ten animals, and another six of mine and twelve animals. Then the remainder of your pilgrims with the last of your animals, and the last of mine: pilgrims and animals. You shall appoint someone to lead each of your groups; I will do the same with mine."

"We'll all dismount," said Pater Venformir. "As I hope your company will."

"That might prove a little difficult in some instances, as I know you are aware. I am certain that Sorer Imogen will have to be led across on an ass, just to make sure she can be made to stay in place, and not risk herself and all the rest of us in a foolhardy act." Sieur Horembaud could not conceal his annoyance with this prospect.

Sandjer'min considered the recommendation. "Yes. I agree that would be best," he said.

"And Bondame Margrethe may lead the ass, and Lalagia attend to her. You, Sandjer'min, can lead their animals for them. On foot." Sieur Horembaud offered Sandjer'min his least sincere smile. "You'll agree to that, won't you."

"Of course," said Sandjer'min imperturbably.

Pater Venformir studied Sieur Horembaud for a moment, then said, "It all seems providential, that we should be brought here together, and this bridge is like the ladder revealed to Jacob, but for worldly, not holy, safety. Those cables are stout and in good repair."

Pendibe rode up to the group. "Are you planning to make camp on the far side, or just gather in preparation for moving on?"

"What would be the point of stopping unless we're near dawn?" Sieur Horembaud asked, getting ready to hold forth.

"If we are going to camp, you should appoint someone to be in charge of it, and to supervise its set-up," Pendibe went on.

Sandjer'min translated his Coptic for Sieur Horembaud and Pater Venformir. "It will be decided by how long it takes to get across the river; if the night is largely over, then we camp, otherwise we move on," was the decision Sandjer'min passed on to Pendibe. "I think it would be best to build a fire on the far side, whether or not we go on tonight."

After a flurry of discussion in three languages, the fire was agreed upon, and as the pilgrims continued to come up behind them, Sandjer'min made another, cautious suggestion. "Might it not be best to have the guides—yours, Pater Venformir, and Sieur Horembaud's— cross ahead of the rest of us, then you two leaders can choose which is to lead the pilgrims, and who is to follow at the last. The guides will know better than we what will be needed once we're across." As he repeated this proposition in Coptic, he saw Pendibe nod.

Tsega added in Amharic, "Watch the planks; not all are in good condition." Pendibe translated this into Coptic for Sandjer'min, who translated it into Anglo-French and Church Latin for the Europeans.

"How do you think we should go across, Pendibe?" Sieur Horembaud asked before Pater Venformir could inquire further of Tsega.

"I would recommend that after whichever leader crosses at the head of the companies, through which two or three servants or slaves cross immediately behind him, to help build the fire and attend to simple cooking; they can also lead over some of the pack-asses, with enough food for a small meal before we continue on our way toward the Monastery of the Redeemer. The animals will need to rest after crossing the bridge, and so will a few of the pilgrims." Pendibe waited without impatience while Sandjer'min translated, then continued, "Both groups will want time to get their animals ready for travel again once we're all across. Some of them may be restless after the crossing and will need water and a handful of figs to ease them while they become used to solid ground once more."

"There is much in what you say," Sieur Horembaud grumbled. "I'll go last; it is fitting that if you go first, I should be last. I'll have Olu'we go across behind you, Pater Venformir, along with Almeric. Both of them are reliable and do not dread bridges, or they haven't done so that I know of. That way, both pilgrims and servants will know it can be crossed without mishap. You may choose one of your servants to cross with them."

"This is a wise notion," said Sandjer'min to Sieur Horembaud, hoping to soften his increasing resentment. "Ruthier and I will see that they have the ass carrying food to lead across with them."

"Very good," said Sieur Horembaud with obvious indifference. "Tell the others. Including Olu'we and Almeric."

Pendibe went to look for Pater Venformir's guides: Teklile Brehane—who spoke Ge'es and Coptic and a little Arabic, but no other tongues—and Tsega, whose language was Amharic but who knew some Arabic, some Ge'es, and a little Egyptian Coptic, along with a smattering of Oromigna and a few words of Greek—to tell them what had been decided. He saw them a short distance back in the line, and went toward them, swinging his lanthorn.

"Shall we start working on the order of crossing? Shouldn't we line up the two companies into the order we have agreed upon? The path is narrow enough that jostling could be risky, could it not?" Sandjer'min asked with a deferential ducking of his head; he wanted to give Sieur Horembaud no more opportunities to take umbrage at his comments. "The sooner we have organized that, the sooner we'll all be across."

"No doubt," said Sieur Horembaud, and called out, "Frater Anteus!"

"Sieur Horembaud?" the monk asked as he sidled through the tightening crowd. "How may I assist you?"

"You may make note of what I tell you, then inform our company of where each of them will walk. Have them all dismount and prepare to lead their animal over the river; the servants and slaves will lead two animals each, and there will be one or two pilgrims and such who will want to lead their own mounts, like Sandjer'min intends to do. We will have no argument about this. Temi and one or two others will lead the extra animals. Ruthier is good with horses; use him. He'll go behind Sandjer'min." He spoke decisively, as if he had come to these conclusions on his own. "Pater Venformir will tell you who in his company will make assignments."

"I will speak to him when I have received your instruction," said Frater Anteus; he was pale and Sandjer'min suspected he was ill or frightened.

"Then let us make our assignments. It will be best to have the women go with the first group of six—at the end of it. Sandjer'min will cross behind them; it puts him just ahead of the first group of servants, but he will not protest the order. The women may need his help." He shot Sandjer'min a look that dared contradiction. "So it would be best, I believe, to have Vidame Bonnefiles go first in the first group, don't you see the advantage?" From his expression, Frater Anteus knew better than to question him.

"I will inform them directly," Frater Anteus pledged.

"Why don't I go and explain this to the Bondame?" Sandjer'min said, tired of being so relentlessly bated. "The sooner we have our line of crossing in place, the sooner we may begin. The women will need a little more time than the rest to organize themselves to cross if all three of them are to be safe. Frater Anteus need not concern himself with Sorer Imogen: the Bondame and Lalagia will see to her care."

"Very sensible of you, Sandjer'min," Sieur Horembaud approved without enthusiasm. "Be about it now." He pointed at the line of pilgrims, servants, and animals slowing to a halt behind them.

Sandjer'min went back along the line of pilgrims; he could see the three women on their mounts about mid-way down the line, and he increased his already rapid stride to reach them quickly.

"Oh. Thank goodness," said Margrethe as she caught sight of him approaching. She lifted her lanthorn to make out his face. "I hoped you'd come."

"I have information for you," he said, moving more slowly for the last dozen paces so that he would not alarm Sorer Imogen, who huddled on her ass, hands wrapped around her rosary and the raised pommel at once.

"We are going to move up a few places in line," Sandjer'min told Margrethe. "When we cross, you and Lalagia will lead the ass and tend to Sorer Imogen so that she will not become upset while on the bridge. I will come after you as soon as you are at the mid-span, so that if there are difficulties, I will be with you shortly to do what I can for her." He was aware of her dismay at this plan; he took her hand and said, "You know better than anyone that she requires careful attendance, and I will be as near as the bridge allows. It will be better if she can be kept . . . inattentive of the water below. You will know how best to accomplish that."

Lalagia answered for her. "Then I should lead the ass, and the Bondame walk near the ass; Sorer Imogen trusts her more than she trusts me, and I have led asses and camels since I was a child." She glanced over at Margrethe for endorsement.

"She's right," said Margrethe, carefully letting go of his hand. "It should be borne in mind that she becomes troubled when she fails to recognize those around her." She faltered. "How steady is the bridge?"

"Pendibe has described it to me: it is anchored in four iron pillars, two on each side of the river; they are thick as tree-trunks and sunk deeply into the rocks. The bridge itself is made of thick, hempen rope, with heavy netting under the planks of the bridge-road, which have bored holes at the edges, and those holes are used to anchor the planks to the under-webbing with thick cords, to keep the planks in place, and to provide a more secure footing. He says the planking shifts little, and the sway doesn't cause trouble for those crossing, as the sides are chest-high for most travelers. We will have lanthorns at both ends of the bridge after the first crossing and until the last."

"How long is the bridge?" Margrethe asked him.

"Pendibe says it is thirty paces, more or less." He had perused the bridge when he approached it earlier, and reckoned that the length was slightly more.

"Will you give us something to help calm her?" Margrethe took his hand again, and this time, there was more in his grasp than worry.

"I have two treatments in my medicaments bag that should reduce her fright," he said, struggling to keep his mind on the crossing and not to be distracted by Margrethe's eager desire. "I'll go get them and explain them to you."

"You are very good to us," said Margrethe.

"And then we'll move you up in the line," Sandjer'min told her as he stepped back from her, then turned and made his way along the narrow track to where Ruthier waited, Jiochim Menines immediately behind him, two of Pater Venformir's company ahead of him. He raised his hand as he neared Ruthier.

"Has the crossing been arranged?" Ruthier asked in old-fashioned Spanish for Menines' benefit.

"For the most part," Sandjer'min said in Imperial Latin, though he was aware that Menines understood a good deal of it. "We will have to move farther up in the line, so we can cross behind the women. Sieur Horembaud wants you to cross with other servants, but you will be just behind me, so that will put us on the same side of the river at almost the same time."

"And I take it we're to look after the women?" Ruthier asked without seeming too surprised.

"Yes. Better us than Howe, or Micheu, don't you think," said Sandjer'min with a sardonic smile.

"Or any of the others, including myself, given how Sorer Imogen sees men," said Menines, his Imperial Latin stilted but comprehensible. "How long before our crossing begins?"

"A while yet, but Sieur Horembaud is in a hurry to have us on our way again, and that should speed up our crossing." Sandjer'min went to take his medicaments sack from one of their two asses saddle. "I have something for Sorer Imogen that will help her during the crossing."

"No doubt she will need it," said Ruthier. "Should I move up now, or wait a bit?"

"If I were you, I'd move up now, and escort the women forward," said Sandjer'min. "The more confusion she encounters, the more distressed Sorer Imogen is likely to be."

"I'll attend to it, my master," Ruthier told him.

"Bring Melech with you. I'd prefer he stay in your hands until I lead him across." Sandjer'min slung the strap of the bag over his shoulder and started back along the line toward the three women. "I have something for you," he said in Anglo-French as he approached the three women.

"Tell me what to do," Margrethe said to him.

"That I will," Sandjer'min assured her, slipping the strap off his shoulder and opening the bag. He withdrew two round jars, both about the size of a lemon. "The one with the glass stopper is the more potent, and must be diluted in water or it will sting her mouth. The one with the leather stopper is soothing and is to be used after the first." He reached into his sack again and brought out a shallow cup. "One full measure in the spoon you have of the first in a cup of water, then one full measure directly to her of the second," he said. "And if you will follow me now, we will find you where you are to be in line to go across."

For a while the activity along the narrow path increased as pilgrims, servants, slaves, and animals jostled to their appointed position, but finally Pendibe stepped onto the bridge, leading his horse. Tsega and Teklile Brehane followed him out onto the bridge, each leading a horse, as Pendibe passed the mid-point of the span. After them came Pater Venformir, leading the ass he preferred, since the Bible reported that the Christ had ridden an ass into Jerusalem before His sacrifice; as a priest, Pater Venformir was eager to emulate his Savior.

It took the three women more time to cross than it had the men before them: Lalagia kept the ass at a slow walk, not only to diminish the sway of the bridge, but to ensure that Sorer Imogen was not twisting or squirming in her saddle. Margrethe walked beside her, speaking reassuringly over the noise of the tumultuous Atbara, repeating the *Magnificat* when Sorer Imogen seemed restless or anxious. Once Sorer Imogen kicked out at Margrethe, and once she tugged on the two leather straps that held her in the saddle. As the women passed mid-point, Sandjer'min led Melech onto the bridge and set his pace to the women's. Reaching the far end of the bridge, Sorer Imogen began to sing the *Agnus Dei*, gesturing to those who had already crossed to join with her in this expression of gratitude for their deliverance. Soon a few of the pilgrims on both ends of the bridge were praying together, their prayers a chant.

Sandjer'min was almost at the center of the bridge when somewhere off in the night, a lion bellowed; Melech froze, legs locked, neck craned out, and ears flat back as the roar sounded again. Everyone in the two pilgrims' companies stopped what they were doing and peered into the night. Horses and asses fretted and strained on their leads; one of the asses that had just crossed the bridge broke away from its handler, hurtling into the darkness, screaming in dread.

Lalagia pulled firmly on Sorer Imogen's ass' lead and got the animal moving again so they could get clear of the bridge; Margrethe did her best to reassure her sister-in-law, keeping her voice much more composed than she felt. She looked back to be sure that Sandjer'min was moving with them.

"More lanthorns!" Pendibe shouted from the broad clear space on the plateau. "Build up the fire!"

Sorer Imogen moaned and rocked in her saddle, transfixed with fear, while Lalagia patted the ass the nun rode and Margrethe did her best to dismiss Sorer Imogen's terrors by reciting Psalms.

From his place at the end of the line of those waiting to cross, Sieur Horembaud shouted, "Torches! We need torches around the camp!"

"We haven't enough wood for torches!" Pendibe called back.

Sandjer'min cajoled Melech with kind words and a promise of figs, and gradually the gelding stopped panting and tucked in his head; he moved watchfully forward, the lead still taut as he minced along.

From some distance away they heard a sudden scuffle, a sound between a bark and a growl, then thrashing, then a kind of predatory rumble, a low, sinister noise from many throats.

"Lions," said Pendibe to Pater Venformir. "They found the ass."

"They're nearby," said Pater Venformir, crossing himself. "Am I right that there is more than one lion to be dealt with."

"Probably a group of females with young, and a big male or two to scare away others," said Tsega when Pendibe explained what had passed between him and the Moravian priest. "You don't often find them here, but the Inundation must have driven them to higher ground; they'll be hungry."

"Are we in any danger?" Pater Venformir asked, not persuaded by Pendibe's equanimity.

"Everyone, everywhere is always in some sort of danger," said

Tsega, and turned away, his remarks untranslated for Pater Venformir.

"Let us hope we move on tonight," said Pendibe in Coptic.

Pater Venformir crossed himself. "Amen."

More leonine muttering came from the kill, and a shriek of complaint from one of the hungry cats.

"How are we to protect our animals?" Vidame Bonnefiles asked Pater Venformir. "We must keep the lions at a distance, or all the horses and asses will balk at crossing the river."

"With torches and lanthorns and guards with cudgels, I should imagine," said Pater Venformir. "And prayer."

There was a bustle at the bridgehead as Lalagia stepped off the last plank, and urged the ass to come on. A small spate of thanks to God rose into the night as Margrethe joined the other two women on the west side of the river; on the bridge, Sandjer'min urged Melech to move a little more quickly, which the gelding was willing to do, walking carefully, his ears turning to catch any sound of lions ahead.

"Are we going to erect tents here?" Margrethe asked Sandjer'min as he and Melech came off the bridge.

"Sieur Horembaud wants us to continue on tonight, and both of the companies agree, especially since the lions arrived. There will be a supper here, and the animals will be fed, but unless something delays us, we should be a league away from here by dawn. That should put us at the monastery near midnight tomorrow night."

"And then we climb into the mountains," said Margrethe, adding, "I wish I could go back to Alexandria with Lalagia and Temi."

"Do you?" Sandjer'min was surprised to hear her say this.

"Yes. I know it is wrong of me, but . . . I think of my husband and I wonder if he will even know me when I return to Creisse-en-Aquitaine. He forgot Guillaume des Grossierterres, his seneschal, when he had been away for a summer; I will have been gone more than two years and I have failed him so badly, how can climbing mountains erase any of it?"

"What answer do you want? what the Church expects, what your family expects? Do you want approval or disapprobation? Or something else?" He felt her pale eyes on him, and he turned to meet her gaze.

"I want your answer," she told him, putting a little emphasis on *your.*

When he spoke again, his voice was more musical than she had ever heard it. "I think that so long as you find merit in the pilgrimage, you deserve to remain with it. If it no longer comforts you or reveals what you seek, then it becomes a torment, and loses whatever virtue it may have had, and you need not remain."

"The pilgrimage is to test the soul, not to provide comfort, or strange lands to marvel at," she corrected him. "You know that; we've talked about it."

"Do you still believe that it does?" he asked her gently.

Instead of replying, she pointed to the bridge: Ruthier was coming off it with a horse and an ass behind him; he went to set up their remuda-lines. He offered Sandjer'min a sardonic Roman salute, then set a ringed spike into the rock, his mallet thudding at every blow. "It's getting noisy," she said as an excuse for not answering his question. "I'd better help Lalagia with getting Sorer Imogen out of the saddle."

Sandjer'min kissed her hand. "I have more calmative in my red-lacquer chest; I'll bring it to you after the midnight meal."

"Will we all be across by then, I wonder?" she mused.

"I trust so," he said, and went back toward the bridge to help unload the heavily laden ass that Vitalis led.

The perimeter of the camp and the approach to the bridge were bristling with lanthorns and occasional torches, providing rich, golden light for all those still coming from the far side. There were sixteen more pilgrims and servants to cross, and twenty animals; Sieur Horembaud stood at the bridgehead, urging the men to cross without stopping. He was growing hoarse from shouting orders, but his face was alight with purpose, and he persisted in his task eagerly, reminding the pilgrims that at the end of the following night, they would rest on holy ground at the Monastery of the Redeemer. He admonished them all in very poor Church Latin to be diligent, to do as they were pledged to do, to show God the strength of their faith. Beside him, the copper-dun chafed at her bit, taking his state of mind for her own.

An old man from Pater Venformir's company faltered as he approached the bridge; he crossed himself, and hesitated moving forward, clearly terrified of walking on the swaying span. Behind him, Magister Clothwig murmured encouragement to the frightened man, who turned to Sieur Horembaud and said something incomprehensible, which only served to annoy him. With an oath that bordered on blasphemy, Sieur Horembaud grabbed the old man's arm and shoved him forward. The old man howled with terror.

"Please," Magister Clothwig said, reaching to pull the old man back. "He's scared."

"I can see that," said Sieur Horembaud.

"Let me speak with him, reassure him, and then—"

Sieur Horembaud cut the scholar short. "We haven't time for that."

Magister Clothwig was prepared to object, but Sieur Horembaud paid no attention. "Micheu! Get this man across! I'll have someone else lead your horse!" He stood blocking the bridgehead so that the old man could not come back off the span until Micheu de Saunte-Foi walked up to him.

"How shall I do it?" Micheu asked Sieur Horembaud.

"I don't care." Sieur Horembaud gave a loud whistle. "Sling him over your shoulder if you must, but get him over the river—alive, if you please."

"As you wish," said Micheu, and stepped around Sieur Horembaud, saying as he approached the immobilized old man, "There, Grandfather, don't tremble so. I will protect you. Give me your arm and we shall cross together." He said this easily enough, but there was iron purpose in every movement.

"I . . . I . . . can't," the old man quavered out.

"Then lean on God and me, and we will get you to the other side." He took hold of the old man's arm and, by pressure on the man's back, propelled him reluctantly forward. The old man shuddered and almost sank to his knees, but Micheu kept him up.

After what seemed half the night, the pair reached the other side. "No more bridges. Go get something to eat," said Micheu with unexpected kindness before he turned and waved to Sieur Horembaud at the other end of the span. As he watched, Sieur Horembaud signaled again, indicating his desire to finish the crossing soon.

"Not too many left to cross," said Sandjer'min as Micheu came up to him.

"Thank God," said Micheu, blessing himself. "As things are, we should be a league or two nearer the monastery before we camp."

"We won't leave here until everyone's on this side, including Sieur Horembaud," Sandjer'min reminded him.

In the center of the ring of lanthorns and torches, the cooking-fire was alight, and the men whose work it was to cook were readying their griddles and cauldrons to make supper.

"That should urge them on," said Micheu, nodding in the direction of the fire, then went toward it himself. "The lions will be curious, too."

Those who had the first lentil cakes and onion-and-eggplant stew were finished with their meal by the time the last slave came across, bringing three asses and two horses on a very long multiple lead-line with him.

At the far end of the bridge, Sieur Horembaud swung up onto the copper-dun mare; on guard at the bridgehead, Sandjer'min muttered, "Stupid and vain," in a language no one on the pilgrimage spoke except himself.

"God save him," said Almeric, and, like the Copts, raised his arms with palms turned toward the starry heavens in prayer.

The copper-dun mare took a few steps, then, as the bridge swayed, she balked and attempted to back up. Sieur Horembaud slapped her rump with a hunting bat and spurred her sides; she moved forward, but stiffly, in little steps, her head up, the whites of her eyes showing, her head tossing as she moved farther out on the span.

"Dismount!" Vidame Bonnefiles shouted.

In the camp everyone but Sorer Imogen stared at Sieur Horembaud, some eagerly, some in dread. One of the Moravians called out in Church Latin, "Anyone want to make a wager on his chances?"

"Don't say such things," Pater Venformir admonished him. "You'll pray the Psalms for that remark, and beg your bread once we reach the monastery."

The Atbara's furor kept the silence of the two companies from being eerie, and as Sieur Horembaud gripped the mare with his lower legs, forcing her to go on, it became noticeable that the horse was favoring her injured leg.

"There's too much for her to balance. No wonder she's having trouble," Temi said quietly to Lalagia, who stood with him at the edge of the remuda-lines.

The pilgrims whispered and pointed as the copper-dun moved, hesitating as the plank under her front hooves moved; she was inching forward when a loud roar a quarter of a circle away from the feeding pride, and no more than twenty paces away from the lanthorns and torches, shredded the stillness, and set off an exchange of challenges. On the bridge, the copper-dun reared and tried to spin; Sieur Horembaud stopped her from turning more than a little, and she came down with her front legs straddling the upper southern cable, which put her into a full-fledged panic. She reared again, pawing at the air, and it was clear her splint was worse. As she came down, she bucked, screaming in pain, and threw Sieur Horembaud from his saddle, and over the side of the bridge.

The lions were in the heat of battle now, roars and coughs and screams drowning out the shrieks of the horse and the ominous thud as Sieur Horembaud landed on a narrow shelf about nine cloth-yards below the end of the bridge.

"Get more fire on the west cliff!" Pendibe shouted; Tsega, Olu'we, and Teklile Brehane all rushed to obey him. As Temi realized what they were doing, he and two of the Bohemians joined them.

In a last, desperate attempt to free herself from the ropes and cables of the bridge, the copper-dun mare leaned heavily against the south side of the bridge which was now swaying and dangerously canted. The mare struggled to pull her damaged leg free, and rolled off the bridge, dropping to bounce off the stones and into the flooding Atbara, vanishing immediately from sight as the river swept her northward.

The stunned silence at the mare's fall from the twisting bridge was broken by a howl from below the bridge. *"I'm HURT!"*

The pilgrims were seized with confusion, no one knowing what to do. Finally someone shone a lanthorn down in the direction of his voice. Sieur Horembaud lay on his back on the narrow ledge, about two cloth-yards from the bridge; he waved his arm as the feeble light from the lanthorn reached him. "Get me *UP!*"

Sandjer'min signaled to Ruthier to bring rope, then he turned to Frater Anteus, who had come to the bridgehead as Sieur Horembaud had started across it. "I'll go down to him, to see what his condition is."

"Yes," said the monk distantly. "That would be kind of you." He turned away from the river, and heard the rumble of many voices as the pilgrims tried to decide what was to be done.

Sieur Horembaud yelled again. *"I'M HURT!"*

When Ruthier handed Sandjer'min the rope, he said in the dialect of western China, "I'll secure this rope to the southern pillar and let myself down to the ledge. If I can make a sling for him, you and a few of the others can haul him up, then drop the rope to me again. If there is a problem, I'll let you know and you can lower what I need."

"Do you think it will be—"

"He has broken bones at the least," he said in Anglo-French, "and he may turn cold from them."

Micheu shoved through the knot of pilgrims at the bridgehead. "What do you want me to do?"

"Keep these people from falling off the cliff, if you can, and have Pendibe and his group plant their torches and move back," said Sandjer'min as he bent to tie his rope to the iron pillar. "These men are worried and frightened. In a short while, they'll be skittish as well, and that will do no good for anyone." He saw Micheu give a sign of agreement, so he added to Ruthier, once again in Chinese, "If I pull twice on the rope, send down my bag of medicaments. If I pull once, haul him up."

"Yes, my master," Ruthier said in Anglo-French.

Even with four lanthorns now aiming their beams at the rock-face, Sandjer'min was relieved that he did not require much more than starlight to see clearly. He descended fairly rapidly, keeping close to the wall of the canyon; as he reached the ledge, he tested his footing before moving along it. He went carefully, for the nearness of running water distracted and disoriented him. He called out, "Sieur Horembaud. It's Sandjer'min."

Sieur Horembaud raised his hand. "I'm over here. Did you bring a lanthorn?"

The question alarmed Sandjer'min, but he answered in a composed voice. "No. I only want to see what your condition is so we can raise you."

"The mare fell . . ."

"Into the river, yes." Sandjer'min approached him slowly. "How do you feel?"

"I hurt," was the curt answer.

"I understand that, but where?" Sandjer'min could smell the blood welling from a broken collar-bone.

"My shoulder hurts like Lucifer's brimstone. There's a bone broken at my shoulder, and I think the arm . . . may be, too."

"What about your head, your back, your legs?" He knew what the answer would be.

"Nothing. Below my shoulders, no pain at all. I can't move them, either." He paused, as if he was beginning to understand his injuries. "That's a bad sign, isn't it?"

"Yes. It means your back is broken, and it may not be safe to move you," said Sandjer'min, and shuddered, for it was one of the few injuries that could give him the True Death as surely as it would kill the living.

Text of a letter from Pater Fridericus Schallensang, secondary Papal secretary in Roma, to the Assistant Vizier Yerga-al-Ahmad bin Issa to the Sultan of Egypt in Alexandria, written in Church Latin on parchment, carried by Papal courier and delivered to the Master of the Hospitallers in Alexandria for official presentation twenty-three days after it was written.

It is my honor to address you, most highly renowned Assistant Vizier Yerga-al-Ahmad bin Issa, who serves the Illustrious Sultan of Egypt, Malik-al-Kamil bin Ayyub, on behalf of His Holiness, Pope Honorius III on this, the 21st day of August, in the Year of Our Lord, the Savior of the World, 1225.

Esteemed Assistant Vizier Yerga-al-Ahmad bin Issa,

It has pleased His Holiness to approach your Sultan on a matter of mutual importance, and one that must surely command the attention of Malik-al-Kamil bin Ayyub for the sake of his people, for which I ask you to read what follows.

His Holiness is minded to suspend the pilgrimages currently taking place in Egypt and lands beyond Egypt to the south. He has considered the situation, and is likely to bring forth an Encyclical directing good Christians who wish to visit holy places to confine themselves to their own lands and Jerusalem. With so many pirates and other rogues preying upon those companies of pilgrims that are abroad in the world, it would reduce the need for guarding the companies and pursuing the miscreants who have abused them, allowing the Sultan to dispatch more of his soldiers and officers to places where there is new fighting.

If this action should be met with approbation from the Illustrious Malik-al-Kamil bin Ayyub I would be most gratified to so inform His Holiness upon receipt of your notice of such, and to turn the matter over to the Cardinal Archbishops for official action.

Most cordially,
Pater Fridericus Schallensang
Premonstratensian and secondary Papal secretary
at Roma

6

Shortly before dawn, as the two companies of pilgrims passed through an avenue of palm trees along a road that merchants had used for two thousand years, Sieur Horembaud began to moan, a despairing sound that spread through the two companies like a disease, draining them all of hope and filling them all with anxiety at what such agony might portend, for it was known that when a leader was stricken, his followers would suffer with him.

"What can be done about that?" Pendibe asked Sandjer'min as they moved steadily through the night.

"It will grow louder," Sandjer'min said to Pendibe, regretting to have to tell him something so unwelcome.

"You've seen it before, then?"

"I have," said Sandjer'min, recalling the Greek sailor who had been struck by the boom on his fishing boat, and was only found by other fishermen searching for him because of the ferocity of his screams.

"Is there nothing you can do?" Pendibe inquired, his voice low. He held up his hand to halt the pilgrims.

"There is, but it might shorten his life," said Sandjer'min as Pater Venformir rode his ass up to them. Sandjer'min translated greetings for them both, then cast a glance at the jagged eastern horizon.

"Should we camp for the day, if this is going to continue? I know we agreed to keep going until near mid-day, but we need rest now. We're all tired, aren't we?" asked Pater Venformir, as he and Pendibe halted their groups on a stretch of level ground studded with small boulders and resinous scrub. "I know we must care for him, but is there nothing that can be done about that . . . that noise?"

Sandjer'min answered the question. "It would take a miracle for him to survive, but I can ease his suffering. It's not much, but it is the best I can do under the circumstances." He was running low on syrup of poppies, but he had some oil of blue lotus that would reduce Sieur Horembaud's pain and give him visions as well. "The sooner we reach the monastery, the better."

"No doubt. If he is to die, let it be on sacred ground," said Pater Venformir. "Surely God will give him strength enough to reach the Monastery of the Redeemer."

"Are you suggesting that we ride through the entire day?" Pendibe asked Sandjer'min, and shook his head. "You pale people are not made for it, Sidi, nor are Sieur Horembaud's pilgrims. You with light skin suffer in our sun. Those with light eyes and hair suffer the most."

"We know," said Sandjer'min. "But if we wrap our heads and keep covered, might we be able to endure it, for a day?" He knew it would be as bad as the road to Damascus for him, but this was not a time to hesitate.

"For a full day, no. It would bring more ailments than you expect, ailments that cannot be addressed on the road, and would ultimately slow our progress," Pendibe warned, his eyes narrowed in thought. "If we rest at mid-day, it is possible to reach the monastery not long after sundown, if we do not have to stop to attend to Sieur Horembaud or Sorer Imogen, or anyone else. Not all of the two companies will want to travel so relentlessly." He waited to hear if Pater Venformir would agree.

"It is our duty to care for our pilgrim-brothers, and sisters, whether it is convenient for us or not," said Pater Venformir with the stubbornness of righteousness. "If we fail in our duty, where is there virtue in our pilgrimage."

"A commendable sentiment," said Pendibe as Sandjer'min finished his translating. "But it will do us all more good to reach the monastery as soon as possible than to delay on the road. Surely you agree with that, Pater."

"I should have mentioned this sooner, but I thought it would not be a problem." Pater Venformir lowered his head and crossed himself. "Frater Tone has a bad swelling in his ankle, and it is worsening. He needs relief from traveling."

"Why is his ankle swollen?" Sandjer'min asked once he had translated Pater Venformir's words for Pendibe.

"He claims not to know," said Pater Venformir. "I find I believe him."

Sandjer'min sighed. "I'll have a look at it when we stop," he said. "For now, I assume there is an oasis ahead?"

Such observations no longer shocked Pendibe, but Pater Venformir regarded him in astonishment. "Why do you say so?"

"Because there are trees on the side of the road—have been for half a league—and trees mean water," said Sandjer'min, and repeated this in Coptic. "When we reach the oasis, we must water the animals and refill our water-casks. I'll deal with Sieur Horembaud and Sorer Imogen then, and may do something for Frater Tone, depending on what I find. Then we can go on until mid-day. Tents and sails to go up as quickly as possible when we stop for our mid-day rest to provide shade; cooking and care of the animals will have to wait until there is shelter for all the two companies, and the horses and asses."

Pendibe thought this over briefly. "The stop is necessary, so turn it to good use, Sidi."

"I will do my best," Sandjer'min assured him, and a short while later, the companies were moving again.

At the small oasis Pendibe had chosen, Sandjer'min moistened a tiny, narrow spoon with oil of blue lotus and rubbed it on Sieur Horembaud's lips while Sieur Horembaud howled and struck out with his one arm that remained undamaged and fulsomely cursed Sandjer'min. As Sandjer'min left him on the pallet pulled by one of the asses, Sieur Horembaud suddenly yelled, "What have you done to me?"

Florien and Almeric stood nearby, both of them silent and hollow-eyed, exhausted and affrighted by the awareness of Sieur Horembaud's impending death.

"Given you a way to suffer less. You should be asleep shortly, and will sleep until we stop again, when your servants"—he gave the two a single glance—"will help you to eat and care for your body until you sleep again," he went on to Pendibe as he gathered up his materials and continued on to the three women, sheltering at the edge of a stand of leathery-leaved bushes, Sorer Imogen still mounted on her ass and strapped into the saddle. "This will help calm her, and lessen the pain of the sun," he said as he came up to them; already Sieur Horembaud's screams were less appalling.

"Torquil made that apparent to us all," said Margrethe in a disheartened voice.

"If Sorer Imogen will keep to her veil and wimple, she should not be at too great a risk," he said, wanting to provide Margrethe some cause for seeing promise in this part of their journey.

Margrethe took a vial of syrup of poppies he held out and asked, "How much will she require?"

"Half the vial now, with water, and half when we stop, with food." He took a step back from her. "You're looking tired."

"Because I am tired," she said, then yawned. "I have to say something to Lalagia, something between us."

"Your monthly flowers are about to come and you need rags and lint," he said. "You have almost none left."

She blinked at him, wanting to know how he had come to notice her cycle. "Yes. I do need those things, for the reason you describe. Lalagia has offered me some of her own—being pregnant, she will not bleed for several months, and by then, I would hope to be . . ." Her words trailed off, suddenly embarrassed by speaking so openly to him on such a matter.

"We'll meet later, once we reach the monastery," he said, going away from the three women, looking for Frater Tone.

The monk was sitting on a stack of small chests, his face ruddy from being in the direct sun. He stared disconsolately at his swollen foot and ankle, not bothering to look up at Sandjer'min. "You're the magician, aren't you? The one who has the medicaments. You're the one who brought Sieur Horembaud up from the ledge."

"I am." Sandjer'min squatted in front of him. "May I look at your foot?"

"If you must." There was a note of hostility in his response. "They say you can work wonders. But they say that of many foreigners."

Sandjer'min loosened the broad linen bands that wrapped Frater Tone's leg; the foot was the size of a gourd, and his ankle was as round as a foot-soldier's helmet, the skin stretched and shiny. "How long have you had this swelling?"

"Two, three days. It got worse yesterday." He stared at Sandjer'min. "Do you have anything that will help?"

"I don't know." Sandjer'min examined the ballooning tissues, but found no bites or scratches to account for it. "Has anything else happened to this foot?"

"I twisted the ankle four days ago," he admitted. "I almost fell over."

"Perhaps you should have," he said, and reached into his bag of medicaments, bringing out a jar that contained a smooth ointment. "This contains willow-bark and alum. I want you to rub this into the swollen part of your leg three times a day for the next two days. We'll see how you go on after that." He stood up. "I'll speak to you tomorrow morning. In the meantime, wrap it loosely in cotton or linen, to keep the sun off."

Frater Tone thought this over. "I will. For now."

When the monk said nothing more, Sandjer'min turned away, seeking out the three guides at the head of the line.

"Sidi," Pendibe greeted him. "Will you tell your company that they have only a little time to fill their casks with water and to be ready to move out."

"Gladly. Is there anything else I can do for you?"

Pendibe frowned in thought. "Tsega saw signs of jackals nearby a while ago: make sure the pilgrims don't wander beyond the torches."

"Certainly," said Sandjer'min; he went among the members of Sieur Horembaud's company, urging them to prepare to leave shortly. Cristofo d'Urbineau and Agnolus dei Causi asked him about Sieur Horembaud's condition, and expressed pious horror at what they learned.

"I have given him something to ease his pain, but there is little more I can do," Sandjer'min told them both, and informed Noreberht lo Avocat that because they had left Gudjei at a small oasis with food enough for three days did not oblige them to do the same with Sieur Horembaud or Sorer Imogen.

"But they are both getting worse," Noreberht protested.

"It is a Christian duty to care for the sick," Sandjer'min re-

minded him, and continued on his very short rounds before returning to where Ruthier was loading their chests and cases on three
asses; the horses beside him were not the usual two.

"I've put Melech on the remount line," Ruthier said to
Sandjer'min, and nodded in the direction of a grulla mare with two
white feet. "Eyael is rested and will move along smartly."

"Thank you, old friend," he said in Imperial Latin as he mounted
up. "I don't think I've seen you on that—"

"That dark-chestnut gelding? I've ridden him once before." He
paused, and his faded-blue eyes glinted with amusement. "The horse
dealers always want to sell us geldings, so we won't start breeding
our own herds, I suppose." His chuckle had little amusement in it.
"As if travelers can care for foals and pregnant mares."

"A strong animal, that chestnut, and sturdy. You'll lead asses?"

"Pendibe has asked me to," said Ruthier, then went silent for a
long moment before he asked, "How much longer?"

Sandjer'min's answer was remote, but filled with distant sorrow.
"Sieur Horembaud is very strong. He may last through tomorrow."

"No chance he'll improve?"

"None," said Sandjer'min, and set his grulla mare trotting toward the head of the line that was forming for the grueling morning
ahead. As he took his place with Pendibe, he saw the east begin to
pale, and steeled himself for the ordeal of bright sunlight and leagues
of trotting along old, rutted roads.

By the time the two companies stopped for their mid-day meal
and rest, Sieur Horembaud was wrawling again; the jenny-ass pulling his pallet had her ears laid back, and her tail twitching nervously.
Almeric rushed to Sandjer'min as soon as the companies drew rein,
his face now haggard.

"I'll attend to him at once," Sandjer'min said in Anglo-French
and then Coptic before he hurried to treat Sieur Horembaud while
Pendibe and Pater Venformir supervised setting up the camp.

Sieur Horembaud's color was not good—an ominous combination
of bruise-gray and dull-red—and he seemed unable to focus his eyes.
He struck out at Sandjer'min as he knelt beside his patient's pallet and
lifted the improvised hood that had protected Sieur Horembaud from

the worst of the sun. Sandjer'min administered the oil of blue lotus, saying as he did, "This will take your pain away for a time. I will see you have more of it before we go on in the afternoon." He brought out a small skin of water and held it to Sieur Horembaud's mouth.

"Will you? Do you think I'm a fool?" Sieur Horembaud challenged, and tried to strike out at Sandjer'min; Sieur Horembaud groaned in frustration and tried to spit the oil off his mouth. Then his face softened as he tasted what Sandjer'min had given him. "Oh. This. I like this," he muttered and made a clumsy attempt to take the vial from Sandjer'min. "More."

"Later," said Sandjer'min, preparing to rise.

This time Sieur Horembaud managed to snag the cuff of Sandjer'min's sleeve. "More!" he repeated loudly.

Sandjer'min put a very little more oil of blue lotus in the tiny spoon and spread it on Sieur Horembaud's lips. "There." He got up as soon as Sieur Horembaud released his sleeve, turning to the two servants. "He will sleep heavily with so much of the oil in him. If he should have trouble breathing, come to me."

Florien ducked his head respectfully. "We will, Sidi," he said, adding impulsively, "How are we to get home, once he dies?"

"Speak to Frater Anteus. He will know what to do," said Sandjer'min, and hoped that the monk would be willing to assist servants for the sake of their master.

Almeric glowered at him. "Foreigner. Who is to say you aren't making him suffer more, not less?"

Aware of the threat in Almeric's remark, Sandjer'min answered, "It is because I am a foreigner and not a Christian that I direct you to follow the orders of Frater Anteus, who is the Pope's monitor for the pilgrimage, and who is responsible for your protection, whether or not Sieur Horembaud is leading the company." He saw the servants exchange startled stares. "Didn't you realize that?"

"I thought it was d'Urbineau, that all his talk about being defrocked was to throw us off the scent," said Almeric.

Florien shrugged. "We will talk to him. If he will not help us, we will implore you." He went to unhitch the pallet's drag-poles from the disgruntled jenny-ass.

Almeric gave Sandjer'min a measured scrutiny before saying, "It won't be much longer."

"No. A day or two at most. I'd speak with Frater Anteus now, if I were you." He saw Sieur Horembaud wince as the hood over his pallet was taken away, exposing him to the refulgency of the sunlight. "Get him into his tent as soon as possible. The sun is bad for him."

"Then why not put his hood back over him?" Florien asked impertinently.

"Because it is bad for me, as well, and I need to shelter from it at once." Sandjer'min hurried toward his tent that Ruthier was just beginning to erect. "Which is—" he began in the language of the Khazars.

"The lower chest contains your native earth; can't you tell?" Ruthier answered in the same tongue.

"Not in this light. It is all like the rays off a polished mirror, like pins in the eyes," Sandjer'min admitted, his body beginning to ache, leaving him queasy and weak, in response to the gathering might of the sun. "I ask your pardon, but I'm growing edental." His attempt at a joke got no laughter from Ruthier.

"Toothless is the least of it." He set the last cross-bar in place. "Sit down and restore yourself, my master. Even I find this sunlight harrowing, and I'm only a ghoul." He helped Sandjer'min to move the trunk of clothes that rested on the larger one that contained his native earth. Watching Ruthier attend to getting their tent up, he indulged in wondering what this group might do if they became aware of his true nature. "More to the point," he whispered in the long-vanished language of his people, "what would Bondame Margrethe make of it?" He had been wondering since he joined the pilgrims how he would explain his vampirism to her without giving her a disgust of him, or worse, a loathing.

"You can go in now, my master," Ruthier's voice speaking Anglo-French cut into his disturbing reverie. "I'll bring your chest for you."

"I appreciated that," he said, hoping most of the camp would shortly be asleep, enabling him to go to the remuda-line to recruit his failing strength with a little blood from the horses being held in reserve; a cup or two of their blood would keep him from becoming so enervated that he would have to rest until sunset. Having Sieur Horembaud in so perilous a condition made Sandjer'min keenly aware of how untenable his own situation was becoming. He looked toward the tent-flap and made for it as if he were in the river and had seen an uprooted tree in the current, for as miserable as running water could make him feel, riding a log was preferable to having to attempt to swim. As soon as the sun was off him, held at bay by the heavy sail-makers' canvass, he began to relax, to let himself seek out his mattress, to help Ruthier spread it on the chest of his native earth. The vertigo that had possessed him began to fade.

"Go to sleep if you can," Ruthier recommended.

"After I have visited the horses," Sandjer'min said.

"Better to visit Bondame Margrethe," Ruthier rejoined.

"But much less safe," said Sandjer'min. "At least Sieur Horembaud is silent. That should help everyone to sleep."

"I will wake you when the pilgrims have fed. You should be able to get what you need from the horses," said Ruthier, knowing better than to argue this with him. "Two monastic Hours' rest should help you."

"I suppose it should," said Sandjer'min, and let himself lie back, slipping quickly into the profound stupor that counted as sleep among his kind. When Ruthier shook him awake some time later, the sun had moved westward overhead, and most of the two companies were asleep. "What is it like outside?"

"The cooking-fires are out, the griddles and pots have been cleaned and put back in their chests. Pendibe has said we must go on when the sun reaches the fork in the rocks to the west."

"And how many guards are there?"

"Five, two at the remuda, the other three at opposite ends of the road, and one in the center of the camp," said Ruthier.

"Two at the remuda," Sandjer'min repeated, sounding displeased.

"They're from Pater Venformir's company," said Ruthier. "I told them that you will come to bleed the horses suffering the most from the sun, and that you may find some way to dispose of the blood, in order to keep the lions and wolves and jackals away from the camp that might otherwise be drawn here by the scent of blood, and follow us." He said it all seriously, but Sandjer'min knew him well enough to hear the mirth in his voice.

"How very . . . useful of you," said Sandjer'min with a sleepy smile. "I'll bear that in mind."

"The cooks will be preparing a light meal shortly, when most of the two companies—"

"—will be sitting down to eat. I do understand," Sandjer'min said as he got off his bed, his black linen old-fashioned dalmatica dripping a little coarse-grained sand onto the mattress. "If you would, brush this before you pack it away again."

"I always do," said Ruthier. "The sand would wear the cover to tatters if I didn't." He pointed to a shallow basin. "If you'll wash your face, I'll shave you."

"Most welcome," said Sandjer'min. "Perhaps while we're at the monastery you would trim my hair?"

"I plan to," said Ruthier. "It must be the very Devil to lack a reflection."

"Often it is," said Sandjer'min as he went to wash his face.

When Ruthier was through with him, Sandjer'min rummaged in the smaller clothes chest and came upon a wide-brimmed straw hat with thin leather chin-straps. "This will help," he announced as he removed his dalmatica and put on his least-damaged paragaudion. "I smell bean stew and salted greens. Nothing of meat, and none of it raw." He added this last with a note of warning in his words.

"I am told there are birds along the Atbara and Nile, vast numbers of them. I will dine well in the next few days." He adjusted the angle of Sandjer'min's hat. "Tie your chin-straps and have what the horses can give you."

"I will, thanks to your cleverness, old friend," said Sandjer'min as he raised the tent-flap to leave.

Under the watchful eye of Frater Jurg, one of Pater Venformir's pilgrims, Sandjer'min drained a small amount of blood from the necks of three horses, tasting each in turn. "These three are too hot to be ridden; their blood is imbalanced and they must be allowed to become cooler," he announced when he was done. "See they are in the remount line."

The Slavic monk shook his head in astonishment. "Your servant said you could discern much from blood, and that you might drink a little of it, to be sure the horses did not have so much choler that they would not be able to carry a rider safely. I didn't quite believe him, but now I see he spoke the truth."

"As I have asked of him," said Sandjer'min so smoothly that Frater Jurg was wholly unaware of the relief welling inside him. "When do you saddle the horses and asses?"

"Shortly; Vidame Bonnefiles has gone to ask the guides if he may ride with Sieur Horembaud. He says it is his duty to stay with his countryman and his leader." Frater Jurg thought briefly. "I would probably do the same thing in his position."

"Ah," said Sandjer'min, and heard Frater Anteus call out loudly in Church Latin that it was time to strike the camp, that everyone had to wear a head-covering, and that servants were to carry hunting-spears, not to kill game but to keep lions and leopards and wolves at a distance.

"I'd best go and tell the Ethiopians what Frater Anteus just said," Sandjer'min remarked as he turned on his heel and left the remuda-lines. Once he had taken care of the translation, he searched out a small patch of shade, sat down, and let the horses' blood infuse his body, slowly regaining a measure of strength from it, even as the weight of his loneliness bore down upon him; as simply nourishing as the horses' blood was, there was none of the nourishment of close-ness that came from a knowing and accepting partner. For a sus-pended moment he contemplated the intimacy that Margrethe so poignantly sought from him, and which he desired as ardently as she did, but then reminded himself, she might not welcome his true nature once she learned of it, and that would be worse than what he felt now.

A short while later Ruthier found him. "The horses are ready," he said, troubled by the inaccessible anguish he saw in Sandjer'min's blue-shot dark eyes.

Sandjer'min got to his feet. "I should examine Sieur Horem-baud," he said, and stepped out into the glare of the afternoon, con-cealing the pain it gave him as best he could. He mounted the grulla mare. As he started her at a walk through the crowded camp, he was aware that Ruthier had mounted the dark-chestnut gelding and was leading three asses. Turning in his saddle, Sandjer'min called out in Visigothic Spanish, "Where is Sieur Horembaud?"

"Behind the guides and Vidame Bonnefiles," Ruthier replied.

"In other words, ahead of where we are," said Sandjer'min, working his way to the front of the line.

"There you are," Almeric yelled as he saw Sandjer'min coming nearer. "Stop. He has started moaning again."

"He has had a great deal of the oil of blue lotus," said Sandjer'min, dismounting to have a look at Sieur Horembaud as he lay under the improvised hood. "Have you given him water?"

"Yes, Sidi, we have," said Almeric.

"He needs more," said Sandjer'min. "He will need two large cups of water once I put the oil on his lips."

Sieur Horembaud turned glazed eyes in Sandjer'min's direction. "Who . . . is that?"

"I am Sandjer'min," he said, removing the vial and small, narrow spoon from his medicaments bag. "You have no reason to fret."

Sieur Horembaud blinked. "It's you. You have the oil. I want it." It was an effort for him to speak without yelling, but he managed it.

"No doubt," said Sandjer'min, removing the vial and the spoon from his bag. "Here."

"How long will it last?" Sieur Horembaud asked.

"That will depend. I will check on you from time to time, and your servants will attend you as we travel." He put a little of the oil into the narrow spoon, then smeared Sieur Horembaud's mouth with it. "You should feel its relief shortly."

"Not soon enough for me." Sieur Horembaud swiped at Sandjer'min, missed him, and cursed, exhausting himself with his minor effort; tears leaked from his eyes. "Too many foreigners. The other pilgrims are foreigners. You are a foreigner. You're not even a Christian."

"If you will try to rest, you will feel relief sooner," said Sandjer'min, rising and getting back on Eyael.

"That hat is foolish," Sieur Horembaud shouted.

"Perhaps; but it keeps the sun off." Sandjer'min tapped the grulla mare with his heels and she moved off at a fast walk.

Ruthier followed after him, glancing over his shoulder once to see how the three women were managing in the afternoon heat. "Do you want me to assist the women? Sorer Imogen seems a bit upset."

"What is she doing?" Sandjer'min asked as he reined in.

"She's refusing to mount," said Ruthier. "If you wish, I will hold our place in order of march. You can see to Sorer Imogen."

"This shouldn't take long," said Sandjer'min, taking his bag of medicaments and slinging its strap over his shoulder as he dismounted; he went back along the forming line of march to where Sorer Imogen was kneeling and praying loudly, her face covered only by a thin veil. He looked at her, and then at Margrethe. "How long has she been—"

"She started when we went to eat. She wouldn't take food or water," said Margrethe, who was standing beside her horse, holding the lead to Sorer Imogen's ass in her hand. "Now she insists we wait for night."

"Has she said why?" he asked as he approached the nun. "Good Sorer Imogen, it is time we were away from here. The Monastery of the Redeemer is near and it is our duty to go there with all haste."

She glared up at him, but continued her prayers.

He came to her side and said, "Let me help you to mount, Sorer. You will need to keep your place in line, and this can only happen when you are in the saddle."

"We are night pilgrims. We should not be abroad in the day," she said suddenly, her orisons stopped.

"For the most part, that is true. But Sieur Horembaud is in need of treatment, and it is essential that we bring him to the monks, who will care for him." He bent down and joined his hands on his knee. "Use these to mount."

Sorer Imogen shivered and resumed her prayers, ignoring everything around her.

A moment later, Micheu de Saunte-Foi came up to her, picked her up, and set her down in the saddle, securing the leather bands that held her in place. "There," he said, giving Sandjer'min a hard look. "Now we can leave."

Sandjer'min studied Micheu, then went to offer Margrethe a leg up. "I will leave a calmative with you. It isn't as strong as the syrup of poppies, but it will keep her from being anxious as we move on."

"She is worried about Pater Venformir's company, though they are Christians," Margrethe said, impulsively touching his shoulder as she prepared to get into the saddle, then self-consciously averting her eyes. "They are strangers, and that frightens her. Her world is growing smaller as we go farther and farther from places she knows." Before he could speak, she set her foot in his hands and swung up, adjusting her skirts before she gathered up the reins. "In all this vast-ness, she longs for a convent cell."

"You cannot give her what she seeks," he said gently. "Had you to offer her what she says she wants, she would refuse you, because it must come from God."

She nodded. "You do understand," she said as she gave a tug on Sorer Imogen's ass' lead-rope.

Taking this as a dismissal, Sandjer'min went back to his mare and returned to his place in line. "I believe we're almost ready to start now," he said to Ruthier in Imperial Latin.

"Yes. Pater Venformir is hearing Confession, but will be through quite soon and as soon as he is, we are off."

Ruthier was right. A little bit later, Pendibe raised his hand and called out "Onward!" in Church Latin, one of the few words he knew. In response the line began to move, following the westering sun; they moved at a slow trot, keeping to the merchants' road as they climbed into the hills. Day faded into night, and the pilgrims lit their lanthorns, arranging themselves in two columns. Coarse sand gave way to hardpan in a small valley where there was a stream with small trees and thickets with thumb-sized orange fruit marking its course. The night rustled with the sound of animals in the under-growth, and the horses and asses grew nervous as the two companies of pilgrims circled to have their midnight meal.

Sieur Horembaud was listless, drinking only a little water but refusing all food, and Sorer Imogen was caught up in a kind of day-dream that held her attention more than anything offered to her.

"Don't worry. The monastery is not far, and she will be welcome there," said Pendibe as he accompanied Sandjer'min among the pilgrims and servants.

"Pray God it is so," said Margrethe, and pointed her lanthorn's beam toward the bushes with the odd orange fruit. "May we eat those?"

Pendibe laughed. "If you want, but the taste is very bitter."

"Are they poison?" Sandjer'min asked.

"No, but they aren't good for much," Pendibe said. "The little black kernels that grow at the base of the goats'-ears bush are sweet but few in number."

"I may pick some," Sandjer'min said, planning to offer them to Margrethe. "If there are any at the monastery."

They continued on as soon as the meal was over; the road rose gradually toward a shoulder of the mountain. Reaching the crest, they looked down into a broad, green valley in which a long line of lanthorns were shining in the night, approaching the huge opening of a cave halfway up the valley's far side.

"What are those?" Pater Venformir asked Sandjer'min so that he could ask Pendibe.

"Pilgrims, of course. You didn't think you were the only ones, did you? Pilgrims come here from all Christendom, to pray for healing or to die in a holy place," Pendibe answered. "The Monastery of the Redeemer is inside that cave."

Vidame Bonnefiles stared. "A monastery inside a cave!"

Sandjer'min translated again, then said, "Do we join the other pilgrims? At the rear of the line?"

"Of course," said Pendibe. "Come. We will be at the cave by sunrise."

Text of a letter from Viviano Loredan at Arsenoe in Egypt to Virgilio Ca'Sole in Venezia, written on vellum in the Venezian dialect, and carried by Venezian courier ship; delivered thirty-nine days after it was written, along with a demand for ransom of two hundred ducats for the release of Viviano Loredan and his servant from someone signing himself Al-Ahbad.

*To the most august merchant, Virgilio Ca'Sole on the
Campo Santa Fior of the Serenissima Reppublica, the
greetings of Viviano Loredan in the Egyptian city of Arsenoe, on this, the 2nd day of September in the 1225th Year of
Grace,*

> *Most accomplished Signore Ca'Sole,*
>
> *After long months of travel, I have reached a small Or-
thodox church here in this ancient place, and I am assured
that the monks here will see to it that this letter is put in the
hands of the Hospitallers or the Venezian legate of Alexandria for delivery to you. Until now, although I have often
availed myself of the virtuous reception offered by the
Copts, I have not been persuaded that any message could
be safely entrusted to them, if for no other reason than there
is much conflict now between the Sultan's officers and the
Coptic bishops. These Orthodox monks know more of the
Christian world than the Copts do. I concede that the Coptic faith reaches farther than I thought, but it is isolated as
Roman and Orthodox are not and that creates its own
problems. I apologize for the long time it has taken me to be
able to write to you, but that, too, has been unavoidable. I
had to wait until the Inundation began to subside to make
any progress moving down-river.*
>
> *I am now at Arsenoe, and I will shortly go to Alexan-
dria on one of the travelers' barges. I have paid for my passage, and need only find a boatman willing to carry me
down-river. My servant Salvatore is with me, as he has
been since we left the Gold Camp. He has suffered from a
fever that he has not been able to entirely banish from his
flesh. There was a translator with the company of pilgrims
who was something of a potion-maker, and I have wished
that we had him with us now. If Salvatore continues to ail,
then it will be difficult for me to get him aboard one of our
galleys; passengers with illness are not usually welcome
aboard ship, for fear the sailors and oarsmen will take any
disease he may carry. If that is the case, I must linger at*

Alexandria until there is a Captain who will take Salvatore as well as me to the Bascino di San Marco. You have my apology if that is what God Wills, but you will agree it is necessary for me to attend to a servant who has been loyal.

About the Gold Camp: it does produce a goodly amount of the metal, and the quality of it is most excellent. I have no doubt that in time an arrangement can be made with the men who run the camp, supplying us ore for our ducats and the ornamentation of our glass. From what I was told, by those ordering in quantity, there are many advantages that I am sure the Signoria will find most acceptable. I urge you to select a delegation to come prepared to bargain. A few presents to the Masters of the Camp would be wise to bring with you, for they will gain the good opinion of those who are in charge of the mines if the gifts are fine enough. The journey is demanding but it can be made. We reached it at the beginning of summer, when the desert is at its most savage, but I am told that in winter it can be far more mild, and the Inundation would be over, so the river would provide a swift journey upstream and down. There are more travelers at that time of year, and there are more robbers and kidnapers about, but guards can be hired. With a sufficiently large donation, the Templars will lend us a few of their men-at-arms for such journeys.

We should be in Alexandria in ten days, or so I am told by our host in this inn. If that is so, then it should be an easy thing to take passage to Venezia within the month. I would hope to be back with my family by the Nativity; if the winter storms are as ferocious as the Nile's Inundation has been this year, I will remain in Alexandria until spring, though I pray this will not be necessary.

If the Console still wishes to dispatch merchant-adventurers to the Christians of Ethiopia, let me recommend that they mount a larger group of them so that they need not have to ally themselves with pilgrim companies, and are in a better position to commandeer a place aboard north-bound craft. A dozen young men, used to the rigors of travel, would be more likely to accomplish the Console's will than another like me. Yes, I have been twice to the Stone Tower, but I was a decade younger when I made the second trip, and I find the years tell upon me. So I recommend all those sent on such a trek be under thirty and capable of enduring privation. I will enlarge on all these matters when I am once again hearing Mass in San Ezzichiele.

May God bless the Serenissima Reppublica, and all who dwell on her islands.

Viviano Loredan
agent and adventurer

7

"She says she must remain here, at the monastery, in one of the penitents' cells; anything else would be Hell for her," said Margrethe as she came into Sandjer'min's tent, her demeanor flustered, her gestures nervous. She lingered two steps from the flap as if she were too close to him, for he sat on the chest that was obviously his bed, awakening all manner of dangerous fantasies within her; her cheeks grew ruddy, and she took hold of the support pole at her elbow. Since their arrival at the monastery six days ago they had seen each other infrequently, and always in the company of monks and pilgrims. It was now four days after Sieur Horembaud had been buried in the little cemetery outside the massive cave that was reserved for Roman Christians; there were over forty crosses marking Catholics' resting places, and a crude statue of an angel holding a crucifix kept silent watch from the center of the graves.

It was almost sundown, and the two companies of pilgrims were camped on a broad expanse below the monastery's cave, sharing it with three other companies; all three were northward bound, having completed their visits to a number of holy places in the Ethiopian

Highlands. Set aside for Roman pilgrims, it currently had over eighty tents erected within its borders; the space half a league away was reserved for Orthodox Christians and currently boasted six tents. With evening came a breeze out of the north that was strong enough to flutter the heavy canvass of the tents, and set the cooking-fires throughout the cluster of pilgrims' camps to flapping like flags.

"Pendibe and Pater Venformir say we must go on, and shortly, and most of the rest agree," said Sandjer'min, both apprehensive and pleased that they were alone together; Ruthier had gone off toward the stream to catch one of the water-birds for his evening meal and would not return for some time; if the tent-flap were tied closed, Ruthier would not attempt to get in. Sandjer'min wondered if Margrethe knew this, and waited nearby until she could find him alone; it had happened before, in the Khazar Empire. He smoothed the front of his black silk paragaudion and inclined his head to her.

"Pendibe knows the country and Pater Venformir knows the way of pilgrimages; they have been meeting today, to decide how they will continue. I understand that Tsega has said that we should try to stay ahead of the weather: there are storms coming and we want to have reached the high plateau before such tempests burst upon us." She paused, pressing her lips together as if to keep her words from tumbling out, without success. The air prickled between them.

"Do you want to go on?" he asked her gently. "Into Ethiopia?"

"I fear I must: I can't remain here. Aba'yam Emerta Hodilleilo has said I cannot stay in this camp unless I take monastic vows, which I cannot do, not having my husband's permission to abandon him. And I have no vocation, had Sieur Dagoberht given me leave to do so. So I must think of something else." Margrethe stared at him; Sandjer'min felt her like a magnet, attracting and repelling him with equal force. She rubbed her face and started to pace in a small oval. "Lalagia and Temi will leave shortly, going down-river. They have already arranged for a boat. They will take the Pilgrims Road to the Nile in a few days." This was the principal road that pilgrims traveled to reach the Monastery of the Redeemer after they left the Nile at the once-thriving market-town of Dofunj.

"Do you want to go with them, down the Nile? Or leave with

another company of pilgrims?" If she went with north-bound pilgrims, it would mean she would be gone in three days, if the pilgrimage leader allowed her to accompany the monks from Carinthia—seven if she waited to travel with the pilgrims from Ravenna. He rose from his place on the chest filled with his native earth.

"I don't think they want my company, though Lalagia expressed it very nicely," she said reluctantly. "And I would be foolish if I were to travel with returning pilgrims I do not know. I would have to rely on the leader in a craven way, and be beholden to him for everything from shelter to food to chastity." She saw him raise his brows. "Oh, most pilgrims may be relied upon to keep their vows of virtue, but not all will, the more so because their pilgrimage is ending, their penance complete." She stopped pacing, licked her lips, and resumed her restless walking. "Who knows what might become of me?"

"Yes," he agreed. "That would be foolish, putting yourself among strangers."

There came chanting from the interior of the cave, droning on two notes, unlike the chants of the Roman monks, announcing the beginning of evening Mass.

"Strangers," she repeated as if the word itself were frightening.

"Does Sorer Imogen attend services in the monastery's church?" Sandjer'min asked, as much to provide Margrethe the opportunity to consider her situation with less dread as to gain any useful information.

"No. She insists that she be allowed to pray in her cell, in isolation," she answered, sounding disheartened. "She has no desire to leave it for any reason. She said that God has called her to be an anchorite nun, and Aba'yam Emerta Hodilleilo is willing to accept her as such. "

"Then it would seem to me that you are free to choose where you will go," he said, feeling Margrethe's consternation as if there were a dust-devil inside the tent. "You can do nothing useful for her; the monks will guard her now."

She trembled. "But how can I abandon her? I promised to see she came to no harm." She stepped a little nearer to him, as if she had just realized how close he stood to her.

"And that you have," he assured her. "You say she wants to remain here?"

"She says it is fitting to pray in a cell carved out of the heart of the mountain, for it is a preparation for death, and one that readies the soul to leave this world." She blinked, took a deep breath, and asked, "What is to become of me?"

"You will have to decide that for yourself," he said, the directness of his observation offset by the kindness in his voice.

"What choices do I have? Everything that I might do is bound up in the decisions others make. I could ask among the pilgrim companies going north if I might join their companies, but whom shall I trust? I have some money, but it is not sufficient for me to pay guards and guides to take me to Alexandria—or even to Luxor—on my own, and what is to keep guards and guides from holding me for ransom or selling me to a slaver? Once I am traveling alone . . ." She gave a tired sigh. "Lalagia and Temi will want to travel as married partners, and will have no use for me to monitor them. I can be of little use to Lalagia in her delivery; I am no midwife. Pater Venformir has already told me he wants no woman in his company of pilgrims, for the presence of women leads to jealousy and lust. I cannot remain here, or so Aba'yam Hodilleilo has informed me, since I am not needed to tend Sorer Imogen any longer. I told you that, didn't I?" She gazed at him, her yearning for him stark in her face. "I could send a letter to my husband, requesting an escort from him to see me back to Creisse-in-Aquitaine, but I would have to wait for the greater part of a year for an answer, and longer if he agrees to dispatch an escort for me, who will have to come from the Aquitaine."

"What do you intend to do?" he asked in a voice that was both steadying and tranquil, though his thoughts were agitated.

"I should go home. It is what I want to do, it is what is expected of me though it will be a difficult return, since Heneri and Sorer Imogen will not be with me. Sieur Dagoberht will not approve of my failure to protect them, if he is aware at all. Without Heneri and Sorer Imogen with me, I have no reason to continue as a pilgrim, for I cannot achieve what I pledged to do. I have no oath to fulfill now that my sister-in-law and her half-brother are no longer with Sieur Horembaud's company, since my primary oath was to them, and my secondary to Sieur Horembaud. What use is my supplication for Sieur Dagoberht to be healed if his heir and his sister do not join with me? The priest who attends to my husband was most firm on these points: that all of his family must seek his restoration to sense and health, and that anyone attempting to pray alone at the holy shrines would not suffice." She stood still, pinching her nose to keep from weeping, but the tears came silently in spite of her efforts. "I want to appeal to you to give me escort north, but you have obligations here. They require a translator if they are to go on."

"With Sieur Horembaud dead, I wonder if I am obliged," he said. "Frater Anteus would be pleased to have me gone, and although Pater Venformir has said nothing directly, he is wary of me. There must be someone among the pilgrims camped here who would take on my task."

She spoke as if she had not heard him. "I think and think, but I see no solution. God has shown me nothing, though I pray for wisdom morning and night, nor has the Devil," she said in a rush of despair; she was hardly listening to him at all now, but railing at her own precarious circumstances. She resumed her pacing, as much to keep some distance from him as to relieve her anxiety. "I am alone here; I hadn't understood what that meant until yesterday. It is not just the distance, though I am a hundred leagues from any Christian stronghold. Few people beyond these pilgrims speak my language, and I do not speak the languages of those around me. It would take me months to find a place where I would be among my own kind, and during all that time, I would be wholly at the mercy of foreigners, though I am the foreigner, not the people who live here, and this is their land, not mine."

He responded to her misery, to her aching loneliness, going to her and taking her in his arms, gathering her close to him. "You will not be left to wander the world, Margrethe. You have my Word on it."

"But you wander the world." She was a hand shorter than he, and that made it simplicity itself to kiss him, feeling him answer to her arousal, his passion ignited by hers. The depth of his response to her increased, made her venturesome, and her embrace became more amplectant.

As their kiss finally ended and she gradually pulled back from him, he said, "You humble me, Margrethe."

Her laughter was quick and breathless. "And you me," she said, holding his shoulders as if she were dizzy. "But I must not surrender," she added more firmly. "I must not falter now." She made herself release him. "I don't know what you may think of me for what I have done, and said."

"Nothing to your discredit," he said, holding out his hand to her; she almost touched it, but not quite.

"Easily declared now, in the moment. But what will you think when you rise tomorrow?" She looked away from him. "You will not want to be burdened with me, will you?"

A much larger choir began to chant, the droning notes now loud enough to create a formidable echo within the cave that boomed out across the tents into the night.

"Tomorrow I will feel much the same as I do now, and have done for some time," he assured her; he felt her conflict increase as she listened to him. "I hold you in high regard and great affection." It was as effusive a statement as he could make without causing her to worry what he wanted of her. "I ask nothing of you that you do not choose to give me: believe this." He could see she wanted to be persuaded; he waited for her to speak.

"You have assisted me and shown me particular attention: do you think that Frater Anteus has been unaware of those things? He has complained that you do not Confess, though you are not a Christian, for in Christian company, you are expected to follow the conduct of Christians." Her pulse was beating more rapidly now, and her face was softening, lessening the sting of her sharp words.

"Frater Anteus is enjoying his authority," said Sandjer'min.

"He tells me that he must be responsible for the company's souls, including those who do not share our faith," she said. "He guards us from the corruption that pursues all pilgrims, the temptations that the Devil sends us to test our resolution." She hesitated, glancing in his direction. "He has warned me against you. He says you're a servant of the Devil."

"That does not surprise me; he needs someone to show as dangerous, and I am not a pilgrim, nor a Christian," he said, aware of the ambivalence that warred within her and not wanting to add to it. "He will warn you most of all. You are a lady of position, you are kindhearted, and you are comely."

This time her blush was bright and sudden. "How can you say that?"

"I mean you no disrespect, Bondame," he said formally. "You are of a generous nature, and you have shown me courtesy when many another have not. D'Urbineau also thinks I am an agent of the Devil, and dei Causi agrees with him, and the Vidame. Jiochim Menines is curious but not from any kindness to me; he simply finds me unusual. You have more grace than they."

The chanting stopped abruptly only to recommence after a moment of silence.

"Thank you," she said in some confusion.

"There is no subterfuge in my admiration; in demonstration of my high regard for you, I will pledge to see you back to the Aquitaine, if that is what you want." He spoke in his most courtly manner.

"How can you do that?"

"I have means, more than you would think," he said, trying to relieve her worry. "I can arrange for passage in a merchant's ship. You have but to tell me what will suit you and I will—"

"Don't promise; you are as far from your home as I am from mine, and have no certainty of reaching your fiefdom safely. If you are willing to make an effort to deliver me safely to Alexandria, I will be deeply grateful," she said, a bit startled to realize that what she told him was true. "I have dreamed about you for months."

There was no light in the tent, but a glow from fires and lanthorns around and throughout the camp imparted enough luminosity for her to see him if they remained close together; he could see by starshine, so the crepuscular light in the tent did not hamper his vision, but he remained close to her for other reasons. "You say you have dreamed of me. What have you dreamed?" It was a blunt question, but he was sure she would prefer it to hints and teasing and troubadors' lyrics. "If you will tell me, I will hold it in confidence, my Word on it." Again he waited to let her frame her answer.

"I am not sure I remember them clearly," she fibbed, trying not to reach out to him, although she did relent enough to take his hand, and allowed herself to be distracted from his probing. "How beautiful your hands are. I hadn't noticed that. And small. Yet you have such strength in them."

He studied her face. "You needn't answer me if you would prefer not to."

This gentle regard lessened her reserve, though she continued to address his hand, not daring to look into his compelling eyes. "I dreamed, more than once, that we lay together, that you wanted to please me. And I allowed it." She almost whispered this to him, not out of embarrassment, but to enforce the secrecy of their developing liaison. "You seem to know what I want, so my dreams tell me that I am correct. Frater Anteus has told me the dreams are the work of the Devil, when I have Confessed them to him."

"I would like to give you pleasure, for both of us, and not leave you to dreams alone," he said, remembering the many times he had become a dream for a sleeping woman to give her pleasure and to gain sustenance for himself. He was standing less than half a step from her, but aware that she would not trust any attempt to rush into her desires. "When you are ready."

"I have been ready since Edfu; I felt drawn to you as saints are to God. I had not known until then that such fire was within me, ready to ignite. If it is God's work, then I thank Him most fervently for His gift. If it is the Devil's, I cannot cry shame upon him for it, since I am taken by it willingly," she murmured, her eyes once again brimming with tears. "I might have said something before now, come to you, but Heneri and Sorer Imogen would have denounced me at once, and I would have been stoned for my hopes, and you would have been left in the desert much as Gudjei was. For pilgrims, the thought is the same as the deed and the punishment for the deed must be enforced." She recited the last as if repeating a lesson.

"That hasn't changed," he said, stepping back from her.

"But there is a need within me, one that I have never known, and though the monks would damn me for this need, if it is of the Devil, still I'll welcome what it brings, for now. The joy may not be lasting, but it is still joy." She crossed herself, and was surprised when there was no odor of brimstone or pain in her body.

Sandjer'min did not move. "Consider what you're saying, Margrethe. I will gladly give you all that I have to offer you, I will do all that I may to provide you what you seek. I will be honored to give you pleasure, but not if it costs you your life."

"I'm not afraid." She did not raise her voice, but there was a steely shine in her light-blue eyes like the glint off a polished blade. "Now that I am alone, I am in my own hands. Neither the King of England, nor the Church, nor my family, nor anyone in Sieur Horembaud's company will care what becomes of me, and neither God nor the Devil have moved me according to Frater Anteus, but the Devil is prepared to corrupt me. What must I do, then, but listen to my heart."

"Perhaps you should be," he said, "afraid."

"I don't think I am important enough to stone, even if I should be accused of adultery," she said distantly. "My station in life is known but it means little here, I believe. The Aquitaine is very far from this place, and Sieur Dagoberht is only a baron, and an invalid. I will return to him, but I will not deny myself the—"

"Stoning is a painful death," he told her, recalling what it had been like at Patmos, nine centuries ago; he had come close to the True Death then, and his ribs had taken almost a year to heal from their several breaks.

"All deaths are painful," she corrected him. "Those that seem less so still hurt, for it is the soul leaving the body, and what worse separation is there for the living?" She turned in a circle, her face showing no emotion.

"Your faith teaches that you will return to your God," he pointed out, wanting to find some way to lessen her distress.

"Or burn in Hell for eternity, or wander in Limbo, with unbaptized souls. God will choose who may sing His Glory in Heaven, and we can but praise Him for His Grace. I fear I am among the damned, or God would have made it possible for me to pray for Sieur

Dagoberht with Heneri and Sorer Imogen. But that is not before me now—you are." In the next breath, she took a long step to his side, reached for his hand, and placed it over her small, firm breast; she gathered her courage and met his eyes. "I may never have another chance."

"Bondame . . ." he said cautiously.

"Does this please you?" she asked, rubbing his palm against her cotehardie to stiffen her nipple.

"Very much," he said, "but you know you are taking a risk."

"I know. I feel condemned already. But I cannot endure this loneliness. I am lost in this place, as if all the expanses we have traversed are nothing more than cages with invisible bars. If my pilgrimage is to ask God to restore my husband, then why does He impose this isolation upon me? How can that bring healing to Sieur Dagoberht? It is as if I were suffocating, or that I were drowning in a swift river." She opened the front of her cotehardie and moved his hand inside, to touch her skin. "If we lie next to your bed, no one will see us."

"They may hear us," he warned her.

"I will keep silent. Will you? I know you will." She opened the front of her cotehardie to her waist. "Before I lose my courage, Sidi, let me know my dreams."

"There is no reason to rush," he said, slowly easing her cotehardie off her shoulders to drop onto the canvass floor, leaving her naked but for close-fitting drawers; he reached for the light coverlet on the bed and handed it to her. "Put this where you want it. I'll tie the tent-flap closed."

"I will," she said with a quick nod.

He took three steps, then bent to tie the three canvass strips together; as he turned to her, he saw she had spread the coverlet on the floor next to the chest and was removing her drawers, stepping out of them with care. She was thin and her muscles were taut from their travels, but the look that suffused her face was beguiling; he went to her, and dropped on his knees between her and his earth-filled chest. "I'm sorry I have no pillows to offer you," he said, holding out his hand to her.

She dropped onto her side, rolled onto her back, and extended her arms to him. "Take off your garments," she urged quietly.

"Perhaps later," he said.

"Why not now?" Her voice was sharper.

"I have . . . broad scars. They are not pleasant to look upon." He stretched out next to her.

"Oh. Then how will you . . ."

"Let me show you," he said, and kissed her half-open lips, feeling her desire increase as his tongue touched hers.

She moved her leg over his hip, straining to get completely close to him in spite of his clothing. When she pulled away from the kiss, she was breathless. "You burn like the wings of angels," she whispered.

He kissed her again, this time as lightly as a butterfly alights on a flower, and she shivered with the sensations that coursed through her. "Lie back, Margrethe."

She moved her leg off his hip and did as he asked, her hands at her sides, her eyes on him, filled with wonder and eagerness.

"Tell me what you dreamed, what gave you the most pleasure," he said softly, "and I will try to make it so."

"Kiss me. Kiss me all over, in diverse ways," she murmured, excitement taking hold of her.

Now he kissed her brow, her ears, her eyelids, her nose, her cheeks, the sweet indentation at the juncture of her jaw and her neck. As he did this, he began to caress her breasts, slowly, tantalizingly, evoking delicious responses that left her astonished. His kisses moved down her neck and replaced his fingers on her nearer breast.

She gave a soft sigh and tangled her fingers in his hair. "That is so good," she whispered.

"Then I will do it some more," he said, moving to her other breast and blowing lightly on her nipple before taking it in his mouth.

Margrethe inhaled through teeth clenched to keep from moaning. She was trembling again, her passion seeming to be greater than her body could contain; as his hand moved down her abdomen toward the cleft between her thighs, she wanted to tell him to go more slowly, that she could not stand to have this end too soon. Responding to her need, he moved his hand languidly, taking time to touch the arch of her ribs and her hips as well as to stroke her body while his mouth dallied at her breasts. As her pulse became more regular, he recommenced to move his hand downward, into the light-haired tangle that concealed what the poets called *her most lovely rose;* his mollescent touch stilled the sudden twinge of uneasiness that had rattled through her as his finger found the bud hidden in the sea-scented folds. She stretched with sinuous grace, her fervid fancies of her dreams now seeming girlish and trivial compared to the ecstasy building within her, expanding through her torso into her limbs so that there was no place he could touch her that did not enhance her arousal. When he slid two fingers inside her, she felt her spasms begin, and sighed that it happened so soon even while her senses rioted in rapture. His kiss this time was long, luxurious, and certainly not like a farewell.

"Take a little time to rest," he said very quietly. "There is more for you if you want it."

"For you, as well," she said. "You only used your hand. Or did I not notice you tupping me?"

"Only my hand," he agreed.

"Then you are not satisfied," she declared, speaking more loudly than she had intended; she dropped her voice, "Unless you released your—"

"No, I didn't. I do not . . . function that way," he told her, aware that she was not yet prepared to deal with his true nature, or his impotence. He drew her close to him again. "Do you want more?"

"Yes, of course I want more," she said, struggling to keep quiet. She wriggled to get nearer to him the whole length of his body.

"Then you shall have it," he murmured. He stroked her back, from shoulder to leg, his hand light, warm, and clever; there were sensations she had not until this night, imagined were possible. She marveled at each one as he explored her, occasionally biting her lip to keep silent, but reveling in what he was doing to her, and the occasional kisses he bestowed conveyed a sweet delirium that left her stimulated at a level that she was amazed she could sustain. His esurience was growing keener, the sound of her heartbeat summoning him to the sharing of her fulfillment. There was such magnificent release building within her that he restrained himself from pressing to her gratification, feeling from her that there was a greater awakening occurring within her than she anticipated. He continued his sensual ministrations, exalting in her discoveries of the delectation of her body.

This time when she felt the gathering within her, she pulled him as close to her as she could without disrupting the work of his hands. "It is nearly here," she said, her lips against his earlobe.

He did something wonderful to her, and the spasm was once again upon her, but more intensely than before, an experience of transports that could not possibly be other than heavenly. The jubilant waves continued while he bent to her neck, delicately taking what he had sensed in her from their first meeting. Their unity enveloped them both, and lasted for longer than he had expected. As her culmination faded, she lay back, sublimely replete, and stared up at him, her eyes shining.

"How did you do that?" she asked, astonished.

"I followed where your desire led," he answered, brushing wispy tendrils of pale hair back from her brow.

"But you didn't use me," she said, and then clapped her hand over her mouth because she had spoken too loudly.

"Not as you mean, no; I share your own fulfillment." His quick smile gave her a frisson that was an echo of her rapture. "Those of my blood seek touching and knowing."

"Is that why you . . ." She fingered the two small cuts in her throat.

"Yes, so I can know you more completely," he said. "You offer me your self, and what is more your self than your blood?" He kissed the place he had nipped her, little marks no larger than flea-bites.

She pondered this. "And this enables you to touch me without . . . without . . ."

"Yes."

"What do you gain from it?" she asked, trying to decide if she believed him.

"Life. To touch you so closely brings me nourishment in body and soul," he said, then held up his hand in warning as three men walked by the tent. One of them carried a torch, and its flickering light gave a short-lived brightness to the interior.

She gazed at him. "What are you?" she breathed.

". . . and we will have to depart in two days, according to Frater Anteus," said one of the men speaking in Bohemian.

"What does Pater Venformir think?" another man asked.

"He has said nothing yet," the third remarked. "He'll announce his position after Mass tomorrow morning."

"So it is go south or go north, but go?" said the second man, his voice fading as they moved beyond Sandjer'min's tent.

"It seems so," the third man said; his voice was deeper than the other two's, and it carried farther. "Tsega agrees, or so Teklile Brehane told Pendibe." The light from their torch became a bright spot, and then faded into the general glow of the camp.

"So we leave in two days," said Sandjer'min softly as the men passed out of earshot. "We'll have to prepare quickly."

"Which way will you go?" She did her best to keep the worry out of her voice. "I know what you said before I implored you to love me, but men will say many things at such a time."

"Do you mean will I escort you back to the Aquitaine? I meant it," he told her, and felt her wince at the tenderness he offered with his pledge. "And I will require nothing from you for doing it, unless you care to offer."

She sighed, welcoming his reassurance. "How will you arrange this?"

"I will inform the Aba'yam of my intentions in the morning, and I'll set Ruthier to getting us ready to depart." He sat up, angling his knee so that she could lean against it. "We will travel separately from any pilgrims. Going with pilgrims could lead to problems."

"What problems?" she wondered aloud.

"Suspicions. Accusations. Punishments." He kissed her forehead. "We need to get beyond this place without attracting attention."

"What are you, Sidi," she asked him again, "that you should fear these things?"

He was ready to answer her, at least in part. "I am an alchemist."

She gasped as softly as she could. "And a physician?"

"Yes; among other things." He could feel her uncertainties return. "You have nothing to fear from me, Margrethe."

"But from others?" She touched his face. "Are you in danger from others?"

"From time to time," he answered, his memories ranging back three millennia, and what had befallen him.

"Could we go with Temi and Lalagia? Wouldn't that help?" She sat up. "I could convince them to travel—"

"We could, but it wouldn't be wise for any of us," he said.

"We will go by river?" she persisted.

He shuddered inwardly. "I believe we must. The Inundation is largely past, and the river is faster than the desert." He did not add that three foreigners alone on the sands would surely attract the attention of robbers, slavers, and kidnapers.

"I will have to say good-bye to Sorer Imogen, to let her decide if she wants to remain an anchorite here." She frowned. "If she has changed her mind, she will want to go south, into the mountains; she'll want me to go with her."

"I doubt she will leave." Sandjer'min got to his feet, then helped her to rise. "I'll give you a vial of medicaments for eyes; if anyone questions you for being out, tell them you wanted something to stop your eyes hurting."

"I'll do that; thank you." She reached for his arm to help her up, and was surprised at the strength in it. "Will you arrange for the asses and horses?"

"Certainly. Tell Ruthier what you require of him, and he will put himself at your disposal." He went to untie the tent-flap closures. "You must be careful to behave toward me as you always have, and I toward you."

"Yes. Yes." She took his hand. "Will this be the last time, though it is the first time?"

He answered with an unguarded smile, infusing his face with an emotion she could not identify, but which held an element of hope. "I trust not, unless it is your preference. I would be most appreciative of any opportunity to gratify your longings." There were many things he had to tell her, particularly if they were to lay together more than six times, but that was for another time: now it was sufficient to kiss her thoroughly, give her the medicament from his bag, and lift the flap for her departure into the starry night.

Text of a safe passage from Aba'yam Emerta Hodilleilo of the Church and Monastery of the Redeemer, for Rakozcy Sandjer'min and Bondame Margrethe de la Poele of Rutland, wife of Sieur Dagoberht Gosland, Baron du Creisse-en-Aquitaine, for a voyage to Alexandria, written in Coptic, Arabic, and Church Latin on papyrus to be carried the duration of the journey, along with three messages to be delivered to Coptic churches along the Nile.

> *Be it known to all, Christians, and followers of Islam, and worshipers of ancient gods, that the man who carries this, Sidi Rakoczy Sandjer'min, is acting on my behalf, performing a service for the Church and Monastery of the Redeemer near the old city of Meroe, known for its care of the sick, injured, and dying as well as those troubled in their thoughts. I, Aba'yam Emerta Hodilleilo, extend my protection to this man and to his servant, Ruthier, the noble lady he escorts, Bondame Margrethe of Rutland, and to the horses and asses that may travel down-river with them. Any who do not honor this safe passage, in any way, insults me and traduces the honor of the Church and Monastery of the Redeemer, and will be cursed from now until the End of Days when all men shall be judged before God. Any who extends himself on behalf of Sidi Rakoczy Sandjer'min will be rewarded in the life that is to come.*
>
> *The letters Sidi Rakoczy Sandjer'min carries with him are not to be opened or removed from his care, for it is his sworn duty to see them safely into the hands of the Aba'yams for whom they are intended, and those who interfere with his mission stand in the way of sinners and will answer for their insolence. For those who assist him in his duty, praise and glory to them.*

Sidi Rakoczy Sandjer'min's two companions are to be shown the same regard as he and are not to be used to bargain with or influence him in the accomplishment of his tasks, for that will be the same as if Sidi Rakoczy Sandjer'min were treated in like kind. Any breach of honor will not be absolved, nor will deliberate encumbrance receive the blessing that is repentance.

By the hand of Aba'yam Emerta Hodilleilo
The Church and Monastery of the Redeemer
The Feast of the Holy Sepulchre

8

Along the docks at the base of the Pilgrims' Trail there was a great deal of activity. With the Inundation finally coming to an end for the year, the water level had begun to drop and the current was less tempestuous than it had been a month ago; the reflection of lightning in the southern clouds still flashed in the night sky, but not as furiously, nor as often. Pilgrims were once again arriving at Dofunj to begin their overland journey into the Ethiopian Highlands, or to depart from having been there. Two large barge-boats had just arrived from down-stream, both with large companies of pilgrims in them. On the far side of the most up-stream dock, a double-hulled barge-boat waited, its elevated fenced deck with raised platform at the rear was fixed to the two long, narrow paddled boats that were manned by six oarsmen each. Amidship was a structure that could provide shelter from the inexorable sun and housing for animals traveling on the Nile. A steering-oar attached to the rear of the elevated deck, and it was in the hands of a tall, lean man who stood on the raised platform in clothes Sandjer'min had come to recognize as Ethiopian. Drawing in the reins of his horse—an older gray gelding with a mottled coat and dark-gray mane and tail—Sandjer'min pointed to the barge-boat. Behind him, Margrethe pulled her mare to a halt. Ruthier, bringing up the rear, led their other horses and their pack-asses bearing all they were carrying down-river.

The man holding the steering-oar had been scanning the confusion on the docks, one hand lifted to block out the burnished afternoon sun from his eyes; the air was a babble of languages and the rush of the Nile. He caught sight of the three travelers, two in pilgrims' blue, one in black, with horses and laden asses. He shouted in Coptic, "You in black! On the light-gray horse. Are you Sidi Sandjer'min?"

"I am," he called back in the same language, then indicated Margrethe and Ruthier and their animals. "The two with me are my company. The horses and asses are our beasts. We are here to set out to the north at your convenience, if you are Nohe BetreMussie."

"I am. You are here in good time. My slaves are in the market getting food and water for our journey, and the oarsmen are finishing their meal," he said, waving his hand to indicate the empty elevated deck. "They should return shortly."

"Then we should be away before sunset?" Sandjer'min inquired.

"That is what you requested and what you shall have since you are generous; the oarsmen are willing to travel by night because you are paying them handsomely, but if there is trouble, we must go by daylight," said BetreMussie. "Aba'yam Hodilleilo's courier was quite specific. I purchased more lanthorns and oil for them with the money you provided."

"Very good," Sandjer'min approved. "I have the payment you require for the journey to the Third Cataract, in gold as stipulated, when the balance for the voyage to Alexandria will be paid to you, and we will use other craft to reach the sea. If you will lower a gangplank, we will come aboard before your crew returns from their meal; we will try to be stowed and settled by day's end." He was more fatigued than he wanted to admit, for he, Ruthier, and Margrethe had left the Monastery of the Redeemer six days ago and traveled through all but the mid-day, when they took time to rest, to feed and water their animals, and to provide Margrethe with a proper meal. The strain of this demanding pace had taken a toll on them all.

BetreMussie laughed as if this were a great joke, but unfastened the ropes that held a gangplank with low cross-bars to make loading and unloading easier out of its housing on the deck and put it in place, connecting the dock to the barge-boat. "I will string the arm-pulls, if you will give me a little time."

"Of course," said Sandjer'min, and repeated to Margrethe and Ruthier what his exchange with BetreMussie had been. "From what Aba'yam Emerta Hodilleilo's messenger told me when we encountered him bound south on the trail four days ago, this craft is sturdy and you, the captain, are reliable."

"Do you know what the messenger told him about you?" Margrethe asked, feeling uneasy with this unknown boat-captain.

"That there were three of us in this company, two pilgrims, one a woman, and me, your translator. The messenger informed Betre-Mussie that you and Ruthier would be in blue and I in black, and that I had served Sieur Horembaud's company as a physician as well as a translator, and I have shown the notification of Sieur Horembaud's death to BetreMussie. If there was more, he didn't mention it to me." He put his hand to the purse in the sleeve of his worn cote-hardie. There was gold enough for their travels, but not so much more than that as he would have liked; he would not be able to make more until he reached his apartments in Alexandria, behind the offices of Eclipse Trading Company. "I will pay for the boat to which we transfer at the Third Cataract, and the one we will use after the First."

"Understood," said BetreMussie from his vantage point on the platform of the deck. Fixing round posts topped with near-circular iron cuffs into prepared holes at the sides of the gangplank, Betre-Mussie listened to the three of them converse in Anglo-French, taking care not to betray his knowledge of the language; he knew the advantage such information gave him was lost if his comprehension was discovered. Once the ropes had been strung through the cuffs on the posts, the captain stepped back and made the traditional Coptic gesture of welcome. "Come aboard, Sidi. You and your companions are welcome. My men will be here shortly, and when they and their belongings are aboard, we will leave."

Sandjer'min made the gesture of thanks before he dismounted and, after a moment's hesitation as he recalled Sieur Horembaud's fall from the bridge over the Atbara, led his gelding up to the gangplank, feeling the vertigo that running water always awakened in him; he took hold of the ropes that served as railing and stepped aboard. On the deck he steadied himself and moved the horse toward the covered portion of the barge that would serve as a stable and sleeping quarters for their northward journey. As he came up to BetreMussie, Sandjer'min slipped the purse out of his sleeve and handed it to the captain. "Venezian ducats, as you asked."

BetreMussie winkled the purse away from him, slipping it into a sack that hung from his braided-leather belt. "God give you good fortune and peace."

"And make the voyage a safe one for all of us." Sandjer'min led the gray gelding out of the sun, into the double row of stalls on the raised platform, where he traded his bridle for a halter, and secured the lead-rope to the side of the open manger. "We will have food for all the horses and asses; my companion will see to it."

"Very good," said BetreMussie, and went back to the top of the gangplank to direct Margrethe and Ruthier aboard the ship. They were soon on board, all but one of their chests piled and secured in place by nets fastened to cleats in the deck of the barge. Ruthier took over the task of caring for the animals while Sandjer'min set up his chest of his native earth on the rear of the stable, a heavy dark canvass tarpaulin rigged from the stable roof to make a partial tent. Margrethe came to see how he was progressing with this secondary structure, saying, "You were right: I'll take one of the stalls and make it my sleeping place; it is the most private place on the deck. The horses and asses will be able to guard me."

"That they will," Sandjer'min agreed. "You can use straw to make a pallet to sleep on, and Ruthier will sleep at the other end of the stable."

"Sleep in straw, like rushes at home? I liked to sleep in the rushes when I was a child, in Rutland." She touched his hand, then took a step away. "Three oarsmen in each of the long boats, you said?"

"Yes. We will travel as much at night as we can, and rest during the heat of the day, or so BetreMussie promised Aba'yam Hodilleilo through his courier." He looked around at the small open boats working among the barge-boats, their oarsmen crying their wares, their foods, their services. "Pilgrims and merchants. Dofunj has managed to survive because of them, though Funj itself has faded from a city to a village, or so Tsega told me."

Margrethe stopped a sigh. "How long will it take us to reach the Fifth Cataract?"

"The current is still running fast," said Sandjer'min. "Three, perhaps four days, with the oarsmen adding to the flow."

"Coming up-river was slower."

"We were going against the current, and even in spring, it is powerful; it's strongest at the height of the Inundation," he told her.

"Which has passed, hasn't it?" she asked him, staring out at the small crafts jostling at mid-stream. "I can feel it coil and twist."

"As I can," he said, fighting down the queasiness that was rising in him; he swayed as the craft rocked gently. "I . . . I fear I must lie down, the river is bothering me."

"Does it bother you, being on water? They say Lionheart had the same malady."

"Then he must have had a difficult journey to the Holy Land," Sandjer'min remarked.

"Why not sit on the chests? You'd best wait to lie down until we are underway." She pointed toward the gangplank and the first of the oarsmen coming onto the raised barge-deck, the first of them carrying a canvass bag filled with sand.

He nodded. "A good thought," he said, and gritted his teeth against the incendiary presence of the sun.

The oarsmen were Nubians, although one had facial features that revealed a few Egyptian ancestors; most were dressed in smock-like chamises over loose, knee-length femoralie, and were barefoot. Two wore their hair clubbed at the back of the neck, and the rest confined their hair with broad bands around their heads above their eyes. They deposited the items they carried—casks of beer, more sacks of sand, a small barrel of olive oil—near the center of the deck, then went to their stations, adjusted their seat-planks, and prepared to go down the river. BetreMussie came to the edge of the deck and called out questions to the oarsmen, first on the right, then on the left side of the craft. The answers he was given were satisfactory, and he returned to the steering-oar at the back of the boat; he stood on the platform four steps above the deck to give himself an unimpaired view of the river. He watched as a larger barge-boat than this one, coming from up-river, slowed carefully and swung in to the dock below this last one.

There was a commotion at the foot of the gangplank: the slaves had arrived with provisions. They came aboard with crates and sacks which they disposed in low-lying trunks built into the foredeck, working efficiently. The most senior of the slaves—a man of perhaps thirty or thirty-two—bowed to BetreMussie, then to the three passengers. "There is food for tonight that is already cooked. Later we will have to prepare what we eat," he said in Egyptian Coptic. "In the morning, the eggs we bought will still be fresh."

"The oarsmen brought sand to line the pit for the fire, so we may cook safely. Will we have to go ashore to get more?" BetreMussie asked, more for Sandjer'min's benefit than his own; he knew his ship's routine better than anyone.

"Of course we will, if it is needed," said the eldest slave. "We will attend to the cooking-fire night and day if it is necessary."

"I know you will," said BetreMussie, glancing in Sandjer'min's direction.

The larger barge-boat had finally sidled into position, and was tying up to the wooden stanchions on the dock, the slaves on its high deck already preparing to unload the boat.

"We have a chance now," said BetreMussie, raising his voice. "Prepare to leave." The activity on the deck increased, and two of the oarsmen nearest the dock loosened the lines on the stanchions they used, gathering in the heavy ropes to the long, narrow boats that bore the platform of the deck. "Sidi, is your man going to stand guard on the bow this afternoon, or will he wait until tomorrow morning?"

"He will take up his place as soon as we are beyond Dofunj. I will take his place at night, after he hands the lanthorns over," Sandjer'min replied. "For now, I will rest so that I will not doze tonight."

"What about food? Shall we wake you?" BetreMussie asked.

"It won't be necessary; I'll dine later," Sandjer'min answered, and prepared to lie down on his mattress-topped chest of his native earth. Before he pulled down the flap, he said to Margrethe, "You need rest as well as I do. Build your place in your stall. Ruthier will make sure you are not disturbed."

She nodded and helped him to secure the flap, then stepped out of the sunlight into the shadow of the stable, where the smell of horses and asses was so strong it was a physical presence in the confined space. She noticed the two long slots at the edge of the lines of stalls and realized that it was an open trough with a baffle which allowed the ordure and sullied straw to be swept into the river without having to brush it across the deck. With a faint smile, she went into the unoccupied stall and used one of the rakes in the containers outside the stall doors; she began to heap up the straw, shaping it like a pallet, then went to claim the light-weight blanket she had slept under for their journey from the Monastery of the Redeemer,

"Would you like my help?" Ruthier asked her as she came back into the stable; he was tending to the animals, making sure each of them had grain and bundles of drying grasses.

"No. I can manage with what I have." She unrolled the blanket and used it to keep the shape of the straw.

"There are knots of camphor leaves that will keep the pests away," he suggested. "I have enough and to spare."

"All right," she said, recalling how effectively such knots had kept flies, fleas, and other biting insects away. "And thank you."

"I'll wake you when my master relieves my watch at the front of the boat," he said. "If you want some figs, I'll have some for you later."

"That would be welcome," she said, sinking down on the pile of straw and taking her place on it.

For the rest of the afternoon and into the luminous evening, the barge-boat slipped along the Nile, going at a fairly quick pace, passing some of the smaller vessels, held back by others. As the night deepened, the number of boats diminished, some to tie up at the shore, others to anchor in eddies, still others to gather in clusters around a central location, and to rotate slowly through the night.

"They're like a clock," Margrethe said as she came up to Sandjer'min, who was keeping watch at the bow of the deck; she stayed an arm's-length away from him, aware that they were being watched.

"That they are," he agreed, a bit surprised that this would occur to her.

"I saw a clock in Noirmoutier once, at the Abbey de Sant-Marc. It sounded the Hours for the Fratres." She thought a long moment. "Sieur Dagoberht had wanted one for Saunt-Felicite, but then he had his fall and the fever, so nothing came of it."

"You've had your food and you're growing tired in spite of your nap," he said as sensibly as he could, feeling her desire mounting again; the night they had spent an hour together on their journey to Dofunj had ended with kisses; now he felt his esurience flare again. "Perhaps we should talk tomorrow evening."

"Do you plan to sleep all day?" she asked, curious as to why he might do so.

"No, only for the mid-day when the sun and water are omnipotent," he said, "but in the afternoon, I'll need to consult with Betre-Mussie about what lies ahead; I've never been here before." Hearing himself admit so much startled him; he explained as much for himself as for her. "I want to find out what landmarks and villages lie between here and the First Cataract, so I will know what to look for when I stand my watch."

"Then you'll be keeping watch in the night all through our journey," she said.

"Yes. Those of my blood see well at night, and sometimes can be blinded by bright sunlight if it is shining off water all day long." Two decades since, he had experienced what was called sand-blindness on his journey to Karakhorum, and some centuries earlier he had another case of it, on the road to Damascus. "This way, I am being most useful with the least risk." He reached out to take her hand and bowed over it. "I have pledged to see you back to your husband, and I'll strive to fulfill my promise."

She yawned. "I lack your diligence, Sidi," she said, and turned away to return to her stall.

On the slopes down to the river, scrub and fine pebbles gave way to hardpan and dust, which became rock and sand as they moved northeastward on the last of the yearly Inundation. When they passed the Atbara, Sandjer'min was surprised to see how much its water was reduced from when Sieur Horembaud had attempted to cross it.

BetreMussie laughed. "In a month it will be only a stream; in two, it will be gone until next year."

At the Fifth Cataract the river was still swift and high, so they took two days to pull the barge-boat to the shore, dismantle it, load it on the asses and spare horses to carry it down the zig-zag path beside the Nile for reassembly; they were among a dozen other crews doing the same thing with their boats. At the end of the narrow road there was a broad landing where boats could be reassembled and crews could camp for the night. From sundown to sunrise, groups of armed boatmen patrolled the edge of the camp, carrying lanthorns and torches to keep away the creatures of the night. In the morning, a number of crocodiles gathered at the edge of the landing, sometimes coming near to the men and animals waiting to return to the river. As BetreMussie's men got the deck-platform into place, a crocodile rushed the slave nearest the water, rushing up onto the shore to bite his leg. The slave yelled, dropped the shim he was working into position, and tried to break free of the crocodile. The boat shifted and canted onto its side, half into the current.

Sandjer'min shouted to the fleeing men, "Go back and get your comrade!" Then he reached for one of the iron grappling poles and ran to the water's edge, using the hook at the end of the pole to attempt to break the creature's skull, though he was finding it difficult to see the crocodile in the glinting reflections spangling the river. When the fourth blow struck home, the hook sinking through the tough hide behind the skull, the crocodile writhed, its long tail thrashing the water to foam. Sandjer'min held on, fighting off the nausea and weakness that threatened to overcome him. One more jerk on the pole brought the slave within reach; Sandjer'min leaned on the pole, not only to stay on his feet, but to immobilize the crocodile; memories from his ordeal in the Roman arena returned as he struggled against water, sun, and crocodiles. The current here made it worse than the Circus had been. After a last attempt to wrench itself free of the hook, the crocodile opened its jaws, and Sandjer'min bent down to pull the slave from harm. The man's lower leg was torn and bleeding, so that when Sandjer'min tried to raise him to his feet, the slave shrieked and lost consciousness.

"There are more coming!" BetreMussie shouted, and pointed toward long, dark shapes coming toward them, eyes and snouts above the water, the rest beneath. "Fend them off! Don't let them get near us!"

Struggling to resist the enervation of the water, Sandjer'min fell back, his eyes aching, his attention unfocused. He sensed the crocodiles moving nearer, some of them going toward the boat, the others toward him; he strove to regain his nidus, and through that his intent.

Then Ruthier came, taking hold of the slave and handing Sandjer'min his Japanese sword. "There are more coming," he said in Imperial Latin. "About a dozen, I count."

"That they are." Sandjer'min clambered backward on unsteady feet, his eyes fixed on the crocodiles. "Get the man back and wrap his leg above the wound, tightly enough to stop the bleeding. I'll sew the tears closed if I can, when I'm through here," he ordered, drawing the blade from its scabbard. "I'll get the rest to move away from this place."

"I'd rather remain here," Ruthier said, lugging the slave by one arm to pull him all the way to safety.

"Go. He needs immediate help."

"So do you," said Ruthier as he moved to obey.

"Tell BetreMussie to get his craft into the water as fast as he can. If I can redirect the crocodiles, it won't be for long; they will keep coming until we leave."

"I will," said Ruthier, picking up the slave and slinging him over his shoulder before he trudged off to the landing.

Sandjer'min flung the scabbard up the bank and found a low rock near the landing; he took up his position on it, willing himself to shut out the pain, the disorientation, and the sense of peril that wore on him. He studied the approaching crocodiles, then waded into the river and shoved the dead crocodile away from the landing, hoping those others of its kind would follow the body away from where he stood, seeking an easy meal in the swollen river. Cramps ran through him as the river leached his strength, pulling at him as if luring him to surrender to the current. He held the katana over his head as he staggered back to the rock and heaved himself out of the Nile, as exhausted as if he had climbed the outside wall of a castle, or had been caring for the stricken in a time of plague.

One of the crocodiles did not go after the body, but came on toward Sandjer'min, who was still on his knees when the crocodile surged out of the water less than a forearm's length from Sandjer'min's foot; he kicked out, turned halfway around, and struck down with the sword an instant after the crocodile's teeth scraped along his right ribs with its teeth, paddling back as its snout fell away from his head, its blood reddening the water beneath the rock on which Sandjer'min huddled, the wounds in his side growing more encaramined. For an instant he was glad that he had no pulse to drive his blood from his veins as it did with the living, but that quickly gave way to the realization that he would have to bind up his injuries or risk being reduced to something as ravening as the crocodile.

Two of the crocodiles that had almost reached the shore stopped, then launched themselves at the injured beast, pulling the dying crocodile under the water, where the two began to pull it apart.

Slowly, painfully, Sandjer'min heaved himself to his feet, light-headed and filled with growing agony. He stumbled toward the landing where BetreMussie's men were trying to deal with the wounded slave and, at the same time, reconstruct the barge-boat, all the while keeping uneasy watch over the water. He tried to call out for help, but could not draw enough air into his lungs to make more than a duck-like quack; he sank down on his left knee, wondering how much blood he would lose, even without beating heart, and dreading the devouring need such a loss was starting to waken in him; he had experienced that craving before—not often nor recently, but the memories of the five times it had occurred since he came to the House of Life shamed him—and was certain he would have to do his utmost to keep from savaging anyone on BetreMussie's boat if he did not find his way out of the sunlight and away from the water, where he could tend to the rents over his ribs. His body was growing weaker and he could not summon enough stamina to stop the continuing erosion of his condition; he tried not to despair, but the appalling thought of what he might well become shook him like a fever, and he asked himself if the True Death would be preferable to the possibility of being transformed, famished beyond all reason.

Then he heard Ruthier's voice and felt himself lifted and moved along the shore away from the water. The shadow of some large object fell across him, and he took a deep breath of relief.

"I have your red-lacquer chest, my master, and I will do as you bid me," Ruthier said, then raised his voice, calling out to BetreMussie, "I'll attend to your slave as soon as I have done with my master."

"Keep Margr—" Sandjer'min gasped.

"Away, I will," Ruthier told him.

BetreMussie made some diffuse comment from where his men had largely prepared the barge-boat to return to the water. "Will he be able to travel with us?" he asked as he came into the shade of the stone slab that angled up from the end of the landing.

"I don't know," said Ruthier, then looked over at the slave. "I doubt he will; the muscles in his leg are shredded and he is clammy to the touch. He could be dead in an hour. My master is gravely injured, and I need to close his wounds."

BetreMussie bent over Sandjer'min and made a face. "Exposed ribs: four of them." He shook his head. "Neither he nor the slave have much of a chance," he added, speaking in slightly stilted Anglo-French.

"It seems so," said Ruthier, making no comment on BetreMussie's skill with the language. "And I must be about treating him now."

"We'll pull to the bank a little farther down-river for tonight. In the morning, you will tell us how we are to proceed." He gave a single, explosive laugh. "What about the woman? Does she stay with my boat or with you?"

"Let her decide," said Ruthier, and saw Sandjer'min wince. "For now, I know what I must do."

BetreMussie cast another cursory glance at Sandjer'min, unaware that he could hear and understand everything. "If we lose him, I suppose we will lose the rest of the fee, and the work."

"Let us see what the morning brings," said Ruthier, opening the red-lacquer chest and taking out a folded and rolled swath of linen. "I doubt you want to see this."

"Probably not," BetreMussie said, and left the shelter of the canted rock.

Once he unrolled the linen, Ruthier removed a coil of silk thread and a steel needle. "Do you hear me?"

"Yes," said Sandjer'min faintly.

"Is there anything I should use on the wounds before I close them?"

"I don't know," Sandjer'min conceded. "It would be wise to wash the open flesh with the tincture of pansy and willow-bark, though it won't lessen my hurt." He fell silent while he made another effort to regain a modicum of composure. "If there are animacules in the rents, they will breed and have to be lanced later."

"You want nothing more than that?" He threaded the needle.

"If it would do some good, yes, but not even syrup of poppies will relieve the pain for the undead. I'm prepared to deal with it, if you will give me the smaller biting bag, so I won't alarm the Captain or Margrethe."

"I will," said Ruthier, and opened one of the four bottom drawers to remove the leather-covered bag of sand, which he bent down to place in Sandjer'min's mouth. "I'll start now."

Sandjer'min bit down hard and gave Ruthier the sign to begin.

After rinsing the wounds, Ruthier carefully pinched the lips of the wounds together and sewed them closed. He worked quickly and efficiently, pausing often to study Sandjer'min's state before continuing. When he had completed the task, he sat down on the folded sail that had often sheltered the asses and horses, and using some Padovan soap, washed his hands to be rid of the blood on them, then wiped the needle and returned it to its place in the linen roll. He studied the sky to judge how long the closing of the wound had taken, then went to see how the slave was faring; the man had sunk into a coma, barely breathing, his color tinged with an ominous shade of blue-gray. Ruthier shook his head, fetched some oil of arnica, and spread it on the man's thigh above the ruined leg, which he surmised could not be saved.

Day faded; fires were lit along the shore where boatmen and watermen would spend the night. Lanthorns and torches were set out to keep the hunting creatures at bay; many tents were erected and guards were posted; prayers and chanting arose from various pilgrim companies: still Ruthier remained where he was, his whole attention on Sandjer'min.

"Ruthier," Sandjer'min said weakly when the constellations overhead revealed that the night was more than half over.

"My master," said Ruthier in Imperial Latin. He left his place on the folded triangle of canvass.

"You did well, Ruthier," said Sandjer'min.

"I wanted to see you safe before I caught a duck," Ruthier said.

"Go eat," Sandjer'min said, and sank back into the stupor that was his version of sleep. When he wakened the night was nearly ended; Ruthier was sitting on the folded sail once again, his attention flagging as the events of the previous day bore in on him. Sandjer'min made an effort to raise his right arm, trying to bend sufficiently to see the bandage that Ruthier had tied around his chest; the pain from his injuries made this impossible and he lay back. "I know what I would like you to do for me," he said, a bit more loudly than earlier, and with greater cohesion in his speech. "I hope you will agree to it."

Ruthier swallowed a yawn and got up, going to Sandjer'min's side. "What is it?"

"I can't travel yet," he remarked without distress. "But if you will arrange a shelter for me, and leave an ass and a pair of horses with me, I will come to Alexandria as soon as the wounds are healed." Ruthier started to speak, but Sandjer'min went on, "I want you to escort Margrethe on her way home; I have pledged to do it, but it would mean not setting out until next spring, and that will not do. She has been gone too long as it is. To add another four months to her stay in Egypt would be no kindness to her."

"Probably not," said Ruthier, and listened intently.

"When I am able to travel, I will go to Alexandria where I will stay at Eclipse Trading, in my personal quarters." He stopped and took three hurried breaths. "I would not ask this of you, but I cannot think of Margrethe traveling alone, but neither can I ask her to remain here. I would not trust the Templars to escort her; the Hospitallers might consent, since she is nobly-born."

"Her presence could be useful to you, my master," said Ruthier, making the suggestion as indirect as possible.

"I don't think she would accept my true nature; she is troubled enough by my being an alchemist. She does not know what I am, and she will not know; I don't want her to fear she has been set upon by a minion of the Devil. She has not tasted my blood at all, and I have only tasted hers twice. She is in no danger of waking to my life." The spurt of energy he had summoned up all but vanished as he closed his eyes, frowning.

It was useless to argue with him, and Ruthier was not surprised to hear this. "Then, if she consents, I will see her on her way back to her husband."

"I am very much obliged to you," said Sandjer'min, trying to hang on to his last small reserves of energy. "If I were to try to—"

"You must rest until the scars are gone," he said.

"That is not what vexes me. I don't want to be tempted to impose my will upon hers." His quick smile was wry. "There is vellum and ink and trimmed pens."

"In the second drawer," said Ruthier.

"Yes. I will write several notes for you to deliver, and entrust you with the missives from Aba'yam Hodilleilo."

"I will arrange for a courier to carry them."

Sandjer'min did his best to smile his approval. "Margrethe should be able to travel before the winter storms make the seas unsafe, if she does not dawdle here."

Ruthier felt increasing relief, for he could tell that the worst of Sandjer'min's anguish had passed. "And I'll speak to BetreMussie about where you might remain; there is a trading village not far away, or so I've been told, and I will go there once the sun has risen."

"Thank you, old friend."

Ruthier stood up, then thought of something. "Would you rather dictate your letters and let me write them? With your right side so damaged . . ."

Sandjer'min shook his head. "I write equally well with my left hand," he said, and no longer fought the fatigue that held him.

"And Margrethe? What shall I tell her?"

It took Sandjer'min a little time to answer. "Tell her I would like to see her toward day's end; I'll think of something to tell her by then."

Text of a letter from Bondame Margrethe de la Poele, written in Anglo-French on vellum from Creisse-en-Aquitaine, carried by Ruthier on the Eclipse Trading ship *Santa Laetitia,* and delivered in Alexandria, forty-six days after it was written.

To the most dear, most excellent Rakoczy Sandjer'min, Gro-fek and Sidi, the greetings of Margrethe de la Poele, on this, the 23rd day of May in the 1226th Year of Salvation,

Most adored Sandjer'min, or as Ruthier has told me you are, Comes Saunt-Germain, I want to inform you that I have reached Anglo-French territory, and to thank you for your generosity and care that brought me safely home. Our voyage from Alexandria to Genova was interrupted at Messina when the ship lost its minor mast in a sudden wind, and we, perforce, had to stay on in Sicily while needed repairs were made. We continued on, though there was already a turn in the weather, and so traveled into the Aquitaine in rainstorms, arriving much later than either Ruthier or I had anticipated, nearly ten months after we left the Monastery of the Redeemer.

It was all for naught. Sieur Dagoberht died well over a year ago. I am now a widow, and with Heneri turned Islamite, Sieur Dagoberht's lands and titles will pass to his cousin, Aluradus, who has vowed he will provide escort to return me to Rutland. With my father and two brothers dead, I cannot believe that Persival will be pleased to have to provide for an older, widowed sister. I am pleased that I have not been ordered to take the veil since Sorer Imogen's example has given me many reasons to avoid the cloister. Perhaps I can be useful to him because of the pilgrimage, telling what is true and what is not about Egypt, and in that way assist him. I met an English merchant in Messina who told me that he would find experiences like mine most helpful in his line of work.

When you can, will you write to me, and tell me how long you had to stay in that abandoned bird-coop? You said it might be three or four months; I hope it was fewer than that, and that your recovery is complete. I trust you are well. I hope you are no longer in Egypt, but have gone to your homeland as I have to mine.

I have heard nothing of any of the other pilgrims in Sieur Horembaud's company since we parted from them at the Monastery of the Redeemer. It is as if the desert has absorbed them into its own silence, as it does the dust-devils and the bones of those who die in its embrace. When I first saw a forest again, I longed to weep for the joy of it. I never understood why the pagans of old worshiped trees; now I have learned a little of their faith.

There is so much I want to tell you that I cannot summon up the words. I do not want to dither on foolishly, so for now, I will take my leave of you. Ruthier has given me a number of places to which I can direct my letters to you, if there is need to contact you again. If you send me letters, I ask that you send them through Sieur Aluradus; he will know where to find me. I am sorry we had so little time alone. Every night I have dreams, the same kind that I described to you, and for that little time, I feel I am again in your company. Pray remember me with the same kindness you showed me in Nubia.

With my thanks for all you have done for me,

Bondame Margrethe de la Poele
by my own hand

EPILOGUE

Text of a letter from Sanct' Germain Franciscus, in Ragusa to Atta Olivia Clemens at Lecco on Lago Comus, written in Imperial Latin on vellum and delivered by hired courier twenty days after it was written.

To my enduring and fondest friend, Bondamma Atta Olivia Clemens, at Villa San-Germanno at Lecco, on this, the 9th day of September, 1231,

My cherished Olivia,

Thank you for sending me your letter; I will bear in mind that you will be leaving Lago Comus shortly. When you have decided where you are going, I ask you to send me word. I will soon depart this wolf's-lair of a city for Viendona, as they are calling Vindabona these days. It is in the County of Austria and has recently benefited from the increase in mining in Moravia and Bohemia, which intrigues me. I may go to my native earth for a while, as well; there have been rumors of increasing hostilities with Hungary. It would benefit me to protect the place I was born, though it was more than thirty centuries ago.

Rogerian is presently in Venezia where he is delivering some contracts to expand Eclipse Trading there. The Console has decided to tax me for every Venezian port-of-call we use as a condition of using their escort ships and their trade routes. I am willing to agree to their stipulations in part because it helps me to link Eclipse Trading in China with Eclipse Trading in the West. It is also a way to get *around the demands of the Templars in the Holy Land who are busy shoring up their accounts at the expense of merchants. I am also planning to see what arrangements I can make with the Hanseatic League, for with as much upheaval as we see in trading, having more, not fewer, options will do much to make Eclipse Trading strong enough to remain in a good position no matter how chaotic some parts of the world become. Increasingly I value Eclipse Trading, which I began as a way to escape from foreign lands, and now have found a most successful enterprise. I am astonished to see myself endorsing trade in this way, but it is ever more useful and I would be a fool to eschew it.*

You inquired about any attachments I have formed since my short-lived association with Bondame Margrethe de la Poele of Rutland: I must confess that there have been none. I have limited myself to visiting women in their sleep, and rousing dreams in them. It is not the same sort of nourishment as there can be with knowing partners, as you yourself have remarked, but it is enough to suffice my needs for now. I was pleased to hear that Ruporecht has been willing to stay with you past six encounters; he seems an excellent partner for you. Will you take him with you when you go to Brabant, or will you leave him in Lecco?

By the way, I had a letter from Bondame Margrethe about a year ago; she had been in London with her uncle, who introduced her to a merchant from Bruges, and who had asked for her hand in marriage, since he valued all she told him about Egypt and the places she had gone to and from with Sieur Horembaud's company of night pilgrims. She said it was not a relationship of passion but one of liking and shared good opinions. He is a few years younger than she, but a mature man of good sense and respectable enough to win the approval of most of her family. She believes that is because she had no intention of marrying again, and the family did not want her to be a cost upon their purses. This way, she will be married, if somewhat below her station, to a man whose wealth exceeded almost all her kin. She said she regrets that we spent so little time in close association. She promised to love me always, which is meaningless, but still a great compliment. Yet I wish her happiness in her marriage: may she and her husband achieve their goals in business as well as in more domestic matters.

And yet, and yet, I find it within myself to want to see Gonder and Lalibela and other holy sites in Ethiopia, and I will try to find my way there before too many years go by. I hope I will not be compelled to travel up the Nile, but perhaps find a way in the routes along the Red Sea. But imagine it, Olivia: buildings as grand as the Lateran, Churches dug into the stony earth, and chapels more than a thousand years old dedicated to Jesus of Nazareth well before the wild men of Europe had embraced his teachings. I must save this for another decade, but I cannot turn my back on these remarkable places.

Rogerian, who brought her from Nubia to Alexandria, said that she saw the earth as static as the Roman Church does, and therefore finds it difficult to accept change of any kind. Rogerian is of the opinion that she would not have been willing to accept my true nature, had I revealed it to her, and because of her education, he may be right. The Roman Church promises stability and the Rule of Heaven on earth as if it could be possible. Much as it rankles with me, I am inclined to agree with him on that point. Still, I cannot help but be grateful to and fond of Margrethe: in Sieur Horembaud's company, she was the only one whose curiosity about me did not include dread or challenge. She has seen beyond the strictures of her faith, which takes courage more than sense, no matter how prudent faith may be.

You tell me that you will want to buy some Barb mares from me; you may have them gratis if you will tell me where I am to bring them; give me one in four foals for my horse-farms and I will be more grateful than you can know. Lighter horses will help the armies in the West hold off the

Mongols when Jenghiz Khan finishes ravaging Russia and what is left of the Khazar Empire. You and I will be able to supply them. Were it possible, I would drink to our success, but as you know, vampires cannot share blood with vampires since there is not enough life in it, and I do not drink wine.

With more than a millennium of devotion,
Rakoczy Sanct'Germain Franciscus

7/14 cm